4 Bones Sleeping

To my three darlings, Emma, William & Adele

Also by Gerald Wixey

Salt Of Their Blood
4 Bones Sleeping
Small Town Nocturne
The Police Inspector's Daughter
Beaneath

For more information about Gerald Wixey,
visit his website: geraldwixey.co.uk

COPYRIGHT © 2012 BY GERALD WIXEY

ISBN 978-1-4717-6059-4

The moral right of the author has been asserted

All characters and events in this publication, other than those clearly in the public domain are fictitious and any resemblance to real persons, living or dead is purely coincidental

Printed by TJ International
Trecerus Industrial Estate
Padstow
PL28 8RW

4 Bones Sleeping

Gerald Wixey

1

1945 – TEDDY

He woke up in the same bed. Always the same bed, his mind flew randomly around like a moth battering into a streetlight.

He understood most things, except for the depravity around him. The dim awareness that he was being dragged down. Deep down into the abyss with all the other degenerates.

He had to keep swimming away from these dark waters.

Only two more days and he'd be safe.

Watching the depraved. Watching.

But not getting involved... yet.

Teddy shivered in amongst the sweat. He must have a fever or something. Irritable and uncomfortable in an indefinable way. He wanted to run away, to be able to run for cover like a cat that manages to escape on the night before a disaster.

Teddy sat bolt upright. No longer dead inside... he wanted the boy.

No.

The pretty young man with cheekbones like Veronica Lake.

Please no.

There's a shadow, cloaking every breath. Making every promise empty. Pointing every finger. All the others around him with their roasting rectitude. Their loathing, their weakness and his guilt all kept him alive.

But for how much longer?

He was wading knee deep into the depravity of it all.

Going in deeper, never to come back again.
He'd already gone under twice. Keep swimming.
Swim.
Swim.
'Teddy – can I come in?'
Teddy lifted his head and stared at the young man's sculptured cheekbones for a few seconds.
Too late!
He gestured with his head and the young man crept through the cell door and sat on the lower bunk.

1945 – JACK

I'd named them both. No real claim to fame and hardly original I know, but Harry the Ox and the Dashing Major they became. Harry liked nicknames and always called me Jack the Scribe. Wyn had given himself the sobriquet of the Major, I added the prefix. Wyn wasn't the most glamorous of names, but giving yourself the title of Major when you had no actual military experience was a dangerous game at the best of times. In 1945 it could be considered reckless. But Wyn needed danger in his system almost as much as I needed a drink.

I didn't name them as part of my job. I wasn't some high flying sport's writer. Just a jobbing hack that wrote crime features for the Daily Mirror. And lucky to get that job so quickly after being de-mobbed from military intelligence.

The Major always called me lucky, "better lucky than rich" he always said. I guess that not one person in the world, thought that he ever believed that himself. But there was an element of truth in it. I even had more than my fair share of good fortune during my military service. The army didn't think me robust enough for active service. Military Intelligence was a grandiose title. It effectively meant that instead of the Normandy beaches, I spent most of the time wandering around London looking for spies, spivs and deserters. The last two much the same beast I always found. A soft life, spending most of my days in East End boozers.

Occasionally arresting a sharp-suited spiv, or a cowering runaway. Once we arrested a bewildered, old Italian pasta-house owner. He'd wandered back to Soho from an internment camp in Wiltshire. That was as dangerous as it got for me, a soft life, never smelt any danger, until I bumped into the two brothers.

We first met in the York Hall, Bethnal Green.

How could I forget?

Not that you could call me a regular frequenter of boxing halls just after the war. I always found them one up from a fascist convention. All of the wild eyed, shrieking hysteria that went with the whole package. But I had gone with a friend who was a boxing correspondent on the Daily Sketch. Ringside seats as well, that's where I first saw them. Well I saw Wyn first, Harry was back in the changing room somewhere, pacing, shadow boxing, threatening anything that came within a boxer's reach. Where his manager should have been you would have thought. But Wyn knew his brother too well, stay out of range and leave Harry alone with his temper to warm up punching fresh air.

Anyway Wyn had company, a glamorous woman sat next to him. Not that you'd expect any woman in his company to be anything other than beautiful. He looked fabulous himself with his fur coat draped around his shoulders. Despite it being an especially mild evening, the coat remained steadfastly in position. That and the handmade brogues on his feet, an early indicator for me of his ostentatious nature. Like a young Edward G Robinson, Little Caesar and a woman wrapped around him like a scarf.

The woman I recognised from somewhere, statuesque and blonde. I'd seen her photograph in the newspaper, or on a billboard. Famous for something and she looked trouble in that blonde way that does it for most men. Lana Turner or Jean Harlow, a femme fatale that twisted and turned men into whatever shape she fancied creating at the time. Had she got her hooks into Wyn? I thought so at the time, but Wyn was a shrewd operator. It took me months before I realised who was manipulating who.

I struggled to take my eyes away from her and she knew that I had stared her way. She kissed Wyn's neck and gazed right through me at the same time.

Like what you see?

Yes actually.

I quickly glanced back down at my program, Harry Watkins. I just about remembered the name. Useful boxer but like many, the war had taken his best fighting years away. Then the booing began, I turned around and there he was, walking down the gangway. No shadow boxing for him, nothing apart from a slow, slow walk and the two fists of his boxing gloves pressed tightly together in front of his chest. That and a frown that made me want to look the other way.

The dense smell of embrocation and sweat wafted under my nose. Then I almost choked on my cigarette as he passed me. Too short for a boxer surely? Too short for any sport, his opponent a foot taller and a good stone heavier.

He climbed through the ropes to be greeted by a wall of booing. He apparently thrived on this attention. A pantomime villain with a smile ghosting across his

lips and he put his gloved hand up to his ear.

Is that the best you can do?

Some idiot behind me started bellowing, 'Knock the short fat cunt out.' I turned and stared at him, bulbous nose, wild, staring eyes. A trilby hat perched on his head. 'What are you staring at four eyes?'

You actually.

I turned back as the booing reached a barrage; a few programmes were tossed into the ring. Harry laughed, mocking a thousand screaming fight fans. He beckoned them with his gloved hand. An invite into the ring if they fancied their chances. Then he mimed "c'mon then" and laughed again.

The idiot behind was out of his chair. 'Let me get in there – look at the short, fat fucker, let me get at him.'

I felt him leaning over my shoulder and waving his fist. Hysterical like most of the others baying for the shorter man's blood. Wyn had climbed into the ring himself by this time, a brisk couple of paces over to Harry and he slapped his brother across the cheek. I heard it from fifteen feet away, a rifle report that shot through the bedlam of noise.

Concentrate!

Harry didn't even blink, just the frowning stare across the ring at his opponent. Wyn shouted, for the opponents benefit as much as his brothers. 'Calm now, you can take
that donkey out – calm.'

Calm? I looked at the few women scattered around me. All wide-eyed, sat forwards in their seats. Hands bunched into fists. What excited them? The reek of liniment? The sweat that glistened off the two fighters muscles? The unwashed brutality about to be unleashed on us all?

I shook my head, women always confused me anyway.

Then the clanging bell broke into my puzzlement. But it never stopped me frowning as I proceeded to watch a man box like I'd never seen anyone fight before. Perhaps his lack of inches meant that he had no choice. But all he presented to his opponent was the top of his head. As he leant forwards with the gloves protecting the whole of his face. Anything thrown his way was taken on the elbows or forearms. Whenever he got close, Harry grabbed the bigger man and held him in a clinch tighter than a blacksmith's vice. Then his forehead went to work, always in the taller man's face despite the referee's frantic efforts to part them.

I could just about make out the over-worked referee screaming, 'Watch your head. Break, break when I say.'

Wyn never said much, no advice forthcoming like you'd expect from a wise manager. He just sat unmoved throughout most of the action. At times he paid more attention to the woman. Apart from just before the end, when he jumped to his feet as the taller boxer crumpled under the frenzied barrage. Wyn's eyes bulged, his whole demeanour switched from relaxed spectator to lunatic in a less than a second.

Then he began to scream, 'Hit him, spear his eyes out – hit him.'
He needn't have bothered.
Silence in a crowd this big is an unusual thing. As if someone off stage had quickly turned the volume down. No doubt, the crowd had been cowed into sullen obedience at the ferociousness. A Jewish fighter thrashed in his own back-yard just wasn't meant to happen.

I turned and stared at my big-mouthed friend, he looked back, a sullen gaze and he muttered, 'Sheep shagger.'

In the meantime, Wyn swaggered back to his seat like he'd won the bout himself. Strutting the short distance, an occasional cheery wave sent back in the same direction whenever a shout of derision came bouncing his way.

The woman, like the rest of her gender, had watched the fight in a state of orgasmic, eye stretching disbelief. She sat back in her seat afterwards, took several deep, deep breaths.

That was good.

She put a cigarette in her mouth and leaned forward. Wyn, attentive from the moment I first met him, played the lighter around her cigarette. Even that took on an erotic dance as they hovered around one another in a teasing, ritualistic mating. Eventually lit, she dragged deep and flopped back into her seat. Wyn looked deep into her eyes and eventually, they both laughed.

Then he too sat back and reflected on a good night's work. He stared around, glanced past me, did a double take. The first time he had noticed me and his soft brown eyes came back and fixed on mine. Anyone with a front row seat must be worth talking to. Wyn leant across and said, 'What a fight, the boy's a bruiser that's for sure.'

Looking back, an incongruous place to start a friendship that would last well over thirty years. But there you are and here's the second incongruity of the evening. I warmed to him instantly, despite recognising what he was. The clothes, the big coat and bigger attitude. Pretentious and he didn't care who that bothered. I'd spent the last couple of years following black market crooks that mirrored this man's appearance. Wyn shouted venality and a flamboyant venality at that. Everything I despised... and yet I liked him.

He nodded at me, 'You a reporter?'

I nodded, his eyes spotting my press pass that I'd deliberately left just exposed in the breast pocket of my jacket.

What did that make me?

One who disliked pretentiousness in all of its manifestations. And yet I wanted people to recognize my own status. He gave me a card with a name and address, then a casual invite. 'Come and have a drink in my club. Don't bother to bring your wife.'

Then the look ... we're all men of the world. He winked and my face must have given me away.

Oh that sort of a club.

I looked away and down to the address on the card, Beak Street, Soho. Not tonight I think. Another deterrent, the name, I laughed at it, I mean, "The Suede Tangerine" – c'mon.

Well it sounded like a queer boys club, or at the very best, a low class café.

1945 – TEDDY

Teddy stood in front of the boy, leaned forward slightly and rested his head on the mattress of the top bunk. He felt the boy's hands fumbling with the buttons on his prison trousers.

Teddy groaned and his mind drifted. Back – way back.

He always dreamed a lot. But then there was nothing else to do in this shithole. He liked to touch his mother's auburn hair, once he crouched in the shade and touched it as she passed by. Her reaction stayed with him for ever, an ear drum-splitting shriek, a spin around, eyes bulging away as she backhanded him across the head and told him to fuck off.

Did he hide in the shadows a lot? Probably.

Did that make him unpopular?

Probably not.

Although he could be a morose child, not loathed so much, as generally just overlooked by his large family. This didn't mean he disliked his siblings, or his parents come to that? He was just never smart enough to avoid confrontation. Not that he ever tried that hard to avoid it, perhaps that became the only way to gain their attention?

Arguments got him going almost as much as the noises that came from his parent's bed. Sharing a bedroom with your parents had its compensations. Not a voyeur yet, just an adolescent with a harmless infatuation for spying on adults. He listened to their noises, watched his father's violent thrusts. Lay in bed thrilled, if a little perplexed. More confused when his father and his aunty regularly went through the same routine. This left him as delighted as any other morbid schoolboy would be. The sound of a man on the cusp of an orgasm.

He couldn't wait.

The noise of the young man slurping away dragged Teddy back to the here and now. At least he wasn't pacing the cell. Constantly, like an agitated polar bear in a small compound. Two steps, turn. Two steps turn, until he came back to square one. Then another circuit, then another, then another. It seemed that he'd spent the last six months
pacing the floor. At least he was alone; virtually six months spent alone. Well that suits me he thought, the idea of months banged up with another smelly old lag, or a ponce, or worse, some little queer boy, turned his stomach.

No, solitary did him fine; he couldn't have coped with someone in his cell with him.

Punch a guard and bingo, a cell on his own.

Teddy Lewis didn't need anyone, he thought of the birch that went with the solitary and he punched the hard pillow on his harder bunk. Bastards, the old lags always preferred the cat because it was always applied across the shoulders. The birch went across the arse. The humiliation of bending over with your trousers around your ankles worse than any pain involved. In this dump, you just never knew who was stood behind you. Then the token administration of first aid afterwards still bent over and you knew then all right. Always some little poof of a half-trained medic rubbing ointment over your arse.

Fuck it.

He shuddered, all things considered, the administration of pain was more his style.

Soon.

Another day, one more night and then what? All that catching up to do, that's what.

Teddy blinked and looked down at the young man's thick, wavy dark hair. He'd done what he always said he'd never do. Spent the night with a little queen. At least it was as dark as a crypt. He couldn't see the eyes, especially when the young man was face down on the hard mattress with Teddy doing something else that he'd vowed never to do.

He imagined a blonde head nuzzling its way around his lap. Teddy shut his eyes again.

Shirley.

Teddy had been hard for most of the night, still hard now. He started to move his hips.

Shirley.

Hard thinking about. I'm coming baby. Shirley.

Then he heard the scrapping metal on metal sound of the spy hole on his cell door being drawn back.

A harsh cockney voice – south London Teddy guessed.

'Lewis, can we come in? Has he stopped fucking you up the arse yet?'

Arse?

He wasn't a poof.

Teddy stared down at the young queen wiping his mouth in the grey prison issue blanket. The young man lifted his head and their eyes met.

'What are you looking at you cunt?'

The young man quickly looked away as the door opened and the guard gestured with his head and the little queen bounced out.

'Lucky boy Lewis – us giving you treats like that when you're supposed to be in solitary.'

Teddy stared at the two guards until they both looked down at their highly polished boots.

He snapped the words at them, 'That's better – show some respect you fucking half-wits.'

2

1980 – TEDDY

Mad.

She was mad.

Deranged, certifiable, demented, unhinged, stark staring raving.

He knew all there was to know about crazy women as well. This one took the fucking biscuit. Still, he shouldn't have rifled his way through her bedroom like that.

Sleeping dogs.

Better never to have found all that gear. A sleepy village in Berkshire, an expensive school – where did she get that stuff from?

He blamed his wife.

Or did he?

The outer life. After all that time of peace, the outer life had become as unbearable as his inner life.

His inner life had contrasted nicely with this period of calm. All through this time, his inner life had tormented him, all the shocking images. The made up conversations. The horrific dreams, the insomnia. Two men with their throats cut. All the queer boys looking at him in prison. Four men burning to death. Two brothers that had mugged him and worse, made him look stupid.

All of those things and more.

But it was the most recent thing that tortured him more than anything. Not all of that stuff from just after the war.

That kiss.

That two year-old kiss, or was that a kiss from two years ago? Why did she do it?

She was twelve years old. The sweet smell of pre-pubescence on her after two hours in her gymnastic class.
When he picked her up in the car, she leaned over and kissed him. Not on the cheek either. He pulled back like he was avoiding a punch between the eyes.

She stared at him with those dazzling almond eyes of hers. Then she said, 'Why won't you let me kiss you like mummy kisses that other man?'

He'd done nothing wrong, but his wife… now she was cracking up as well.

And he should know, after all he knew all there was to know about mad women all right. Mad, sane, normal, whatever that was.

Thirty five years down the road and he could only think of one woman. All the others became subconscious images somehow. The blonde was the one that always came into sharp focus.

She wasn't crazy, dangerous, but not crazy.

'Shirley. I wonder if she still tastes the same?'

His wife said, 'What did you just say?'

He shook his head, 'I never said anything.'

'I thought you said something.' His wife sighed, 'What are we going to do about her?'

'Who?'

'Your – our daughter. What are we going to do?'

He shut his eyes and massaged his temples with thumb and index finger.

Over and over.

'She's in trouble.'

'I know.'

'What can we do? She shouldn't have gone back to school. Whatever can we do?'

Eventually, 'I don't know.'

1980 – JACK

I sat in my office, tapping my teeth with a pencil, glanced down at my watch, just before midday on a frosty Wednesday. Copy for the week finished and a long lunchtime beckoned.

Stuart sat back in his chair, with his feet on the desk, hands clasped behind his head. I smiled, he did a few hours a week for me, the rest of the time he worked in his father's pub.

An obvious act of nepotism on my part, but I liked Stuart and owed everything I had to his father. Harry saved my life and giving Stuart a job a tiny price to pay.

'You going for a pint?'

I raised my eyebrows at Stuart, 'What do you think?'

I looked at my secretary. She smiled, knowing exactly what Stuart was angling after. 'Jack's Wednesday afternoon public bar discussion group. Membership by invitation only.'

Carol couldn't be called a beautiful woman in any sense of the word, eyes were probably too narrow and the thin lips gave a hint of meanness. But whenever she smiled like she did now, her mouth became suddenly generous and she lost her solemn, intenseness. Suddenly the intuition came to me that she would be all business in bed, I smiled to myself at this image. A sympathetic woman and a good listener too, strong and certainly no pushover.

How did she put up with that lout of a policeman for a husband?

'Where you going?'

I shrugged; Stuart's insistent questioning meant that he was angling for an invite. Stuart even began to count his change, I sighed, patronage comes at a high price.

'Go on Jack – you can afford to buy the poor boy a pint.'

I pointed at Carol, 'You can be quiet as well.'

We lapsed into a comfortable silence.

Just the noise from the printing machines out the back. Sometimes they clattered and rattled like an Edwardian threshing machine. God knows how my three printers coped with it. Not that they were especially well rewarded for their efforts either. But two of them had been here since their schooldays.

Three printers and two in the office, the sum total of my staff. As it happened, just enough to keep a provincial newspaper ticking over. Better still, all mine, an independent newspaper owner. I smiled at Carol and she smiled back, a bitter sweet affair that said, it's nice to work for an honest man.

If only she knew.

Carol glanced over to Stuart and then back to me. 'I can lock up if you two want to get off.'

Sweet woman, relieved of my gate-keeping duties gave me a clear run at my favourite watering holes. Before I could thank her, my phone clanged into the collective consciousness of the small office. Stuart's feet lifted clear and he swivelled his chair my way, sitting to attention at the same time. Carol's eyebrows went up, she took all the calls, only two people had my extension and we all realised the potential significance of this call. My pulse quickened at the prospect of a decent story filtering my way at last.

A soft, even voice, instantly recognisable. 'I know you've probably wrapped up for the week, but I think you'll be interested, a girl has either just fallen, or jumped, or maybe even been pushed out of a third floor window in St Mary's. That's the school not the convent. Just one thing, please don't bring that hooligan you employ as a cameraman.'

I smiled and glanced at Stuart. Calling him a cameraman was perhaps a touch grand. Calling him a hooligan would have been accurate ten years ago. The police and Stuart. In a way it summed up the beauty of a small town. Everyone knows one another. The police knew all of the tearaways. I got rules bent here and also scratched backs there. All so convenient, but it goes with the health warning that everyone always knows who's doing the scratching and bending.

That's why Inspector Mably's call was such a surprise in a way, he never usually took chances. Perhaps the article I put on page one about the charity efforts of his police station made him feel especially benevolent towards me?

'First day back after the holidays as well.' Apart from that comment, he was all business, brief and with no introductions, just that simple message, with a final instruction. 'See you in a couple of minutes.'

Then I heard the phone being placed ever so carefully back, like you would a baby back into its cradle.

Once again I tapped my pencil against my teeth a few times, not caused by boredom this time however. St Mary's was recognised as a public school with an unusually high standard of scholarship.

Well that's what the prospectus would have you believe. According to Harry, nothing other than a load of parasitic, St Trinian style hooligans marauding around the shops of a lunchtime. Despite their age, that didn't stop him serving them whenever they crept into his pub though.

I jumped up, 'There's either been an accident. Or a young girl may have been pushed out of a window.'

'You'll need a body guard then?'

I smiled; my insecurity meant that I always needed some sort of protection. It used to be his father, now I had Stuart. A fair substitute I felt, although Harry would dispute that.

'You'd better stay here. I'm meeting our erstwhile Inspector outside St Marys.'

Stuart's mouth turned down and he glanced at Carol and shook his head.

I stood and took a deep breath at the chance of the first decent copy for months. A possible scandal at a posh school more than compensated for the interruption of my afternoons boozing. I stood and wrapped my scarf around my chest, dragged the heavy overcoat on. Placed my trilby at an angle set to impress Humphrey Bogart. I gestured for Stuart to stay put and I walked out into the midday air.

The coldness crashed deep into my lungs as I walked up Grove Street. The sun low at this time of year, as it glistened off the frost still clinging to the rooftops. Frosty flowers of ice, frozen onto the pavements still in the shade. Freezing air and an almost cloudless, dark blue sky. Just a few broken red clouds arcing towards the horizon and my breath frozen and snorting out from my mouth as I marched on. An edge to the whisper of breeze, a breeze that would have felt like a gentle kiss in the summer. Now, it nipped like an agitated Jack Russell and made your eyes run.

I hurried past the Indian restaurant, evocative smells of cumin and cardamom drifted towards me. Mixing with the stale urine, left against the restaurant windows by the same louts that ate in there. I needed Stuart now, he knew everyone under thirty. He had his finger on the heartbeat of this little town's pulse all right.

I carried on up Newbury Street until I was alongside the imposing, redbrick school. My messenger had been on the ball because no ambulance, no doctor even. Just Inspector Mably watching two policemen labouring away with a stolid purpose. They had fenced the area off with hazard tape. One of the policemen glanced up and down the street, catching my eye.

'Watch out sniffer's on the job.'

They both laughed, but the underlying impression was a nervous one.

Where's that ambulance?

Ignoring their sarcastic epithet, I joined Mably and we both stared up at the tall redbrick building. One open window on the third floor, with a muslin curtain hanging limply out of it in the still winter air.

Mably lifted the tape and ushered me through.

'It's a mess.'

He pointed at what was obviously the point of impact. Splattered red and lumpy grey bits, rather like poorly made porridge. The high wall had broken her fall, not that it had saved her. Head first onto its sixty degree corniced top and dead in the blink of an eye. I noticed her legs, slim and shapely.

Her grey uniformed skirt well above her waist, no tights, light blue knickers. Both arms under her waist. Head over at a crazy angle, but her face unmarked and still beautiful. Almond eyes staring into space, classical cheekbones, strong chin and perfect teeth exposed in some sort of obscene, grin of a death laugh.

I shivered and looked back up to the window. The four story building had been encased in scaffolding for months and I knew the builders well.

'Jack, I thought I told you not to bring him.'

Mably was staring at me and pointing south towards Hungerford. I took my gaze up the street and groaned. Three builders stood ten yards away. All smoking, rubbing their hands in the cold. Sometimes the youngest of them looked up at the open window, as if expecting an action replay.

Stuart stood at their centre and they inscribed a ragged, semi- circular arc around him.

'Oh God.' I groaned again, 'I told him, sorry David, I'll get rid of him.' Mably took hold of my arm, 'All three might be suspects, I've told them to stay put. That long haired one is trouble. Look at them all talking as if nothing had happened.'

His expression that of a straight-laced verger, viewing a rampaging, drunken mob.

1980 – TEDDY

Two policemen stood in the drive.

What the?

His wife opened the door.

'Mrs Schwartz?' She nodded.

'Can we come in?'

Teddy stared at them, the older of the two policemen nodded.

The younger policeman looked down at the floor.

'What do you two pair of…?'

'Shhhh!' His wife put her hand on Teddy's wrist. Turned

to the policemen and said. 'What's happened?'

What's happened? Teddy knew. He sat down and waited.

The older of the two policeman cleared his throat. 'We've got some bad news for you.'

But Teddy knew.

3

1945 – JACK

I stared at the card Wyn had given me for most of the journey back on the tube. I got out at Oxford Circus and would normally have walked east along Oxford Street. But something dragged me south towards Beak Street and Wyn's club. I used that closeness to my flat as an excuse. Despite the laughable name, I found myself walking in. A piano played away to one side. I might not have liked the name, but the sweet, slow jazz piano that accompanied the darkness and the cigarette smoke matched my mood.

I paid for a bottle of outrageously over-priced beer and took it over to a table. I saw her straightaway, she stared at me freely. As if she dared me to look at her, or more likely, dare me to look the other way. I did look away, glanced at a room full of women and tired looking men in shiny suits and cheap black shoes. But my eyes went back… and there she was. Close to Wyn, but she gazed around the club, constantly looking for eye contact with other men – and there were plenty of takers. She sipped her gin with one hand and held onto Wyn's fingers with the other.

She didn't greet the other men with any degree of reverence or awe. But head on, everything was always head on with her. She looked at men with no inhibition and certainly no guilt. Yet to a man, we would all think that she only had eyes for the one she was looking at the time.

In this instance, me!

In a room full of attractive women, she was the only truly

beautiful one. A pearl necklace at her throat, an expensive watch on her slender wrist. She'd changed into a white evening dress, cut low. The impression of a woman that had never been hurt or scarred by a man and not likely to be either. She smiled at me and walked my way, her breasts moving against the sheerness of her dress. Sat down next to me and crossed her legs, waved back at Wyn with a dismissive flourish that said won't be long, her crossed leg kicking slowly back and forth.

'Well twice in one day, aren't you a lucky boy?' Then her knowing smile, she inclined the head a touch and she left her mouth slightly open. I was surprised by her voice, clear of the whining cockney vowels and the nasal awfulness that bombarded me all day long. Not Home Counties, Gloucestershire or Wiltshire maybe as she said, 'You're a reporter aren't you?'

I nodded; beautiful women didn't walk over and talk to me unless they wanted something. She made me defensive, cautious around women at the best of times. I needed to know what she wanted and probably sounded abrupt in manner.

'I've seen your picture in the paper.' I remembered that she was hanging onto a man built like a concrete pill box. I took a flier at it, 'Where is he... the big boy friend.'

'A sharp man.' She blinked, glanced Wyn's way and then back to me, fingering her pearls at the same time. 'I like my men a little on the dim side. I hope you're not too clever for your own good.'

'Remembering faces is my job.' I couldn't place either of their names and it drove me wild, 'What was his name?'

She leant back in her seat, 'Teddy Lewis – have you heard of him?'

Then she stared right through me.

Her answer, something about it annoyed me. As if someone so beautiful could drop the name of a psychotic tearaway into the conversation and I should be impressed. Stupefied or terrified probably, I tried to stop my eyebrows from going through the ceiling and all the time my heart pounded like a tattoo on a snare drum. Teddy Lewis, doing time and Wyn was doing…

I shook my head, 'Teddy wouldn't like you seeing other men would he?'

'It's all over now… anyway he's a pussy cat.' Then the same dismissive gesture with her hand. The same hand fluttered over towards me and she rested it on the back of my wrist. 'Don't look so shocked.'

The eyes held me, trapped I fumbled for my cigarettes and the escape of distraction it might bring. No good, hooked liked every other man in here would have been.

She smiled, another one in the bag.

I said, 'What's your name again? Remind me?'

'Shirley Mathews.'

Yes!

Shirley Mathews and Teddy Lewis made the second page of the Daily Mirror a while back. To call them an attractive couple was an understatement. Teddy complemented her beauty. He was an eye-catching man himself, with his dark-skin, broad shoulders and those sculptured cheekbones. I remembered staring at their photo and wondering which one to fantasise over. The photograph gave no indication of the power of his eyes. Hard, cold even, a bit like polished ball-bearings. Both of them dressed to kill, out on the town, snapped stepping into a club in Mayfair. My rabbit's eyes blinked into the powerful headlights, Shirley just stared back.

'He's a striking-looking man.' I never mentioned him being psychotic, unhinged, unstable and all of the other synonyms that neatly summed his character up. Or that I felt oddly attracted to him.

'He's dynamite.' Shirley's eyes clouded a touch and she sighed. 'But all in the past now.'

I struggled to change the subject, 'You're not from around here are you?' Blindingly banal, but all my wit strangled by her sexuality and a vicious ex-boyfriend.

'Small village in North Berkshire originally – years ago.'

A country cousin who had left home and here she was one up from being on the game. A good time girl and trouble with it, what a potent mix. Shirley's eyebrows relaxed and she smiled, as you'd expect, her teeth were perfect. Small, even and brilliantly white, she leaned forward. The way you do when whispering to a fellow conspirator. 'Would you like one of the girls to come over – bring a drink maybe?'

I shook my head, a touch too quickly probably. 'I'm going to have a drink with Wyn.'

'You'd rather talk to the Major?' Shirley inclined her head a touch, 'What's up, don't you like girls?'

What did I say to that one?

Fortunately I never had to answer her question. A small man came over, thin faced. A countenance that would evolve in a few years, into a full weasel featured face, complete with six o'clock shadow across his sunken cheeks. His eyes darting everywhere, up and down me a few times. Then around the club, before finally settling on Shirley. A little man you felt would always be happier in the shadows. Certainly not someone comfortable in the sun. His de- mob suit hung loosely across his sparse frame, fitting where it touched.

He pointed at Shirley, 'You going to be long?'

She rolled her eyes back and shook her head, 'You know I have to stay, it's my job.'

He lowered the pointer that was his right arm and stared at her. I twisted in my seat, his expression indicated an argument, a shouting match, or at least a one sided accusation directed Shirley's way. But a deep breath later and he turned, muttering away about sorting all of this out tomorrow and scuttled away. Looking for the shadows I imagined. I lit a cigarette and glanced across at Shirley. I'd just sat in amongst some sort of brief and one sided argument. A sudden squall on a calm August afternoon.

She just shrugged and stood, I watched her as she smoothed the silky evening dress down. I felt my eyebrows arch, in profile it stood out like a barrow or tumuli in a flat meadow.

Was this perfectly formed young woman pregnant?

Shirley whispered goodbye and left in a hurry. I stood up

and took the short walk across to Wyn. The first thing that stood out, he wasn't a drinker. He sipped a glass of orange juice. He'd tell anyone else that it had gin in it, but I watched him pour the orange into an empty glass. He smiled my way, gestured me into a seat and I asked him. 'Do you ever take a drink?'

Wyn frowned a touch, glanced up at me and smiled. 'Not really – I prefer a good cup of coffee my boy. With Shirley around I need a clear head anyway.'

I wondered if he wanted his sexual performance razor sharp or because she couldn't be trusted, a bit of both probably. I wanted to ask him if she was pregnant and who the father was, instead my eyes went towards the piano, 'Who's the piano player?'

A small woman, in Army uniform and playing like Theloneus Monk or more accurately, Jelly Roll Morton and she hit her stride with "Fickle Fay Creep" Just my sort of music, perhaps she was looking to follow in Jelly Roll's footsteps. After all he started his musical career playing in a brothel.

Wyn opened the palms of his hands and shrugged. 'She played here throughout the war – when she was on leave that is. I've been here two months and she comes in and plays, get her the occasional drink – doesn't want paying. Good isn't she?'

'Good? An understatement. You should offer her a contract – you could be her manager as well.'

Wyn's glance back my way suggested grandmother and sucking eggs. 'Oh I've asked her – not interested. Only has eyes for my brother for some strange reason.'

'Are you talking about me?'

Harry, soon to be Harry the Ox, with his gigantic shoulders and bullet head. A distorted massiveness due to his height I guessed. I glanced up to the belligerent face set atop of them.

Wyn said, 'This is Jack'

He placed two drinks on the table and rested his cigarette on the ash tray. I stood and he gripped my hand like a clamp.

'That's a powerful grip – is that full power?' I stated the blindingly obvious in the hope that the vice of a hand would loosen a touch.

Harry frowned, 'What sort of questions that Jack?'

'I think it's one of the easier ones.'

He smiled and relaxed the grip and wandered back to the piano with two drinks in his right hand and a cigarette in the other.

I inspected my fingers expecting dislocations in all four. Wyn laughed, 'He's still got time – all those war years without proper food. We'll get him fit and strong again and who knows? The trouble is no one wants to fight him.'

I sipped the awful beer; and thought, no one wants to fight him, that could be no surprise. He moved like a tank, slow and predictable maybe. But he dished out the same punishment a Sherman tank would, once he caught his opponent that is. Armour plated, impervious to punches, he hit harder than an irritated donkey kicked. Harry used his elbows, forehead, thumbs – everything went his opponent's way. He frightened me as I watched him smiling and chatting to the pianist. The bruised eyebrows and fat lip testament to his trade.

Wyn's soft voice brought me gently back, 'I need some photographs – and a few lines. Who do you write for again?' He looked disappointed when I reminded him. He raised his eyebrows a touch, beggars can't be choosers. 'What do you think?'

I think that my editor wouldn't want to be seen promoting some cheap little brothel in Soho. Unless one of the girls was on offer of course. I shook my head, 'Not really – what's different? What could sell it that sets it apart from the rest?' I answered my own question, 'Nothing except the piano player maybe.'

Wyn smiled, 'Oh yes the divine Peggy, how about this for a headline then. "War heroine plays for free. Mystery woman plays at The Suede Tangerine " What do you think?'

I smiled back at him, it might work. Wait until Friday

night and the editor comes back from his usual three hours in the Old Bell in Fleet Street. "Did you hear about the war heroine playing jazz piano"?

The old editor's red faced, leering presence might just give me a sympathetic hearing. If Wyn threw one of his attractive women into the equation then he'd get half a page.

Wyn gazed my way, hopeful, eyebrows raised a touch. I wanted to ask him what regiment he was in and how come he had been demobbed so quickly. I glanced around, taking in the girls and the business suits, all drinking heavily – group flirting progressing nicely. The smart appearance of the girls couldn't disguise a collective hardness about them. Well behaved with just the right amount of communal submissiveness needed to keep the men interested. They had been well schooled that's for sure.

I've seen this sort of woman in other clubs, most of them wore a garish blouse and tight skirt. Many of them took on the appearance of a thirteen year old girl who had raided her mother's make up. Lashed the foundation across their cheeks with a distemper brush and then used the same frenzied approach to the lipstick and eye shadow. It gave them the terrifying, expressionless appearance of a sociopath in high heels. I couldn't see it myself, but in other clubs, the tired business men, dust covered builders and the occasional sharp suited banker seemed untroubled by a woman that appeared made up like a circus clown out on the prowl.

These girls were much more understated, Wyn had gone upmarket that's for sure.

I said, 'You did well to get all these girls organized so quickly.'

Wyn balanced his cigar in the narrow edge of the ash tray and smiled. 'Shirley sorted all of that out. Contacts – their all good girls as well. No drippers, all under twenty five and no deranged pimps to worry about either.'

I wanted to smile at the oh so certain man sat opposite me. But I feared for his life and that of his brother. I didn't show the same concern for his little tart, feeling deep down that Shirley would always survive anything thrown her way. Either Wyn had a naïve streak that I'd missed somehow, or he'd got plenty of muscle hidden away somewhere. But what I'd learned about this business, muscle had to be upfront. The potent threat omnipresent.

'I know what you're thinking. No one's ever bothered me with threats, no demands for protection.' He picked his cigar up, played the lighter beneath and made the flame jump about as he lit up. 'Of course I've also got the boy – You've seen him in action. Not that I'm expecting any, but Harry will nip any aggravation in the bud.'

A burst of laughter from the table next to us, six business men mingled with the same number of women. To a woman, apparently in awe of the men, laughing at whatever they said.

Oh you're the funniest group of men we've had in – well for at least half an hour anyway.

We both exchanged a smile, all that champagne – all those girls, all that money. Wyn's self-belief was impressive, the world and his wife respected and believed in a self-confident man – but.

I said, 'Do you know Teddy Lewis is out soon?'

His expression hardly changed, just a small cloud passed across Wyn's moon shaped face for a second or two, before the smile returned. 'He might still be a young man, but he's an old time crook – times are changing.'

'It's none of my business...' I trailed off; Wyn must have known that Shirley was his constant companion at one time. I'd heard somewhere that Teddy even wanted to marry her.

He read my mind. 'They couldn't have married, that would've been impossible.' Wyn's belief in that assertion total, he tipped his head a touch and leant my way. I felt confirmation of his earlier statement coming towards me. Wyn never disappointed, 'She's married, her husband's just got back. He spent the last five years in a Polish prisoner of war camp. I think you've just met him.' He smiled, then spread the palms of his hands as he said. 'Complicated enough for you?'

Complicated?

I shook my head.

I imagined her husband tagged, shaved from toe to head, de- loused, de-humanised. Stood in a line, hungry and shivering. While his wife…

'Does he know?'

'Does who know?' Wyn shrugged and smiled again, showed me the palms of his hands. 'Her husband? Teddy Lewis? Do either of them know that she's my personal assistant? No to both I think.'

Personal assistant?

I leant forward, opened my mouth, but thought better of saying anything. After all what business was it of mine? A pregnant personal assistant? No make that a pregnant mistress, a returning husband and a psychotic ex-boyfriend. I shook my head and we sat there. Wyn leant back staring around his fiefdom. One of us serene the other anxious, one of us wondering whether a returning husband or an avenging angel sweeping down from Wormwood Scrubs would wreak a violent revenge on this totally self-assured man.

Wyn relit his cigar, smiled as he stared, calculating, forever calculating how much was in the till. Perhaps he should pay more attention to the woman, pregnant or not, I'd lay money on her being trouble.

After all she'd hypnotised me from the minute I'd set eyes on her.

1945 – TEDDY

'C'mon Teddy, time for a walk.'

Teddy stared at them, both with truncheons in their right hands and frightened eyes looking his way. Wide-eyed and if not ready for a fight, then expecting one at least. Teddy stood right in front of them and stared from one to the other. Not now, not another fight – out tomorrow. Another fight meant three more months inside. Teddy knew that this thought emboldened the guards too.

'C'mon you cunt and let's get going.'

As they marched him down the corridor, the random prod in the ribs to help him on his way, 'Move it. March c'mon – one two, one two.'

Marched up to the door of the governor's office, made him mark time on the spot, prods in the ribs again. 'We never told you to stop.'

'Come.'

Into the governor's office, up to the desk. 'Stop – stand up straight.'

Stare down at him, full faced, cheap suit – Teddy knew about sharp suits. Teddy mocked the suit sat in front of him. His heavy lips sneered away until the florid faced governor pulled the jacket together and coughed a couple of times.

'Lewis.' He sighed, a patient father administering a gentle word of advice to an errant son. 'Lewis I think you know that you've not done yourself any favours.' He sighed again, shook his head, picked his pipe up from the oversized ash tray and pushed the tobacco down with his thumb.

Placed it in his mouth and …

'Get the fuck on with it.' Teddy stared down - the hard cold eyed, unrelenting gaze that unnerved most and caused the pipe smoker to squirm a touch in his seat.

From behind him, 'Shut your mouth Lewis.'

The governor raised his hand, calm everyone. 'You're out tomorrow – another outburst and I could give you an extra week for your troubles – you're nothing but a menace. I think ….'

Teddy's attention had gone, caught by the back page of the Daily Express's banner headline.

Welshman humiliates local boy.

Last night at the York Hall, Bethnal…

'Lewis – Lewis.'

Teddy couldn't believe it – local fighter beaten by some

sheep shagging Welshman.

'Fuck it.' He said.

'Lewis, you'll be out tomorrow and good riddance.' The governor lit his pipe, great big sucking sucks until he'd got something going that resembled an allotment fire in late September. Through the dense tobacco smoke, a voice filtered up towards Teddy. 'Oh just take him away – get him out of my sight.'

Teddy didn't move, just stared out of the window, he noticed the sky and the powerful morning blue, the moon long gone in the west, along with the soft pink blush as the sun soared up on its late spring climb in the east. Irregular dark buildings contrasted harshly against the sky, the mist that bubbled up over the canal, long gone too. A warm day and he imagined the women in their print dresses. He never knew what to say to young women, they interested him like nothing else in his adolescent life.

But they never liked him and it took Teddy a long time before he got to find out what they wore under their cotton dresses The rattle of a train wrestled for his attention, that and the bell of a racing police car.

Teddy stared on, thinking of her blonde hair and dancers legs. He brought his gaze back to the governor's newspaper and stared down at the picture of a boxer, his arm around a well-dressed man that could be no one else but his brother. One bruised and blood stained, the other like he was straight out of Burton's window. Teddy gazed at the boxer and compressed his eyebrows.

He's too short to be a fighter surely?

4

1980 – JACK

'You get a favour thrown your way, I expect…' Inspector Mably's voice trailed off and he walked away from me at the same time.

'I'll get rid of him.' Spoken to a man that wasn't listening. I turned and walked towards the builders. Old drinking companions all of them. Although, to a man they wouldn't look at me. I went up to Stuart first, I said nothing. Just shook my head at him. My admonishment would have to come later.

He just smiled at me, a naughty schoolboy… again.

I turned to the builders. They had a communal strength about them, only one of the group had heavy shoulders, all three had hands like gravel, bare knuckle prize-fighters hands. A granite solidarity about them – they were a handful. Cold eyed, never polite and a collective look bounced towards me.

Don't get too close!

They should come with a health warning.

'See anything?'

I said this to Stopcock Arthur, probably the most superstitious man on the planet. He finally dragged his coruscating blue eyes my way. His face blistered red brown after a lifetime working outside.

He pointed and whispered. 'Just jumped out head first – six feet away from me.' His eyebrows saucered wide open as if to confirm his next few words, 'Can't believe it.'

Arthur rolled his substantial shoulders, the hawk nose pointed my way like a road sign and his mouth froze open like a disbelieving man-hole cover. We stared at each other until

Arthur closed ranks and took his unblinking gaze in the same direction as his two colleagues.

I moved around the builder's self-imposed wall, getting into Tommy Doyle's eye line. Tommy was Stuart's father-in-law and an uneasy truce had always existed between the two.

Tommy had said It enough times to his errant son-in-law, "hurt my daughter you bastard and you'll get a fucking half-brick across your thick head."

I smiled and despite the fact that I'd know these men for over thirty years, I never expected much joy. Tommy, cold eyed, white cheeked and unshaven, with tired, tired eyes. Almost fifty five now, thickening around the waist a little, but still the boyish expression and the fearless appearance.

Bleak and silent he tried to light a cigarette, his breathing shallow, he stood waiting, staring like a condemned man who'd just finished his last breakfast. A man of moods, at the same time he could be melancholic, stubborn, violent and funny. Now his lighter shook randomly around a quivering cigarette, a fraught encounter as he wrestled the shakes in a bid to light up. After a long Saturday night boozing, his hands often shook on a Sunday morning. He'd walk blinking into the pub; find a spare table, read his Sunday Mirror and smoke. A glass of Irish and a pint close by as he snorted the cigarette smoke and watched as it climbed like the pernicious column it was, until it met up with the nicotine coloured ceiling ... a meeting of minds somehow.

And now, with Tommy's face as closed as the tightest of vaults, I turned to the youngest of the three. A close friend of Stuart's but it counted for nothing as the invisible wall came between us and I was on the outside, frozen out on a freezing day.

I stared at the younger man, Patrick the Hod, with his pugnacious frown and thick, dark blonde hair. He still wore it cut too long, thirty one and not married. Local hard man, slight framed but don't let that fool you. A hod carrier since he was fifteen, a man of few words and many girlfriends.

Nothing from him either, I sighed and tried the collective

approach, 'Were you all up the scaffolding at the time?'

Just like the truth, a lie makes no noise, but silence often screams like a wailing tom cat sat staring at the full moon. The traffic slid past, a backdrop like a round of polite applause. The three smoked and stared and occasionally stamped cold feet.

I said it again, 'Were you up the scaffolding when it happened?'

Tommy spat an answer my way. 'Arthur and me were working.' He nodded up towards the highest level of scaffolding and then pointed at Patrick. 'You better ask that cunt what he was doing, whatever it was it wasn't work.'

Patrick stared at Tommy as if some Fenian brotherhood's darkest secret had somehow been blurted out to the world in general. The silence screamed again. I gave up and walked back to the gate in the wall, perhaps Stuart would have more luck on his own?

Mably noticed me approach and turned his back towards me. I felt a period of penance coming my way. Stuart was impulsive and he had his father's temper; an interesting cocktail. Now he had damaged a carefully cultivated relationship.

I crept back under the tape. The impact was close to the school kitchen. The smell of frying onions and plates being rattled, shouts and curses coming through the air vents of the kitchen. They were in a world of their own, kitchen staff, oblivious to the outside world and the chaos ensuing ten feet away from them.

'That's close enough sniffer.'

The policemen both chortled away, as I felt my chest tighten, resenting the soubriquet and the accompanying intimation that I was a journalist who only ever reported on village whist-drives, crib, funerals and the odd shoplifter in Woolworths. All too true I'm afraid. I was touchy about taking the easy life above hard journalism, three decent stories in thirty five years.

I shrugged and stared at the body.

The air compressed out of my lips like exhausting air

brakes and I felt my eyebrows stretch skywards.

Why didn't I recognise her a few minutes ago?

It was the girl in the Chinese restaurant a few weeks ago. I was convinced of it and what a painful night that turned out to be.

'Out the way you.'

A familiar voice shook me out of my reverie. Talk of the devil and Don bustled through, pushing me out and away from the body.

'Crime scene you know, what's happened lads.'

The town's ace detective, also the town's only detective. Don stared at his two uniformed colleagues, then took his eyes up the length of the girl's legs. I imagined him enjoying the experience. All the time I strained to keep my eyes on his coarse features. I watched as his thick lips formed a perfect circle, the olive skin drained like a litmus paper in reverse. He turned and threw up in one smoothly violent motion.

I didn't show him any sympathy and turn away. Never gave him some discreet distance, instead I crowded him and just stared as he retched and retched. I wanted to look into the eyes of a compromised policeman.

Saying nothing, I turned and beckoned Stuart.

He hurried over and stared at Don, 'What's up with the fat man then?'

I brought my finger up to my lips and we walked briskly away from the grim scene. My mind was buzzing with all of these questions.

'That was the girl in the Chinese restaurant.'

Stuart said, 'I know. What a night that was. Carol was drunk; Don was staring at a fifteen year old schoolgirl. And you looked pissed off with the pair of them.'

I couldn't argue with that. I'd taken Carol out on her birthday, just an employer, employee arrangement of course. That's all it ever was with me anyway and everyone in town knew that. Her husband joined us, like many policemen, the thought of a free meal too good to miss. Too lacking in sensitivity to leave us alone and let his wife use me as her father confessor.

'It was one of the few occasions I was pleased to see you.'

Stuart frowned, 'It was an awful night.'

God knows what had been festering between them. Carol smoked too much and drank too quickly. Her drawn features relaxing apparently in direct correlation to the amount of rum she'd consumed. Even in the middle of an argument, Don couldn't take his eyes off her legs. But he would gaze at any woman's legs that way.

And true to form, his focus soon strayed. Don stared at other women in the restaurant. Carol tried to keep his concentration, but like a distracted seven year old, he kept staring at the other women and one girl in particular.

I said, 'Don was watching the girl like a hawk.'

Stuart stopped me, 'He was obsessed with her. Took her out in the police car a few times.'

'He's such a sleaze-ball.' On reflection, I should have asked Stuart how he knew that Don had been a chauffeur to the girl. But I couldn't take my mind from the policeman's mood in the restaurant.

It made no difference to Don, even with Carol sat alongside, he scrutinised the adjacent girl with no feelings of guilt or inhibition. Lust was a cheap commodity for Don as he dreamed about other moist possibilities. That's when I first saw the girl, I watched Don as he watched the young woman in the restaurant. In his defence, she looked at least twenty. A stunning beauty, but Don's eye had been ensnared not so much by her exquisite features, as by the movement of her heavy breasts against the clinging wool of her dress. I could see his mind working, Don wanted to lean in close and smell where she'd applied her perfume. She crossed her legs and kicked her free leg back and forth, staring at him all the time.

Stuart said, 'How old is he?'

'Forty three I think. Too old for a schoolgirl that's for sure. Carol was fuming; she asked him who the girl was. Don never answered her. Then she said the girl was a bit young even by Don's standards. He told her to get on with her food.'

I had invited them out and yet it seemed that I was intruding. Luckily, that's when Stuart and Patrick came in. He joined the girl and Carol invited Stuart to sit with us. That made me smile for the first time that evening. Don and Stuart hated each other and Carol was well aware of that fact.

In the meantime, when the girl spotted Patrick, she jumped up and kissed his cheek in a very middle class, typically public school way. Patrick rolled her a cigarette and they sat. Heads together like two close friends in playschool. The young girl twisted her long hair constantly, platting it, combing it back between her fingers. Her movements, quick and bird like, she blinked constantly, her expressions seemingly changed with every blink. Attractive, but highly strung, like a two year old, well-bred racehorse impatient for the reins to be loosened.

Don ignored Stuart, he just had eyes for the girl opposite anyway. Don stared on as the soft light fell on her hair and shoulders and breasts. Carol had gone quiet, staring at the couple sat opposite. She stared openly their way, first at Patrick and then at the girl. Carol's gaze suddenly went down into her lap. Where they remained as though she was considering something important.

Mind made up, she brought her eyes back up and stared over Don's shoulder as if he were not there. She turned a touch in her chair, bringing her legs out into the open and into play as it were. The restaurant was busy, a burst of laughter and a predictable uproar from a table of young men, most of them staring at Carol's legs. Jealousy brought Don back, annoyed because Carol gave them a show every time she moved. I saw Stuart smiling as the anger bubbled away inside Don.

He even shook his chopstick at her and scowled down the table and said, 'Keep your knees together.'

Carol blinked, 'I bet you never say that to any of the other girls you talk to.'

Patrick and the young woman stood and she led the way imperiously, head up, shoulders back. Patrick nodded our way and stopped close to Don.

'You better ease up on the driving lessons, what would the inspector say?'

Don mouthed something and his eyes followed them out of the door. Don's gaze settled on the girl's swaying hips and arse. Craning his neck to peer around Patrick and get a clearer view.

And now that same young woman was lying broken and dead. I blew a steaming mist of warm air out from my clenched teeth. I think my observation of people and relationships better than most. I would have put money on Don being close to this girl somehow. Stuart had confirmed my worst fears, despite Don being nearly thirty years older than her, that look between them in the restaurant was worth more than a thousand words.

1980 – TEDDY

Strangulation – kicking, wrestling against oblivion. Shitting your pants as you go. Trying to drag air in through a blocked windpipe. Unable to see whose doing the strangling.

He breathed in – deeply. A maniac on the loose. Not yet!

Past lives, his thick, short sighted brother. What about his past life? Was he even alive? His bloody stupid daughter was dead. She was past tense now.

He rushed the few hundred yards back home, animated and frightened. Dejection pulsed through him like a thorn being dragged backwards through his femoral artery. Up the spiralling staircase two at a time and into the bathroom, two steps across the floor and close to the mirror and stared. What did he see? Why did he look like his father? How did that happen? His breathing didn't want to slow down, he tried to breathe deeply but his chest ached after his short run back. Burned like a chest infection, he tried to remember the last time he'd run.

His eyes flicked all over the mirror, you're scared.

He heard a dog bark, answered by another on the other

side of the village, but no police siren, no ambulance, nothing apart from his rasping breathing. It was the worst day of his life and he'd had a few of those over the years. It wasn't as though someone he knew had gone forever. Gone in a flurry of intense activity, a rain of efficient punches. That was always easy for him to visualise, not like someone falling, it wasn't like that. He clutched his chest; the acute sensation of his heart plunging through his diaphragm wouldn't leave him alone.

His chest rasped in and out like an asthmatic accordion, he breathed with a fervent intensity. He tried to smile at the mirror, no pleasure or warmth in it, he tried for neutrality, if she knocked on the door, he had to appear calm – but he'd convinced himself he would sound angry or agitated or both.

Worse than that he might cry.

He rubbed his eyes, sleep … he needed sleep more than anything. Apart from her that is. Shirley had been his religion for years and years, but now sleeplessness had become his new belief.

He walked through to the bedroom, despite the exhaustion, he felt too warm and he knew sleep wouldn't come tonight. His brain wouldn't slow, he tried to focus – something momentous had just happened and he couldn't focus on it, his mind darted everywhere. No not everywhere, always towards her. His daughter had become his magnetic north and his thoughts always pointed her way now.

Why did she do it? What did she expect him to do?

He thought of the prison cell, things were easy then. Nothing to worry about, get sucked off by the queen now and again. Treated with reverence, even the governor was scared of him. In the unglamorous confines of the cell, his emotions were always in check. It was never the worst of times, despite the deprivation. He enjoyed the simple boundaries to the brutality. Stress and deceit were never in his mind – only revenge.

Now?

The images started to come back. He shut his eyes; he wanted the Old Testament world of barbarity and retribution back in his life. The fantasies of rapists and pederasts. The bloody perverts and sex offenders. His mouth dried and he felt humiliated because of his erection. Fuck knows why? They were few and far between these days.

He threw his clothes off and slid into bed. He pushed the erection between the cheeks of his sleeping wife's buttocks.

'What are you doing?'

Someone must pay for his stupid daughter.

But despite everything she'd done, he wanted her back.

'What's up with you? Jesus Christ, our daughter's just… what are you thinking of?'

He blinked and turned away from her.

5

1945 – TEDDY

Teddy rubbed his eyes, he needed sleep, why couldn't he feel drowsy at night? After all, he couldn't stay awake in the daytime. Then he always felt like a dog in the midday summer heat, all he wanted was a lethargic crawl into some cool shade and the chance to dream. He needed sleep now more than anything – apart from her that is.

He walked through the gate, ignored the prison officers comment.

'See you in a few weeks Teddy.'

He felt better standing, whenever he lay down the constant burning began, acid? Perhaps he had an ulcer? Whatever it was, in the morning his stomach still burned sour like an acid drop wedged up his anus. His brain wouldn't slow, he tried to focus. The heavy gate slammed behind him. The car across the other side of Braybrook Street, his brother grinning myopically his way, elbow sticking out of the car window. A blonde sat in the back seat – movement in his trousers, he wanted her so much. He couldn't stand the disappointment, perhaps it was just some old tart his brother had found for him.

Perhaps it wasn't her.

He climbed in the through the back door, slid alongside the woman.

All the time looking ahead. He couldn't stand the disappointment. He felt a warm hand on his thigh, 'Teddy, I've missed you so much. Look at me.'

She took his hand, placed it on her thigh, directly on the

stocking top. Teddy slid the dress up and stared down and over her legs. He slowly brought his eyes up to the woman's face.

Shirley!

Five minutes later, Teddy spotted Eyeless watching in the mirror. 'Keep your fucking eyes on the road.' Shirley jumped and Teddy felt the involuntary bite into his erection. 'Careful you stupid cow.'

Minutes later, she said it, 'Move up north of the river, all the money's there. No more putting the squeeze on fish and chip shops. No more running spotty faced tarts up Coldharbour Lane. Big money's up west.'

He was an east-end boy, making a crust south of the river. No more.

Up west for me, Soho, me and the blonde.

Then she said it.

'Fix the fight.'

The fight!

Get all his mates to bet on the fight.

Clean up and then everyone will know that Teddy's the man.

'Come and look at the club. It's really smart – that's what we need. Something smart. He's in my back pocket, he does anything I want.'

She wouldn't shut up, on and on.

'I've organised everything for your party – even got a few girls…'

***

He noticed that journalist straightaway. They'd met before, but Teddy couldn't remember where. There he was, sat in the club, staring at him, all the time. The sneaky glances. Until he let their eyes finally meet. That look between two men. The implicit understanding that goes with it.

Those little poofs in prison – the same look.

Most men avert eye contact from strangers. Poofs look

straight into his eyes when others wouldn't dare.

He knows – or thinks he does. He knows fuck all.

1945 – JACK

I called it a coming out party at the time. The estimable Teddy Lewis had invited the usual suspects, a few policemen, a couple of reporters, local councillors. I say Teddy had sent out the invitations, nothing formal of course, I assumed a phone call here and a whispered word there. My editor gave me the time and place, who contacted him I never knew until much later.

Teddy's club full of his cronies, with their scarred faces and broken noses, all this contrasted nicely with their dark, expensive suits. Cheap cologne enveloped the group and the music struggled to break through the denseness of the cigarette smoke. The choice of song made me smile, Cole Porter's "I've still got My Health". I sat back and watched, jumping once when a champagne cork popped behind me. The women gaudy and blonde most of them, as they twittered away. Not the joyous chirping you'd expect from a dozen or so women drinking and eating for nothing. A collective, cold-eyed edge as they stared at the financial options spread around the room. The men must have felt like an untidy bundle of used notes being viewed by a group of voracious and opportunist women.

A click of Teddy's fingers and the drinks materialised as if by magic. I looked around at the other tables, all of us on the take. I stood up and wandered over to the bar. Ordered another drink and slipped a ten shilling note out from my pocket. The girl's eyes went towards the big framed man stood alongside me, he nodded his head.

The man lifted his glass my way and said, 'Cheers.' He was a thick set man with thick lips and thicker glasses. 'It's diabolical what they done to Teddy, he's a peaceful man – everyone knows that.'

I stared at the man, who turned out to be Teddy's older brother. I called him a body guard, but Teddy would have bridled at the suggestion that he needed such protection. I listened as the accolades flowed from the short sighted man's mouth. Like a bad actor that had at least learned his lines well. He spoke with earnestness and in the manner of a cockney who carefully tried to enunciate every word.

I interrupted his uneasy monologue, 'How many police here?'

I'd talked to this man before, months ago, naturally defensive like all of them. Given the chance to brag about how powerful they'd become, caution quickly replaced by effusive carelessness as the chance to impress took over. He looked around the densely packed club, 'Ten, eleven… eleven, cost a fucking fortune. But it keeps them off our backs.'

The police turned up a bit like me I supposed, looking for a free drink and scraps of gossip. A chance to turn a minor villain in, a more than better chance of an approach from one of the women. Teddy had crossed the line last year, putting a blade across his wife's cheek in front of two dozen people. A high profile attack in a Lyons tea room on a Monday afternoon.

Overstepped the mark just like they all do eventually. Believing their own publicity, the legend, their own invincibility. It cost him the best part of a year in the Scrubs and now he sat like a morose Kaiser looking to fill a void in his life.

My large friend hit the nail on the head, 'When you lot tell the punters that they should be afraid – then they are afraid. It works well… cuts down on the beatings.'

A surprisingly perceptive thug.

Oh well – pleased to be of service.

I scanned the room again, the men talked in whispers, uneasy with Teddy's silence and I drank on the house, along with policemen and local councillors and high flying legal eagles. The established Fleet Street tenet called make the most of it, meant that I necked Teddy's gin. I glanced across and he sat, dark skinned and sleek, hair brushed neatly to one side.

Moustache clipped and the ubiquitous trilby on the table in front of him. Large coat and trilby... everyone tried to look like Humphrey Bogart back then. We had run a series of articles about Lewis just before he was put away. That's when the photograph with Shirley had been snapped. My battered notebook bent and buckled as I scratched away. Every word of Lewis's noted, every glib quote, all the thinly veiled threats.

I supposed that the newspapers were no different back then, more interested in the legend than accurate copy. Truth shoved way back as we all took drinks and the free theatre tickets and the girls.

Right and wrong not a chance, it was never in the frame. I wanted to enhance these people's image not shoot them down. Teddy Lewis used us to make his position more secure and a sanitised revue of his benevolent activities appeared in the paper periodically. I gulped his gin, knowing the next would be along smartly.

'You having another?'

I stared at the man's thick glasses, hypnotised by how myopic he must be. My unconscious thoughts made a sudden and unwelcome appearance as I said, 'Blind as a bat.'

He squinted, then stood up and came close to my chair. 'What did you say?'

'Some people in your line of business.' I had an ability to think on my feet, which was lucky, even if I was sounding more and more like Wyn. 'Short-sighted, never see the bigger picture.'

'I don't know about that.' He sat down again, 'Look at the girls. Look how well they mix. They do Teddy's work for him. We don't need violence.'

I nodded; I could see that they would be more effective than all of the bribes and the free booze. But extortion needs policing and not the boys in blue either.

But my new friend only wanted to talk about the women and he confirmed this by saying. 'Poke one of these women and ...'

I never said anything, but he was right, sleep with one of

these girls and blackmailed straight away probably, though not for money necessarily. Power, leverage – networks springing up again and hey bingo, Teddy's back in business. He needed immunity, but the large amounts of cash going into corrupt policemen's pockets was no longer a guarantee. Teddy had become a marked man in many ways now, they might still take his money, but gone were the days when he strutted around with impunity and immunity.

Oh, but we still took all the booze and women on offer. I mean if someone is that stupid to throw it your way, well why not? Where did all of this leave me? Principles, ethics, morality – I glanced across at Teddy sat back in his chair, gin in one hand and a large cigar in the other. A woman stood behind his chair and gently rubbed his neck. Then she bent a little and whispered in his ear, he never smiled. She blinked a couple of times, her mouth formed a circle. Her irresistible offer rebuffed by a surly man with other things on his mind.

Teddy's eyes scanned the room. If I were sensible and in control I would have looked away. Eye contact with a barracuda? But I couldn't resist staring at such a handsome man. Again I couldn't answer another question, was it the danger, the power of the man? Or his sexuality? Teddy comfortably held my gaze and I knew. One of my questions had been answered. I shook my head, this was a dangerous game to play.

I turned to my companion and said, 'Where's that good looking woman that was always hanging onto Teddy's arm? Before he went down that is.'

'Doing some administration for Teddy.'

He laughed and I frowned as a small electrical charge of discomfort shot down my spine. I asked my companion another question. 'Are they still together then?'

'Well, I picked her up outside of East Acton station. She sat in the back. We drove on to the Scrubs and Teddy came out a few minutes later. Got in the back seat with her. Then he told me to keep my eyes on the road and off the fucking mirror.'

I shuddered, hoping against hope that we were talking about different blondes. 'She waited for him then?'

My companion nodded, then pursed his heavy lips and sucked the smoky air in. He slowly shook his head, 'If she looked at another man, Teddy will go fucking ape-shit.' He took his glasses off and rubbed his eyes and sent a short sighted squint my way.

She wouldn't dare.

And there, right in front of me, the implied and thinly coded threat of a razor blade across the cheek if she ever crossed him. I frowned into my gin; these people would never last long. Short lived thugs they might be, but what was Shirley playing at?

Messing about with recklessly violent men?

Wyn felt that they could be persuaded to work together for the greater good. Business before anything else, but it wasn't their philosophy, cunning and not very bright, petty jealousies and greed had turned most of them into a directionless mob.

If she wasn't already, Shirley would soon be out her depth. Teddy must know about her and Wyn, after all they had hardly made any effort to keep their relationship discreet. Although things had become marginally more so since Ronny's arrival on the scene. He seemed happy enough working for Wyn. Just about accepted his wife's closeness as some sort of business arrangement, he appeared unaware. Or maybe he pushed things to the back of his mind and hoped for the best. Like most of us would do, Shirley had a talent. Able to blind us all, twist us into believing whatever she wanted us to believe. A natural gift for deception maybe, but she was either not very bright or mad. She should know better than most why Teddy had gone inside.

***

Michael Parlane was a good editor, old school, effusive and abrupt at the same time. The many broken veins on his bloated cheeks an indication that he pursued the god of alcohol like most members of this profession. When I got back to the office, Michael was waiting by my desk. I knew that under normal circumstances he would have gone himself. But it was meant as a snub to Teddy, high flying editors couldn't be seen alongside razor happy thugs.

Michael put his shirt sleeved arm around my shoulders, 'How did it go?'

'Usual stuff – lots of girls.'

Michael raised his eyebrows, never one to refuse hospitality, especially attractive prostitutes. He winked at me, 'Pity I couldn't make it. How was Teddy?'

I wanted to get back to work and write a few lines about Teddy. I needed to think this was a harmless enough trade off. I didn't need Michael regaling me with his tales of just how generous a south London yob could be. I tried to keep a straight face. 'He's turned over a new leaf and hopes to get into the night club business. All legitimate this time.'

I sometime surprised myself and wondered if I sounded at all cynical. No one could believe that one and no one would, but I pushed it all to the back of my mind as best as I could. When reality made the occasional foray into my consciousness, I pushed it back as effectively as Canute might the tide.

Forcing myself to believe that I belonged to that bibulous, collegial group of principled journalists that exposed corrupt politicians and crooked business men.

I think Michael understood, he patted me on the back, 'Don't worry, you're young. Still got one or two principles left. Write it up, you know the rules.'

I knew all right, our strict libel laws and our neurotic legal team always gave us the excuse for not exposing, often holding back the best stories, the ones that we never printed. Perhaps they would have made us all famous and loved even. How I wallowed in self-pity – twenty one years old and starting at the bottom. How unjust my working life had quickly become, well down the list behind the political correspondents and the war correspondents, the diary editors and show business reporters.

Bottom of the pile and remunerated accordingly.

I sat in front of my typewriter, what did all of this make me? Someone happy to take free drinks from Wyn and yet more from Teddy. I told myself that I would never take anything else, oh maybe the occasional theatre ticket either of them sent my way but never the endless offer of girls, I couldn't be tempted by that one. It would be fair to say that the first couple of months of the post war period were certainly not dull and I was on the take like everyone else.

Justifying taking most things that came my way by wallowing in a glorious and self-righteous indignation.

***

Later that night, I walked into Wyn's club. Happy to be in the company of people, who had quickly become firm friends. I had fallen under the collective spell of a club owner and his deranged mistress. A woman with a blatant sexuality that she wore as proudly as any medal. A woman who I knew was betraying her husband and now it seemed, her lover as well.

As was her custom, Shirley sat close and I always felt I wanted to use her much like you would a priest, sat close by like I was in a confessional box. Talking to Shirley despite the sense of suspicion she always brought out in me. I started to tell her what a bad lot life had become for me, when I should have been asking what she was doing with Teddy earlier this morning.

Instead I said, 'What do you want out of life?'

'Have fun and be happy – not too much to ask is it?'

Shirley stared at me and said, 'I always enjoy playing cards and having a laugh. But it's not the same, I loved it when it was packed with servicemen.' She smiled and said. 'No – not just because they were mostly men either. It was lively and I felt safer even when the air-raid sirens were going off. It's become dangerous now, I hear what the girls whisper and listen to what Harry and Wyn won't tell me. That's the biggest giveaway – what's not said.'

'I went to a party Teddy Lewis threw this afternoon.'

Shirley never blinked, she out stared me and I eventually glanced across to Peggy, who gave a little wave and started to sing, "You're a bad influence on me".

I watched as she sang, saw her eyebrows lift a touch and Peggy nodded in the direction of the bar. I did a rapid double take, Teddy Lewis waiting to be served, dressed conservatively – a man out to impress. I turned back to Shirley... gone. She had an intrinsic sense of survival that went way beyond a formal education. I stood up and rushed towards the back office, heart beating erratically, my eyes fixed on the floor. I knocked and walked into the centre of Wyn's plush little universe. Neatly panelled with dark wood, table to match. Box of cigars and a large lighter close by. Wyn leant back in his chair; Shirley leant against him, her fingers stroking his neck.

I blurted the words their way, 'We... you have a visitor. Teddy Lewis is sat out the front.'

I knew that I had become an adroit reader of expressions. I studied him now, the smile, followed by the slight inclination of the head. The brown eyes, I would never call him careless with his own life or that of others. I mean he had so much to lose for a start. But he did appear unconcerned with consequences. He studied me with a look that openly calculated and weighed me up. Then like a door being slammed shut, he smiled my way.

Relax.

'I've just heard.'

They never said a word; it was as if they had rehearsed this moment many times. Shirley slipped a lightweight jacket over her shoulders. Picked her handbag up as Wyn lifted the phone out of its cradle. He gave the number slowly and waited, he drummed his fingers once on the mahogany table. Sat forward as the connection went through. He spoke, 'Yes it's the Major here.' The first time I'd heard him use that epithet, under normal circumstances that would have made me smile. His voice carried calmly on, 'Taxi – yes Beak Street, around the back please. No longer than five minutes.'

Then the phone went back into the cradle. He stood and they embraced, oblivious to me. I felt that I was intruding, their long stare into each other's eyes, his arms around her waist now.

Shirley ran her finger along his cheek as she said, 'Be careful.' We walked out of the office, along the corridor and along to the fire exit. She gave me a cheery little wave and disappeared out of the door.

Wyn came up close and gently gripped my bicep, 'I'm going to face the music, are you coming?'

I was being drawn inexorably somewhere, a place that I didn't know, accompanied by the strong intuition of dark consequences. It seemed that Wyn saw nothing and I felt everything. He picked his coffee cup up, sipped away as the clock ticked away on the wall behind. I closed my eyes and tried to concentrate, did I walk back into the club with Wyn, or go out of the same door that Shirley had just walked through?

I felt a reassuring grip on my elbow and with no resistance from me, felt myself being guided back into the club. Wyn pulled two stools across and we sat at the bar, he nodded at the barman and a bottle of single malt appeared in front of me. I sat unsteadily, my temples throbbed and the world fell silent.

Wyn poured a generous measure and I gulped most of it in one. It changed nothing; I wanted to lose myself in a mindless fug of smoke and booze. Surround myself with drunks, perverts and the dissolute. Not the psychotic sat somewhere behind me.

I turned and looked for him, my cigarette stuck in the middle of my lips. As the smoke drifted up and stung my eyes I saw him. Sipping coffee just like the man sat alongside me.

Coffee? What's up with everyone?

Teddy's cold colourless lips matched his cold, cold eyes. Colder than a pair of marbles on a frozen, December morning. The face of an emotionless assassin? It wasn't that he saw things that others missed so much. Rather that he saw what he wanted to see and most of the time that displeased him. Why did I keep glancing his way? I forced myself to stare at my half empty glass. That's when I felt the tap on the shoulder, I spilt good scotch on my trousers and waited stoically for a punch in the kidneys.

'Get your fucking head out of your arse Jack, he's gone.'
Harry!

***

Much later, when most of the punter's had gone home, we all sat and talked the night away. Wyn with his pot of strong smelling coffee and his jug of fresh orange juice on the table in front of him, neither item available for most of us. The black market had blurred class boundaries. Decent people from all walks of life wanted the good things. Most of which could only be supplied by spivs and other shady people of the night. Organised crime had come to London. I say organised, chaotic in its infancy as gangs jockeyed for all the opportunities that dangled tantalisingly in front of them. The gangs of hungry dogs made for an unseemly and often violent scrap as they chased after the juicy bones.

'What was Teddy Lewis doing here?' I asked the question simply because Lewis was an east London boy and he operated strictly south of the river... until now.

'I don't know, spreading his wings. West End is where the real money is after all. Don't worry, there's enough to go around, if we're sensible that is.'

'He's everything but sensible. You've just had your card marked.' I looked up at Wyn, 'You know how it's going to start – a fight breaks out, a few tables overturned. Glasses broken, women insulted, customers pushed and shoved.'

'Not here.' Wyn gazed evenly back at me, 'I'm legal – extortion only works in illegal drinking dens.'

He sat back, glanced at one of his girls as she slinked passed heading for the last unsuspecting business man. Propping up the bar and staring glumly into his drink.

Wyn smiled at me as we both watched the woman as she ran the back of her fingers down the man's cheek. He smiled up at her, apparently unaware that he had suddenly turned from a drab and inoffensive little man, into a magnet for an attractive woman. Wyn shrugged my way, just another public servant providing a valued service and another soon to be contented customer.

I took my eyes back to Wyn; it had fast become a favourite pastime for me, trying to disturb his equanimity. 'They wouldn't have issued a drinks license if they knew you had never been in the Army.' Wyn back handed away, despite giving himself the grand sobriquet of the Major. Laughably everyone believed that one and they happily called him Major Watkins. He traded under that name despite never being near a uniform. Unless you count the times he was stood next to a squaddie at a urinal. Had I chipped away the veneer of imperturbability?

Maybe... his mouth turned down a touch, 'What are you suggesting?'

'You only got the license because the magistrates thought you were a war hero.'

'Whoever told you that lie?'

I said nothing, Harry's grin widened and his eyes creased as an awkward silence enveloped us, Wyn stared across the table towards Harry. 'My brother can be so indiscreet.' He said this, apparently hurt by the revelation.

I pressed on, 'Your drinking might be legal. The women and the gaming aren't. You're treading on these people's toes in more ways than one. Sooner rather than later and you'll get a call.'

There, I'd done my duty, a caveat duly imparted. But words of warning broke over Wyn as ineffectually as waves across granite outcrops. No sign of fear or caution, merely mock outrage that I suggested he ran something like a glorified knocking shop.

He confirmed this when he said, 'You think I run a brothel – I find that offensive.' His face reflected that, as though something rancid had been thrust under his nose.

I could've argued that point, the illegal gaming tables and

the women brought Wyn over a thousand pounds a week. That very illegality made an approach from any one of half a dozen thugs inevitable. Their offer of protection as reassuringly certain as the neap tide always follows the full moon. It wasn't as if Wyn's operations were in any way covert either.

The women made their trade apparent, happy to not only drink with customers, but soon place their cards well and truly on the table. Wyn even kept a couple of rooms upstairs. Covering every eventually, I mean punters with no hotel room available could soon be drinking his over inflated booze again after a quick and probably soulless coupling.

Just then, the sound of a woman laughing drifted over from the bar, followed by a man saying, 'How much?'

Harry laughed, I smiled and Wyn sighed.

I sat back in my chair and my mind kept wandering back to Teddy. Shirley had branched out it seemed. She was romping in the back seat of a car with Teddy. Not content with sleeping with Wyn behind her husband's back. Shirley was sleeping behind her lover's back as well. All these dangerous complications and pregnant too.

'What are you thinking about Jack?'

I sighed, 'Life's complicated isn't it?'

He backhanded this away, 'I do all the right things. Politically I mean, policemen drink for nothing. Things are going nicely, complicated? I don't think so.'

I briefly thought about telling him what I knew. Shrugged and said nothing. Instead I scanned the club, Wyn was right.

Business was booming all right. Everyone was on the make; policemen put the squeeze on plenty of illegal drinking dens. Doubling and trebling their weekly incomes at the same time. And there were a few sat in here tonight. Happy to drink still wearing their uniform. The dull, deep, deep, dark blue contrasted nicely with the garishly lit club. Sipping what should have been expensive drinks and watching the women. Despite all the free drinks and the women Wyn dispensed their way, an unstoppable chain reaction was in motion and the money rolled in.

It appeared that he had the police on his side, but not his lover.

6

1980 – JACK

My mood didn't match the setting. All the lights were off, except for the dart board spotlight. That solitary light had been turned through one hundred and ten degrees and shined away like a guiding light onto the piano. Peggy came out on occasions like this, rather in the same way the Lutine bell is sounded whenever a ship is lost at sea. Someone dies in town and out she comes, turns all the lights off, plays the piano for an hour and then disappears again.

The only other light came from the two fires at each end of the bar. Casting a carroty softness over the customers and the walls, turning the nicotine browned coloured ceiling into an orange sunrise. A relaxed, yet sombre setting and I was feeling agitated about a young girl's death. It seemed that I was the only one showing any concern. A fragrant darkness and I watched Stuart as he worked away in the gloom.

'Has Patrick said anything?'

'You're joking.' He shook his head, 'Quiet, the police will pull him in if…'

Stuart trailed off, I finished the sentence for him. 'What, if they knew he was fucking a fifteen year-old girl?'

I rarely swore, Stuart blinked a couple of times and then stared at me for a few seconds. 'Something like that.'

I shut my eyes, sleeping with someone had a much softer, less threatening sound to it. Is that why I used a vulgarity to describe the situation? An underage girl getting fucked gave the whole thing an imbalance that my idealised mind needed. I whispered, 'Something like that. What can you tell me?'

Stuart raised his eyebrows, 'Not much really. Don's

driving lessons, that's about it.'

He wasn't going to mention what his mate got up to with the girl. Fifteen and grown men sleeping with her. One nearly old enough to be her grandfather. The other twice her age. I listened to the piano and the steady murmur of conversation. This suited me fine, blue music, a good pianist and a calm end to a tumultuous day.

A chance to reflect on the day's events.

I picked my glass up, threw some beer down my throat and glanced at Harry. Still the argumentative nose that glowed before any confrontation. Still the hair-trigger temper, still the awesome power. But with that package, comes the health warning that he was too slow and his hands too brittle. I'd made sure he was always close by in those post-war years. The years when I was suffering some sort of shell-shock and needed his protective cloak around me.

I watched Harry and Tommy sat on bar stools resting their elbows on the counter and smoking. Stuart stood opposite the pair and they formed an irregular triangle, son, father and father in law. Hardly the holy trinity, but entertaining if nothing else. Stuart wore his status as licensee like a military campaign ribbon. Comfortable with the little scandals, arguments, brushes with the law that seem to go hand in hand with the pub trade.

Stuart's gaze settled on Tommy. 'Someone falls out of a window and the police have three men on scaffolding as witnesses.' Tommy's eyes flicked around the bar, a muscle ticked away in his vacant cheek, finally he smiled, but said nothing. Harry punched his son on bicep and said, 'It's amazing, three men working a few feet from a window, some girl hurls herself out and they see fuck all.' Harry turned towards me and said it again. 'They see nothing, what do you make of it all Jack.'

'Three wise monkeys – the difference is that all three say nothing. They all saw what happened though.' I stared at Tommy who gazed steadfastly into his beer.

Nothing for me here.

'Where's your brother?'

Harry snorted towards the other bar, 'Where do you think?'

Stupid question, I sighed, turned and wandered through to the Smoke Room. Wyn beamed my way and Shirley stared down at the floor. Wyn's right hand rested insouciantly in the expensive sports jacket pocket, the left elbow rested against the mantle shelf. He took his look away from me and stared down at the fire for a minute.

Wyn had become the perfect combination of discretion and seediness. A connoisseur of good looking women that, to some at any rate, made him even more interesting. Perhaps his age had added just a touch of vulnerability. Wyn absent mindedly fingered the scar that ran diagonally down his broad cheek, like a railway embankment viewed from a hot air balloon. A permanent testament to a singularly, violent act of retribution. Aside from this startling feature, his face reflected pious corruption somehow I thought. Old fashioned manners, serious expression, matinee idol's moustache.

Never beaten, plenty of reversals – but he always won the war. He'd reluctantly dropped the epithet of the Major after our escape from London all of those years ago.

I said, 'Nasty business.'

Wyn nodded before saying, 'Nasty, young girl too.'

I glanced at Shirley, preparing to leave it seemed, putting her cigarettes into her handbag. Dragging her kid-skinned gloves on. She stared at Wyn as she spoke, 'I heard that she liked older men.'

Wyn glanced back over towards Shirley and said. 'Well I wouldn't take much notice of anything he says at the moment.'

Who says?

I stared at her, she met my gaze comfortably. Nothing new in that, Shirley intimidated me and she knew it. Everyone knew it; perhaps our antipathy towards one another caused Wyn to change the subject. 'I'm thinking of selling up – what do you think?'

The George Hotel had made Wyn a steady living for over

thirty years, I couldn't see him giving that up. I said, 'Why?'

I smiled and Shirley brought her gaze towards Wyn and her nose flared, a frown firmly in place. 'Yes… and what would you do? You'd be bored witless in a few days and waste most of your money in the bookmakers.'

Shirley's fingers drummed away on the table in front of her, she nodded silently, the sound of the piano from the public bar drifted through like morning mist over the canal bank. All followed by the heartening burst of shouting from Harry, mingled with a regular curse from Tommy. They looked at each other and smiled. But they were both preoccupied I thought. Shirley's immaculately applied make-up inferred a pending encounter. I might have known her for thirty five years, but I hadn't trusted her for a single minute of that time.

I listened.

Wyn said. 'I could just sell it all, get the solicitor's moving, sell up, make a lot of money and take things easy.'

I watched Wyn as he glanced back at Shirley, with her thick blonde hair, blue eyes and those cultured cheekbones. Wyn smiled and no wonder, in her mid-fifties and not a grey hair in sight.

Shirley uncrossed her legs and pressed the knees demurely together. 'You need to stay busy and you're better off watching all those gorgeous young women you employ – have you thought about that?'

'All those young women?' Wyn moved away from the fire and stood directly in front of her. 'At my age.'

Shirley lit a cigarette and stared at Wyn for a few seconds, 'They all love you.' Shirley glanced my way, raised her eyebrows, 'They keep you young.' She shook her head, glanced at her watch, a touch impatient I felt, 'I have to go soon.'

'Are you going to have another one?' He nodded towards her empty glass.

Shirley sighed and stood, brushed her skirt down and then smiled up at Wyn, 'Early night, things to sort out.' She buttoned her long raincoat and picked her hand bag up. Wyn walked the short distance to the door and opened it for her.

Shirley rested her elegant fingers on the back of Wyn's hand. 'Old friends.'

She stared my way and raised her eyebrows again. Shirley kissed him on the cheek and closed the door behind her.

'Old friends.' Wyn said this as though he was the only person in the room.

I shook my head, I didn't ask him what was going on. He'd tell me soon enough. We stared at each other, his soft, brown eyes sparkled my way, first time I'd seen that for a couple of months. 'I've asked Shirley to come down to Cornwall for a few days.'

I smiled at him. 'Lucky man.'

He laughed, 'You're always the lucky one.' Then Wyn frowned and his lips turned down, he sighed and I watched as his hand came my way and it gently gripped my bicep. How many years has he been doing that? I felt warm and shivered at the same time. Wyn's soothing words drifted my way. 'Listen... Shirley's life's a bit complicated at the moment, she needs to get away and let things calm down here.'

With that he turned and walked into the other bar. I stood and thought about Shirley's complicated life style and didn't know whether to smile or grimace. She copes well enough, but then she's had forty years practice. I opened the front door and carefully sniffed the air. A smoker's always cautious when he walks from a hot room and outside into the cold air. With lungs already ruined by thousands of cigarettes, the shock of ice cold air was enough to cause the heart to stall. I let the frosty air filter in through my nose rather like a cautious foot soldier sniffing the air after a mustard gas attack. I glanced up the hill and then down the other way.

That's when I saw them, walking away from me, hips together and arms linked. Shirley's walking slowly alongside a bulky figure that was so familiar. They walked around the back of the terrace. I hurried after them, I knew the place so well, I knew it would be library quiet, bathed in soft street lights and solitude. Immaculately clean, steps recently scrubbed, a couple of cats were sat uneasily close and about to argue over possession of what would be the early morning sun trap. Ears back and staring, distracted by two people wandering along at this god forsaken hour, the smaller cat broke off and scuttled away.

The couple stopped in front of number six, the man looked down at his watch as Shirley slid the key into the door. He pulled the kitchen door up behind him. I crept close, watching through the un- curtained kitchen door window. She leaned forward and they kissed and walked towards the small living room as they kissed. A room that didn't reflect either her personality, or the way she dressed I thought. Everything neatly understated, a dark coloured sofa, one soft table lamp. No television, music coming from somewhere bathing the room with some sort of soft soul music. Shirley always banked the fire right up, a fierce heat, disproportionate to the small hearth would envelope the man in its redness. He was about to be enveloped by a hot fire and a red hot woman.

He wouldn't notice the carriage clock, or the small brass ornaments either side on mantelpiece. Never realise that there were no photographs of her late husband. Perhaps he might glance at the solitary photograph. One of Peggy, Harry, Stuart and Shirley stood behind the bar with their arms around one another, broad smiles from all four. Taken just about the time Stuart started messing about with Shirley's daughter-in-law, no wonder he looked so happy.

I sighed, turned away and walked back up Grove Street; reflections of Shirley muscled their way into my mind. What's better I wondered, images of a compromised Shirley or images of a compromised policeman?

It wasn't the two lovers that stuck in my mind though, as they writhed and twisted all over the living room floor. Don had no principles and seemingly, no preference about the age of his women, fifteen up to fifty five was a generous tolerance by anyone's standards. Although the bottom limit was as yet unproven, if it ever could be now.

***

I slept the profound sleep of the wicked until the alarm clock smashed its way into my head.

No!

Just me, alone as I fumbled for the clock and as the erotica fuelled dream receded, the same thought pulsed through me. Her words from thirty five years ago, as her hot breath tingled against my ears and she whispered. 'I had you down as a queer – I'm not usually wrong.'

I gave up and my head went back against the pillow and my mouth hung open, surrender.

Do what you like.

Not that I was an expert, but it's how I imagined a lover felt when seduced, overpowered by an overpowering lover. Was this how the young girl felt? Out of control, out of her mind because of her uncontrollable feelings for her lover?

I frowned, annoyed at being distracted by a woman I'd known for so long. Distracted by a policeman that I hated, angry that three men I'd known for years had closed ranks and cut me off completely.

Patrick would be the key, the unspeaking Patrick. How do you encourage him to talk? Only one man could do that and Stuart would become my interpreter, my key.

You see I didn't want Patrick to be implicated, I wanted to nail Don, I'd convinced myself that he had become the catalyst in all of this. I shrugged, even if he wasn't, he deserved some sort of comeuppance. One thing was for sure, perhaps he didn't realise it now, becoming involved with Shirley was a hazardous game.

He was about to find that out.

1980 – TEDDY

'Bernard.'

Her voice, but not HER voice.

'It's not your fault. It was no-one's fault.'

He shook his head, rubbed his eyes and stared at her. 'I

can't sleep, what am I going to do now?'

He watched, she slowly shook her head, then tried half a dozen times to open the packet. He waited until she'd got the cigarette to her lips and fired the lighter up.

'Don't smoke in here.'

She held the unlit cigarette between her heavily made up lips. Sighed deeply and then tried to slide it back into the packet. Her fumbling fingers caused the cigarette to break; she threw the tip towards Teddy. It fell on the bed halfway between the two of them.

'Jesus, what's happening between us?'

'Perhaps she just took after her mother?'

'What do you mean by that?'

Teddy sat up and pointed at her, 'Supposed to take after their mother's aren't they?'

'I've done nothing to feel ashamed about, perhaps you should look at yourself first.'

Teddy's lips compressed first, then his forehead tightened. He slid down the bed and turned on his side, away from her. She should think herself lucky he thought, not so long ago …

Women! Mothers, daughters – fuck them all.

No, he didn't mean that. Teddy never moved, held his breath as she walked past the bed and went out through the door. He waited until the door was gently pulled shut. Waited for her to go down the stairs. Teddy heard the radio burst into life, she turned the volume up, she always did that, her little act of rebellion.

Christ, Teddy thought, not this bloody song again.

The words battered their way up the stairs and through the closed door.

> "Call me immature
> Call me a poser
> I'd love to spread manure in your bed of roses
> Don't want to be rich
> Don't want to be famous
> But I'd really hate to have the same name as you."

Teddy clamped the heel of each hand over his ears, then he started to sob. The song title repeating over and over.

"Too much. Too young."

Over and bloody over.

He rushed out of the door, up and into his dark room. He threw photographs everywhere until he found the letter. It had lost its perfume years ago but never its emotion. He looked at the date, the 27th of August. The year wasn't there, but it was engraved on his heart well enough.

My dear, darling Teddy ...

His breathing slowed and then, the racking sobs stopped as well.

He sighed.

My dear, darling Teddy.

7

1945 – JACK

Teddy came in the next night, with his short sighted brother this time. Eyeless immediately ordered drinks and then refused to pay. Wyn signalled the barman to stand down. Teddy stared at me, I looked away, felt my eyes go back towards Teddy's icy gaze. I looked away again like a scolded dog avoids his vicious master's stare. But like the dog, my eyes went back to Teddy. All the time I wondered where Harry was. Adrift as I was, bobbing around in a minefield without my minesweeper.

Teddy didn't swagger so much, as glide over and he towered over Wyn, never held his hand out and I wondered if Wyn would have shaken it anyway. Teddy nodded and looked around the busy club, Caesar meets the Kaiser. Wyn never moved, apart from his eyebrows stretching a touch, nothing. Impressive I felt, perhaps his heart hadn't stopped like mine.

Peggy played some Cole Porter, 'I've got my eyes on you.' Just as Harry hove into sight, his frown clicked into place and over he came. Levered himself in between Wyn and myself and gazed at the gazer. Mexican standoff and the world stood still. People moved past us, all out of focus. Blurred movements past the two men facing us.

Harry broke the spell, 'What do you want?'

Teddy's gaze measured, us, the distance between us, my shoes, my jacket. I shivered and waited for someone to make a move.

'Nice place.' Teddy's voice inflected a little tension, perhaps he didn't get the deference he expected from the brothers stood either side of me. I could sense their breathing, Wyn's calm and even, Harry's short and rapid. One at ease with life, the other expected World War Three to break out at any second. Eyeless had his hand in his jacket pocket, wrapped around a blade of some sorts no doubt.

Wyn stared at Teddy and in his calmest delivery said, 'And what can I do for you? Drink? Cigar maybe?'

'Ever get any trouble?' Teddy answered the question himself, 'Not yet by the look of it.'

Then his deadpan face abruptly loosened and turned into a question mark as he stared at me again. 'Jack – slumming it a bit aren't you? What brings you in here?'

I stared frantically around.

Where's Shirley? What do I say?

'I only live fifty yards away.' Which not only sounded lame, it practically gave him my address. I watched Teddy write it down in the back of his head.

'Got an office?'

Wyn nodded, 'Of course, shall I bring anything?'

A nice looking girl?

Teddy pointed at Harry, 'He stays here.'

Wyn nodded, 'That's ok, Harry will wait outside the door though.' Then he gestured my way and said, 'My press secretary will be with us though.'

Press secretary!

Does he mean me?

Teddy looked around the office, huge oak table. Walnut inlay, table tennis size. Pictures on the wall of boxers and racehorses, cigar case on the table, the smell of fresh coffee, bowl of fresh fruit. One wall hidden by dozens of crates, hundreds of bottles of single malt whisky. Teddy raised his eyebrows, his thoughts transparent enough, Wyn did have contacts. Teddy stared as Wyn sat back in his chair, half-smoked cigar stuck in the corner of his mouth. Hands clasped behind his head and his brown eyes twinkled Teddy's way.

My god I thought, Wyn's either a good actor or a better card player. I watched Teddy fumble around in his trouser pocket, once again the thought that the cut throat razor was coming out and Wyn was about to be striped right now, right across his fat cheek. I wondered if Shirley could fancy a short balding with a long scar like that. Teddy pulled his hand out of the pocket and sat down, placed his hands palm down on the table and stared at Wyn.

Wyn gazed back, his soft eyes calmly fixing into Teddy's eyes.

Finally, 'Sorry – I haven't offered you a drink – I've only got whiskey or coffee.'

Teddy nodded and watched a bottle of Jura being uncorked. I smelt the scotch and needed more than a sniff myself as he said, 'Cheers.'

Wyn sat back again, showed the palms of his hands to Teddy, then he laughed, a self-assured laugh. 'Let's not beat about the bush.' He lit his cigar and said, 'What can I do for you Teddy.'

I began to wonder who was putting the squeeze on who? I soon found out as Teddy said, 'Your boy fights next week – how's he going to go?'

Wyn tipped his head a touch, 'Oh he'll win – he's stronger than ever. And his moods just right, no beer, women or fags for a month makes you a bit touchy.' Wyn leant forward, 'As you well know.'

He laughed again as Teddy clamped his lips together. That was cheeky, too cheeky as Teddy leant forward himself, their faces a couple of feet apart. 'He's going to lose, he's going to lose and lose in the sixth round as well.'

Teddy sat back and watched, Wyn disappointed him once more. Not a flicker, apart from the spectre of a smile in the corner of his heavy lips. 'Teddy – why didn't you say it was a business proposition you had in mind.'

Wyn placed his cigar on the ashtray, brought his elbows up onto the table and his fingers steepled together. 'The sixth you say... what if the boy gives your man a right going over for five rounds. You can get a better price if you load your bets up as the fight goes on.'

'Maybe, but he goes in the tank – round six.' Teddy stood and pointed, 'Round six or he'll never fight again. Or walk properly either.'

'I'm a business man.' Wyn shrugged, 'We can all make a lot of money out of this. Business – nothing personal.'

'You bet on my man, you're dead.' Teddy stood, Eyeless a split second behind him. Teddy said it again, 'The sixth and stay away from the bookies.' Eyeless opened the door for his master and Teddy walked out and stopped in front of Harry, 'What are you staring at?'

Teddy's dog came alongside his master, a small pack ready to kick off together. Wyn's voice came across the floor. 'Calm down Harry – everything's done and dusted.'

Teddy laughed in Harry's face and they wheeled away. Pack leader out in front and so happy I guessed, maybe the niggling thought tapping away in his head.

Wasn't that all too easy?

My own thoughts galloped around the meadow of my mind, good job Shirley was upstairs, good job Harry never heard what deal was being cut. Harry paced the floor looking for something to punch as it was. Wyn poured some coffee and said 'Watch those knuckles now, don't punch anything too hard.'

'Fuck off. What did they want?'

'Nothing really, testing the water probably.'

I didn't point out that Teddy's type never tested the water, just jumped straight in with their threats. Harry turned to go several times, from the waist up only as confusion whistled through him. Questions to ask, but Wyn introduced Harry's favourite topic into the unstable equation. 'Is Peggy ok out there on her own?' Wyn smiled my way as Harry closed the door behind him. He whispered, 'Dangerous times.'

I nodded. 'What are you going to do?' Desperately trying to keep the anxiety out of my voice.

Obviously failing as Wyn said. 'Don't worry my boy.'

He placed a whiskey tumbler and the bottle of decent scotch in front of me. Went back and made himself another pot of coffee, inspected his box of cigars before coming back and sitting down.

I said, 'How can you sleep drinking gallons of that stuff at this time of night?'

Wyn smiled, 'Clear conscience – sleep like a baby, always – unless Shirley's close by of course.' He smiled again, 'Don't look like that my boy, things aren't what they seem.'

I poured myself a decent measure and reached for my wallet, Wyn shook his head.

Don't insult me with money.

I smiled then said, 'It's chaos out there, drinking clubs and gaming clubs all getting the treatment. Beatings, fights kicking off everywhere except here – until tonight that is.'

'Oh there won't be any fighting.'

'No fighting, but he's putting the squeeze on you. He won't last long, if you can just hang on a few months, he'll be back where he belongs.'

Wyn held his hands up, 'Don't tell Harry any of this, about the fight I mean. No mention of six round defeats.'

I felt my mouth hang open, 'But…' I stood up and leaned on the table. 'Harry won't go for that one.'

'I know, I'm not even going to mention it for a while.'

'Harry's likely to win. What do we do then?' I stated the obvious in the hope that Wyn would reassure me in his inimitable way.

Silence, Wyn folded his arms and stared at me. Finally he said, 'I don't know. I was hoping you would come up with an idea.'

We stared at each other. I felt a tingle of excitement rushing up between my shoulder blades. Life was getting more dangerous by the minute and I was about to suggest something reckless. Sometimes I thought I needed sectioning for my own good.

I took a deep breath, 'You're a business man – think about it.'

'Never mind what I think.' His soft brown eyes suddenly took on a hard look, 'What are you thinking?'

'What are the options? We could do what Teddy and his cronies are doing, load hundreds, probably thousands on the other man.' I frowned as I said this, knowing exactly where I was going. Yet somehow still unable to believe what I was about to propose. How could Harry be persuaded to throw a fight? It didn't make sense, he wouldn't do it. Surely the better financial option was to do the opposite and bet on a long priced outsider. That's the sensible move, financially sensible, if not giving due consideration to one's own safety.

I considered myself a sane, calculating young man. I liked to balance everything up before acting. But recently I'd discovered money and in amongst the balancing act that my existence had suddenly become, money moved the fulcrum of my life. Nothing balanced at the moment. Money making schemes throbbed through my head. Most men my age were fixated by women. With Wyn, women and money in equal measure became the motivating force… whereas me? The fulcrum suddenly lurched off centre again as a heavyweight, hair-brained scheme sat one end of the see saw and a lightweight Jack at the other.

I couldn't believe the way my mind worked sometimes. We were skating on thin ice anyway. What did it matter? I took a large gulp of scotch, waited as it scorched its way down my throat. Then a final deep breath before saying, 'What does the bookmaker do?'

'I'm not familiar with bookmakers.' Wyn's head twisted a touch, 'What do you mean? Explain.'

'C'mon, what happens to the book – how do they balance the book?'

For a man well used to all things shady in nature, he wasn't a gambler. Not with bookmakers anyway. All of his risks involved a cocktail of illegal deals and irritable husbands. Dealing with bookmakers could be considered less than life threatening. Usually that is, not with what I was about to propose however. This meant something so risky that tossing lighted matches around in a fireworks factory should have been a more attractive option.

But I'd hooked myself and now I threw the bait Wyn's way.

'What's going to happen to the odds after all of Teddy's money goes on his man?'

'He'll become a red hot favourite, odds on I suppose.'

This was gaining a momentum of its own, I couldn't believe what I was about to say, it came out anyway. 'What would happen to Harry's odds?'

His mouth turned down at the corners and his eyebrows rose. He twisted his head a couple of times at his sudden realisation of an outside chance to make a lot of money.

He started to convince himself, 'Thinking about it, Harry will never throw anything, let alone a fight of this importance. What are you thinking of.'

I reinforced the direction he was heading, 'The odds lengthen on Harry, if you think that he has a good chance of winning – put some money on him.'

Surely Wyn wouldn't consider such a crude double cross? He sat back in his chair, folded his arms and sent a wink my way. He has considered it, this had turned into some dangerous farce. Perhaps we both had a death wish, or maybe he just didn't care about himself or his brother.

My frown intensified as Wyn began to get into the swing of it all. 'There's two issues here – the first and most important, I'm not bending the knee to some old school gangster that tries to put the squeeze on me… ok?'

'That's a very principled stance, but someone's going to torch this club of yours – or worse.'

'Maybe – but you have to admit that there's no way Harry would ever throw a fight and I would never ask him to.'

Wyn poured some single cream into his coffee, carefully placed a sugar lump onto his spoon and lowered it into the coffee. He watched as the whiteness of the sugar changed, turning a sandy colour from the bottom up. Finally collapsing, only then did he stir. He smelt the pungency beneath his nose, smiled across at me and sipped away.

He said, 'What would have happened if I'd have said no

to Teddy?'

'You'd have got a razor across the face – or worse and then he'd burn your club down. With you in it probably.'

'Exactly – which leads me onto the second issue. Harry won't play ball and neither will I. Don't forget, Harry's opponent has to make it last as well. He's not expecting a real fight. Oh I know what you're thinking – two horse race anything can happen. Lucky punch, Harry breaks a bone in his knuckle – distinctly possible that one. But the likelihood is that he'll win. Teddy will have distorted the book with his crazy bets.'

It was a fair point; Harry had five rounds to get his retaliation in first. A clear run in a way. I wagged my finger Wyn's way. 'Just a straight win, don't get carried away now.'

Wyn shook his head, 'We'll load up on the same round as Teddy's laid all his money and make a small fortune.' He sat back.

Easy money.

What have I started?

I pointed Wyn's way, 'Just a straight win, or at least cover yourself, and only lay half on the round he'll take the other man out.' Wyn poured himself another coffee and went through the same ritual again. I thought about leaving this madman alone and wandering off into the night. Find myself some friends without a death wish, but the magnetic force held me hard in my seat. I disliked Teddy, especially now that he considered me as just another one safely in his back pocket. I wanted to be my own man and resented Teddy and his free drinks. If I was to get free drinks then I'd get them from Wyn.

I said, 'It's still a huge risk – how do you know Harry will put this man away in the sixth.'

Wyn laughed, 'When I tell him what's going on – well you can imagine. Fixing the round will be difficult – but, I agree with you, we'll cover the bet with one for Harry to win in any round.'

The illegal bookmakers were scattered all over London. They survived by word of mouth, often operating from their own living rooms. They weren't organised, the concept of laying big bets off, virtually unheard of. But big bets going against the book would soon be on the grapevine. We had to lay the bets as late as possible.

'We have to be careful with the bets, the afternoon of the fight is best. The day before maybe.'

Wyn pointed at me, 'How many bookmakers?'

'Hundreds. It'll take me days to find out their locations and what sort of top limit they operate.'

'You can do it. We'll be careful, we can clean up here.'

That's the trouble with Wyn, always so plausible. So believable – he'd got his thinking right about the fight, but the repercussions? Neither of us had considered the aftermath. Crusades take on a life of their own.

Oh well, in for a penny.

'You're going to need a few people to lay the bets for you – I've not got much on at the moment.'

Wyn leaned across the table, 'My boy – you won't regret it.'

I poured another drink and sighed.

Won't regret it? I think I might.

'One thing.' I pointed at Wyn. 'Don't tell Shirley.'

He frowned, 'Why ever not.'

'Women can't keep quiet, you know what they're like.'

He nodded, 'You're right of course. Not a word to Harry either… yet.'

'You ought to get Shirley out of the way.' Consequences had started to muscle their unwelcome way into my mind. 'Somewhere safe I mean.'

He ignored me, 'Shall we start putting the money on tomorrow?' No such consequences for Wyn, just pound signs rattling around in his head.

I sighed, 'No, haven't you listened to a word. The same day of the fight at the earliest.'

That's how we left it

1945 – TEDDY

Teddy stared at her, she had some face that's for sure. Is that why he couldn't stop thinking about her? The way she whispered in his ear as he fucked her. 'C'mon Teddy, it's so good. Don't stop – Teddy I love you so much.'

He shouted, 'Don't fucking stare at me, who the fuck do you think you are?'

She carried on looking, he could feel her eyes on him 'I need a man right now, I always need you Teddy. You excite me so much.'

Now that should have been funny, he never excited anyone and he never had an issue with that fact.

'Look at me, why won't you look.'

Teddy dragged his eyes into hers. They shone like a pair of highly polished, tinted blue mirrors. He couldn't work her performance out, her wide-eyed excitement agitated him. He was disturbed, angry and aroused.

Aroused!

He had become turned on by this humiliation and she knew it.

'I can see Teddy. C'mon on, come to Shirley. Don't fight what comes naturally.'

So much confusion, he didn't know whether to hit her or fuck her. Which neatly demonstrated his bewilderment. He was capable of either, never done both at the same time though. Still, never too late for a first time.

'I can see inside your soul.'

He believed that one. He watched her mouth open and her eyebrows raise. He shouldn't have said anything. Punched her in the mouth and walked out. He blinked at the bright, early morning sunshine tumbling through the window, then told her to shut her fucking mouth. Carefully adjusted his erection and stumbled towards her bed.

Much later, 'I'm pregnant.'

'You're fucking joking, you've got a husband. What's he say about it all?'

'I haven't told him. It's not his, he doesn't come near me.'

'What about the fucking sheep-shagging' Major?'

'Don't be silly, he's my sugar-daddy, that's all. You're the only one Teddy. What are we going to do?'

He said nothing, let her do the talking.

'The fights in the bag – we'll be rich.'

We'll?

8

1980 – JACK

Her name kept bouncing around in my head, not Celia – that's a common enough Christian name for a well off, middle class girl. Her surname fascinated me, Schwartz, maybe Hungarian originally, certainly Jewish. But most Jewish immigrants softened their names. Made them more acceptable to our sensitivities. Even our own little town's member of the chosen race had changed his. Or more likely his parents had, from Goldstein to Goldstone.

But Schwartz?

I guessed her oh so British public school chums would have found it all mildly amusing, in their civilized and slightly anti-Semitic manner. But they would have had enough to gossip about anyway, more important issues. Like drugs and a fifteen year old girl's promiscuity. Both confirmed by the medical report, levels of both marijuana and heroin in the blood. All this plus rumours of L.S.D and God knows what else. What was up with the girl? Was she abused as a child? Full of self-loathing, was that it? Drugs and predatory men lurking close by, what a mixture.

How many men another unknown, but there was evidence of a recent sexual encounter. This wasn't necessarily an indicator of promiscuity in itself, but the gossip abounded. Most of it coming from Inspector Mably and all given to me freely over a pint. With the finger pointing squarely towards Stuart's closest friend. Of course Patrick had conveniently disappeared, just wandered away and no one knew where.

I stared at Stuart, he knew all right. 'Where is he?'

'Dunno.' He shrugged, 'Shacked up with a woman

somewhere probably.'

I sighed and glanced back down at the pathologists report. Another privilege granted to me, another favour pushed my way by Inspector Mably. He'd forgiven me for Stuart's intrusion the other day and even photo-copied the juiciest bits for me, of which there were plenty. This was more than the gossipers tittle-tattle about a disturbed young woman, all in front of me in black and white. How recent is recent I wondered? The night before, a few hours, minutes?

All these questions and no answers. Who throws themselves out of a window after a mutually satisfying coupling?

I shook my head and stared at Stuart, unusually reticent about it all – but I knew him well enough and it would all come my way eventually. I went back to the report, evidence of something in the anus, Patrick's calloused finger I dare say. If there were only some brick dust visible that would confirm that one. I groaned, the age of the girl tempered my humour. Fifteen, sexually active and deeply troubled, is that why Patrick was suddenly lying so low?

'Can I see?' Stuart stared at my reading matter. I folded the report and placed my hand firmly on it. 'Please yourself, you know I'm the soul of discretion.'

We stared and eventually I smiled, 'More than my job's worth. I do need to talk about a couple of things though.'

Like our erstwhile detective's involvement.

The door rattled open and talk of the devil… Don's bulk hovered over the threshold. No sneer across his face, unusual in itself. Nothing, just a closed expression, although it was soon apparent that he was open and ready for business. Don quickly glanced Carol's way and gestured with his head.

'Give me a minute with this tosser.'

Carol stared back, raised her eyebrows as if to say no arguing please. Sighed at the impossibility of this simple request. Stood and went out the back.

No pleasantries from Don, he just pointed at Stuart. 'Where's your mate?'

I watched Stuart's eyes, just a momentary flicker. He lifted his legs off the table and swung around to face Don. 'Which mate?'

Don frowned, 'You know which one, where's the Paddy?'

Stuart shook his head, 'Not a clue.'

'You were seen driving him out of town last night.' Don's temper was always on the edge at the best of times. Like an oil man desperately trying to cap a gusher, Don was having trouble right now. Stuart had become Patrick's personal chauffeur recently, driving him somewhere for a night out, not in itself a rarity.

'I took him to the Swan at Great Shefford.' Stuart had learnt the best technique during interrogation is to drip feed information. Saying little, offering up stuff we all knew. 'He hasn't got a license thanks to you bunch of bastards, I drove him to darts.'

Oh yes, we took our drink driving seriously around here, Patrick enjoyed doing it and Don's colleagues had been out to nail a soft target. His second drink driving offence in eight years and Stuart took it all too personally. Not because he condoned the offence necessarily, he just hated Don.

The feeling was mutual and Don kept pointing Stuart's way as if to confirm this widely known fact. 'But did you bring him back into town though?' Don's question coming back too quickly for my liking. He knew something that I didn't.

Stuart said nothing, just waited, he didn't have to wait long.

'Did you bring him back into town last night?'

'Course I did, pretty late though.'

'Your car wasn't in its usual parking place at seven this morning when I went past.'

Stuart shrugged and waited.

I helped Stuart with a change of direction, 'How come Shirley knows so much about the girl?'

Don's head went back; he blinked and stared at me. Pointed at Stuart and said, 'Find him, he's summonsed for the coroners this morning and we all know he's not going to show.'

Stuart pointed back at Don, 'What about you? Anything to say about driving lessons in a police car?'

Don's dark skin reddened a touch and he sighed, a deep heaving groan. 'Don't get lippy with me. See you in court; tell your mate he'd better be there.'

'You tell him yourself, you fucking…'

I shouted, 'Stuart!' Then I watched as they stared one another down. I tried to dismiss Don by saying, 'See you in court.'

He ignored me and glowered Stuart's way. 'We'll talk later.'

Don finally nodded at me and left.

I stood and walked close to Stuart. 'You shouldn't provoke him, it is his job after all.'

'Why did you mention Shirley?' Came back at me as quick as a flash. 'Do you know what I know?'

'I know nothing, just bits from the pathologists report.' I shook my head. 'Why don't you tell me?'

He raised his eyebrows, steepled his fingers together, before saying, 'I don't know much, only what Patrick's told me.'

We stared at one another, I brought my finger to my lips. Carol wouldn't want us discussing her husband's infidelities in front of her. I gestured for him to continue. Which he did, quietly and somewhat reluctantly I felt.

'She was as mad as a March Hare, drank anything, snorted, injected… you name it. You know they had the scaffolding up against that wall for the best part of three months. She would leave curtains and windows open, walk around half naked. Patrick said that she just came right on, wouldn't take no for an answer. You could see how attractive she was. What would you have…?'

He trailed off, done nothing was the obvious answer and he well knew that. I said, 'She was fifteen, Patrick's over thirty.'

'Just over.'

'Don't…'

He raised the palms of his hands, 'Patrick never touched her. I believe him.' Stuart must have seen my frowning, look of disbelief and offered a reasoned defence for his absent friend. 'You know how we are, if there's something going on we can't wait to tell each other. He told me from the beginning, she used him as a priest. He liked her and she told him that she liked them his age, or older even.'

Then he stared, enough bait there to hook an overfed barracuda.

'Patrick puts women on a pedestal, he's not pushy, he listens to them. I believe him, it wasn't age that stopped him though. It was her being so barking mad. He didn't want to exploit her, he tried to help her. I'm sure the thought of a prison sentence was always at the back of his mind though.'

Did I believe that? Maybe, 'You make him out to be some sort of agony uncle.'

Stuart laughed, 'It's why he's so good with women. Try this for size, one of her teachers and her mother's lover.'

'Teacher? Mother's lover?' I felt my eyebrows arch, fumbled for my cigarettes and whispered. 'And let's not forget Don.'

I already had three or four red top newspapers on the story, if this got out we'd get the whole of Fleet Street. I flicked ash into the heavy glass ash tray and said, 'Which teacher?'

'Geography, slight chap. Wispy moustache and weak chin.'

I knew that all the male teachers were heavily vetted, only the plus fifty five's or the queer ones got jobs there... I thought.

Stuart must have read my mind, 'He was a limp wrister, but not that limp evidently.'

'How do you know him?'

'I played squash against him once, tidy player although he minced around the court like Liberace. He was in bed with her, until her schoolmates walked in that is. She liked an audience.'

I frowned, 'Don't the police know?' I knew the answer to

that one and answered it myself, 'Don't tell me, the governors hope to keep it canned and then quietly sack the teacher.'

Stuart nodded, 'He's gone and I don't think the police know.' He put his finger in the air, and then pointed it towards me as if it were a pistol about to be fired. 'Patrick got caught as well.'

'I thought you said he never touched her.' The palms of Stuart's hands came up. Listen will you.

'As I said she liked to shock. It shocked Patrick too and that takes some doing. He was talking, clambered through the window, sat on the window sill. She stripped off, slowly like some burlesque queen. Lay down on the bed, propped her head up with one hand. Like she was waiting for her schoolmates and sure enough, they burst into the bedroom a few minutes later and she just lay there. Legs open, showing the lot.'

'You've only got Patrick's side of the story mind. Going missing has made all of this worse. You have to get him to the coroners, he'll go to prison.'

Carol came back through and said, 'No he won't, not with other men involved.' She sighed, 'Women know these things, and Patrick's not interested in schoolgirls.'

How would you know?

Stuart smiled at Carol, she lowered her eyes a touch and a glimmer of a smile crossed her lips at the same time. I felt I was missing something here. 'She thought they all loved her and she fell for all of them. Loved them, fell completely.' Stuart was still looking at her as he spoke, 'And she was relentless, she wouldn't take no for an answer.'

Stuart swallowed hard, 'Relentless.'

'That's no excuse.'

Carol blurted, 'What about the mother's lover then, or the recently departed teacher? He's the one that rolled her joints for her as well.'

'Did he now?' I stared at Stuart, all the time wondering how Carol knew so much about this. Stuart didn't want eye contact, he gazed at the clock and I talked to the side of his face. 'Patrick has to make contact, Carol's right, it will change things with others involved. You've got time before the coroner arrives. Go and get him, it looks so bad if he doesn't show.'

Stuart looked down at the floor and said nothing, the seconds ticked by. Finally he dragged his eyes my way. 'He... I can't get him back.'

'Where is he?'

'I gave him a lift.' He lowered his gaze and swallowed hard as I stared, the horrible intuition within me that the young man opposite had implicated himself somehow. He showed me the palms of his hands.

You'd do the same for a mate.

'Where did you take him?'

'Holyhead.'

'Oh God.' Whispered from Carol's lips.

I groaned and sat down, a suspect safely ensconced in some bolthole in deepest rural Ireland by now.

***

I stared around the darkly lit, wood panelled courtroom, glanced across at the reporters from the dailies. Nosing around, ringing the office, casually bumping into me in the pub. Asking me questions, what was she like? Why did she do it? But I told them nothing, this was my coroner's report to write up, my dead body to gossip about. Not a clutch of minor crime reporters from the red top newspapers.

We sat in the corner of the darkly lit courtroom. With the entrance diagonally opposite, I had every angle covered. I had become well used to the coroner's dull monologue over the years.

He had an unfortunate delivery, whatever the subject matter, I felt his wooden delivery rendered everything to a list of names in the phone book. On and on he rambled, until he read out the name of the father that is.

Bernard Schwartz?

I shook my head in disbelief; Bernard Schwartz was the real name of the actor Tony Curtis. I craned my neck but could only make out someone with thick, black hair swept straight back over his scalp. An expensive black suit, a powerful neck and wide shoulders.

'My name is Bernard Schwartz and I live at Rose Cottage in Sonning.'

I blinked twice, three times. My throat dried, I thought I might faint. The voice jarred. A mongrel accent, cockney and something continental. Despite this, alarm bells clanged away, a voice from my past. I never realised that they could speak, but I'd just heard the voice of a ghost.

1980-TEDDY

Teddy listened to his wife, giving her name and address. Her head down, speaking so quietly.

Speak up you slag.

He stared at the fat coroner and his mind drifted away, a beach in Spain, a camera. A zoom lens, a couple kissing. Not on a beach though. Somewhere much cooler, Abbey Meadows in Oxford. He had followed them from the gates in front of Trinity College. Hand in hand, shoulder to shoulder at times. She kept kissing the man. Weedy little fucker, hippy looking little cunt. He knew the man, her geography teacher. Shook his hand once, like grasping a wet lettuce.

They had sat close to the river bank. Even from this distance, the zoom lens picked her exquisite jaw-line. It certainly picked up her hand all over his cock. It couldn't miss the man's hand going up her skirt either.

The fucking bastard, someone else on his growing list of scores to settle.

'Mr Schwartz.'

That little ginger moustache nuzzling into her neck. His zoom lens picked her saying something – "I love you"?

'Mr Schwartz?'

She always said that to me – right up to the end. 'I love you daddy.'

'Mr Schwartz, Mr Schwartz – are you all right?'

He looked up at the coroner, blinked at the fat face and nodded. But he kept thinking of his gorgeous daughter and that song. That bloody song was making him cry now. The bloody, fucking, sentimental fucking garbage.

> "And I miss you
> And I'm being good
> And I'd love to be with you If only I could
> When flowers bloom and robins sing."

'Mr Schwartz – do you need an adjournment for a few minutes? He felt his wife's arm come around him, he shrugged it off.

It was his voice, but he didn't remember speaking. 'Get on with it. Just get the fuck on with it.'

9

1945 – JACK

I tracked Shirley down later, a broad smile and she rushed over to greet me, up on tiptoe and she kissed my cheek.

'Jack – stranger, how's things?'

Jesus she looked so good, low cut gown, but a cut above her surroundings here. She dealt cards for the poker games, I'd watched her many times before – a player of no little skill. I think most poker players struggled to take their eyes from her breasts as she dealt the cards. Her eyes always fixed on the player about to get the bum hand. Making sure his eyes were on her cleavage. Always the breasts pushed up like some regency courtesan.

I said, 'I've not seen you much since Teddy's been out.'

She stared hard at me, 'No?' The gaze came unremittingly my way, I looked around at the market traders, finished for the day and having a few hands before they made their way home. I felt her hand on the back of mine. 'Why – are you worried?'

How long have you got?

I told her about the fight, although not mentioning the intended double cross.

'I knew something was going on.' Shirley's articulate eyebrows went up a touch. She tugged at her silver earring, looked away and smiled. 'Poor Jack – life's complicated for someone like you isn't it?'

Shirley glanced at the poker players, one of whom waved frantically her way. Shirley fixed me again, 'I have to get back to the game, listen... have no doubt that Wyn's well in control of the situation. Me too, don't forget that I've got the perfect way out of all of this if things go wrong.'

'I think that you should get out for a while, it's going to get hot.'

'How?'

'We're about to come under the protective arm of Teddy Lewis and you know how unpredictable Teddy is.'

No wonder she was so good at cards. I got nothing from her except a sigh, then she said, 'We'll see.'

With that she turned on her heels and left me. It seemed that everyone had this collective complacency around them.

I went out into the evening sun. Blinked into it as I walked south west along Conduit Street, blinding me… but to what? I didn't know if Wyn and Shirley might be stitching Teddy up. Or more likely, Shirley and Teddy were double-crossing Wyn. And all the time Teddy was marauding around out there. Either way it became an explosive equation, all these questions, even down to the small bite on her left breast.

Who did that?

***

Women had always felt comfortable talking to me, I never understood why. Always smart in appearance, not especially good looking and certainly no athlete. But talk they always did. When Peggy asked to meet me at lunchtime, I never questioned meeting at short notice. We arranged to meet in the Bag of Nails in Victoria, a pleasure for me, not a duty that needed to be reluctantly discharged.

Two suitcases alongside the table where she sat alone, sipping her Gin. Peggy's eyes red after recent burst of tears. She refused another drink, I sat opposite, and proceeded to chatter away mentioned the weather, how was she, everything but her suitcases.

I needed shutting up and she duly obliged.

'Jack – stop a minute, listen.' She sighed, 'I'm clearing out, I've heard about the fight being fixed, you've all gone mad.'

I put my glass down, offered her a cigarette and lit it for her.

Peggy sat on the edge of her seat and stared down at the table. After several deep breaths, her eyes grudgingly came up to meet mine.

I shook my head and dragged the smoky air in with a hissing intake. 'Well, I'll be sorry to see you go, it's the sensible thing to do mind.'

Peggy let go of my hand and sat back, 'I've got enough money.' The ghost of a smile tweaked the corner of her mouth, 'Don't tell Harry, not until after the fight. He thinks I've been detailed to the barracks at Chelmsford for a few days. I'm going back to my cosy little town and all the reassuring gossip that goes with it.'

'Do you need any money?' Cash had suddenly become something as disposable as a bag of dolly mixtures. Something I could throw around, after all I had it coming out of my ears. I had a job, not for much longer mind and Wyn had me on his payroll as well.

I pulled my wallet out, Peggy put her hand up, a policeman on point duty.

Stop!

'Keep it Jack, its all blood money, murder money.' She said it again, 'You've all gone mad.'

We both stared the same point on the table, I talked, directing it towards the table. 'Where are you going?'

'My sister to begin with, her husband... he never came back from Burma.' Peggy sighed, 'She lives between Oxford and Reading.'

I pointed towards her suitcases, 'Coach or train?'

'Paddington – taxi's coming in a few minutes and don't offer to pay for that either.'

'What about the army? You've signed on for five years.'

She shrugged, 'Told them I was pregnant. Shirley gave the sample, I hid it in my handbag. Pretended it was mine. Dishonourable discharge, my feet never touched the floor. Listen, you know where I'm going, if things die down and he still wants to see me. Point him in the right direction will you?'

I watched the taxi pull away – took a deep breath. Both of

our world's changing, hers becoming safer, mine about to fall apart. I imagined Harry and Wyn, putting the barricades up.

Getting ready to go to war.

Six years after everyone else maybe, but ready nonetheless.

***

I shivered into my jacket, stayed close to the wall of the terrace. The air heavy after summer rain. I looked down at my watch and waited.

Wyn whispered, 'There he is.'

I had found out the name of the referee, a dockworker from Bermondsey. He'd had a few fights himself, but was relatively new to refereeing. Just over forty, heavy, with abundant black hair, a hooked nose and surly mouth.

He took our approach badly, wild eyed stares up and down the street. Wyn soothed him, guided him through his own front door. His wife stood over the badly stained kitchen sink, forever washing children's clothes. Some sort of stew, nothing too rich by the smell of it. We walked through the narrow hallway into a tiny living room, paper roses the centrepiece in a bowl on the small table. Peach coloured wallpaper and a sagging sofa. He fumbled around and found his tobacco pouch. Wyn gestured to me, I offered him a tailor made cigarette.

'I know who you are; you could get into a lot of trouble with the fight coming up so soon.' He blinked at me, 'Get us both in a lot of trouble.'

I tried to reassure, 'We know what's going on, don't worry, we're not after any trouble.'

Much.

Wyn took on the mantle of smoother, 'We just want you to reassure us about the fight.'

'Me – I can't do anything, it's a done deal mate.'

Wyn reached across and touched the man's leg, 'Listen, its best if my brother hands out a beating first. Before losing the fight, makes it more credible don't you think?'

His eyebrows went up, 'Go on.'

'We've talked to Teddy about this, his lot are going to place more bets as the fight goes on, the odds will get better the more Harry belts the living daylights out of Teddy's man… don't you think?' He stubbed his cigarette out, stared into the ashtray and then brought his eyes our way. 'I've got no choice, three kids and her out in the kitchen. I had no choice.'

'How much did Teddy …'

'Nothing, not a penny, he'll just cut me fucking throat if it goes wrong.'

'Don't worry, it won't.' Wyn pulled a roll of banknotes from his jacket pocket, sent him a bundle and said it again. 'Don't worry, he'll get roughed up and my boy will go in the tank in round six.'

In the tank.

Wyn was becoming familiar with the terminology of the whole stinking operation. I wondered if he considered the consequences for the man sat next to him. Unlikely I suppose.

***

It was a fortnight later before Harry found out. Wyn told him ten minutes before we left the club and drove across London to the fight. Poor Harry, the woman he loved suddenly out of his life and now this. Some Mozart drifted out of the radio and filtered into our consciousness like an unwelcome visitor at Christmas. I glanced across towards Harry, a reluctant curiosity on my part. Frightened by his temper and threats, more frightened by the likelihood that he'd carry them out. He stared towards the empty piano – a symbolic headstone for his embryonic romance.

I couldn't stand this any longer. One of them wanted to strangle Teddy, the other wanted to carry on and operate normally, I said to Wyn, 'What have you told him?'

Harry frowned our way, I looked down at the table – even if it wasn't directed my way, a glare too much for me to cope with.

Harry glared on.

Wyn twitched a couple of times. 'You're supposed to take a dive – round six.'

Harry stood up and shouted. 'What? Fuck off, the pair of you with your schemes. I'm not throwing anything, just going to throttle the bastard and fuck off back to Wales.'

'What and work down the pit again? Listen, Teddy and all of his mates I guess – well they've all bet on you losing in the sixth. He came around here and told me to make sure that's what happens.'

'When? Why the fuck didn't you tell me?'

Wyn sighed, 'I didn't want it to upset your training.' Harry's blood vessels in his neck stood out like worms wriggling away under damp tissue paper. Wyn showed Harry the palms of his hands. 'Jack and me, we've loaded some money and put it on you to win… in the sixth of course.'

Harry brought the flat of his hand down onto the bar; I jumped and thought about ducking in the same way I used to when the V1 bombs were screaming towards the ground. He shouted at Wyn, 'How the fuck do you think I can stop a good fighter in that round? In any round come to that.'

I said, 'He's not expecting a fight.' Reluctant to become too involved, I pressed on nonetheless. 'It's a shot to nothing – we cover the bet with another on you to win in any round.' Harry's frown relaxed a touch as I continued. 'Of course you still have to win. We've spread it across town, small bets with every bookmaker in London.'

'Whose idea was this?' Harry glared at me.

Wyn nodded my way too, I had the feeling that if Harry come up with the goods, my idea may well turn out to be Wyn's brainwave.

Wyn said, 'Get your revenge this way – as long as you don't get knocked out in the sixth, Teddy and his goons lose and lose big. Think about it, like Jack says. It's almost a shot to nothing, think about it … a small revenge I know, but it makes him look like a loser at least.'

1945 – TEDDY

Teddy tried not to laugh when he heard the muffled conversation from the kitchen. People were so predictable, none more so than the couple downstairs. Laughter preceding them up the stairs, minutes later the strange noises, animal somehow, then the rhythmic grunting, all the time getting louder. Skin slapped against skin, sounding like an old fashioned leather drive belt on a thrashing machine. Then she wailed out something indistinguishable. A man's voice, someone apparently reaching the end of a sprint of a journey, closely followed by the sound of air brakes hissing.

Then she whimpered.

He imagined the blonde's legs still wrapped around him, as the breath jolted out from the pair of them.

No, that was too painful.

He went back to his teenage days, how he looked across at the camp bed in the corner – another night in the attic listening. They had stamina that's for sure, but there was no sexual jealousy on his part, it was down to them the way his talent developed – he laughed out loud at his clever use of words. Developed, that reporter would have liked that. He pursued this quest with macabre, schoolboy eagerness and it had never lessened over the years.

A secret and no one suspected, he breathed easily and he felt his eyes close. Suddenly raised voices from below woke him, he heard his own name being shouted out, then heavy footsteps down the stairs, a door being slammed and his mum shouting "fuck off then". Teddy tried to place the jigsaw together – it would have to wait until after the fight – he rubbed his hands together. Oh we'll soon be together again.

Where?

He came back abruptly, sat and stirred his frothy coffee, his mind spun like the top of his cappuccino. He rubbed his eyes and flinched.

Had he cracked up?

Blown out by that bitch of a wife of his and she's probably worrying some other bloke half to death. Teddy felt that things should be on the up, but obviously not, as he started another long slide down into another abyss. His latest little scheme meant trouble heading his way. He shouldn't have hit her, when he punched the old woman things began to close in again. Dirty old dripper offering him a free fuck. She deserved it, lucky it wasn't a blade.

Enough.

No more of that, yet his mind raced on.

Drag those bastards down and then he could settle down. A club owner with Shirley. He needed her, it would be different at her flat, she would see reason.

He always had his photographs to fall back on. Now he felt secure again, convinced the old woman would say nothing. Why had he got involved with her anyway? He had little interest in sex, except when he was with Shirley. He likened it to pornography, it bored him quickly. Watching was different, the constriction in his throat, the tight chest, the blood throbbing into his penis. Afterwards a low groan as something had been satisfied deep within.

He took a deep breath and the pain shot across his chest, half an hour earlier and he had walked out of that club, no blonde. Plenty of blondes, but not the right blonde that's for sure. He expected to see them, both of them laughing like love struck teenagers.

Sweat came into his palms, 'Anything else love.' Someone cooed in his ear. He brought his hand down onto the formica topped table, the noise of condiments brief jumping journey causing eyes scattered around the small café to round on him.

Fuck them.

He smiled at the thought of the blonde, but then the memories came flooding back and the hurt never lessened. Turning the clock back and watching them together again hurt him. The bad memories came back like a deluge. Coming home from school, his auntie always held him, made him a drink and talked. Then it all changed, overnight it seemed, coming through the door that afternoon; there they were, sat at the kitchen table, drinking tea, gazing into each other's eyes. A half empty bottle of Gordon's gin on the table, her eyes were especially sleepy.

'Hello Teddy.'

That was all she said, pouting her lush mouth at him, she smelt of smoke and gin and something else, wild and earthy. Heavy breasts straining against the confines of her coffee coloured lace top, all luxurious curves – a body that shouted sex at you was gaping, showing four bruises, two on each breast. All four the same bite size and perfectly round, standing out starkly against her white skin. She saw him staring but made no attempt to cover up.

Teddy took his eye reluctantly across the table, eventually coming to rest on the dapper man, check jacket, cravat, and Ronald Coleman moustache – smiling at him. Why did his old man grow that stupid moustache? After a while, the moustache spoke to his aunty. 'It's a nice afternoon; shouldn't you be out playing with your friends?'

'What are you doing with my Dad?'

She stood and came over and pulled him to her and planted a big kiss on his cheek. There was a strange smell on her breath, a sickly sweet smell that disgusted him. He pushed her away and rushed out leaving the back door open.

For years, the nightmare tortured and tormented him. No wonder he had moved out as soon as he could, eighteen and running wild, often earning good money. Then his mind span back again, she was another one always happy to flash the gusset of her knickers at all and sundry as well.

As he drained the dregs of his cup, he noticed the old woman coming his way, strapped into her coat like some Russian peasant woman scrapping for kindling. A cheap old scrubber that said, 'Hello love, you look like you need a fuck.'

She'll do!

10

1980 – JACK

A ghost.

One that no longer dwelt along the Vauxhall Bridge Road in London, but someone that still lived close to the Thames. In the salubrious village of Sonning now, just east of Reading. Not the tenements and the flashing, slashing razor blades of old. The ghost had not only come back to life, but had become a social climber who had somehow moved upwards. His wife appeared much younger; I imagined too much make up on her face. I could see the expensive, glitzy jewellery and the well-tailored suit. Like her husband, the blackest of black.

She confirmed her name, but without the cockney drone. Home Counties and well educated too, but dull. Flat monotone that indicated someone grief stricken and trying to retain some control over her emotions. Or maybe someone heavily sedated, perhaps both.

I turned across to Stuart and whispered in his ear, 'Get outside and take some pictures of the father when he comes out. Stay out of the way when you do it though.'

Stuart leant back and stared hard.

It's cold out there.

I ushered him out with the back of my hand as the coroner briefly listed the injuries, lung and kidney damage. Either of which probably would have killed her. If the damage to the back of the skull hadn't done the job instantly that is. He detailed the drugs and then came to the more interesting detail. The sex a couple of hours before the fall. I let my mind drift, two hours? One hour? Minutes? The voice droned on, something inserted up the anus. Not full anal penetration though, then the coroner stopped, raised his large head and addressed the parents.

'I'm sorry to have to tell you this, but Celia was pregnant.'

Pregnant?

Mably had kept that from me. I felt the air whistle out from my lungs. I heard the mother gasp and lean against her husband. He never put his arm around her. Just stared at the coroner. I thought the coroner unused to such a withering gaze. He coughed a couple of times and then began to read the witness statements out. Both Tommy and Stopcock Arthur breathed sighs of relief that neither parent wanted to question them.

Then the coroner apologised for itemising all of the distressing detail and then promptly announced an accidental death verdict. Don groaned and shook his head, vigorously enough to catch the coroner's eye. Who blinked a couple of times at this show of dissent, before releasing the body for burial, once again commiserating and then he stood. Despite his dullness, a sentimental and sensitive man who had tried to spare the parents more pain. He'd done that to the best of his ability and upset the local constabulary at the same time. I closed my notebook and watched the coroner sweep out with all the elegance of a bulky tramp steamer bobbing up the river Clyde.

The usual murmurings from the gallery, like a swarm of bees buzzing away in the background. I glanced away to my left at the half a dozen reporters. Shuffling out, avoiding my eyes... good. My feelings of bitterness hanging over me diverting any offers of a drink and halting the fraternal farewells. Farewell to the outsiders muscling in because they see a rich, suicidal public schoolgirl with a penchant for older men and various drugs. I watched them off the premises, gone forever I hoped, they'd lost interest. Not even a suicide verdict, what an anti-climax for them.

My glance went back to the grieving parents, both with

heads bowed and both sitting resolutely in the chairs. Then he stood and without the merest of words to his wife, he strode for the exit. I felt my mouth hang open. I thought he was going to glance my way and my heart stopped, my chest stopped as well in apparent sympathy.

But he just stared fixedly in front, there could be no mistake. Fuller of face that's for sure, but the cheekbones, the skin colour and most of all those piercing eyes. Teddy looked good, not much younger back then and not much older right now. He pushed the door open rather like a rugby player's stiff armed hand off. Never bothered to wait for his wife and the door swung back into her face. Well used to this sort of behaviour I guessed, she just sighed and then followed him out of the building.

I sat back down, spread the fingers of my right hand and massaged my pounding temples. As Harry would have put it… "fucking hell". If I hadn't have been so shocked, so disoriented I could have sat back in wonderment at how fate had knitted all of our lives together like this. Treachery apparently woven to longing, aspiration chain linked to resentment. Throw in some romanticism, more adoration, lust, a murder or two, probably a missed bus in their somewhere. Hurl a late train or two and a cancelled flight into the equation and then the ringmaster pulls the strings and we all dance the dance. Surely it couldn't be another dance of death? It was thirty five years ago. Back then that tango was to the death and now forever etched into my memory. And here we are once again, fate, or coincidence?

Either way I had the feeling of a solitary rabbit cornered by a fox out on the prowl. I crept out into the car park, the earlier winter sunshine replaced by heavy cloud and an icy blast straight down from Greenland. I scanned the scene, saw Stuart hurrying away, camera in his left hand. He was going to the same safe haven as I intended to. After the ghost had driven his black Ford Grenada out onto Church Street and past me.

Mr and Mrs Ghost, both with expressionless features, faces clamped tight. After all, you'd expect nothing less from a pair of phantoms.

I rushed headlong down Grove Street, raced past my office and on towards friendly faces and comfort that I craved. Past Goldstone's shop, I noticed him out of the corner of my eye, mouth open and ready to exchange pleasantries. I flashed past, crashing through the door and into the public bar. Hit between the eyes by the heat from the blistering coal fires that blazed away at each end of the bar. Stuart was leaning against the bar talking to Shirley, he smiled my way and pulled me a pint. I sighed, what is it to be nothing less than predictable, ah well that's reassuring in itself I suppose.

Shirley stubbed her cigarette out and looked across, about to speak.

I beat her to it. 'Where's Harry?'

Stuart shook his head, 'Out the back.' He tipped his head a touch, 'Are you ok? You seen a ghost or something?'

I threw some beer down my throat as Shirley spoke softly, 'Suicides are bad enough at the best of times, a young girl… well.' She shook her head and stared down at her bright red, beautifully manicured nails. 'Changing the subject, guess what? Some idiot in a car gave me a mouthful of abuse five minutes ago…'

Sorry Shirley, drivers shouting her way was a common enough event. I put my hand up and whispered, 'Go and get Harry – it's important.'

Shirley raised her eyebrows at me, unused to being interrupted in full flow, she glanced at Stuart. Stuart shrugged and said. 'I'll get him.' As he started to turn, the front door opened and Don came through. Stopped in front of Shirley and stared freely at her.

She never looked his way, calmly stood, brushed her skirt down and said, 'I'll get Harry for you.'

She still moved fluidly, hips and shoulders synchronised to perfection. Don watched her, her arse to be precise as she slinked out through the door. Well, enough sexual tension between those two to keep us gossipers going for weeks. I wondered what happened the other night between those two, or never happened perhaps.

Don's sarcastic tone brought me back. 'Didn't see you in there, were you skulking away at the back as usual?'

He smiled my way, but his sneering, leering face never expressed amusement as such, just a mocking contempt for the whole world it seemed. Full faced and heavy lips that turned down whenever he talked. I shouldn't have taken this too personally, he addressed everyone this way, but it still got to me. Just like it did for everyone it seemed.

'He was just doing his job.' Stuart spoke for me, 'I wonder who the father was.'

I tried to hide my smile in my pint glass; Stuart knew how to get the rise out of him. Don took the piss, but didn't like it coming back his way.

I'm an important man, show some respect.

Harry burst through the door, smiled my way and snarled at Don.

'What do you want?' Harry's jowls bristling like an aged bulldog looking for one last fight. His square forehead slowly lowered, the impression that it was finding the right position and range, ready to shove it into Don's face. 'Why don't you do some work instead of sponging free pints in here?'

Good old Harry, coming up to sixty and still fighting. I breathed easier, lit a cigarette to celebrate this and watched the cabaret begin.

Don's eyebrows came up and he pointed at Stuart. 'I am working – where is he?'

Stuart shrugged, a gesture that his uncle had perfected years earlier and passed onto the next generation. Stuart had refined it enough to get right up Don's nose, evolution in action is a wonderful thing. Stuart leaned forward and in a level voice said. 'I don't know who you're talking about?'

All said with a smile that indicated the opposite. Don's breath rasped out, he immediately tried to drag it back into his wide deep chest. Went close to the bar and started to jab his finger Stuart's way. 'Don't get smart with me.'

Stuart's smile widened, as Don glanced down at his watch,

gave a great big heaving sigh, before saying to Harry. 'Can I pop through and have a word with Shirley before I go?' Then the smugness, the impression he wanted to give.

Me and Shirley.

Harry just ignored the implication sent his way and shook his great big head, 'She's out the back with Peggy, not to be disturbed she told me.'

Don frowned back Harry's way, swung his head in Stuart's direction. 'I'll talk to you when your bodyguards not around – let's see how brave you are then.'

He turned and did his John Wayne walk out of the bar, I pushed my empty glass Stuart's way and we all waited for the door to shut. We watched as Don's head went across the window and disappeared. We gave it a few minutes grace, I stared at the head of my fresh pint, Harry offered me a cigarette, closely followed by his lighter. I dragged deep and said, 'We need to sit down, with Wyn and Shirley – something's happened.'

Harry ignored me, went up close to his son and shouted, 'Where is he – you're a stupid fucker. Stay out all night, Kathy's worried, kids are worried, your Mum's worried.'

I smiled to myself, of course Harry would never admit to being worried himself. He just choked on his cigarette, smoke coming out of nose and mouth as he coughed and tried to point at the same time. Stuart carried on in an even voice, 'I wasn't lying, I haven't got a clue where he is… now.'

'Well we all know which country he's in.' I stated the obvious, one of my less redeeming qualities according to Harry. 'You know he was seen in the schoolgirl's room that morning?'

Stuart dragged a stool across, scraping the feet along the flagstone floor. Harry rolled his eyes.

Lift it, don't drag it.

Stuart smiled at me, he knew what he was doing. He'd had years of practice perfecting and twisting his father's spring steel of a short temper into tight little knots. He sat and leant forward, elbows on the counter – just like his father.

'I gave him a lift – anyone would do that for a mate.' He stared at Harry, 'How many times have you baled Tommy out?'

Harry glanced across at me and shook his head, as the living room squeaked open, Shirley's head craned slowly around. She whispered our way, 'Has he gone?'

She answered her own question by walking into our little huddle. Gestured to Stuart with her icy blue eyes and as if by magic, Stuart placed a gin and tonic in front of her. She slid the stool over and climbed up onto it, brushed her skirt a couple of times. I offered her a cigarette, which Harry lit for her. Shirley took a heavy sip and then dragged deep on her cigarette.

Stared at Stuart and she said, 'What's the gossip then?'

He shook his head and looked across at the dartboard, stared at it and frowned. As if the numbers had suddenly been shuffled around the perimeter and double twenty now sat in the double eight bed. Shirley glanced at Harry and then across to me, graveyard silence enveloped our little huddle.

'Oh I see.' Shirley frowned, tapped her cigarette three times into the ashtray. 'Nothing for Shirley's ears then?'

'I've got something that will shake you up.' I hadn't forgotten about Teddy Lewis, how could I ever? Talking about his daughter just made me make the inevitable comparisons. Disturbed daughter of a disturbed father. Nothing new there. Was madness hereditary? I needed to know how he had influenced her. Sleeping with her mother's lover and making sure they'd be caught, why? My mind slid back Teddy's way, I couldn't work out who frightened me more, him or Harry? I emptied my glass, gestured around the others. Glasses replenished, I gestured for the attention of the others.

'When you realise who the father is, perhaps it's not surprising that she turned out as disturbed as she did.'

A single word from Shirley, 'Who?'

'The St Mary's schoolgirl.' I answered, sipped some beer and raised my hand. 'I saw her father in court this morning. You're not going to believe this, but there can be no doubt.

Teddy Lewis, alive and kicking his way back into our lives.'

Then more silence, until Shirley's glass smashed into the floor and her mouth formed a perfect circle. 'It was him; he drove past me, in town. Someone shouted at me from a big black car.'

Harry's breathing took on that of a sprinting racehorse in the winner's enclosure. His fingers drummed a tattoo on the counter. He whispered… fucking hell I think.

Stuart frowned and said. 'Who's Teddy Lewis?'

1980 – TEDDY

Teddy stared at the coroner. The fat bastard.

He wanted to shut the noise out. All those words. On and bloody on.

Lung and kidney damage, fractured skull, drugs still in her body. Sex just before… evidence of anal…

The coroner lists all of this shit. On and bloody on.

Who does he think he is?

Teddy struggled to stop his hands from covering his ears.

Anal intercourse? He'd never done that. Not with a woman anyway.

On and bloody on.

Pregnant!

Pregnant?

He never asked questions anymore, in fact the question became more important than the answer. The question to Celia, better off never asking it and he didn't, his mind went off at tangents. Tangents went off at tangents to tangents, what is real? He thought about it for a while, eventually decided that luck or chance was the only reality.

He thought about the dream that woke him this morning, somewhere he couldn't recognise, but a safe place. He walked on now, looking for this safe place. Of course he didn't know the town and all of its streets, but no matter where he stood the feeling of being lost swept over him. Lost in a small town and lost inside himself. He tried not to think, becoming just an unthinking camera brought him a degree of calm. He saw but stopped thinking and a solitary calm, an empty tranquillity came alongside him.

Everything had changed within seconds it seemed.

He walked out of the courtroom, into a blustery wind that he thought had honed itself just for him. Walking became the key, just by following the flow of his body, all places turned into a blurred equality; he floated on with the reassuring sensation that he was nowhere. He remembered whenever anyone asked him how Celia was, he told them that she had always wanted to go to boarding school anyway. They weren't really his friends however and they knew he lied.

Fucking bitch.

The day she did it, he wanted to be dead. Now, while he was certainly not glad to be alive, but alive he was and Teddy thought that it was marginally better than being dead – but only just. He walked on, eyes down and ears closed to the sound of rain beating on parked cars. He had a craving now, a hunger that only a special kind of food could satisfy. He didn't plan on stopping eating until he became bloated on its singular qualities.

Geography teacher for a start.

Questions, questions, what was she doing in a police car? Why did he start following her? Should he have even been following her?

He drove the car around the small market square. His wife couldn't drive, too much Valium floating around inside her. He could fuck her now and she wouldn't feel a thing.

Not that he wanted to touch her again… ever.

Fucking pedestrians, get out of the fucki…

His head span away like a multi-coloured top. It couldn't be?

It was.

Seeing her again in this poxy little town. As if he wasn't confused enough as it was, fat bastard coroner, gloomy little courtroom with all of those eyes staring into the back of his head.

Well they can all fuck off.

There she was. The belted raincoat, high heels and the blonde hair. He recognised her immediately, braking the car and staring after her.

I wonder if she still shaves her chuff?

Oblivious to the car horns behind.

His wife shouting. 'What's up with you? Why have you stopped in the middle of the road?'

It took forty minutes before they got home and as soon as he stopped the car in the drive, Teddy burst through the front door and rushed up to his dark room, unfolded the letter.

My dear, darling Teddy. I love you so much and I always will. I have to go away, I almost mis…

***

Much later, he walked on and tried not to think about her, but he thought about her anyway. Wondered if she had a son or a daughter? Wondered what a man of thirty odd did? Wondered what his name was? Thought about his own life and when he stopped being real? If he lived at all, it was through this imaginary person he had become. A walker that didn't see, a listener that couldn't hear, oh well he thought, everything that could happen to him had happened and this thought made him surprisingly composed.

He's got a son out there somewhere.

I bet he doesn't wake every day like me, re-born every morning. A baby when the alarm clock clatters away. Growing rapidly, ageing so that by lunch time I'm a teenager. When I'm my father's age, it must be tea time. By midnight I die and hope that by morning I won't be born again.

He shook his head and stared at the faithful few filing into church, if he stared long enough they disappeared, he could make things invisible.

He said, 'No one else can do that.'

The people vanished, but he could see his words, arc out

from his mouth like a cartoon caption and then they died and vanished as well.

'I had a father once... and a mother.'

He watched the words float over the small redbrick wall of the Catholic Church.

'Bernie – I'm so sorry, how are you?'

He shook his head again, his mother-in-law came into sharp focus, why did she call him Bernie?

She wrapped herself around him, he stifled within the smell of Woodbines, fried eggs and her hounding personality.

'Poor Bernie, all you've had to put up with and now this... poor Bernie.'

Who the fucks Bernie? Where's my baby? Where's Celia? Where's Shirley?

'What did you say – speak up, stop mumbling. I can't hear you. Who's Shirley?'

11

1945 – JACK

Harry caught him early, not with a punch though. Harry's forehead crunched into his opponent just below the left eye. I think if it hadn't been the first round, the referee would have thrown Harry out of the ring. Or, more likely, Teddy's threats had the referee's mind focused on one thing.

You make sure that fight lasts until the sixth round!

It wasn't the effect of the butt, it didn't scramble the man's brains, he didn't need to hold on for his life. But the eye began to close, by the end of the first round it had shut completely.

The referee was called over during the interval, much waving and pointing towards Harry's corner. The referee's face strained and pale despite the exertion. I thought he was about to disqualify Harry.

I glanced across at Wyn who had stood by now and his face looked on the point of a serious explosion. A burst blood vessel at the least.

He shouted advice at the referee, 'Let them fight, let them get on with it – it's a man's game.'

I didn't think Harry heard a word. He stared at the corner opposite, watched an ice pack being pressed onto a badly swollen eye. Never even noticed the referee's finger being waved under his own nose. Ten feet away and I heard it, 'One more and you're out – behave understand?'

His opponent couldn't see properly, perspective that was the problem and Harry kept throwing right hooks, loads of them. It became a massacre and I think that he had forgotten his lines. We needed a sixth round KO to pocket all the money. at the end of the round, Wyn was up again and round into Harry's corner.

'What are you doing? Ease up ... remember for God's sake.'

Harry tried, held his opponent up for a couple of rounds. Cuddled a lot, pushed and shoved a bit. Never landed a worthwhile shot.

Until just before the end of the fifth, then another right hook crashed onto the temple. Harry claimed later that he meant to hit just that bit high. Any lower, cheek or point of the jaw and it would have been curtains – the man wouldn't have woken up for a week. It was just enough to scramble his brains for most of the minute while his seconds worked frantically. I worried that they might pull him out, his head was down on his chest, exhaustion or oblivion just one punch away.

The bell sounded and for a split second I thought he was going to remain on his stool. But I guessed he was pretty aware that not only Teddy, but most of his thug mates had their shirts, houses –everything including their dinners on him winning in this round. I supposed he thought Harry would have been reading from the same song sheet. He pulled himself onto unsteady legs and his corner men pushed him out to finish the job and pocket some extra from a grateful Teddy.

He walked out to be greeted by a flurry of wild hooks, he grabbed Harry, he wondered why... I half expected him to say –"c'mon it's my turn". Harry ripped uppercuts onto the chin then drilled a couple into the solar plexus. The gloves came down and three, four, five hooks flew onto an unprotected chin. Down, eyes shut before he hit the canvas. The referee never bothered to start a count, raised Harry's right hand and he ducked straight out of the ring.

We had it all worked out, never even went back to the changing rooms. Wyn had already put Harry's clothes in the boot of the car. I walked up the aisle with them. Straight out into the cold night air, into Wyn's car. What a sight, Harry with the gloves still on. His boxer's robe carried by Wyn and me hurrying alongside. Wyn fired up the engine and we left into the night and back the short distance to Soho.

It was a tense gathering, only Harry, still high as a kite wanted to drink and sing and dance. Wyn and me sat there and said nothing. We expected the wrath of Cain to descend at any moment, sometimes silence speaks a thousand words and I looked from one to the other and sighed. 'I've had enough of this.'

Wyn brought a pot of coffee over and a bottle for me, I wanted to fall face down onto the table and sleep like that. I'd placed bets all over London the previous day. Thousands of pounds loaded onto Harry's broad back. In a few hours' time, we would have to venture out and collect. I had started to, no – I did inhabit a dangerous world and despite being terrified, I rather enjoyed it all.

'You're going to stop here the night?' Wyn touched my hand as he spoke.

I nodded, despite me finding this new life exciting, the short walk to Poland Street was just too much of a good thing.

I said, 'Tomorrow's going to be tricky.'

He nodded, 'We'll collect the money, stay tight together and hope for the best. I wonder what the bookies made of it all?'

For days before the money went on Teddy's man. Some bookies closed the book on him. That's when we started putting it down on Harry winning in the same round as his opponent.

What did they make of it all?

I wonder if Teddy was made aware as to the situation? Probably not, but Wyn took no chances anyway. The changing room became a dangerous place, no security, no one about – a place to avoid.

'How much did we make?'

'Thousands.' Wyn spoke through a wide grin. 'Enough to get away somewhere safer.'

There ... he'd said something sane at last. Then the collective feeling of anxiety spread amongst us.

When are they coming?

Wyn poured coffee, sat back and looked at me.

I tried to smile, but the thought of the doormen stood around oblivious to the danger they were in. Tethered like two sacrificial goats, their foot on the first ladder of the low level criminal. Doing a bit of door work. It's that or thieving, that's the usual attitude around here, who wants a proper job that pays nothing? I popped out periodically and had a word with them. Nice boys, big and no age. Pleased to have a job for the night – longer than that they were told if they did a good job. Brothers and I'm sure their mum was proud of them. Clean shaven and smart looking, polite and wary at the same time. The dimly lit street casting menacing shadows across their faces.

'Would you like a coffee later?'

They both nodded, one said 'I'd like something sweet.' I knew what he meant, a bar of chocolate, the smell of rain on cut grass, a woman maybe? That was the last I saw of them.

I went back inside and glanced around at the usual scene. The degenerate, the debauched with the occasional pervert loitering around the edges. Two attractive young men sat at a table opposite.

Both leaning forward – their heads close together over the centre of the small table. One of them squinted at the rising fog of smoke from the cigarette clamped between his lips. I sighed at the same time as a pair of warm hands came around my neck.

'Got a minute?' My eyebrows stretched upwards as she spoke again. 'Wyn's made arrangements for me.'

Shirley squeezed past me and smelt divine – recently bathed I guessed. Dressed for work or seduction? Perhaps they were the same thing with Shirley. My pulse quickened, I thought it must be visible at my temples – moving like a tiny heart.

'Don't look so miserable.'

I hadn't realised I was looking that way. Shirley sat down next to me and squeezed my arm as she did so.

'You're still here then?'

'Oh feel free to be so abrupt with me – how are you Shirley? You look well.' She made an attempt to look agitated, scrambling through her handbag. Compressing her cigarette between her ruby lips. Sticking her chin out expecting me to light it. I passed my box of matches over, she sighed and lit up. Blew the smoke into my face and said. 'You need straightening out.'

We stared, her mouth tight, smoke tumbling from her nostrils. Finally she said. 'You're in trouble, we're all in trouble.'

I said nothing, perplexed by her sudden awareness about life's dangers.

'Why didn't you tell me? About the fight, all three of you said nothing.' She frowned and hammered her cigarette out, then pouted my way. 'You don't like me do you Jack?'

'I know about you and Teddy.'

'You know nothing, Wyn asked me to get close and you all cut me out of the loop. Why don't you like me?'

Shirley pouted like a thirteen year old schoolgirl being denied a night out with her friends. I shook my head, 'You get confused when a man doesn't fall at your feet – I don't dislike you. I always thought that you were just out to fleece Wyn that's all.'

'Cheeky bastard.' Shirley snorted, all tobacco smoke and bile, 'I'm just out of my depth, that's all. You think that I'm the one playing one end against the other don't you? All I ever wanted was Wyn, he's the one directing me this way and then that.'

I couldn't believe that one, but I couldn't believe anything at the moment. I changed the subject, 'Have you talked to Peggy?

'I'm getting out too.' Shirley nodded, kept her head down as she spoke. 'My flat was broken into, we all know who that would be. No damage, nothing taken. Just the feeling that someone was waiting in there for me. I'm off right now.'

My first impressions of Shirley floundered on the rocks of her despair, a tear sat in the corner of her left eye. A few weeks ago I would have thought that the tear stayed there until Shirley gave it instructions to tumble down the ridge of her cheekbone. Now I wasn't so sure, as she stared down at the ash tray and slowly wrung her hands together. A couple of heaving sighs burst from her and my eyes slipped down to her blouse. Shirley had a careless nature when it came to buttoning blouses and I stared at her breasts, rather how I imagined the gullible card players did when they should have been watching her hands.

Temptation without satisfaction and the same thought pulsed through me. I wanted to throw myself against her – despite me being street wise and aware of more than most. I'd never even held a woman properly, let alone kissed one. Even on VE Day I'd managed to avoid the thousands of rampant women on the loose. I wanted to get close, but always frightened off by their imagined sexuality and scared of being found out as inadequate.

'I just wanted you to like me, you're different.' She wanted everyone to love her more like, Shirley talked like this was the most important thing in her life.

I struggled to make any sense. 'I never said that I never liked you.'

'It's okay.' But her frown said otherwise, 'Lots of men don't like me. You're no different. Don't like me, but want me just the same.'

'What do you want me to say?' Whenever I sat alongside her my spirits soared like a swallow in August. A small, erotic island of pleasure in my ocean of menace, dressed in black. Blouse, black with buttons undone that exposed breasts and a black bra. Loose trousers, patent black shoes. The startling whiteness of her hair sat on top of it all.

Shirley raised her right hand a few inches above the table, she smiled, 'I'm going, soon.' I felt the light, warming breeze from her breathe on my cheek. The club plunged into a freeze frame of silence. Punctuated by the high low call of an inadequate trumpeter as he struggled to reach the right notes.

'I just wanted to say goodbye, thought you might be

hiding from me.'

Much too quickly I said. 'No. I like you too much for that to happen.'

There I said it, my jumbled outpourings of the last few minutes laid to waste.

'Good job you said that, don't forget, I can make you talk – I'm an expert.' Her pink tongue exposed for a couple of seconds. Shirley laid the palm of her hand onto the back of mine just as Wyn hurried back in.

'Taxi's out the back, trains off in half an hour. It's deserted out there.'

I walked out the back with them and we walked out into a persistent drizzle, the pavement shining, dark grey roof tiles glistening away. My own private weather system that matched my mood precisely. Her hand slipped through and linked onto my arm.

Shirley looked up at me and smiled. The final dislocation from my world that had just spun away from its orbit like a clay pigeon soaring briefly. Either to be blown apart by a shotgun, or smash itself to pieces in free-fall on its short journey back to earth.

'Perhaps I just like you Jack.'

'You sleep with everyone you like?'

Shirley shrugged.

Maybe!

Shirley glanced quickly up at me, a single tear just below her right eye. Her mascara fanned out like an ink spot on an incline. She laughed, on the edge of tears and the laugh would impress no one. Shirley pulled her compact out and looked at the mirror. Dabbed her handkerchief under the eye and swore.

'Why didn't you tell me? Why did you cut me out of the loop?'

I never had the chance to tell her as Wyn slipped alongside did what I wanted to do and slipped his arm around her. They gazed into each other's eyes and then kissed. Long and slow, heads moving and twisting away. I whispered goodbye and walked back into the club in a daze. I didn't like the feeling of dependency Shirley had induced in me. She had me hooked quicker than nicotine adds another addictive soul to its list. Enslavement seemed to go hand in hand with Shirley. She left with an organised escape route planned, rather like a bomber pilot makes his unsafe way through occupied Belgium.

But where to?

1945 – TEDDY

Two timing fucking whore. The same bile in his throat. Two timing whore.

Twisting, back-stabbing bunch.

The smart money was on that little queer of a reporter organising this.

Smart money?

He would never have another bet as long as he lived. They made him look a mug. All that money.

Yeh, put it all on my boy.

No, not to win. But win in the sixth. Put your houses on it. Teddy's fixed it.

What a mug.

***

He stared at the envelope. The writing was hers, it smelt good too. What else would you expect with Shirley? She always took care of how she smelt, not like some of the other drippers he'd fucked. He lay on her bed and started to weep. What a mug and now a Dear John letter.

He ripped it open and smelt the letter. The same expensive perfume she always dabbed on the gusset of her knickers, no doubt about that.

My dear, `darling Teddy, I love you so much and I always will. I have to go away, I almost miscarried after the fight. They betrayed us, they made a fortune and cut

me out completely. I'm in an infirmary and likely to be here...

12

1980 – JACK

Don came into the office and sat on his wife's empty chair. He stared around the office, smiling. This worried me and interrupted Stuart's frantic burst of energy. Stuart had the bit between his teeth for some strange reason. Phone calls, lists of names, pencil behind one ear. He glanced in Don's direction, groaned and threw his pencil down onto his desk where it bounced up and landed in Don's lap.

He pointed at Don, 'I've got work to do. What do you want now?'

The equanimity balance had changed ownership this morning it seemed. Don just smiled at Stuart, picked the pencil up and passed it back. The unprovoked missile attack ignored as he leaned towards me. Thick lips pulled back into his wolf's smile, his eyes creased – he was about to spring something. I watched him, cold as a bandleader staring at a pianist unable to hit the right notes. He dragged his notebook out, stabbed his pencil into the text a couple of times. Information about to impart and he savoured it. A piece of sirloin steak to chew on, juicy, tasty too.

He chewed some more, before finally saying. 'Did you know Bernard Schwartz – years ago? At the end of the war?'

My head spun, I went for a cigarette, anything to give me time. I frowned at the empty packet, not believing my own eyes. Poking around inside it with my finger to confirm this. It wouldn't register within the dim recesses of my brain that I'd smoked them all. Nothing registered, except the grinning buffoon sat opposite. Count to one hundred, sigh and give him an assessment worthy of a university lecturer. I needed a few moments consideration, time to halt the strolling chickens looking for their roost.

'You're mistaken I feel.'

There… that was hardly worth the wait. Don sighed.

Stuart stood up, 'I bet Carol wouldn't like the way you sourced that information.' The policeman frowned, Stuart winked my as he said, 'I'll say it slower for you – it's not only information Shirley's giving you is it?'

Don stood and went through to the back room, looked both ways and then turned back to us. He wagged his finger at us, his lips moved, but he said nothing.

I said, 'You're ok, Carol's out running some errands.'

I breathed easier, Stuart had stalled the attack at the first hurdle. His brain worked better than mine. Not a fan of blackmail, however, I did feel relieved at the immediate benefit of its slashing interjection.

Don stared at Stuart and finally managed to synchronise his vocal chords with the brain as he hissed, 'You threatening me?'

The fulcrum of equanimity had shifted once more, Stuart nudged it farther off-centre. 'I've heard the parents of that dead girl want tests done to see who the father is.'

'You are threatening me?' A raise of the eyebrows, a slight cant of the head and an eloquent silence from Stuart suggested he was doing just that. Don's voice raised an octave. 'I can cause you so much trouble boy…'

Stuart smiled and eventually replied with the voice of reason, 'I'd get back to the station if I were you.' Stuart looked at his watch, brought his steady gaze back into Don's angry red face. 'Someone you're desperate to talk to is just walking into the police station right now.'

Don frowned.

Who?

The penny must have dropped, 'That paddy bastard.' Don turned and slammed the door behind him.

Stuart smiled his I'm a clever boy smile and said, 'Did you know Bernard Schwartz?'

I ignored his question and sent one back his way, 'What's going on?'

'Patrick rang, not just me. Wyn and my old man. We all said the same.' He raised his eyebrows, then wagged his finger at me, 'We had a long chat. He got a ferry, then a train, I picked him up from Swindon late last night.' Stuart sat down and drummed the table with his fingers. 'I hope I did the right thing, Wyn's getting him some legal advice, what do you think?'

Talk about still waters running deep, I felt a touch of irritation that this had been concocted without my involvement.

I sighed, 'It was the right thing to do.'

'Anyway, what about you and Bernard Schwartz?'

'He was a minor tearaway that I came across – when I worked for the Daily Mirror. The police wanted him for a string of offences.'

That's all I gave him, no mention of his real name, the arson, assault, extortion and murder.

Fortunately Carol walked back in, closed the door and shook her raincoat a couple of times and hung it on the coat stand. She interpreted our hiatus as walking in on the back end of an argument. Raised her eyebrows at the silence and walked through into the back office. Perhaps her entrance distracted him, but Stuart never asked me how Shirley was involved in all of this. He took his silence and his glance back to the list and he began to scratch away with his pencil. He picked the phone up, listening to one sided phone conversations usually amused me.

Not this one however.

'Mrs Schwartz? Yes hello, Inspector Wicks, yes, yes… from the police station. We need to ask a few more questions, yes I know my colleagues have been in touch, but there's a couple of things we need to go over again. A couple of hours. Where's best for you? Sonning, the Bull Inn, lovely, see you then.'

Mrs Schwartz, Inspector Wicks?

'What have you just done?' I stared and all that came back my way was a broad grin.

Stuart placed the phone back in the cradle and said. 'I've arranged to meet the bereaved mother. Don't look like that, I've got a mate to keep out of prison.'

'C'mon Jack.' Carol came back through, 'Things to find out. Innocent man to clear.' Carol smiled, 'A chance for a pair of investigative journalists.'

'Hmm.' I glanced back at Stuart, 'Dare I ask what premise we're using for this interview?'

He shook his head, wagged his finger and said, 'You won't like it, better you don't know I think.' Stuart nodded at Carol, 'And you can keep shut as well. Not a word to your old man.'

Well he never needed to tell her that, I didn't think they were saying anything to each other anymore.

***

We never said much on the journey, I asked him if I should tell Mably that I knew Bernard Schwartz. He didn't think so, just the answer you'd expect from someone with a family background like his.

'Sleeping dogs. I just want some names from Mrs Schwartz for Patrick's defence.'

'I thought you said he wasn't involved, other than a shoulder to cry on?'

'He wasn't, but no one will believe him. It's just some insurance, that's all.'

We spent the next forty minutes in silence. Driving through drizzle and the heavy traffic around Reading, finally pulling up in the pub's car park. It was exactly what you'd expect in an affluent village. A thatched pub close to the river. Not much natural light inside the bar, unctuous landlord, bowing and asking us if we were eating today.

'Two pints of bitter.' Then Stuart's glare gave him an abrupt answer to his question.

Mind your own business I think.

Mrs Schwartz sat in the corner, the huge fireplace to the left, logs smoking like a damp allotment fire. Harry would have started them a good hour earlier. We took our flat beer over and joined her.

Stuart did the talking, as you'd expect from someone just elevated to a detective inspector. Me, just a lowly detective. What a pair, me an elderly, rather frail detective to his very young inspector. He flashed something across at her, back in his pocket within the blink of an eye, his cash point card probably. Not that she would have noticed, around her eyes the skin puffy, the eyes themselves? Bloodshot, tranquillisers and too much alcohol? Masking the eyes with heavy make-up merely drew attention to them. Her bright red lips suggested an unsteady hand, or a lurid sense of what she thought looked good. Her bra miraculously created cleavage out of molehills, certainly enough there to catch Stuart's eye as he offered her his hand.

'Mrs Schwartz.'

'Connie.' Her heavy eyes went to ground, the safest place these days. Well spoken, her voice middle class and in direct opposition to the makeup, bracelets, necklace and rings that adorned most of her exposed flesh. She talked to the flagstoned floor, 'I don't know why you're here. What do you hope to achieve?' A question, but no hostility. In fact, just the opposite, Valium had produced nothing other than equanimity in her voice. Was there a degree of curiosity in amongst the tranquilliser and alcohol induced flatness?

I shook my head as the inspector opened his notebook and licked his pencil. All wasted as she never glanced his way once.

'We have to make more enquiries about Celia's...' Stuart looked my way, lost already.

This was a terrible idea.

'Sexual partners.' Finally tumbled from his lips. 'She had been sexually active for a couple of years.'

She sat back and stared at him, 'Was there a question in there somewhere? What do you want me to say?'

Silence.

I leaned forward, 'Celia possibly had at least three lovers – all over thirty. Maybe the man who never turned up at the coroners. One of her teachers and someone that you knew. We need to talk to them, the teachers gone missing. You can help us contact one of them that's all this is about.'

She sipped the white wine, and then said softly. 'It's any parent's fear that their daughter may be murdered, beaten up or raped. But this… we never got on towards the end either. Forever competing with each other, usual mother-daughter stuff.' She spoke as if on auto pilot, the words tumbled out and yet her mind appeared elsewhere. A safe place maybe, more likely other things on her mind. 'Do either of you smoke?'

I pushed my packet her way, lit her cigarette and she pulled the tobacco smoke down into her lungs. Then a cough before she spoke again, 'I'd stopped for a couple of months, bad time to try and stop eh?' She picked my cigarette packet up and found something fascinating to read. Minutes later she eventually said, 'A confident child, I don't know what else I can tell you.'

'The address of your friend.'

'What good will that do?' Then she frowned, realisation that we knew. She stubbed her cigarette our and steadied herself. 'Celia started having sex before her periods started. She could have been pregnant and never known about it for the best part of a year. She got through that somehow. We didn't know she was pregnant.'

Stuart reminded her, 'Your friend?'

'What do you know about him?'

'That your daughter slept with him.'

Mrs Schwartz hissed, then shook her head, 'I told you she was competitive, cutting her teeth, quickly finding out that it's possible to get what you want out of people.' She turned her hand over and started to beat a tattoo with the couple of large rings. A sharp, regular beat. 'My husband found them in bed together, my lover and my daughter, how about that one.'

I couldn't believe any of this, but all the time I needed to know.

Who seduced who?

Connie smiled, 'It got me out of trouble I suppose.'

'Are you still seeing him?'

'Don't be stupid.' She pushed her chin out.

'We'll need to speak to him.'

Quiet.

After a long time, 'I don't know.' She looked at us, from one to the other… slowly. Leant across and picked Stuart's notebook up.

Scribbled an address and phone number down, underlined them with pressure more suited to cutting someone's throat. Rolled the pencil back across the table and sat back.

'Is that all there is?'

No, I needed to know about Teddy. I said. 'What does your husband do?'

She frowned, took another of my cigarettes, 'I have a photographic agency, he takes the photos – it does very nicely thanks.' Lit up and blew the smoke over Stuart. 'They never got on, he wanted a son and barely spoke to her towards the end. Certainly not after what happened at Christmas.'

She never told us what happened at Christmas; in fact Mrs Schwartz hardly said another word. As Stuart so eloquently put it on the drive back into Reading, 'What a cold faced bitch.'

1980-TEDDY

She was easy to find. Telephone book.

Not many people called Catmore.

S. Catmore.

Six Elms Cottages.

His breathing became short and irregular. As he dialled the number, his lungs stopped functioning completely.

The phone was picked up quickly, three rings then a breathless voice. 'Don. Is that you?'

Who the fucks Don?

He held his breath.

'Don – I need to see you.'

He placed the receiver back in the cradle. Turned slowly and pushed the telephone booth's door open.

No.

Turn, quickly this time and dial the number again. Two rings and pick up.

'Hello.'

'Shirley?'

Nothing. Apart from a sharp intake of breath.

'I need to see you.'

'Teddy?'

'Can we meet up somewhere?'

'Is that you Teddy?'

He forced himself to say nothing.

'I've missed you. How are you, I'm sorry about your…'

'Don't talk about her.'

'I'm shopping in Oxford tomorrow, can we…?'

His breathing turned into short sharp gasps.

'I've still got your letter.'

The line went quiet.

'Did you hear me?'

'I meant every word.'

'Was the baby…?'

'I had a terrible time of it, but I had a boy. He's been in a lot of trouble.'

'Like father, like…'

'Don't Teddy.'

'Where in Oxford?'

He leant against the door of the phone box. The sweat pumped out of his forehead. The same emotion that she always induced.

Fuck her or punch her between the eyes?

Decisions, decisions.

Fight or fuck? Fuck or fight?

Easy, both – eventually.

13

1945-JACK

Half an hour or so after Shirley's escape, a youngish couple came in – him covered in blood. Her covered in a horror stricken, wide eyed, mouth gaping terror as she screamed and screamed. He shouted for help – I was outside before anyone. Two young men, one face down, the other on his back. One with blood gurgling from somewhere. The one on his back had a gashing, gaping slash across his throat and what remained of the blood in his body trickled gently into the gutter. A mocking contrast to the act of terrible violence that caused it.

It started to rush up from deep inside me. I turned and leant against the wall and retched and retched and retched. A rib twisting, vomiting tribute to what I had just seen.

I heard Harry's voice, 'Fucking hell.'

I watched him rush back into the club.

Don't leave me all alone out here.

I told the man who would have normally been on the door to ring the police.

So that's negotiating – a mutually acceptable face saver for Teddy. A sacrifice for both Wyn and Shirley's good looks. I leant against the door, my chest wouldn't work. I couldn't drag air into my lungs. My temples pounded with a steam hammer inside trying to smash its way out from within. My shirt soaked in sweat and vomit.

Harry came bursting out again like a greyhound chasing the hare. Staring, trying to get a fix on an opponent that was nowhere to be seen.

'They've gone and you don't even know where.'

'I'll find him.'

'I don't think you will.'

Safe somewhere – surrounded by his goons. Bragging how he stuck it to the two Welshmen. Well stuck it to the doormen anyway, a mutual back patting orgy as they drank and laughed and toasted good old Teddy.

You should have seen the way they bled.

Harry's chin dropped onto his chest, 'What the fuck have we started?'

Something we can't finish I guessed, in way over our heads. Directed by two people that thought Teddy was a soft target. Intellectually he may have been, sly probably. Street wise definitely, but the message sent our way couldn't have been clearer in my mind. This is coming your way if you cross me again. This is coming your way even if you don't cross me again.

This is coming your way.

We looked at one another and the same thought fired between us. I said it, 'How do we get out of this?'

Harry said, 'Anyone left inside?'

Wyn shook his head, 'No one – all crashed out the back way. That includes staff as well. All the girls, the muscle that was left alive, everyone.'

We talked, most of the time we just sat and drank. The way you can sometimes drink and it has no effect. Little taste either – a pointless exercise, but despite this, we drank the night away. Trying to forget, exorcise a few demons. Stay awake until day-break and with it relative safety of sunlight. Not that we were in any immediate danger, the all clear signal had metaphorically sounded as it were. But I needed sunlight and the safety that went with it.

***

I tried to sleep in one of the upstairs rooms, recently inhabited I guessed from the heavy smell of sex hanging like a heavy fog in the air. The thought of lying on a sheet swimming in another man's semen yet another reason for staying awake.

So I planned and schemed away, I just dreamed of doing something that would put Teddy inside and make me some money at the same time. No one gets hurt, everyone's happy. Apart from Teddy – but he deserves everything that comes his way. I sat and schemed, but whichever way I squirmed, fear tempered my every move. A childhood spent avoiding confrontation and I thought that I would never change the habit of a lifetime.

An unhappy child, the worst thing I could have done was win a scholarship to Chiswick grammar school. I had stood out amongst my peers before this, watching football and not playing. Staring at the play fights, running away from the bigger boys. Then suddenly dressed in a blazored school uniform effectively stamped a bull's-eye between my shoulder blades. I stayed in and read a lot, learnt my Latin and even my parents were worried about the prodigy amongst their midst. Dad had saved and sweated to get me through university, the war meant that his money stayed in the bank.

They still expected me to go when the war ended, but by then I had learnt how to drink whilst nominally tracking deserting spivs. I spent hours watching one flogging watches and anything else he managed to hide in his poachers pockets of his capacious raincoat. I got to know him well; he had an eye for painted ladies and young men. I didn't think he was queer, but he enjoyed young men's company nonetheless. We talked often and I liked him, amusing and arrogant in equal measures. Conceited with a nice line in self- depreciation and I enjoyed this dichotomy in his character. He bought plenty of beer as well, a habit that was going to stay with me forever, I suppose I have to thank him for that at least.

When I mentioned university he sucked his breath in and shook his head. 'No, no – a bright young boy like you – why waste three years when you can live the good life.'

Something my parents never knew, my choice of career had been directed by a spiv. However, for the first time in my life I felt comfortable, enjoying playing at being part of military intelligence. Looking for deserters whilst mixing in the murky world of the spiv and the desperate lives of those on the run. I sat in pub corners and watched, blaming these early years for my voyeurism that I enjoyed so much in my middle years. Never a true voyeur, but comfortable listening into other peoples conversations. Vaguely excited by their changing expressions and if I couldn't hear what was being said then I imagined. This did thrill me as my thoughts ran wild, often way off the mark with my uncontrolled guessing.

Now I had a real scheme to concoct and one that gave me a chance for revenge. For someone that had no real emotions – I suddenly discovered hate in a big way. Hating Teddy gave me a heavy beer drinker's thirst for retribution. But I had also discovered hater's block. Revenge blocked my thought process, a huge some of what might well turn out to be imaginary money dangled away in front of me. Tantalus and temptation without satisfaction teased away in front of my nose. I imagined all of the money apparently within easy reach.

I thought of something Shirley had said to me, 'You live in a dream world Jack.' I said nothing, happy to stare back and wait for her to probe away at me some more.

I awoke and stared out at a grey dawn, mist over the river. A discrete knock on the door, not the Gestapo rattling knock that meant interrogation, torture and a painful death.

'Good morning – a nice morning.' I think Wyn felt that he had to pretend that a certain normalcy needed to be preserved.

'Is it?'

Wyn slipped his arm around my shoulder, 'Listen – the police gave us a hard time after you'd gone. Effectively closed us down, confined us to barracks as well.' Wyn nodded towards his brother. 'Harry – we're slipping out the back, you can stay here it's as safe as houses. Two policeman on permanent guardsman duties.'

'I want to come with you two.' Translated into plain English, I needed to stay as close to Harry as possible.

Wyn slapped me on the back, 'Good man – have a wash, get dressed, we'll sneak out the back and collect our winnings.'

***

Harry was dressed for business. Like his brother, a smart suit and tie. From behind they broad shouldered appearance of a pair of silver backed gorillas wearing jackets. We taxied and walked our way around the city. I imagined being pushed into a car and whisked away to the marshes or somewhere up Epping way and a gangster's assassination. Wyn's features indicated sadness, brown skinned and always attentive. Eternally optimistic and never expecting disappointment. Soberly dressed, restrained and sombre. Browns and dark green the order of the day.

The streets smelled of urine, fried onions from the restaurants and fruit from the street market. Cool in the shade of the buildings. I glanced behind.

Anyone following?

Possibly my last day for this world and I followed them like a spaniel. A supposedly intelligent man offering himself up for a sacrifice.

Wyn glanced at his watch – mustn't be late. He bought some fruit, the weather beaten market woman, head scarf wrapped resolutely around her like a mummy. Her glance suspicious.

Little queer boys out early today.

One little queer maybe!

A normal enough morning, I watched a driver asleep in a parked taxi. Harry's eyes alert, but still the darkness underneath that contradicted his bluff demeanour. Wyn smiled and said good morning to every woman we passed. Shirley told me that he liked to talk. Relaxed in women's company, he liked to make them laugh. An undemanding man in many ways, yet the face of a survivor. Astute and happy to humiliate others and probably a little cruel at times. All this and a survivor too.

My thoughts raced all over the place and he smiled up at me. Here we are in Wyn's dangerous world and he faced it head on. All of the girls liked Wyn, despite him making life unbearable for them sometimes. They liked him and he liked women. I didn't know if he slept with any of them. I guess he did.

A big black Vauxhall crawled past us, usually I felt more comfortable out on the street. But I had begun to fear abduction and I switched places with Harry. He could walk on the outside. Wyn's eyebrows came up a touch.

You've got it bad.

I had become a skilful reader of expressions. I knew what people were thinking.

We walked mostly, sometimes took a cab, we made contact with bookmaker after bookmaker. I had written addresses and names and prices and wagers down when we placed all the bets. Sometimes we spoke, once Wyn said. 'You've not got a girlfriend – have you?'

I shook my head, 'Why?'

'No reason, just that men in that position are sometimes not especially careful with their lives.'

Wyn was right; I had nothing binding me to this life, except life itself. Consequences concerned me though. 'I'm not about to do anything silly if that's what you mean.'

Wyn stopped and stared at me, weighing me up, making the calculations. 'It's a bit late for me to say that you don't have to become embroiled in all of this.' His left arm made a sweeping gesture at the world around both of us. 'You can walk away whenever …' Wyn shrugged. 'Up to you.'

The sun suddenly peeped over the top of the buildings, comfortably enveloped in the early morning warmth. I had been drawn into a situation that I couldn't hope to comprehend. I didn't need some sort of imperious sixth sense to realise that something awful was close to hand. My turn to shrug, 'The deeds done – almost and we all want to get away. Let's hope we can make a safe escape.'

On we walked, narrow streets choked with people milling this way and that. Street vendors, spivs selling from suitcases. Women carrying bread and fruit, old men sat staring endlessly at anything that moved. Eventually we stopped for a drink and as we walked through the door, heads pivoted our way. Harry went up to the bar and I slumped into a chair. My own instinct for survival nowhere to be seen, the usual pub smells, tobacco and this early in the morning, stale beer, wood smoke and shepherd's pie warming on a hotplate.

Wyn moaned about not being able to get a decent coffee, sipping at his fruit juice rather like a gazelle at a water hole.

Danger – let's not dwell here.

The beer helped me, halfway down and emboldened. Whistling by the time we started walking again. The world no longer dangerous, the beer had changed that.

Late afternoon before our tour of London's bookmakers was over. We found a dingy club with music and sat, all three of us exhausted. The quality of the cabaret had a certain value that made it unmissable. Especially when my mood had slumped again after the momentary lift from the beer. We sat and smoked steadily and I drank quickly. The seven piece band, combined age of over four hundred years at a guess. Rehearsing and did they need the practise. A bass player with dead eyes, a pianist with, by the sound of it, four or five fingers missing. An emphysemic trumpeter and a half decent singer. The youngster of the group, just over forty and to round it off, a man in a dark blue dinner jacket and the whitest face in Christendom. I couldn't work out what he played.

'Let's get back to the club.'

Wyn brought his stare quickly over to me.

I make the decisions.

I lowered my gaze, my insubordination over for the day. We watched a plump girl touting away. Wyn said, 'Not red hot and skinny how I like them, but a plump little madam. She pouts and brushes her hair back with her hand. Whinging for the good things, not like Shirley who wants nothing.'

Harry shook his head and shouted, 'She'll bleed you dry, suck ten years off you.'

Wyn's eyebrows came up as he said, 'There's worse ways to go.'

We sat and felt the staring eyes coming our way.

Harry raised his glass, 'Fuck Teddy.' Then he stared into his beer, 'This tastes like swamp water as well.' He frowned towards the barman. 'Couldn't keep decent beer if his life depended on it, I'm going to tell him.'

My mind screamed low profile please, no trouble this far from home.

I watched, Harry sat on a spare stool at the bar – smiled at the barman and said something. The barman's expression froze, he said nothing just carried on wiping the same glass he had been for the last five minutes. Harry pointed and I thought I heard Teddy Lewis mentioned. The previously expressionless barman told Harry to fuck off and called him a nosey cunt.

Whereupon he found himself being dragged over his own counter and then shaken rather like an imperfectly packed bale of straw. This way and then the other – a rat in a terrier's tightly clamped jaws. More words were exchanged before Harry gently placed the rat back on his feet.

A few of the locals got Harry's scowl and he sauntered back and sat down alongside me. He smiled away, but said nothing. He did this when he had something of interest to say.

'What did he tell you?' I asked, quickly tiring of his little game.

'Told me not to go back to the club.' Harry sprawled back into his chair, elbow on the table, large hand propped his head. One eye open as he said. 'Let's just clear off.'

I said, 'Somewhere a bit quieter.' A bit safer was what I wanted to say – dignity dictated that I preserve some element of bravery about my persona. We drank up and headed back to the club.

With a suitcase full of money.

1945 – TEDDY

This was the moment – as the picture appeared in his mind and he scowled at the image presented.

Eyeless was the thickest man on the fucking planet. Now

there's a fucking noose waiting for both of them.

Why? Why? Why?

Stupid cunt, well Eyeless could swing on his own.

Finally, he we are at last. It had been a lengthy slide down to this latest vice. Unlike pornography or women, this had been more like a lesson in dissection.

The fucking blood.

He thought that one day he might find peace. Not this.

For the second time in week, he kicked his way into her flat, nothing – not a stitch.

Gone – he'd find her, one day.

He lay on the bed, turned and buried his face in the pillow.

He could smell her. A familiar constriction in his throat, a sensation those two mugs wouldn't feel again. Their dead eyes kept staring up at him. Like a stargazzy pie, all those dead eyes focused on him.

His heart wouldn't stop thumping, a snare drum played by an epileptic with several fingers missing. One of the bouncers sank to his knees, a low, gurgling grown coming from his mouth. An orgasmic noise defining an end to life, not the beginning.

He saw her in a taxi, minutes before. She saw him too and never blinked.

He laughed, over and over. The blonde could be careless with her legs sometimes, the way her slip worked its way up her thigh as she sprawled over the sofa, the blonde and her slips – her indoor uniform.

Then irritation at the thought of her kissing that man goodbye. Her thoughts as transparent as sulphur smoke over a battlefield.

He'd been double-crossed.

A stern cobalt sky greeted him as he walked into pale sunshine. A certain something in the air, something indefinably bad probably.

Prison?

He followed Eyeless for twenty yards or so, pulled up

alongside and blurted, 'You stupid cunt.'

Eyeless brought his thick glasses Teddy's way, flecked with blood. He could have been a slapdash decorator lashing crimson paint everywhere. His eyes came his way and he took a step back,

'What you wanted wasn't it?'

Eyeless sniffed the air; Teddy wondered what he smelt, something on him? All that blood down my shirt. That and the smell of an old tom cat, or mildew and damp. He wouldn't shave or weeks, his hair needed a wash and his clothes too. Teddy didn't care, an adversary still to be finished off.

Eyeless smiled and said, 'C'mon Teddy, had to be done. You know I'll do anything for you.'

Teddy pushed his way passed him and strode down the Haymarket.

'Teddy – wait.'

He turned, tears streaming down his face, Teddy thought that his heart had stopped or something. He made a fist and punched his chest. Took a couple of deep breaths as Eyeless put his arm around Teddy's shoulder.

'C'mon Teddy – it's important.' He shrugged his arm away.

Eyeless tried for an incredulous expression, wide eyed and open mouthed, finally he said. 'No – Teddy, what about me taking you back and getting us cleaned up?'

Teddy shook his head, 'You slimy bastard fuck dust.'

She liked to walk around the room naked, always went by the long mirror looking at herself, always looked to see if he was watching.

Yes!

His eyes stared at her, he never closed them. What were they looking for? Turning things over and over and over. Re-running things over and over, looking for the starting place, never knowing what the starting place was. All these photographs in his head, thousands and thousands going back years. Trouble was he couldn't find number one, the cause, the starting place, the root.

The last time, definitely the last time, no more, no more.

This overwhelming anger kept drifting back, like mustard gas sweeping along a First World War trench. He kept rocking backwards and forwards.

Anger!
Shit or bust!
Get the boys together.
One day.
Not one day – today, now.

14

1980 – JACK

Stuart's assessment of Connie Schwartz bounced around in my head.

A cold bitch?

True enough, but living with Bernard Schwartz would be enough to shut anyone's nervous system down.

'Do you think she knows Bernard used to be called Teddy?'

I shook my head, but never replied. We drove back towards Reading and our visit to Connie Schwartz's ex-lover. Stuart must have noticed me shifting around in the seat, my sighing and huffing. My hand shaking as I tried to light a cigarette.

'What's the matter with you, too old for this police work? I'll have to have a word with the Super, get you pensioned off.'

I couldn't see the funny side of this, 'Impersonating a police officer carries a prison sentence you know.' I finally lit the cigarette and slumped back into the car seat.

We travelled on for five minutes like this, until Stuart's hand slid inside his jacket pocket. He passed me a small plastic envelope, about three inches by two. I turned it over, his photograph on the right hand side, The Thames Valley Police logo emblazoned across the top. His name, rank and signature tucked in their as well.

I groaned, 'This makes it even worse, I thought you flashed your credit card, this is wilfully impersonating a police officer. Where did you get it from? This is crazy.' I handed it back, twisted away from him and looked out of the near-side window.

'Kathy did it at work for me, she's got a computer. We went to a fancy dress a month or so ago. Cops and Molls sort of a do, we like to get into character for these parties.'

I said nothing and he spun the car into the office block where John Stern worked. Stuart smiled away and appeared very pleased with himself, he liked being an inspector, I wanted to be a journalist again. Through the revolving doors and up to reception. He flashed his card again and said. 'We need to talk to John Stern. Somewhere private would be good.'

'What's he been up to then?' The big haired, receptionist with a slim waist, stood as she made the phone call, 'Can I tell him what it's about?'

Stuart, impressively impassive, just shook his head. She tried for small talk which we ignored.

Please yourself.

She sat back down and pouted, unused to men blanking her. John Stern came through, tanned, black hair swept back. Square, cleft jaw and a hard physique. Attractive to women and Stuart took an instant dislike. I could see his so far impressive Inspector's guise falling apart here. We sat in a small conference room adjacent to reception, he gestured to us with a sweeping gesture.

Sit down please.

Stuart fired off, 'You knew Connie Schwartz?'

He nodded, a hint of a frown, but still confident, blissfully unaware, he said nothing.

'Intimately involved.'

He nodded.

Stuart said one word. 'Why?'

'Why do you think, what sort of questions that?'

'A very easy one.' Snapped back by Stuart, the clear intimation that things were about to get tougher.

John Stern leaned across the table, a man of the world. 'Usual reason, she wanted it, the old boy wasn't up to it.'

He leant back and clasped his hands behind the back of his head and smiled our way.

We're all men of the world.

'You were intimate with Celia as well weren't you?'

His eyes widened, the look of a man approaching a roundabout too quickly and the brake pedal goes down to the floorboards. His hands swept back through his foppish hair, then he swallowed hard. His elbows went onto the table, palms of his hands clamped around his ears. He'd heard too much and steadfastly refused to listen to any more.

'Do I need a lawyer?' Finally came our way.

Stuart knocked the backs of his hands on the table, the man opposite jumped back. Stuart said, 'How did you meet her?'

'She was stood outside the door when I came out of Connie's bedroom, half dressed and looking for the bathroom.'

'You or Celia looking for the bathroom.'

'Me of course.'

'What did she say?'

'Nothing at the time, she waited for me, by my car. Told me to meet her here tomorrow or she'd tell her father.'

'When was this?'

'Lunchtime.'

'When, date.'

'April.'

'She was fourteen.'

He covered his eyes with both hands, shaking his head at the same time. 'No, no that can't be true.'

'Where did you have sex with her?'

'Connie's bed.'

'How often did you meet?'

'Half a dozen times. She kept telling me she loved me, kept asking me to say it to her.'

I said 'And you did?'

He shrugged, 'Of course, if that's what they want to hear then yes.'

'That's just the thing to say to a vulnerable fourteen year old.'

We sat in silence, finally Stern said, 'I didn't see him, he crept into the bedroom and punched me on the ear, my head was spinning.'

'Who punched you?'

'Daddy of course, then he slapped her so hard. I can still hear it, like a starter's pistol. He had a knife, I thought... He frightened me, nasty old bastard.' A couple of tears dribbled down his cheeks. 'Does my wife have to know?'

'She'll probably find out when you go to prison.'

***

We went through the front door to be greeted by a proper fire, the blast furnace effect as hot air whistled out as we went the other way. Harry one side of the bar and Shirley sat on the bar stool on the other. Her anxious, ice blue eyes gazed mindlessly at the fire. Her holy grail of a search for pleasure, or happiness forever ending in apparent disappointment. Although Shirley enjoyed a complicated life style, she always seemed happy enough to be the third side of an unequal triangle.

I went up close, her icy blue stare came my way.

'Why did you tell him?'

'Tell...' Shirley frowned, then her features froze for a few seconds. They relaxed as realisation spread through her just like the redness that crept up through her cheeks.

'Some of us have too much to lose.' I snapped this out, wagging my finger at her at the same time.

Shirley fumbled around in her bag as the shrill, demanding ring from the phone jolted everyone.

Harry never disappointed, 'Fuck it.'

He picked the phone up, said nothing, passed it across for Shirley and we listened to a one sided conversation that appeared to be going in one direction. She smiled and nodded, 'I'd love to.' Shirley inspected her nails as she spoke again, 'You know I don't drink wine, what's up with you.'

She smiled and put the phone down, looked hot and flushed as if she longed to fall down the vertical face of love or passion... either would do. Her perfume drifted my way, expensive and understated. Shirley had some heavy make up on which highlighted the blueness of her eyes and exaggerated the chiselled formation of her cheekbones... oh yes Shirley made up and dressed to kill and a gentle tease in the voice, 'Yes Jack – I'm out on the prowl.'

Stuart said, 'You are dressed for prowling.'

Shirley nodded and pouted a touch, looked at her watch, 'And I'm late.'

Stress did this to me, sometimes I imaged other people's love affairs. I'd dreamt of the women close to me. Imagined how they felt to hold, how they responded. How they prepared for the seduction. I knew that Shirley would always be on the front foot, placing ice filled glasses on the table before coming up behind her lover and slip her arms around his waist. Go up on tiptoe and kiss his neck. Her breasts pressed firmly against his back.

Unwrap her arms and slink away and always sit in the middle of the sofa, her knees together and canted to one side. I tried to recall what Wyn used to say about those legs, what was it – dancer's legs? No, the legs of a showgirl – that was it, a showgirl. I assumed that it would be Don, making the concerted effort to stop his hand from shaking. Failing dismally and the cut glass beat a brief tattoo on the table similar to a one eyed, four year old xylophone player.

Shirley's small living room didn't reflect either her personality or the way she dressed. Everything neatly understated, a dark coloured sofa, one soft table lamp. No television, music coming from somewhere bathing the room with some sort of soft soul music.

Always the fierce heat, disproportionate to the small hearth enveloped the room in its redness. A carriage clock, with small brass ornaments either side on mantelpiece. No photographs of her husband or son anywhere. Just one picture in the room, Peggy, Harry, Stuart and Shirley stood behind the bar with their arms around one another, broad smiles from all four.

I imagined Shirley whispering, 'Kiss my legs.'
Kiss my legs.

I heard that she liked having them kissed. I imagined I was kissing Shirley's thighs as she walked out of the pub. Stuart hadn't watched her slink across the bar and out. He'd stared at me all the time. I tried to hold his gaze, after a few seconds, I glanced down at my beer.

1980 – TEDDY

She looked fantastic. 'I hope you don't shave your chuff.'

'Teddy Lewis – did you just say what I thought you said?'

He shivered, like a drowning man seeking a symbolic lifeline. He didn't know whether to look at Shirley or the tumbling sheet of oilcloth blowing from the lifeboat on a Spanish ferry. If he looked at Shirley, the oilcloth might unfurl and he would become swallowed by destiny. The oilcloth might develop talons and spear his eyes out.

'I trim it anyway. It's the modern thing to do evidently.'

He stared at her, Shirley or the oilcloth? She rested her hand on his.

'Your place?'

'Too complicated.'

'Still married to that little rat?'

She shook her head, 'He died a few years ago.'

He ducked to avoid a big hawk-moth that flapped and fluttered his way. It seemed to come out of the oilskin. He needed to get out of the restaurant. He needed the sense of freedom that would come with fucking her.

What did he say?

She said it for him, 'Why don't we go somewhere more discreet?'

He could've said that, but…

She stared at him. Those fucking eyes of hers.

He looked away.

'What do you think? Perhaps we should start getting to

know one another again?'

He stared at his coffee.

'You know I could always make you relax. It's been so awful for you.'

'Don't mention that again.'

He brought his eyes up to hers and begged with them.

Ask me again – please. Ask me if I'd like to get to know you again… please ask me.

'We don't have to do anything. Lie close and talk. I can make you better. C'mon Teddy.'

He let a long slow sigh out. Did she still perfume the gusset of her knickers?

Only one way to find out.

He woke much later, the sleep of the dead. The first time for weeks that he had slept that deep. His eyes opened and she was looking at him, he felt himself smile and then they began to talk. About her husband, about Spain.

About Connie.

'I contacted the military police, told them about the Major. He got three months.'

Teddy felt himself laughing, good girl.

'I talked to Eyeless as well.'

When?

'Took me weeks and hours stood in that freezing phone box. He said he was coming down to settle things once and for all.'

'When?'

She shrugged, 'February I think.'

'What fucking year?'

'1946.'

'And…'

'There was all sorts of rumours, they won't say anything. Gunshots were heard, but they've never said a thing.'

Gunshots? Eyeless had an old service revolver he used a few times in a couple of jewellery shops.

'Only one person ever talks about it and she's just an old drunk now. Used to be their housekeeper, I've heard all three of them were sleeping with her.'

'Where is she? Who is she?'

'Daphne Miller – gets in the Wheatsheaf. She hasn't aged very well.'

15

1945 – JACK

They read the riot act at us, a burly police inspector cursed and shouted and pointed. How dare we leave, where had we been? Were we all stupid? Didn't we want police protection?

Chastened I crept back up to bed and felt… entombed. And we were, what with two policemen on the front door with strict instructions not to let anyone in… or out. We'd been closed down and I did what I always did at times like this, tried to sleep, bury my head in the sand. To begin with, it went well. I dreamt of tumbling cataracts, Greek columns, snow covered mountains, goatherds, golden beaches. Somewhere safe to sit and all day the sun shone. And with the sun came safety and a small boned man in a crisp uniform serving drinks all day. A couple of hours earlier and I had crawled into bed with the room still heavy with sweat on perfume, cigar smoke and soap. The same bedroom that Wyn had said goodbye to Shirley, dense with the smell of sex. It hung like a cloak and I slept in amongst it and dreamt of Shirley.

Violent and disturbing images burst in amongst my sweet dreams. I woke, covered in sweat and on the edge of a panic attack I guessed. Teddy pointing his finger my way. Or his razor more like. I sat up and tried to get my breath. I got out of bed and walked around the room in a daze. I didn't like the feeling of dependency that two policeman acting as lifesaving sentinels induced in me.

Entombed.

I climbed out of bed and went up onto the roof. An eerie neon light, a hotel sign that winked and teased my way as the city prepared to put itself to bed. The Regent's Palace Hotel, another name to have nightmares about. Music from a film inside my head, was it Brief Encounter? My Favourite Blonde? The Man Who Knew Too Much? A Slight Case of Murder? All four cocktailing into a dream that filled my darkness. Whistling out from the open door of my mind like a newspaper being whipped across the beach in a September gale.

Amid the anarchy of my psyche, I tried to figure the number of murders in the capital. Less than fifty a year. The number of cold blooded assassinations as rare as six fingered leg spinner. The rest, all family disputes, crimes of passion and most of these involving the common denominator that was booze.

Except for the two boys outside the club – no booze motivating this time, just revenge.

I ranted to myself in a rambling, alcoholic induced anguish. I wanted to be sat in the reception of the Regent's Palace Hotel. Somewhere public, somewhere safe. Sit in there and watch Teddy and his underling's crash through the front door on the opposite side of the road. Their knives glinting, coshes, knuckle dusters, lead piping and whatever else came to hand. Sit in this grubby reception area with Wyn and Harry and observe as they all tumbled out scratching their heads. Wandering off with unfinished business collectively etched across furrowed brows. Perhaps a myopic stare across towards us and then off for good leaving us with a leisurely drive into the sunset.

I peered eastwards, the irregular line of buildings, cornices still intact. Roofs complete and unaffected by the best efforts of the Luftwaffe. Night sky still a smudge of dark orange where it merges with streetlights and neon signs. Smells from the restaurants, onions and garlic and fish remind me that I hadn't eaten for hours.

'It's nice up here, we used to come up and gaze at the night skyline sometimes.' I presumed Wyn meant him and Shirley. 'Not going to jump are you?'

Not yet.

I felt his arm come around me, a reassuring cloak of warmth and strength and friendship.

'C'mon, let's go back in.' I smelt his cologne and cigars … his strength. He squeezed my shoulder. 'It's nearly over.'

No – it hasn't even begun yet.

I thought about joining the other two downstairs. Harry drumming the fingers of one hand on the table, a cigarette in the other. Wyn drinking coffee and telling his brother that things would soon calm down. I crept back into bed and pulled the blankets over my head and drifted back to my childhood. I had learnt to steal from quite a young age. Stealing was the easy part, the more complicated venture of selling things on left to an old lag that lived at the end of our street. All the kids used to cut their teeth on him. He'd fence anything – I make him sound like Fagin. He wasn't, he did it because he liked everyone.

Especially us kids, give him a bag of rusty washers and George would still give us a few coppers. Encouraging us in our burgeoning careers, it turned out that I knew the criminal mind, but not Shirley's. I had drank and talked with her, walked her back to her flat a couple of times. A blind man with a whirlpool of internal turmoil as I tried to put the key in the lock. The dance of the door key, no, yes, no – at last the key slipped home. My mind everywhere, thinking back to the time I walked a young woman home in the snow during the blackout. Soft fluffy snow floating down in a windless sky. Crunching under my shoes, my urban scene transformed into a sliver meadow.

Now, I felt like the devil had just tried to tap tackle me. I could have sidestepped, but I let him trip me up. Happy to follow Shirley and Wyn wherever the journey took me, probably to the gallows at this rate.

I crept downstairs, a ghostly scene in front of me. One light on in the far corner, shadows criss-crossing the cavernous room. Harry face down on the table, head cradled by his arms and snoring. An ash tray full of untipped cigarette ends. Wyn glanced at me and tipped his head a touch, his expressive face saying everything. Eyebrows raised, the corners of his mouth turned down a touch as he nodded in his brother's direction.

Asleep on sentry duty – firing squad for him.

He smiled as I pulled a chair up and joined them. His face never actually lied; the truth was in there somewhere if you cared to look closely enough. But no one ever did, distracted by his mellifluent tone and steady gaze, you believed whatever he wanted you to believe.

'Are they still outside?'

He nodded, 'Go and have a look,'

I shook my head; all I could imagine was pounding footsteps and shadowy figures running away and into the night. Blood draining from two young men as they gurgled and spluttered their way to oblivion. I had hoped that when the sun rose, it would burn off my fear, get rid of Harry's heroics for a few hours and inhibit Wyn's vanity for long enough for us to get away from here.

Wyn smiled beatifically my way, not a care in the world. 'Did you sleep?' I shook my head. He leaned across towards me, 'Don't worry.'

But I did, 'Do we go now?'

'Not while the police are stood next to my car.' Wyn appeared to be assessing things, he frowned and thought out loud, 'You pretend to agree to their demands, then you actually agree to everything they want and then you're as bad as they are.'

I assumed he meant gangsters like Teddy.

I said, 'We have to get out.'

Harry lifted his head, eyes still shut as he said, 'Let's go now.'

'What about the boxing?' Wyn shook his head.

Harry's eyes opened slowly. 'I've pushed my head through a brick wall too many times for you. Anyway, with what went on, they might dock my winnings and I'm bound to lose my boxing license, its over.' A sense of relief in their somewhere, Harry spread his arm around the cavernous club, 'This is down the tubes too.'

'You can't leave me on my own to run this place.' Wyn's gaze came my way, he raised his eyebrows, twisted his head a touch.

How long to get back on our feet?

I said, 'It's finished, it'll take months to persuade people it's safe again. Which of course it never will be. Why did they do it?'

Silence as they both considered my question, Harry lit up and Wyn rubbed his chin between thumb and forefinger. I voiced my own idea of how it had started. 'I suppose the boys wouldn't let them in and out came the knives. The trouble is, their business is unfinished. As it is, they've closed us down, but we're still alive and we've made them look fools.'

'It was a botch and we're still their targets.' Harry hammered his cigarette into the fully laden ash tray. Dust and smoke came up like a smoke from a chimney, badly in need of a clean. 'Let's share the money and get out.'

I could see an argument developing here, Harry only wanted to give Wyn his share if he cut and run as well. I felt that Harry should have the lion's share – he did the work after all. But they decided to split the money three ways, without rancour as well. I put my hands up, 'I did nothing, just give me what I put into the pot.'

Wyn looked horrified, mouth hung open for a second and then, 'Oh no, oh no – your idea, mostly my capital and Harry carried it all out beautifully.'

Harry nodded and winked at me. Seemingly less surprised at his brother's generosity than I was. Another quality that threw me, I always saw him as obsessed with his till. But on reflection, that wasn't true. He gave Shirley anything she wanted, kept me in beer and fags and more. We sat in silence, as if no one wanted to appear undignified and suggest sharing it out now.

I longed to ask the question, how much?

Wyn leant back in his chair, clasped his hands behind his head. A benevolent Chancellor of the Exchequer about to deliver good news.

'Just over three thousand pounds... each.' Wyn stood and went round behind Harry as the breath whistled out from inside me. Three thousand, enough for three or four houses, a fortune. He put his arm around Harry, 'You can buy that pub you've always wanted, I can get a hotel – how shall we put it, somewhere quieter. It's all too exciting here. Shall I get the champagne, or is that tempting fate?'

Then the noise, like a medieval battering ram, the splintering of wood, cries of mad dogs at the door. Shouting and baying for blood and Teddy crashed through the front door. Harry stood up, my eyes wide open at the crow bar he manifested from who knows where.

'You fucking slags.' Came our way.

Six of them with knives and snarls and wild, wild eyes. Teddy, not to the fore now, urging the others forward. Harry and Wyn stood, backs tight against the bar, crow bar in Harry's left hand, pointing towards the maul slowly coming our way. Six knives against one crowbar, held by a boxer impervious to pain, ferocious and fearless. Impervious to punches, but not blades.

Wyn hissed at me, 'Get behind the bar and pass me the fire extinguisher – quickly.'

I saw it at once, a huge, old thing that must have held at least a gallon of carbon tetrachloride. I had a job to lift it, heaving and grunting with the effort of it all, I managed to get it up onto the counter. Wyn turned and picked it up with one hand, swing it down to his feet. Pulled the delivery hose out and pointing at the maul like John Wayne would his Winchester rifle at recalcitrant Indians.

The maul stopped rolling about eight feet from us, a collective confusion, a synchronized frown in place. Easily outnumbering us, but a hefty crowbar had a decent reach advantage and who wanted a poke in the eye with that?

'Go on you cunts.' Urged Teddy from a discrete distance, a scrum half at the back of the pack urging them forwards.

I cowered behind the relative safety of the bar, soda siphon in one hand, I had a job to lift it let along use it as a weapon. Harry used the crow bar like a poker. He never raised it above his head, pushed it out like some savage piston.

Eyeless came on first and Harry's piston caught him just above the heart, he went down and I expected blood to spurt out like a geyser, instead only screams came gushing our way.

'Help me – Teddy.'

Wyn started pumping away, carbon tetrachloride doesn't act instantaneously – a few seconds before the eyes start screaming. The application appeared to spur them on, invigorate, not deter and they rushed forward, only to pull up inches from us as their eyes started to burn. Wyn pumped like a demented bilge pump operator. Harry went forward poking away, jabbing into ribs. You could feel them snap. A couple dropped, unsure or incapable of rubbing eyes and ribs at the same time. Harry kept relentlessly pursuing and poking. Wyn pumping and spraying his deadly cocktail around.

It was a massacre, a First World War charge onto a line of machine guns and one by one they all fell. My eyes went everywhere looking for Teddy. Wyn picked a chair up and broke it across the back of a kneeling man.

Where's Teddy?

Teddy had snuck behind the bar, alongside me and he lunged at Harry's back.

'Harry, Harry!'

The knife arrowed towards Harry's neck, but for a bulky man he had some reflexes. Turning, ducking and catching the knife at the same time. Harry screamed, but still got a punch off, just clipping Teddy's chin. Not enough to knock him out, enough for the blade to be released and time for Harry to stare down at a six inch blade sticking into the palm of his hand. A couple of inches of blade appeared out of the back of his hand.

He frowned rather like a confused gorilla does after being stung by a hornet. Harry gripped the handle and pulled, screaming at the same time.

We all watched Eyeless moving towards the door, Teddy close behind, neither gave a backwards glance.

Harry had clamped a bar towel around his hand and began

swearing.

I took my gaze to four badly wounded men, crumpled together on the floor. I wondered what a collective noun for a group of four men with a dozen broken ribs between them was. Wyn shouted at them, 'This way.' He herded them into the adjacent office, easier than an ankle-biting sheepdog manoeuvres four bewildered sheep into a pen.

I walked over and locked the door. A simple enough act, the consequences of which is yet another thing that would haunt me forever.

Wyn said, 'Get the money.' Harry moaned softly to himself. Wyn stared around, took a deep breath and whispered to me, 'Go and get the car.'

I don't want to go outside.

'Do it.' He shouted at me for the first and only time in his life.

I jumped, Wyn threw the car keys my way. I caught them and glanced from one to the other, Wyn still impeccable, Harry wild eyed, his thinning fair hair all over the place. I went towards the shattered front door and peered outside.

Where did the policemen go?

No policemen, no Teddy, no anybody. Two o'clock in the morning and pretty much deserted. Basilica like silence, with just my heart doing a drum roll. I walked over to the car, leant against the door for a few seconds.

Please, please give me the few minutes needed … please.

'C'mon Jack.' Harry barking out instructions, Wyn, suitcase in one hand. His other arm around his brother and they staggered over towards me.

'No choke, don't flood the fucking engine.'

Decent enough advice from Harry, irrelevant if my shaking hand couldn't get the key in the ignition though.

Harry barked more instructions. 'Don't touch the accelerator either, she'll fire up, it's a warm enough night.' I watched him in the mirror as he slumped against the back seat, Wyn soon slipped alongside him, the suitcase clasped to his chest. I pressed the ignition button and the big Humber engine fired on less than half a turn.

I let the clutch up; we slid away from this nightmare, but where to?

I asked the obvious question, 'Where are we going?'

'Just fucking drive.' From one brother.

'You'll think of somewhere.' From the other.

1945 – TEDDY

A broken man echoing around inside his head. Fuck them all, most have nothing inside to break anyway. Scum the lot of them with their freckled faces and clean nails.

'My ribs hurt Teddy.'

What a fuck up, that's me finished, what a fuck up.

'My ribs hurt.'

Laughing stock, finished off by a couple of sheep shaggers, laughing stock.

Eyeless wheezing and moaning didn't help either, shut the fuck up.

Sit down and think, drink tea, whisky, more tea, more whisky…think!

Stare at the empty whisky bottle, find some rag, look for that old Jerry can full of petrol. Fill the bottle up, find a couple more bottles, milk bottles will do.

Fill them up, c'mon Eyeless.

'My ribs hurt.'

Cross Westminster Bridge, redness in the sky to the right. More than fucking redness soon. Along Whitehall, melancholy sighs and Eyeless dawdling along behind. Lost in a painful world of his own. The close heavy smell of early morning in late summer. A woman walked by, plain looking, white blouse and blue skirt, both ironed within an inch of their lives. She stared at the bottle carrying pair.

What you looking at.

She bustled past.

'My ribs hurt. It looks bad, walking along with four Molotov's between us.'

Kick a few pigeons in Trafalgar Square, up the Haymarket, skirt around Piccadilly Circus and up Regent Street. Nearly there.

'Got any matches Teddy?'

Beak Street, too many people out and about now. Around the back, count the windows. That's the office. Silence apart from the sound of a window breaking and the roar of ignition. Two more bottles thrown into the same window.

Roars like a blast furnace. Last bottle.

Fucking hell.

Flames bursting out of the window, glass shattering – screams.

Screams?

That's a bonus, let's hope that ponce of a reporter's in there as well.

More screams, hammering, kicking, scratching – let me out, please god let me out.

Shut up you fucking mumpers.

16

1980 – JACK

I stopped and stared up at the sign. The Wheatsheaf, my house was directly behind me, the office twenty yards farther up the road. Despite the proximity, I never used the pub. Just another dingy little boozer, god knows how anyone made a living there. But I needed somewhere quieter than a chapel on a Monday night. A silent corner with a nicotine stained ceiling and equally discoloured, muslin curtained windows. Somewhere where I could manifest into a nondescript little man, one who had never had a moments excitement in his miserable little life. That's what I wanted, a life of dullness and a couple of drinks to set me up for a day of unremitting dreariness.

I put my hand on the door handle and thought about John Stern, Don, a geography teacher and maybe even Patrick. When does using a young girl become abuse? I could imagine a young geography teacher having a degree of sensitivity to the relationship.

But the other two?

I crept in, the first thing I saw was the fat landlord, who never looked up from his newspaper, he just wheezed a few times, then the rattling smoker's cough. His breathing shallow, puffed his cheeks out every time he exhaled, kept his lips close together and huffed away. Typical of a middle aged, heavy smoker, his cheeks flapped away like an emphysemic bull frog.

He carried on reading until I coughed.

'Oh - hello, just about to… what's your poison?' He looked at me, twisted his head.

Don't I know you?

Recognition, 'Oh hello Jack.'

The landlord's head went back and he seemed to confuse me, I'd suddenly become one of Her Majesty's Custom and Excise. 'I don't water the mild down, or put the bitter slops back into the barrel.' The fat man's vanity took over, pushed his chest out and pulled his stomach in, 'Who's been stirring the shit?'

Pained innocence spread across his jowls, slowly – a bad mime artist.

My spell as a dull little man lasted a couple of minutes it seemed. Forgetting my earlier wish, I tried to bring some direction into this dull man's life. 'Do you get many St Mary girls coming in?' He squirmed, I waited and waited. Silent as a sadistic psychotherapist. The clock's tick got louder; the fat man lit a cigarette. Wheezed tobacco smoke and began to cough – I thought his lungs were coming up – expected them to ricochet off the bar and bounce towards the front door. He dragged in a little air and stared, at me and then back to his newspaper. Up at the ceiling, over to the front door and reluctantly back to me.

Finally, 'Sometimes, not that I serve them of course.'

I showed him the photo of Celia, 'Was she ever in here?' I pulled a stool up as I spoke. The fat landlord kept staring at me until I said. 'It's important and I'm busy.'

He frowned at me, 'No need to be like that.' His glance went down to the photograph. 'Sometimes – why what's up?'

'Was Patrick ever with her?'

He leaned closer, conspiratorially close in fact, and then he whispered, 'It was easier to let him in, you know what trouble he can be. He was always quiet though – they just sat over there and she got drunk.'

I wondered why he had to whisper there's no one to hear a word he was saying anyway. I wanted to shout at him, speak up. Instead I whispered back. 'You served alcohol to a fifteen year old girl then?

He ignored that and then the fat man's offended features ironed out when he said, 'She always ended up crying.'

A bead of sweat ran down an over inflated jowl, he

stubbed his cigarette out and by his expression, he started to ponder something profound. The front door creaked and the fat man's thoughtful spell ended as his second customer came in. I smiled over at the new arrival – his little porcine eyes sparkled back my way as he said,

'Jack – haven't seen you for ages, just the man, just the man.'

Jim, the demon barber, a gossiper of Olympian proportions. By the look of it, an out of breath barber with gossip to tell. He came over and we shook hands. 'Have I got some news for you.'

I put my hand up. Stop!

I broke his flow; Jim's gossip didn't interest me, second, third hand often. Inaccurate and often vicious, the veracity of his rumours never bothered him. He was a nasty little gnome of a man, still he had his uses. I built him up some more. 'Jim always first with the news, you know everything.'

The barber ignored my compliment and frowned. I showed him the photograph.

'That schoolgirl, what a good looker, I always wondered how many would like to give her one?' His face sparkled an answer.

Only every fucker in town, that's all.

Jim whispered, 'Fancy Patrick pushing her out of the bedroom window.'

The fat landlord's head rocked back, 'Fucking hell – no one's safe anymore.'

Jim started to rub his chin, turned to the landlord and said, 'Are you going to serve me or what?' Rubbed his chin some more and waited.

The fat landlord put a pint glass under the Guinness tap, stared down at the flowing, black beer and thought hard. A process he probably used rarely. Suddenly he brought his flabby hands up and wrapped them around his flabby cheeks. 'I'm not surprised really. Do you know what, last time he came in here, he ordered a pint and then insulted me?'

'What did he say?' I needed to know, a good insult might

cheer me up.

The offended landlord was back, 'I offered him a nice pint of this new cold lager I've just had put in.' He nodded at a garish lager pump. 'And all he said was, "no thanks, why don't you just give me that warm, flat, tasteless piss you usually serve up."' A sharp, snorting laugh came racing out from deep within me, the landlord snapped back at me. 'It wasn't funny – he was looking for trouble – threatening me.'

Jim grabbed my jacket sleeve, 'The father of that poor girl was in here.'

'Which girl?' I knew which girl all right, hoping desperately that Jim had made his usual error. Two plus two usually made anything other than four in his perverse and perverted little gossiping mind. 'How do you know who he was?' The words whispered from my lips. Suddenly punch drunk, I wasn't sure what planet I lived on anymore. A sickening premonition burst its way into my insecure existence.

'He asked about her, if she came in here at all, with his strange cockney accent.'

'A cockney accent doesn't make him the girl's father.'

Jim's head went back, 'Don't shout, it's bad for you. Now you've gone as white as a sheet.'

I tried to slow down, 'Jim... how do you know it was the dead girl's father?'

Jim smiled at me. 'That photo of him that you run in your paper.'

He touched my forearm, more to come I fear. I stared down at him.

No more please.

But there was, 'You'll never believe this one, he left here with old Daphne, don't look like that, you know who she is, used to be your cleaner come cook... you know her, lives on the caravan site now. You all used to slip it into her, you know, you remember?'

Oh I knew Daphne all right, I knew her that well that I wanted to run down the hill, rush out of this depressing little hole and bolt for safety. I took a deep breath and turned through ninety degrees and walked straight into Jim.

'Sorry.'

'Jack, hold on, wait up, that's not all. Haven't you heard?' Jim had his mad pixie face on now, bulging eyes and his head twisting this way and that. He blurted it out, 'They've found a body.'

'I have to go.'

He gripped my wrist, 'No, listen up – what a coincidence, a body in old Betjeman's paddock... how about that then?'

I leant back against the bar and patted my pockets for my cigarettes. My chest had a heavy leather belt across it and someone strong was pulling it tighter, notch by notch. My head began to spin, my world spinning off its axis.

Oh no.

'Oh no – please no.' The words slipped out, shock does that, I said it again. 'Please no.'

Jim pushed a cigarette under my nose, 'Are you all right – you're as white as a sheet.' He lit my cigarette, handed it over and put his arm around my shoulder, 'All those rumours, all these years ago and no one ever believed them, except me of course. You lived close by back then didn't you?'

I stood up, wobbled a couple of times and tried to light the cigarette; my hand hovered around like a butterfly in a gale. I looked down at my feet and imagined the world and his dog staring away at me.

What's upset him?

How could anyone find a body down there? I dragged Jim's cheap cigarette deep, it burned and blazed deep into my lungs bringing me back to the demon's inquisitive pig eyes.

I wheezed – one word. 'Who?'

He shook his head, 'Don't know, just a bag of bones. Been there years.' Jim smiled, 'You know they've been working around the clock on that new gas line, I just happened to be walking home. Shook me to my boots, I had to get back and have another drink.' Jim's smile widened, like a gurning, deranged midget with more gossip to deliver. He stared, waiting for another prompt from me to. A cue to tell me more.

'I haven't got time for all of this.'

I pushed past him, his words followed me out of the door like a Jack Russell nipping away at the heels of a terrified sheep.

'You lived down there, all those rumours. You lived down there.' Like someone turning the volume slowly down, his words faded away. I sometimes wished that someone would do us all a favour and put him down.

My pattering footsteps nowhere near synchronised with my clattering heartbeat. Up to the front door and several deep breaths, my hand slipped on the polished brass handle.

C'mon!

The door squeaked and announced my arrival, I tried to smile at the others, be normal I kept saying it to myself, I hung my raincoat up, brushed my hair back with my left hand. Then the philosophical sigh, fate and coincidence, stars and astrological signs, I tried to keep my world balanced.

Harry shook his head as he passed my pint over. 'What was Shirley thinking of?'

I didn't answer the question, Wyn answered it for me. 'No harm done – what difference does it make?' Wyn nodded and poured himself a coffee.

I hissed, but said nothing. Always aware of my melancholic tone, any serious conversations and my voice became confidential and others probably thought slightly dull. These thoughts just a defence mechanism, an excuse not to impart my own piece of bad news. I took a drink, lit a cigarette and then pointed it at Harry and then gestured Wyn to come closer. At the same time my eyes looked down at the floor.

We huddled together as I whispered. 'More trouble.'

I glanced around the bar, empty apart from Tommy sat in the corner in a splendid drinker's isolation. Did they want the bad news or the cataclysmic news?

Bad news first, I whispered to the brothers. 'Teddy's on the prowl.'

'Where?'

'Who?'

'Teddy's been drinking in the Wheatsheaf, asking questions.'

Harry groaned and glared at Wyn, who canted his head a touch and raised his eyebrows. Wyn pointed his cigar at me, 'So what ... you worry too much Jack.' He lowered his eyebrows.

Relax.

That's it then, matter closed as the brother's took their steady gaze over to me, I squirmed somewhat. The squirm became downright uncomfortable as Harry said. 'He's an old man, like us all. What can he do? What can happen?'

Wyn nodded, 'We're ok, perhaps Shirley should be careful.'

Even after all this time, we had everything to lose. I considered this as the world closed in on me once more. Voices coming my way, sound, but I couldn't make out the words. Fraud, perversion of justice, impersonating police officers, oh and last but not least... murder.

Harry boomed, 'You haven't heard a word I've said have you?'

I shook my head.

I thought someone had punched me in the stomach. I stared down at the table, a bead of sweat tumbled down my back. My voice cracking and breaking like an old crystal radio. 'Teddy left the Wheatsheaf with Daphne.'

'He'll have himself a good time then.' Wyn fumbled for another cigar and I could do nothing other than marvel at his self-belief. The world and his wife not only respected, they believed in a self- confident man. I imagined Wyn with his silk dressing gown over silk pyjamas, and leather slippers bought from a small boutique in Knightsbridge. I shook my head and made the natural assumption that Wyn still gave them their daily polish.

'For God's sake.'

Two large heads came slowly up and stared my way, eyebrows up, mouths forming question marks.

What's up with you?

I blurted the real news out. 'They've found the body in Betjeman's paddock.'

I'd had enough, two complacent fools could see nothing, let them chew on that one.

1980 – TEDDY

Some women... most women, all women ... apart from Shirley that is. He had to see her again, tell her everything – she'd understand.

Or would she?

The cold had cemented itself deep within him and the warm room seemed to thaw things too quickly. A trickle of sweat careered down his spine, then tears poured out and ran down his cheeks, and his nose ran uncontrollably. All the time the blood thumped though his feet in a painful tattoo. He sat down and thought about things for a long minute. Teddy's shoulders began to convulse, for another long minute he wondered if it was epilepsy. But he started to laugh, his stomach pumped and he laughed and laughed until his ribs ached and he felt that he might vomit.

Minutes later he stood up, went through to the bathroom and stared into the cracked mirror.

I look in the mirror more than the queen in fucking Snow White.

What was he doing in a caravan? Why haven't the police been to see him? His mouth formed a perfect O, where are they? He'd had a drink with an old woman and then they went their separate ways.

Simple, pick the bones out of that one.

He had been sat in that dirty little boozer, staring into his glass, he'd felt her eyes on him – wherever he sat or wherever he looked the old scrubber's eyes were on him.

It didn't stop him jumping when she said, 'Shame about your Daughter.'

He wondered what this woman would feel like, different

shampoo, perfume. Neither of those smells would be in his nostrils with this old dripper he guessed.

He stared at her great big breasts and felt some movement in his trousers.

She smiled up at him, unconcerned by with his staring. Just passed her empty glass across and said, 'Large rum n black please.'

'Are you Daphne?'

He had two thoughts in his head. Firstly, he hoped no one would see him leave the pub with this woman. More importantly, he hoped she was pissed enough for what he had in mind.

'Where's Elms Cottages? Do you know Shirley Catmore?'

'She lives there, you haven't had her have you?' Teddy's hand went down onto an expansive buttock, her hand came around his waist.

He laughed, 'Just like the old days, two fucks in two days.'

'What did you just say?'

'Nothing.'

***

He jumped, as if he a small electric discharge had shot across between his ears. Followed by a smell – something organic he thought, then the remnants of a dream that he couldn't recall. He tried to fan the smell away, sat up and leaned across to put the bedside light on… and shivered. He suddenly remembered he wasn't at home in bed and looked at the woman.

Who was she?

What was he doing in, Teddy stared around the confined space… a fucking caravan? Then he quivered and shuddered at the memory of that woman's huge buttocks. Dimpled and spotty and her rum soaked breath. Repulsion tore at his throat. He remembered smacking the quivering mass of her arse though.

Hard!

Sweat stood out on his forehead like a tropical disease.

Perhaps she had cholera, clap more like – he trembled again.

He had shoved his hand between her legs and prised her thighs apart. All the time her eyes stayed on his. He was surprised how easily he slipped inside her, then she closed her eyes and he felt her heel on his buttock. He groaned and emptied himself in her. She never looked disappointed, not the way all the others did. She even went down on him later, he wasn't so keen when she pushed his face down between legs. As he went down, he held his breath and shut his eyes. Suddenly a vision of a Bulgarian shot putter's thighs sprang into his mind and he didn't know whether to laugh or cry.

He brought his hands up under his nose, smelt the recent encounter on them – the repulsion disappeared – he might even do it again.

He smiled, things were on the up. She thumbed one of his cheekbones, like an indulgent mother cleaning her only child's face. She removed her thumb and tilted her head and came close and kissed the same spot where her thumb had been, deposited some fresh lipstick on it. He slid his hand under one of her breasts at the same time as the other slipped under the hemline of her slip. She tried not to, but a groan came easily out from her and she groaned again as she felt him hardening against her.

Another escaping moan as his fingers slipped into the crack of her arse and they kissed.

She twisted away from his probing fingers, 'Careful where you put those.' She laughed and wouldn't shut up, 'I think you're living in a dream.' Did she mean he was in a dream? Or living within a dream?

A nightmare maybe?

Later the grey haired woman stared up at the ceiling and smoked. Tipping her head back and sighing her plume of smoke vertically up. At the same time stroking his thigh, as if she was detached and thinking about something else – but Teddy knew that she wasn't. She wanted him aroused again. He watched her stub the cigarette out, chasing the ashtray around the small bedside table at the same time.

He gasped as her hands enclosed the stem of his penis, it felt red hot in her small hands. She moved her hand up and down and looked into his eyes. He shivered and his eyes went back and then closed. He felt her lower herself on him, he groaned and she felt the slow burn inside her – she answered his groan with one of her own.

When had he last felt this calm?

Lying in bed with the blonde and the windows open with the warm August air filtering in.

Then?

'When's the funeral?'

'I don't fucking know.'

'Touchy aren't you? I only asked.'

He noticed the large headline in the local paper.

Body Found In Paddock

He snatched the paper up and quickly scanned.

1946. Londoner. Possible gangland hit. Glasses. Gun.

Teddy felt his heart miss a few beats.
Eyeless!

17

1945 – JACK

Turn left down Regent Street, around the circus and along Piccadilly. I spent so much time looking in the rear view mirror, it was a wonder that I never ran off the road. All the time I looked for headlights, winking and blinking my way. A warning flicker of trailing lights

Oh, I can still see you.

Listening to Harry's great big heaving sighs. Right hand clamped onto his left, a tea towel compressing the wound. Even in the darkness of the car, his face as pale as a ghost. Stoic and no longer angry, just hurting.

Then his brother's whispered words, 'Has the bleeding stopped yet.'

'Think so.' He said this through gasps and groans. I had never experienced real pain. Harry said once that there's a purity to the sensations caused by pain, concentrates the mind somehow. I always accepted that one at face value.

I missed the turn at Hyde Park corner, shuddered at the thought of heading east along the Bayswater Road, back the way we were coming from. I swung south down Park Lane, fully expecting to drive into a car driven by Teddy Lewis, sweeping along Piccadilly like a gunboat up the river Nile. Back on track and heading west. Go west young man, eye on the mirror. See the redness of the sky behind me, go west young man, go west.

'Why did we do a circuit of Hyde Park?'

'Sorry.'

I raced through Hammersmith and along the Great West Road. I knew the route so well. You see I'd planned this escape for months. I had lain in bed staring at a road map, memorising, until the directions were burnished into my mind. Despite this, my concentration was all over the place. My mood swinging ever upwards as we headed west.

An advertising hoarding distracted me.

Wake up perky in the morning.

I laughed as the advert for Ovaltine flashed past. The scantily dressed model in the picture, more suited to a film poster. That's when I clipped the cyclist. He came across the Cromwell road, then turned in front of the car and into Fullers Brewery. I caught his back wheel and sent him somersaulting into the pavement. I braked until prompted to do otherwise from the back seat.

'Keep going. He's alive.'

To confirm the Major's instant medical assessment, the cyclist stood in the road shaking his fist at me. I sighed, unsure whether to laugh or cry. My eyes still on the rear view mirror as I went hurtling through a red light just past Hogarth House.

'Are you trying to get us killed?'

No, was the answer to the Major's question. But I knew a couple of lunatics that were trying to do just that.

I sighed a couple of times, as we slipped away from Chiswick and into the countryside. My mind wandered to Shirley and Peggy, I knew where they both lived. It was simple enough, head along the A4 towards West Berkshire. The daylight bringing me no relief from my congenital cowardice. As the sun rose, headlights disappeared and my twinkling points of reference vanished as well. I pushed the accelerator to the floor and raced towards Slough.

'Slow down – we're not being followed. Try and enjoy the scenery.'

Oh, of course, the scenery. Difficult to appreciate anything given Harry's heaving sighs coming across from the back seat. I said, 'We have to find a hospital.'

I watched Wyn in the mirror, he raised his eyebrows and nodded, 'He'll be all right for an hour or so, distance first.'

That age old equation, as the distance, X, increases. The threat, Y, decreases. Carter's formula for a long and safe life meant that to solve this equation I had to find the value of the unknown quantity. In general, solving an equation relied on keeping it balanced; always add the same quantity to each side of the equation. Therefore, how great did X need to be before Y, vanished over the horizon. Harry would have worked it out quickly enough.

Fucking miles.

An obvious answer really.

Talk of the devil, 'Where the fuck are we going?'

'Out into the sticks. Over the hills and far away.'

I thought the corners of Wyn's mouth turned down a touch. Where are the painted ladies of the night? The street markets and the clubs and a chance to make easy money?

'No need to look like that.' I said. 'What about the chance to live a little bit longer?'

Wyn's eyebrows went up, 'What are you talking about?'

'The country, the sticks and the chance to live a normal life.' I'd never been out of the city, not once. Never seen a cow or a sheep and had no real desire to make their acquaintance either. Rather a cow than a bunch of knife wielding cowboys, shouting and whooping for blood though.

'Do you think that they've got out of the office yet?'

Wyn laughed, a rather soft affair, but a laugh nonetheless. 'Oh I don't think so. I had a steel door put in, kept my whisky in there for God's sake. All my spirits actually, a stick of dynamite wouldn't loosen that door.'

'They'll be getting hungry later then.'

'You left the key in the door though, someone will let them out... eventually.' He laughed again.

Fully light now, countryside and all this greenery. Surrounded by pasture and an empty road. Nothing behind me, X had increased and therefore, Y decreased in direct proportion. I passed my cigarettes back to Wyn; he slid one out and pushed between Harry's lips. Used his expensive lighter and Harry whispered thanks between groans and tobacco smoke. Wyn lit one for me and then brought a cigar out. All of us smoking, sat amongst all of this smoke gave me more of a sense of security that the fields that sped past outside.

I ticked the place names off, Maidenhead Thicket, Reading, Thatcham, Newbury and on ever westward. As we entered the outskirts of Hungerford, I saw the sign for the A338. I swung right, fourteen miles away and our resting place. Twenty minutes later and I drove carefully along Newbury Street, turned left into the market place. Drove another forty yards and pulled up in front of the Bear Hotel. Handbrake on, ignition off, lean back and sighed and sighed. Great heaving gasps like a man given a last minute reprieve by a sympathetic Home Secretary.

Wyn glanced around the market place and shook his head. 'Oh well… beggars can't be choosers. Sit tight, I'll get a couple of rooms sorted out.'

'What about Harry?'

'Ten minutes – they must have a hospital here somewhere.'

He took the suitcase of money with him, I smiled at that, still it was appropriate enough for Wyn to attend to the accommodation details and five minutes later he came back with a couple of keys and a wide smile. 'Gentlemen, your suite awaits you, we have to share a bathroom I'm afraid.'

I thought getting Harry through reception unnoticed wouldn't be easy.

Wyn said, 'Wait here, give me a couple of minutes.'

Wyn went in and started flirting with the receptionist, a plain woman with a good chest. She cooed and giggled and never gave us a second glance. Harry leant against the wall as climbed the stairs, a slow and painful ascent, looking down at his hand every inch of the way. It was my idea to clean him up before we visited the hospital. As well as his hand, he had the customary facial injuries from his fight. Most noticeably, the huge swelling that resulted from butting his opponent. We needed to smarten him up somehow and get some sort of story in place.

In spite of his discomfort, I smiled at the incongruity of it all. Three of us in a small, provincial town's only hotel, one suitcase and not a change of clothes between us. But rich, if not beyond our wildest dreams, then enough to set us up for life if we were careful. One suitcase packed with used notes and the probability that we would be pursued for the rest of our lives.

Discretion was the order of the day. For the next week, year… decade.

I watched Harry, sat on the bed and groaning softly, his right hand still crudely bandaged by the tea towel. The walk from the car had caused the wound to seep blood. I stared across at his left knuckle, red, swollen and broken on Teddy's forehead. Another injury to explain away.

Wyn sat at the foot of the bed, flawless in his appearance and he gazed into the mirror to confirm this. To the uninitiated, the Major might have appeared more concerned with the line of his cravat than the state of his brother. That definitely would be the height of vanity in a way, after all Harry had nearly bled to death saving both of our lives.

We all knew that not to be the case though, both of them unable to show any affection for a sibling. But things were very often not what they appeared to be at first glance. Harry knew that Wyn had a deep affection for him, likewise, Harry felt the same, albeit a grudging, fucking smarmy bastard sort of fondness. Brothers through and through. Two brothers and me. Three of us, still in one piece… and rich.

And the thing that I always remembered most, in amongst the stillness of the hotel room, the heaving, rasping sighs from the injured man. I glanced from one to the other and gestured to Wyn.

'Let's get him sorted out.'

***

Farming accident?

The nurse in the small casualty department shook her head throughout the time she dressed the damaged hand. Not that I was an expert, but we didn't look like farmers. One of our number looking like something you'd see in the window of a Piccadilly men's shop. Wyn had smartened his brother up, but farmers... the nurse talked all the time.

'You need surgery on this. Tendons cut and probable nerve damage. You need a trip to the infirmary in Oxford.'

That never happened and Harry never recovered full movement or sensation in the hand. Such was our collective persecution complex that we stayed away from big town infirmaries. Instead we made our way back to the hotel and shared the money out. Wyn immediately started to open bank accounts. One in each of the town's four banks. It took a lot of persuading, but we agreed to deposit the money in small, weekly deposits. Harry pooled his share with Wyn, two look-alike brothers depositing huge amounts of cash would have been a give-away.

It was straightforward enough, no formal identification needed. He used a false name of course, false references as well. Major Watkins became plain old Wyn Wicks and he resented the sudden demotion back to the ranks. He liked being a Major. We'd agreed, regular payments – the size of an above average wage-packet. I was able to use my real name and the bank clerk's eyebrows went through the ceiling when I loaded banknotes in front of him.

'It's my old aunt, she insists on paying my allowance in cash. Is that a problem?'

'Of course not, thank you mister Carter, would you like to see the manager?'

I shook my head and hustled out.

Harry had turned into some sort of guard-dog and the bag of money his juicy bone. We planned and he sat with his good arm around the bag. It would take months of small deposits before his guard duties would become redundant.

We had so many ideas as well. Hanging in the air like swallows about to migrate. Go our own ways, too risky at the moment. Rent a house together, yes to that. Look for Peggy, not yet, look for Shirley, not yet. Find out what's happening in London, one for me, ring my old boss, he'll know. Harry threw his sling away, stared at his bandaged hand for a long time, before saying, 'Stay together for six months, no R&R visits up to London mind.' He glanced at Wyn 'Not six months in this hotel though.'

We needed a house, Harry's temper encouraged by the confines of a small hotel room. We talked about getting separate rooms, but my instructions were clear. Find a house with a garden. I walked around the market place the next morning, eventually found the only estate agent. Walked around several houses, before deciding on one that I really took to. Down by what was the old mill, a stream running alongside, a small drive running up to a chocolate box of a house. Thatched roof, four bedrooms, all surrounded by abundant hedgerows and bushes and trees.

Six month lease, no, no cash is fine sir.

My next task gave me an anxious moment. I stared at the town's two phone boxes. Both stood outside a pub called the Post Office Vaults. I glanced through the pub window and there was never any doubt what I would do first. A pint or the telephone call?

The beer was good enough, the locals nosey. I didn't realize I had an accent.

Where you from then?

I thanked the landlady, and walked into the phone box. Got my pile of pennies ready and listened as the phone the other end began to ring. Then through two more internal exchanges and eventually the phone picked up.

'Crime desk.'

'Michael?'

'Jack?' Michael Parlane hissed down the phone. 'I thought you'd copped it as well. I thought you were dead.'

I frowned, alarm bells ringing, 'What's happened?'

'Where've you been? That club you used a lot, firebombed. Four bodies, all unidentifiable. Obviously not you though.'

I leant back, another punch to the stomach. Fighting for breath.

'Hello, hello, Jack.'

'Any ideas?'

'Your two friends, Teddy Lewis and his brother. But the bodies are so badly burnt, they could be anyone.'

I couldn't concentrate, images of bodies piled up at the door, trying to clamber over one another and escape from the furnace.

Scrambling, pushing, scratching each other in a frenzied maul of bodies. Screaming for their mothers as their eyes popped like champagne corks from the heat.

'Jack? Was it them?'

Life turns on a sixpence at moments like this. If I hadn't been so scared then the truth would put the record straight. A few hours of tough questioning from the police and with a bit of luck, everything on the straight and narrow again. If I hadn't been so scared that is, surely it would be better if Teddy believed that we had all perished? His hunt for violent revenge would be over on a bonfire of bodies and exploding whisky bottles. The harrying pursuit is over, just one more lie and years of the good life stretched away in front of us all.

'I haven't heard from them for a couple of days.'

'They're checking dental records now.'

Dental records often told the police nothing. Many of these people never went near a dentist.

'Jack, Jack, when are you coming back?'

Never!

I staggered across the market square and lurched into the newsagents, bought the Telegraph and the Express. Rushed the short distance and up to our room. Harry was sleeping, on his back with his bandaged hand across his chest and cuddling the money with the other. Wyn sat by the table writing a letter, more references for himself I imagined.

I tossed the Daily Express his way and said. 'Scan through that.'

I sat in the room's other chair and stared at the newspaper. I found it on page two, a photograph of Wyn and Harry in the ring after their last fight staring back at me.

Champion boxer and his brother missing after club fire.

He read the article and then read it again. He placed the paper down and gestured for me to pass the Daily Telegraph over. He read the article and then read it again.

'I've caused four men to die, unwittingly I know, but…' I let it hang in mid-air.

Wyn turned my way, 'It's not our fault.' His eyes went towards the floor suggesting the opposite. 'This makes things easier I suppose.' Wyn brought his gaze my way.

'My old editor asked me if it was you.'

'What did you say?'

'That I hadn't seen or heard you for a couple of days.'

Wyn nodded, 'Good man.'

I stared at him, 'Have you ever been to a dentist?'

'Are you going mad?'

'Have you?'

'When I was in the south of France. Why?'

'What about Harry?'

We started at him, his mouth wide open showing a full set of strong teeth.

'I'm not sure.' Wyn frowned at me. 'What's up?'

'Police are checking dental records now.'

'Don't worry; I don't think we've got any problems there. You know that it leaves us in the clear. A clear run at a few new enterprises.'

'Not for a few weeks though, your faces are plastered across every paper in the country. You're both staying in this room until I collect the house keys.'

1945 – TEDDY

Everyone called him a hard nut, crazy, a psycho. Yet no one knew that he was frightened of heights, spiders, dogs, some women, most women, the dark. Convulsions have been brought on in the very core of his stomach by any one of the above. He fumbled, where the fuck? Anxious to be rid of at least one of his phobias by throwing the light switch… if he could ever find it. The smell of paraffin oil, mothballs and coal began to penetrate his senses. All those smells that repelled him, confronted him now, paraffin oil, mothballs, coal dust, sex, especially his wife's sex.

He shivered, threw the light switch… nothing.

What the fuck did you expect? If Eyeless's knife had made them both an appointment with the hangman, the Molotov's had meant that the noose was tightening, he could feel its strands brushing his neck. He groped around, a blind man somewhere familiar. Somewhere he spent hours as a boy. He went through the geography in his mind, stood statue still until satisfied. A photo in his mind from years ago. He shuffled and felt his way across the cluttered floor. Felt the damp wall farthest from him and lit the match. Counted up to ten, by which time he'd located the candles.

Boxes of them. Teddy lit another match and transferred the flame to the brand new candle. Blew the match out as one died, another flame flickered into life.

He pulled the old milking stool closer, sat down and surveyed the scene. A fur hat, his mothers, a pile of gramophone records, his uncles. A small axe, his own. A ventriloquist dummy, Eyeless bought it when they suddenly came into some money a few years ago. A push bike with the back wheel missing, his old man's. Used to cycle down the docks to work, until he discovered throwing a half-brick through a jeweller's windows brought about a better hourly rate that is. A wooden crate of Mackeson, his auntie only ever drank Mackeson. Sometimes in his parent's bed which confused his Mum as she pointed at the old man.

'You don't even like Mackeson, why do you drink it in bed?'

Teddy's heart careers away like a brakeless bike being ridden down a steep hill. The silence makes the thumping against his ribs louder, he can smell his own breath down here too, anhydrous, a solvent, meth's or ether. I'll have to stay down here for the rest of my life. The euphoria of the exploding Molotov's and the screams of men being blast furnaced into crisps had long vanished. Quicker than a light bulb filament being turned off. His life has wasted down to this, living in a basement in his parents bombed out house. Dozens of cans of food, eight bottles of Mackeson, a stuffed fox. His grandmother bought if from a pawnbroker twenty five years earlier.

Teddy stared into its glass eyes, flexing his fingers at the same time. A joint cracking symphony that somehow slowed his pulse. He held not only eye contact with the fox, but his rancid breath as well, fifty, sixty, seventy – then an exploded burst of pressurised, hot and stale solvent breath.

He'd stay down here for… he made some calculations. He hated baked beans and tinned fruit. Tinned stewing steak and tinned biscuits.

Nonetheless, enough for a month and it was stuff they'd given his old man. Black market stuff of course, not that the old man ever thanked him.

He was a tight bastard.

But the old man had planned for a German invasion and if that meant staying in the cellar, then so be it. They went down there every time the air raid siren went off. Shelters? Underground? Fuck off, my old man new they'd be safe down here. And they were too, missed everything, except the V2 that crashed through the ceiling in early April. No warning, no siren, just a fuck off explosion and the old man and auntie … well, they went out with a bang. Perhaps that's why he had four crates of Mackeson down here, keep her well lubricated.

The fox kept staring his way, everyone used to kid him

that it had put next doors cat up the duff. They all expected him to belief that one and he did for a while. Until he saw the kittens, they just looked like fucking cats. He stood up and placed a dusty tea towel over the fox's eyes. Nodded with a degree of reassurance towards the now sightless, fox.

Me and you foxy boy – till it all dies down.

Where the fuck did Eyeless get to?

He patted his jacket pocket and felt the letter.

18

1980 – JACK

In the night I'd dreamt of women's hips, wide hips, some too wide, or just voluptuous depending on your point of view. Not like Shirley, she still had hips like a teenage boy. As I dreamt on, I wondered what it was doing outside. Exploding clouds? Yes that would be it, evaporating into little pools, remnants of clouds. The gusting wind that had whipped the puddles, warm and mild not like the frosty mornings that reminded me of Stuart and his sister. When they were young, how they waited in the queue at the bakers. Then the trudge home, Stuart laden with the weekend's bread, his sister unburdened and staring down.

Don't look at me like that, you're the youngest, you carry the bread home.

My dream moved onto Wyn, how he'd stuck his life back together so many times. Twenty years ago when he got a glass pushed into his face. It wasn't the end of the world, although it was the end for Wyn and Shirley. Wyn sat amongst us and smoothed talked and whispered with all the rhythm of a diesel engine, idling away in the heavy morning frost.

***

The smell of last night's beer and tobacco smoke battled with the polish applied to the cleaners mop. Slowly, after much buffing and huffing and against all odds, the polish took over and eventually overran last night's staleness. Just like the Russians at Stalingrad I thought. Then I smiled – I enjoyed military analogies. I stared around the table; Harry had a glass of whisky.

Why not? After all it's much too early for beer.

Stuart sat, elbows on the table, he glanced my way and smiled, 'Here we are then.'

Harry barked, 'What are you having?'

I shook my head, 'Clear head Harry.'

I went through the order of things, ending up with a warning.

'Whatever happens we must remain in control, try to stay calm. Stick together and we can see this through.'

'I can't see why you can't just bubble him. Tell the police who he is and be done with it.' Stuart stated the obvious with the obvious bad taste this left in his mouth. I mean, who would want to talk to… them?

Stuart felt that his father's reluctance was based on the age old tenet of not grassing someone up. But it had nothing to do with that noble principle. The fact was, we had as much to lose as Teddy.

Things from our collective past that just the three of us knew about. Events that could still mean long jail sentences. I shook my head and looked back at the other two.

'We're in need of some sound legal advice.' I looked Wyn's way.

Harry's eyes flashed towards me, 'Any lawyer that knows Wyn, will only be familiar with paternity and bankruptcy cases.'

Although under normal circumstances that would be worthy of a laugh, this morning we looked impassively down at the table. I stared at Harry – his temper was cause for concern. Discretion the order of the day.

Harry's eyes came up slowly; he stared at me… and smiled. Peggy made the coffee and a pile of sandwiches, placed them on the table, glanced at Harry and said. 'It's all too cloak and dagger for me, why do you need a solicitor?'

Harry grabbed a handful of sandwiches, talked through a mouthful of bread. 'We don't yet, but who knows what might come out if Teddy gets arrested or shoots his mouth off.'

Peggy stared at me, glanced across to Stuart, then back to

me. Then she turned and wheeled out, leaving me wondering what she actually knew about her husband.

Wyn stared at me, Harry's physical twin, identical except in their characters. One TNT explosive, the other a calm rather refined man not given to cursing or drinking. His face reflected pious corruption somehow I thought. Old fashioned manners, serious expression, matinee idol's moustache. Never beaten, plenty of reversals – but he always won the war. Two brothers, a formidable pairing... and Stuart of course.

Harry said, 'Well – when do we see your legal man?'

'Woman.' Wyn glanced down at his watch, Cartier he would surely tell anyone prepared to listen. I knew it to be a good copy.

'Woman?'

Wyn pulled his packet of cigars out, gazed at his silver Colibri lighter. I smiled, he knew how to get under his younger brother's skin all right. Harry tried hard, but the heaving, racehorse sized breaths rasping across the table suggested imminent explosion.

Harry drummed the table with his stubby fingers, 'Only you could have got a woman.' He leaned across towards Wyn, 'One of your harem I suppose?'

'She's thirty one years younger than me and a top class lawyer. She's the best... simple as that.' Wyn held Harry's blistering stare and smiled, 'As Patrick's just found out'

Library silence again.

Unimpressed, Harry lit another cigarette, threw the empty packet on the fire, smoke punched out of his mouth as he whispered, 'A lawyer with a speech impediment and just one eye in the middle of his forehead could have got Patrick out. What's the big deal?'

'We'll see her soon, best behaviour I think.'

***

My phone burst into the silence of the office, with all the suddenness of a brick through a plate glass window.

'We need to talk.'

Mably's voice, suddenly singing Stuart's hymn. I shook my head, it was as if he'd been put up to ask that question by my over inquisitive colleague. 'Can you come up – sooner rather than later?'

The thumb and index finger of my free hand began to massage my temples. I sighed and stared frantically around the desk for my cigarettes.

'Oh God.'

'What's up?'

'Lost my cigarettes, that's all.' Lost my fags and beginning to lose my mind. I shook my head, Stuart mouthed, are you all right? I shook my head again and tried to concentrate, whispered down the phone. 'What do you want David?'

He repeated his original question, 'Can you come up here please?'

I felt like the fly listening to the persuasive spider, my neck constricted and my heart thrashed wildly too, I'd dreaded this moment. Attempts to sound normal as my voice croaked and broke.

'Give me an hour or so. Who is it and how long has he, or she been buried there?'

I imagined Mably smiling, he never bothered to answer my question. His agenda and he was going to stick to it. 'Pathologist needs a couple of days, but he said the carotid artery might have been severed.'

I groaned, well that's no surprise, a knife carried in the left hand, a violent meeting between a thugs throat and a left handed assailant. A natural enough meeting place and I remember the noise of the impact. Not like an ostrich egg being punched by a steam hammer. A crushing, split second of impact as a skull is fractured. Just the quiet slicing of a sharp knife through soft flesh, no noise at all. Except for the gurgling a split second later and the screaming noise that only lasted a few seconds. How could I forget? It woke me every night for the next ten years. So frightened that I spent those years living as a lodger in Harry's pub, under his wing and happy to remain there.

'Jack, Jack wakey, wakey.'

I shook my head, 'Sorry – you were saying.'

'In the jacket pocket, a court summons.'

I grabbed the table, this just couldn't be. I'd told Wyn to empty the pockets. He always insisted that he had. Always assured me that he'd cleaned the pockets out. I tried to stop my head from spinning like a top and said, 'Local man?'

Mably said, 'The summons was from Clerkenwell Magistrates Court.' He had more, it was obvious that he had a rabbit and like any top performer he wanted his timing to be spot on. I waited and waited, my heartbeat thumped away in my throat somewhere – tell me. 'The date was the seventeenth of February – the day before that fracas down by the cottage where you lived. How's that for a coincidence?'

I felt Mably was about to take a bow, but like a top class magician, he had another rabbit to produce. 'Forensics have got it now, they should be able to make the rest of the letter out and soon I hope. Oh by the way, he had a gun on him and he was wearing the strongest pair of glasses I've ever seen.'

I could see Mably now, standing up, take a step towards his audience and showing them the palms of his hands. Inviting applause from his dumbstruck audience of one.

'All these bodies all of a sudden, all of these rumours.' Mably laughed, 'All those headlines for you – how's the circulation.'

I assumed he meant the newspaper; the movement of blood around my own body gave me cause for some concern however. Mably droned away, I struggled to listen.

Mably said, 'Me and Don are going up to London this week – see what we can find out.

Oh God.

I placed the receiver back in the cradle and my chin went down onto my chest. Stuart came up close, offered me my cigarettes and lighter. I grabbed them like you would a Red Cross parcel in a prison camp. I lit up and took the biggest drag that my already damaged lungs would allow. I held the smoke for a few seconds. Let the smoke out, sat forwards in the chair and took my glasses off, I rubbed my eyes and looked for a way out.

'Jack – c'mon now. You look dreadful, you need the confessional box and I need to know what's going on.'

He had his mother's sensitivities... when he chose to use them that is.

'Tonight, I'll tell you the lot. Not in the bar – my place.'

He nodded, 'About time too.' Stuart pointed at me, 'Why's a body that's been buried for years suddenly a problem?'

'It just might be connected to everything else that going on.' I could see his glance my way out of the corner of my eye. 'Don't worry, I've said that I'll explain everything.'

***

Stuart's hand shook when I passed the tumbler across and it soon turned from a calm sea of whiskey into breaking waves of good scotch in the glass. His shaking hand only calmed after he'd nailed most of its contents with the desperate swallow of a condemned man. I'd lectured Stuart enough times over the years and the temptation to tell him not to guzzle decent whiskey wasn't far from my lips. He frowned a touch, the only expression that he got from his father. His father's scowl, mother's cheekbones and God knows where the soft, curly, brown hair came from. Some of his braver friends teased him unmercifully that it was a perm. A topic that guaranteed a flash of temper... his father's son all right.

He leaned forwards, 'Jesus, I can't believe some of this.'

'The way you've been acting, it's you that might end up in trouble ... Inspector.' I raised my eyebrows at him, 'You have to be more careful. It's a dangerous game we're all playing at the moment.'

He shrugged and stared down at the coffee table, eventually and apparently reluctantly, Stuart brought his eyes back to mine.

'Please – tell me the rest Jack.'

Stuart held my gaze; I sighed and poured some more whiskey.

'You listen and no more interruptions.'

I had a rapt audience that's for sure. Stuart leant forward in his chair and never said a word. Just stared at me, smiled and shook his head whenever I mentioned Harry's name, or Wyn's come to that. For better or worse, the two major influences on his life, much to Peggy's constant frustration. She wanted him to play the piano, which he did rather well. Harry wanted him to box or at least play football, again which he did better than well. Wyn only wanted him to be happy. A noble motive, but one tempered by his belief that any degree of happiness always involved the relentless pursuit of anything female.

I pushed the plate of sandwiches across the table, Stuart brought his hands up in a gesture that said enough. He lifted the lid on two bottles of Guinness and poured them. Pushed one my way, I took a sip of Guinness and then a nip of whiskey. Material in front of us to talk the night away.

1980 – TEDDY

She stared, grey haired, confused and wild eyed. A puzzled look, like someone strapped into their crashed car, who stared blankly out of the shattered car windscreen at the motorway carnage all around her.

'Why did you just punch me?'

He watched her swallow hard, stared as she closed her eyes as if that memory had become too painful for her. He'd forgotten about it – well she talked too much, worse than that she talked about Celia.

He listened to her rhythmical breathing, he rested his hand on her thigh and she whimpered. He rubbed her thigh with the back of his hand and waited.

'You'd better go'

'You hit me.'
'Why did you want Shirley's address?'
'Why did you hit me?'
'Shirley Catmore's into young men these days ….'
Shut.
The.
Fuck.
Up.

He punched her, the nose splintered – old bones are brittle he supposed.

He watched as she screamed and writhed – the blood bursting over the caravan door. She staggered towards the little bathroom.

He forced her down and bent her over the small bath, he didn't want blood all over him after all. He hadn't been that aroused for years. Fucked her from behind as she whimpered and cried and moaned – with pain. He pulled her hair and yanked her head violently forcing her whole body around. He could see her wild goggle-eyed stare and it made him come straight away. Teddy caught hold of her hair again and rammed her chin against the hard edge. Eased himself out, stood up and stared down at her. She started to retch into the bath, a splattering, stomach voiding vomit. He kicked her in the ribs.

Did he shut the caravan door?

When he walked towards his car the crows squealed, murderer … he laughed at them and pointed their way, what do you know? He looked down at his bruised knuckle and wondered.

How did that happen?

***

'Teddy?'

He didn't know what to say. He went to put the phone down, but the blood on his hand had congealed and phone stuck to the palm of his hand.

'What's funny? Teddy, Teddy are you all right?'

He grunted something down the phone.

'How are you – I've thought about you a lot today.'

He couldn't speak, all these things to say. Shirley, I think you ought to know, I'm a murderer and I'm stood in a phone box, bathed in blood. He's been inside my head and I always believed he'd never escape from the prison of my mind... but he got out. The cold damp recess of my mind, cold and damp like a crypt. It's made me a God, what am I? Human? No, a God and every depravity is vindicated when you're a God. No rules anymore, just dead bodies.

'Teddy, what have you been up to?'

'Nothing, this and that. Can I see you? Let's get away for a few days – I love you.'

19

1945 – JACK

Peace, a time to convalesce and eventually I hoped, a full recovery. That sounds an easy enough concept for the road to a complete cure. Perhaps I got the choice of my nursing care wrong. Instead of quiet country walks, listening to the radio, or reading something heavy, I preferred the snake oil salesman's remedy. Treating myself with strong beer in the bar of the Bear Hotel. Tempering my mood like a lump of wrought iron under a blacksmith's hammer. Despite this crude and not especially effective treatment, I continued to medicate myself this way.

Forever terrified of the darkness, every time my head touched the pillow the same image battered its way inside my head. The picture of burly policeman unable to open a door because of a pile of well toasted bodies the other side. Melted skin stretched across cheekbones, insides well done, eyes popping out like agitated champagne corks. Locked into a crucible by the simplest of acts. By turning a door key, I had not only frazzled my mind, it had torched four men into melted, unrecognisable blob on the floor of an office.

A lifetime of constant pursuit stretched in front of me. Forever harried and pursued by a wolf pack of submarines. All out there somewhere, looking for me, a straggling, drifting merchant ship. Frantically semaphoring for a battleship to come alongside and guide me back to the safety of convoy.

I never made the connection to begin with. I thought the relaxed state was brought upon by the result of a couple of hours in the pub. It wasn't, instead the warm afternoon,
September sun brought relief. Safe in the arms of a deckchair

and the massaging reassurance that the sun on my face brought me. Daylight had become my harbour, sunshine the key to avoiding the nightmares that crashed into my head as I tried to sleep. But even that was illusory, sunshine helped, it took a few days to realise that my main prop had become Harry.

A praetorian guardsman, my own sentinel, a battleship and I followed him relentlessly.

Sat in the deck chair watching Harry. Gardening had become his therapy. One handed gardening to begin with. When the stitches were removed, he tended and nurtured and dug. Burying his memories while I tried to sluice and rinse and flush mine away. His therapy seemed to work better, despite his temper going off like a hair triggered pistol most of the time. But that was pretty much normal for him anyway. I didn't expect a transformation as grand as turning a urinal into the Chevy Fountain for instance.

The point was, unlike me, he hadn't changed much. Except for the fact that he'd taken up gardening. And I sat in the sun and watched him and felt secure. A bobbing merchant ship had its very own battleship support. I watched him take up his new hobby, just like I watched him box. He pursued the two with completely different approaches. For a man who had a temper, he boxed like the most philosophical of philosophers. A calm air of unconcern as he kept himself side on, taking a punch without alarm and dishing out his formidable armoury with a degree of amusement. Whispering into his opponent's ear in clinches like he was offering sound advice to a wayward friend.

I never knew how his boxing had started, his gardening developed by chance. He'd found all of the garden tools in the garage and started digging. You would have thought that he'd done enough shovelling in his working life. Perhaps that's why he did his gardening like he had gout, or toothache. He groaned and sighed, dug and hoed. No apparent pleasure, no obvious knowledge either.

'What are you doing?' I asked him.

He leant on his hoe and stared at me, rather like a pikeman watches the retreat of a defeated foe. No obvious pleasure, just relief and maybe surprise that another day would dawn tomorrow.

'Dunno.' Harry shook his head, 'Pointless asking you.' A reference to my city upbringing I guessed.

I said, 'There's a couple of gardening books indoors.'

And he poured over them like an ecclesiastical scholar scouring some ancient biblical text. I never bothered to remind him that we'd probably be gone before the fruits of his labour could peep through his painstakingly cultivated soil. What was the point? He'd found his therapy and once I'd survived the dread of another night, I watched him and found mine too.

They both accepted my mantra, heads down, stay here until the New Year. Four months the mortgage needed to pay for anonymity.

Wyn got a telephone installed, wrote letters, looked for his hotel and took up cooking. Pined for Shirley, wrote a couple of letters to her and it turned out that she never even opened either of them. He took this badly, although he would be too conceited to admit it. Once I mentioned her, something like have you heard from Shirley? All I got was the habitual shrug, a cant of his head and a frown.

He said, 'I don't know what's going on, just that she doesn't want me in her life anymore.'

Then I got the look. His heavy eyelids, bruised and expressive hooded the soft brownness of his eyes. Usually they beamed like a soft torchlight, now they looked cold and disbelieving. His intention always to convey self-assurance went as flat as his voice.

We won't mention her again.

Instead Wyn got us a housekeeper. A woman just a little older than himself, she had a tangled mass of curls and a ready laugh and one who called herself Daphne. He helped her around the house, watched her as she prepared our meals. He made Daphne's coffee and spent a long time folding the sheets back on the beds with her.

Whilst Harry and me lived the lives of friars, it seemed that for Wyn, life had become more complete than ours.

***

Just before the end of October, I felt strong enough to leave the nest. A destination other than a pub, I needed work. Not the physical efforts Harry had put in all of his working life. Not the slippery social skills Wyn put to good use on his climb. I'd seen the advert in the local paper. Seen it in the office window of the North Berks Herald as well. Walked by it three or four times a day, unable to pluck up the courage. If I'd had two hours in the pub, then bravery wouldn't be an issue. Reeking of strong ale might however. So I walked backwards and forwards past the small newspaper office. Like one of those ornamental sentries outside the Kremlin.

Enough!

The round, polished, brass door handle slipped in my grasp. Is this how low I'd sunk, so feeble that I couldn't open a door? Not quite, it worked in an anti-clockwise rotation. You see determinist logic has its disadvantages. A soft metallic bell announced my entrance, although in my case, the febrile twisting of the door handle had already announced my landing.

I stared across at the oldest man that I'd ever seen. Delicate and with sloping and rounded shoulders. Ash coloured hair, too long in places, missing totally in others. Sunken eyes with panda-like rings around both. both. White skin tinged yellow, coloured like parchment, textured similar to the Dead Sea scrolls you felt. A tobacco coloured cardigan with leather buttons. The sleeves hang loosely at his wrists, his fingers and the backs of his hands are splattered with printer's ink.

His face is all nose and chin, bony and developed to probe the local community for any scrap of news. Local football results, stored in his head. Last week's magistrates court, all down in a battered notebook. Gossip, filed away in another drawer of his mind. His sunken cheeks hadn't seen a razor for a couple of weeks and like the top of his head, the outcrops of hair were patchy. Lush in parts, barren in others.

His whole demeanour one of exhaustion. He fixed me with his dark and deep set eyes. An aged kestrel's eyes had retained just a hint of former glories as they probed me for weaknesses.

'You after a job?' A sombre voice, striking and resonant. Shut your eyes and he could be a world service announcer on the radio. He tipped his head a touch, the hawk eyes getting a sharper focus.

'Or do you have some startling local news for me?'

He scratched his stubbly chin and fumbled around on his expansive desk, found his cigarettes and with a hand that creaked and shook like a one hinged barn door in a gale, he lit up. His chest movements so shallow I thought of him a case for imminent collapse. I glanced around the small office.

Where do you keep the oxygen cylinder?

I said, 'The job you're advertising for.' Horrified that my voice had betrayed the confidence I meant to display. Sat there in my finest, spick and span, standing out like a counterfeit passport. Self- belief holed below the water line as I waited for the certain knock- back.

'Do you have a C.V?' I shook my head.

'References?'

I nodded, 'I can get then sent down from my last employer.' Those references would be from the Daily Mirror and not a certain Major Wyn Watkins. Although, rest assured he would provide a glowing reference. I tried not to smile, 'I can give you a contact name now if you want to talk to him.'

Xenophobic and pleasantly racist, he seemed to find pleasure in the rich anger that spewed from his cracked lips. His profile highlighting his beak nose, as he rambled on. 'You wait and see, win a bloody war maybe, but lose the peace. Lose our Empire, bloody socialist government, nationalise bloody everything.' Then he blinked a couple of times and his beak twitched around to point at me once again. 'Why would you want to leave a national newspaper and come and work in this backwater?'

I'd expected this one and launched into a zealot's exposition.

London had become too hot for me. I wanted to play some cricket, watch some local football. Assimilate into a community that, eventually, I could call mine. Somewhere where I knew everyone and everyone knew me. Work somewhere that I could call my own. Make a difference to…

He held up a transparent talon.

That's enough.

'Do you still have your union card?'

I nodded and pulled it from my inside pocket, along with my press card. He held one in each hand and scanned the two. Back and across, across and back. He dragged his notebook towards him and said. 'Give me you ex bosses name and a number.'

His Schaefer fountain pen scratched away onto a small area of untouched notepad. He liked writing lists by the look of it, I imagined columns of English prime ministers, Saxon kings, chronological lists of rivers with their respective lengths alongside, all enclosed in brackets of course. Names from magistrate's courts, reports from local football matches, phone numbers. None of which he needed, everything would be locked away in his head. All the petty criminals, corrupt councillors, serial adulterers, shop lifters, shirt lifters, choir masters with nasty little tendencies. All filed away in the library of his mind.

A racist, a fascist, probably a homophobe and certainly a xenophobe. I liked him from the beginning. He stared at me, an old falcon viewing a three legged mouse. Finally he said, 'The Oxford Mail, the Reading Mercury, both want to buy me out. The Oxford Mail offered to do all my printing on a sub-contractual basis of course. Printers work out the back, they fleece me of course. But I won't sell, I want someone to take it on for the good of the town. But who would have the time or more importantly, the money to invest in this little circus?'

I might be able to help you on that one.

***

The overweight rucksack of despair had been discarded. Michael Parlane had been his normal effusive self. Of course, if he rings I'll tell him what an incisive and perceptive and hardworking chap you are. I had convinced myself that the job was mine. Not only mine, but the chance to buy the old boy out before he has one cigarette too many and expires with a fag burning away in his mouth.

Time for a drink and not one forced on me as a medicant. A celebration, the future stretched away far into the distance for a change. Not the usual two yards from cliff edge that night time brought. I gazed at the head on my beer, slowly raised it towards my lips when a tap on my shoulder interrupted its smooth progress. I lowered it back onto the counter and turned around. Ronny, Shirley's rat faced husband stared at me. Empty glass in one hand, stub of a smouldering Woodbine in the other. Like the worst of schoolboy actors, he affected surprise to see me. His confidence plainly the product of a few pints. Oversensitive at the best of times, a person who puts insults and slights against him, into the vault of his memory. Locked away until the chance for a sneaky revenge presented itself. The ferret's eyes darting around the half empty bar.

'Buy me a pint queer boy.' Those six words summed him up, a distasteful, spiteful little rat of a man.

With all the insincerity I could muster, I said. 'Ronny, what a pleasure.'

'I've seen you in here a few times. You were too pissed to notice me of course. Why you around this way then, not much for your sort here.' He pushed the empty glass closer, the stub of Woodbine back in the corner of his mouth. One eye shut as the smoke climbed vertically up the cliff face of his cheek and into the affected organ.

I took a drink and the beer tasted sour, poisoned by the man close to me. Ronny had tipped some concentrated nitric acid down the well. He would find sifting through the pockets of the dead stimulating and fulfilling. Dragging the dead from the plague into mass graves, singing as he went about his business. He dropped his cigarette onto the floor and ground it out with his heavy working boot.

There's a carpet on the floor and ash trays everywhere. But I said nothing.

'Where are the other two then? I know that they're not dead.'

'Perished in a fire.'

'Don't give me that rubbish.'

I lit a cigarette and said, 'What do you want?'

He snorted, stuck a finger in my face. 'I've read the letters you know, that's more than Shirley has. Tell the Major that one. Always meet the postman on my way to work, he always hands me all the letters. Very touching tell him, very nice. I'm in a camp in Poland and he's poking my wife. Buy me a drink then, I'm sure we can let bygones be bygones.'

He laughed and scratches away at his stubbled chin. The implied effect of this action one of deep thought, a considered and fair man. Ronny pulled his packet of cigarettes out. 'Sorry Jack last one.'

He lit up, Ronny was one of those that always had two packets of cigarettes on him. One a near full one and the other always had a solitary cigarette left. Just for occasions such as this. Mean in both spirit and deed.

He pointed at me again. 'Shirley's – we're having a baby, how about that one then.'

A smug rat stared my way, I said. 'Good for you, give Shirley my congratulations.'

Now my mind raced, she was a couple of months pregnant when Ronny landed back on these shores. Surely he didn't believe he was the father. I suddenly felt better, we all need secrets and I knew one about Ronny. Not that I'd ever tell him of course, just the knowledge would sustain and nourish me whenever I had the misfortune to be in his company.

'I've got to dash, always a pleasure to see you.' I drank up and turned to go.

Ronny stopped me with a hand on my shoulder. 'Tell the Major that he's got a big surprise coming his way. Perhaps he should move away – right now if he's got any sense.'

Threats tumbled from Ronny's mouth like coins from a generous fruit machine.

'They say it takes a sour man to make good beer – you should've been a brewer Ronny.'

I liked that one, stared at him and waited. He tried for the abstract contempt reserved for people like me. That didn't work, so Ronny smiled to show me that he didn't think me at all funny, like I said, no sense of either humour or irony. I waited and followed him out; the wind had got up and from the north. Autumn began the slide towards winter that afternoon.

Ronny hunched his shoulders, no jacket and defenceless against the cold. He scurried away from me, his breath snorting out in short sharp plumes that twisted up and away. I walked home thinking of Ronny puncturing my brief balloon of optimism. Wondering all the way if I should warn Wyn I decided to say nothing.

The next day, a knock on the door and four red-capped men. Tall and broad shouldered, escorted Wyn away. Military policemen looking for deserters and those that had never signed up in the first place. They were deferential and polite.

He was a Major after all.

* To find out what happened to the obnoxious Ronny, read **"Salt of Their Blood"** by the same author.*

1945 – TEDDY

Two months in a cellar, beat thirty years in a cell he thought. Or the short walk to the scaffold, it beat that all right. Two months in the cellar of a bombed out house. Slipping out at night for a shit in amongst the rubble that was the street he lived on for most of his life. Shitting amongst the broken window frames and shattered doors. Watching all the time, never seeing a soul. Once when he was heaving away, a cat crept alongside, meowed to announce his arrival.

Teddy, well... shit himself.

Goodbye to all that, the cellar and the broken homes. A cabin that was smaller than his cellar. Smaller than his cell even. Getting a berth on this floating heap of bilge was risky. They spoke Spanish and no English which was diametrically opposite to his own linguistic abilities. The captain understood cash though; he even gave Teddy a key to the cabin door.

Followed by the mimed instruction to keep the door locked, miming the counting of money and then most terrifying mime of the lot. A knife drawn under the throat with the implication that his crew were a bunch of cut-throats who imagined a fortune in Teddy's suitcase.

He never washed, shit and pissed in the bucket. His worst fears confirmed halfway across the Bay of Biscay as the bucket slid around the floor as easily as an ice hockey puck across polished ice. Not even a port hole to see the waves. Just the battering, booming noise as they hit the starboard side. Stretching rivets and twisting bulkheads and pounding his head and stomach.

Daylight in Santander.

After four days of blind purgatory. He must have smelt like a two legged cess-pit. That's the impression the concierge gave anyway. Holding the hotel's room key at arm's length and ushering him down the hall and far away.

Por favor – Mierda – Servicio.

Spoken as you do when sponging something awful from off your shoes.

He took the train a week later, down to Murcia. Uncle Jim had lived there for the last... Teddy scratched his head. Sometime between the Spanish civil war ending and the war beginning. He'd got himself a Spanish wife; she was a refugee from the communists.

Well off bit of stuff, even if she did look a bit like a race horse whinnying. Jim was in trouble by this time anyway, so they took a ferry back home. Well to her home that is, last thing Jim said to him as he left. If you're ever in any trouble Teddy …

'Hello Teddy, what the fuck are you doing here?'

'Hello Jim, hello Carmen.'

Where's her fucking nose bag?

'Looking for a bed.' Teddy looked down at the floor, 'I'm in a bit of trouble. Just a few weeks.'

'A few weeks – c'mon in my son. Put your feet up, you look like a fucking tramp, what's happened? What trouble back home? Shame about your old man and my sister.' Jim with his clean fingernails and dirty little habits.

'How did you get here?' Jim studies him like he's a fucking transcript from a dusty old book.

The never-ending circuit for his insomnia looped around and around inside his head. Teddy's throat chokes up, eyes burned with the tears of failure. He had expected Carmen to turn him away, an angel's finger pointing Teddy away from the Garden of Eden.

When it never came he sobbed.

20

1980 – JACK

I walked into the market square with Don's sudden interest in our collective past jolting around in my consciousness. His leering, heavy lipped features drifted in and out of my dreams most of the night. So bumping into Carol made me jump even more. I smiled at her and had to admit it. No matter what Carol's frame of mind, or whether the particular phase of Don's extra-curricular activity was waxing or waning. The children never saw her as anything other than cheerful and bright.

She swung her eyes across to me, 'Are you all right?'

I nodded, 'I should be asking you that question.'

'I'm used to it Jack, see him when I see him.'

'He's busy, lots of things on at the moment.'

Why did I defend him? I couldn't get it out of my head; the thought of Don with someone else had been trapped deep within me for the last few days. I knew Don used his own jealous fears as justification for hammering many a nail into the coffin lid of their marriage.

I stared at Carol, she must have read my mind, her eyes fluttered down, a broken sparrow down towards the two children, 'C'mon – let's get you across to your Nan's.'

Twenty minutes later and walking back towards the office, I stumbled upon them. Whispered conversations anywhere always interested me. In public places they got the gossip hound in me going like a beagle after a fox. Two heads together, constant glances around. He had some bruising around the eyes and a fat lip. She touched his lip. Gently, like you touch a new-born baby's face. Then they both glanced around.

Who's looking?

Carol placed a calming hand on the man's wrist. An attractive couple, wrapped up in each other, perhaps they wanted to kiss. Anywhere else and I was sure that they would. I watched them, her fingers brushed the bruising on his cheeks, just the tips – so intimate. He smiled, eroticism fired across, back and forth between them. Telepathy perfectly in tune.

I watched on and on as they maintained eye contact and still smiling.

Enough.

I wheeled away and went back down to the office and sat at my desk. Stuart stared my way. We'd spent the night. No I'd spent most of the night telling my tale. He'd drunk most of my beer and we shared a good bottle of scotch. He appeared to have slept the sleep of an angel, I looked like I'd been under interrogation all night. In a way, I suppose I had. Layers of lead had been peeled away as the time marched on. My burden passed across, down to a generation that could cope with the pressure.

'You look awful.'

As if to confirm my deep impression that my features resembled something from a Hogarth painting. One he'd sketched in a madhouse. I pointed his way, 'I tell you everything, you've told me nothing. Especially things concerning your mate and my secretary.'

Stuart blinked a couple of times. Appeared to be about to say something when Carol walked into the office, out of breath and smiling my way.

'It's cold out there.' Carol kept smiling after she spoken.

'Sure is.' I nodded and said. 'Patrick's out and about again though.'

Carol's cheeks went scarlet, she turned away and slipped her coat off. Kept her back to me as she hung it up. Slipped through into the annex and left me to my list.

It hadn't taken Patrick long to get back into the saddle.

'What happened to Patrick?' Stuart frowned and gestured towards the door Carol had just disappeared through. I shook my head, 'He's been punched about by the look of it.'

'Two of our finest policemen – there's no place in this town for men that screw under-age girls.'

I raised my eyebrows and whispered. 'Not Don… Surely?'

Stuart shook his head, 'Couple of thick plods, the same two that were outside the school just after the girl jumped.'

I picked up a pencil, studied the point. Slid it into the sharpener and gave it a couple of turns. Stared at it again and began my list. I felt Stuart glowering my way as Carol came back in, back in control and smiling my way.

Don't worry Carol, your secrets safe with me.

'You're a miserable bugger at the moment.' Stuart barked this my way, then whispered, sotto voice…he wanted Carol to hear. 'What's up with you? Patrick getting beaten up in his cell upset you that much?'

I blinked up from my desk, as I've said many times, his father's son for sure. I glanced quickly across to Carol, she acknowledged my shocked expression with a smile. But it was true, I shook my head. Apart from my long exposition last night, I had said little recently. Listened a lot, only spoke when I was spoken too. Drank more and ate less, introspection had become the order of the day.

I sat forward and as if needing confirmation, I asked Carol, 'Am I?'

She laughed, an affectionate gesture that suggested she was fond of her employer. 'Perhaps you're working too hard.' Said it with a touch of melancholy.

We both have lots on our minds at the moment.

'C'mon, let's go down to the burial chamber.'

I blinked, Stuart stood and picked my overcoat up, passed it across and gestured me towards the door.

I said, 'What's up with you today?' Enthusiasm for any sort of work well down the list on his back burner, only one thing worth waking up for in the morning as far as Stuart was concerned and it didn't involve getting out of bed. All I get from him now is questions, constant, non-stop questioning. I felt like I sat opposite some Stalinist inquisitor.

Why?

How?

Where were you when this happened?

'C'mon, before it gets too dark.'

Leave me alone.

We arrived at the old mill, my ears ringing from the questions that he still buzzed my way. Despite my confession, Stuart just wouldn't shut up. We crossed the wooden footbridge and Stuart pointed at the narrow drive that led to a small cottage that lived amongst the trees and dense hedging and shrubbery.

'Mum said that you lived in there with the old man and Wyn for a while. That's the scene of murder and mayhem then.'

I ignored the last bit, 'Just after the war, the three of us – no women.'

Well apart from Daphne.

I stared straight in front, I only ever came down here in bright sunshine and even then, certainly never looked through those wooden gates. I rushed past like a twenty five kilometre Olympic walker. Some people just drink too much, I justified my habit with the simple fact that I'd had good reason to drink too much. How else do you forget what had happened down here. I rushed headlong along the footpath that twisted and meandered alongside Letcombe brook. My younger companion trailed in my wake …I heard him mumbling away.

'Slow down, slow down.'

I stopped, not because of Stuart's grumbling, but I saw a figure in front. Slightly stooped, an elderly posture, pressed up against the police tape that cordoned the area off. It could have been a network of First World War trenches. Gas pipeline trench running away from the footpath at forty five degrees, ten yards from the footpath and there it was. A small area that ran away from the trench rather like the beginning of a communication trench. It had been excavated carefully, rather in the way an archaeologist digs. The smell of recently turned soil made me reel. Not the neutral scent of a tilled allotment, the deeper you got, the stronger the smell.

'Hello Jack.'

Bert Powell!

A coincidence too many and I reeled back at the only witness from thirty five years ago and now… the same, except the police had found a body this time. I took a couple of deep breaths and said, 'Bert how are you?'

Wrong place at the wrong time, I felt a bit like someone sneaking over into Poland from the east, just as the Germans panzers rolled up from the south. I always had a problem with timing Even in this twilight zone old Bert's thoughts appeared as transparent as a sheet of glass as he stared, first at me and then across at Stuart.

What's that troublemaker doing here?

I wasn't sure if Stuart had recognised Bert, he should have, his primary school caretaker and Bert's job for the last twenty years of his working life. But Stuart couldn't shut up, despite me and the anxious old man stood opposite, Stuart wouldn't stop, blurting like a hair triggered machine gun, 'Shall I take some pictures, two bodies in two weeks. Did you know him Bert, you're old enough? Did you know him? You go back to medieval times.'

I noticed Bert's shoulders tense, 'Stuart, leave him alone.'

Stuart took no notice, turned and nodded at the hole, then he said, 'Shall I get close and take a few? It's hardly a crime scene is it?'

I said, 'Stuart – I wouldn't say too much at the moment and it might well be a crime scene.' Advice from one well versed in these situations, keep quiet and save it all for the lawyer some of us are going to need. Stuart just smiled and then looked across at Bert, recognition at last. Bert shivered and I thought he was about to scuttle away. In some perverse way it triggered another burst of activity from Stuart, who slipped under the tape and started to snap away. Flashes going around an empty paddock like an inland lighthouse.

'Stuart.' I said.

He strolled back and came up close to Bert, brought the camera up and said, 'One for the paper Bert.' Stuart quickly took a close up and the flash went into the old man's face.

Bert's eyes clamped shut, blinded, he reeled away. 'You stupid fucking bastard.'

If Stuart had a degree of lucidity left in his body at this moment in time, he would have realised that his own face had become twisted and contorted. The dim street light fifty yards away had deepened his features, coarsened them and probably made him look like a murderer now. Choleric shadows covered Stuart's face and he looked like an irritated Bela Lugosi.

Enough to convince Bert anyway who turned and walked away from us. We both watched him as he walked back to the slow and relaxed moving little brook. On a sunny day the water carried reflections of fluffy clouds and twisting willow trees. A bleak night like tonight nothing, only the sound the rain that pattered down onto a nearby car roof. That and a whispering wind sighing down from the north. A full moon still appeared fitfully behind the heavy scudding clouds. Its bright face casting ashen shadows and when it appeared, the body came into a soft focus again. Stuart got his outsized torch out and he played it over the scene like a frantic cinema usherette looking for a spare seat on a busy Saturday night. As it made its uneven journey around, I imagined the beam as it picked out a dead man's face. One with a pair of very thick glasses on, one form thirty five years ago.

'C'mon, I've seen enough.'

What I meant was, I'd already seen too much.

***

We stopped outside the Bear on the way back; I had hoped that Stuart might have to get back to his wife and kids. I even dropped a hint, 'Don't you have to get back to Kathy, wash the children, read them a goodnight story?'

I wanted to drink alone, but Stuart shook his head and we walked underneath the arch and into the bar. The hotel for the poorly dressed travelling salesmen and midday lovers, women of a certain age taking a pretty average lunch and men of my age… boozing. The losers, the deluded, the fatalists, and those hoping against hope that they'd be left alone in peace.

I stared into the head of my beer, when it frothed as perfectly as this. I felt it invasive to drink through it. Not that invasive though, I threw some beer down my throat, the feeling never lasted long. I gestured to Stuart, 'C'mon, drink up.'

'Jesus, slow down.' His mouth hung open, Stuart's pint hardly been touched. I'd become so preoccupied, I couldn't remember drinking mine. I needed to be alone at this time of the day, as if the night has become my walkway into history, I enjoyed grandiose thoughts, especially after sunset. Night time, a place where, within the blink of an eye, you can be either victim or murderer, it's all the same at this time of day. When I worked in London, I scrounged for gossip, press releases, in amongst the chaos of old copy tele-printer readouts, plastic coffee cups and the phone's constant ringing.

Thank god I was out of all of that, but even small town hacks like me, still twist sarcastic half-truths into headlines. I had made a good living in east-end gutters searching for copy. I saw murders and listened as pink tongued, suspects full of inane gossip and dishonest cunning. Stories appeared in front of me like a phantasm, a mirage with their teasing possibilities. I shook my head, feeling maudlin had slipped unnoticed into my life lately – perhaps I needed some female company, proper female company.

'Jack, Jack.'

I blinked at Stuart, he was pushing his empty glass my way.

'I've got it.' It came to me suddenly, like a blow between the eyes. The shock of it took my breath away. I put my hand on Stuart's forearm. 'I think Shirley needs to be careful.'

'Why - just because Don's spending too much time

around there?' Came quickly back my way.

'No - it's more serious than that.' In fact, if she had any sense of self-preservation, she'd feel a little bit like a fox loitering around the kennels of the Old Berks Hunt at the moment.

Stuart blinked, then shook his head. 'What's up?'

'Teddy Lewis.' I waited until Stuart nodded, 'He used to be so dangerous.'

'He looked like a bookmaker.'

'The point is, he's the type that would bear a grudge big time. He had a thing going on with Shirley as well and he was in the Wheatsheaf the other night.'

'Everyone has a fling with Shirley, except me that is.'

'And me.' I laughed and it felt good. Laughter and a decent pint an instant ameliorant for the blues. I gestured Stuart in close, 'The strange thing was he left the pub with old Daphne, don't look like that, she used to shack up with Stopcock Arthur.'

He smiled, 'I know who she is, she must be seventy that's all'

'And what's up with someone her age having a fling?'

'Nothing I suppose.' He shivered. 'I just don't like the thought of it.'

'I'm sure Daphne's all right, but...'

Stuart finished his pint, getting into the swing of things now. 'I'll give her a ring, give us some change.'

Stuart went to the pay phone in the corner of the bar and went scrolling through the phone directory. Found what he was looking for and gave me the thumbs up sign. Turned his back and began to dial.

He sauntered back shaking his head, 'Nothing, no answer. Drink up, let's go and have a look.'

***

Sunset had long since gone as we walked towards the caravan site; both of us taking a slow, gossip hound walk, pursuing another sad little headline. I glanced around as I walked, I hated the caravan site at the best of times and trying to coax something out of an old woman appeared to be scavenging of the highest order. I tried to justify it of course, whereas Stuart just thought it a grand little caper. I took a couple of deep breaths and knocked on the door, glanced down at my watch and wondered if perhaps she'd be around the Wheatsheaf by now anyway. But I could hear the radio on and expected to hear steps across the caravan floor, soft echoes that became louder as she got closer.

Instead we got nothing, just the crackling radio.

'She's probably down the pub by now.' I wanted to get away. Stuart had the bit between his teeth however, 'There's a light blazing away in the kitchen, the doors shut though. Not a light on anywhere else though. She might have had a heart attack or something. Shall I kick a window in?'

I stared at the lock, not a good quality lock like a Chubb. I thought for a moment, I knew a chap, bit of a rogue I suppose, when I was in military intelligence. We had to get into some office and he became offended when I started to kick the door in. Whoa up he shouted and pulled out what looked like a set of feeler gauges. Until he opened them up that is, most had a tapered tang and different shaped ends. Long, thin tapered ends, some were curly cork screws, there must have had a dozen. A locksmith by trade, he gave me a set and he taught me everything I know.

'What are you doing?'

I hadn't done this in anger for a few years. Kept my hand in picking my own lock now and again. Having someone breathing down my neck tended to affect the concentration. I raised my eyebrows towards the lock and gave myself a running commentary. The spring force increases as the pins are pushed into the hull, but the increase is slight, so we will assume that the spring force is constant over the range of displacements we are interested in. I humffed with impatience, looked back down at the picks.

'How come you've got them then? I thought you could

only buy those if you were a locksmith.' I ignored the question, but more came at me. 'C'mon – Raffles you're not.'

I smiled to myself as I felt the last pin drop and a sense of elation swept over me. My heart hammered with a pulse in my temples that hurt, but the pressure clamped around my lungs vanished and I began to breathe again. I pushed the door open and it was as dark as a crypt, just a hint of wind in the eaves. I stood and waited for my eyes to adjust, I pulled the light cord hanging in front of my nose. Then a blinding, naked bulb cast its stark shadows around the strangest of scenes.

'Fucking hell.' From my fellow burglar, 'Too late Jackie boy.'

Blood.

Blood everywhere, an uneven trail on the floor, it ran from the bedroom door, to the open bathroom door. I stood still. It was impossible to be certain which direction the wounded women would have been moving in.

I'm not going to find out either.

I turned towards the front door, 'Let's get the police.' Footprints in the blood, one barefoot, another a shoe print. No single trail to follow, to me it looked like someone had been doing a conga. From bedroom to bathroom and back again, more blood down the bathroom door, handprints everywhere.

Stuart tiptoed towards the bathroom door, I shouted. 'Don't touch anything.' Stuart's fingerprints were on the record that's for sure. He pulled his shirt out from the trousers and wrapped the tail around the door handle. He slowly pushed the door open, his head came up and back quicker than a Jack in the box. Stuart's face took on the complexion of a mummy.

'Ring the police – let's get out, I've seen enough.'

1980 – TEDDY

He slept next to Shirley and dreamt of chaos, slaughter, disaster and humiliation, Teddy laughed at the suffering poor and sneered at the narcissism of the rest. The reek of full dustbins and the image of new born babies falling from third floor windows jolted him back. He shook his head and brought his gaze back to the shop window and then looked quickly away. I used to be smart, wear decent suit, with a sharp tie and a confident walk.

I looked and felt good, what happened?

I want to be a camera again.

Get rid of any photos taken in the caravan.

When did all of this catastrophe muscle its way into his life? Teddy knew it was when he least expected it, too complacent about Shirley. All he could see was that vile old short arse in bed with her. Fat arse pumping away. The thousands of times he thought of that image and every time he writhed and squirmed in a raging impotence. How he wished he had the chance to push a glass into his fat face instead of …

He sighed, looked across at Shirley. Asleep on her back, he stared at her and his daughter muscled her way back inside his head. That night Connie was out with her lover and his daughter sat close by, filling his glass whenever it was less than half full.

Celia's eyes, why didn't he notice her eyes. Like piss holes in the snow.

What had she been taking? Then she starts talking about school. The conversation got weirder and weirder.

'Why do some theologians take the old testament literally?'

All the time her eyes half shut like she was staring into a setting sun. 'Are the stories symbolic, allegorical?'

He felt himself blink, did he ask her why she was in that police car? Why didn't he mention the geography teacher?

'Were the biblical disasters just payback for human misdemeanours? After Sodom and Gomorrah disappeared in flames, did you know that Lot escaped with his two daughters?'

He shook his head, hypnotised by her cheekbones and the mellifluent voice that had developed after puberty.

'They lived in a cave with no men about. Can you imagine? They got him drunk.'

Got who drunk?

'Their father, got him pissed and both slept with him. Can you imagine?'

No.

'Listen to this, incest amongst the biblical patriarchs was rife, Abraham marries his half-sister; Abraham's brother, marries their niece. Isaac marries his first cousin, once removed. Jacob marries two sisters who are his first cousins and Moses parents are nephew and aunt. Can you imagine?'

His head began to spin, slowly at first. Like a roundabout at a fair picks up speed.

Then he looked at Celia's breasts.

He shook Shirley, wake up, wake up.

'What's up – have you had a nightmare?'

Nightmare?

'Help me, Shirley…'

21

1946 – JACK

'I don't know what all the fuss was about.' Wyn's eyes are forgiving, like a generous father welcoming a feckless son back into his life. Despite spending Christmas in an army prison cell, his voice was calm and devoid of the emotion that he would have been justified in expressing. Even the words didn't trade in resentment and acrimony. He asked the expected questions, how's Peggy? Has Daphne been paid? Have you found a pub yet Harry? How's the job going to me? Finally the question that had to be top of his list.

'Shirley?' His eyebrows formed a question mark as he gazed my way.

I shrugged, 'Mother and baby boy both doing well.'

Wyn's eyes fell to ground, I glanced quickly across to Harry. He tapped his balding head, 'What did you expect?'

Wyn stared at the clock, he sighed. 'I wrote to her – several times in fact. The last one from Chelmsford jail.'

I said, 'She wouldn't have read it.' His face swung my way, question marks still in place. I moaned softly to myself. 'I never had chance to tell you. I'm guessing that Ronny told the military police where you lived. Shirley never saw your letters either. He intercepted everything you, or anyone else come to that, sent to her. I've bumped into him a couple of times.'

Wyn closed his eyes, fighting back tears? Remembering Shirley? Plotting a suitable revenge for Ronny? He opened his eyes, the lightest of dews left after the lids had opened. Despite being knocked overboard into the icy cold water of the north Atlantic. He clung to the vanity that was his life-raft. Elbowing remorse into touch, trudging up the beach to dry land.

He spoke softly, just two words. 'Lucky Ronny.'

'He told Shirley that you had run off with one of the girls, straight after the fight. Took all of the money and did a bunk.'

Wyn tipped his head a touch, 'Which one?'

'Does it matter?'

Obviously it did, 'Which one, it's important.' The first time he expressed any emotion since he walked back through the door an hour earlier.

'The large girl, Jean, or Joan.' I never said blonde one, they were all blonde.

Trying to appear like the cat that's got all of the cream. Not the one left with the saucer of water, he said, 'Little Joanie.' Wyn nodded like Joan would be a good choice to run off with. He confirmed this when he said, 'She liked to play games – enjoyed being a naughty girl.'

He sat back, apparently satisfied with Ronny's choice for his elopement partner. There we sat until the ancient grandfather clock burst into the room. The gears clanked and whirred, the chime took another beating as the hammers hammered out the hour.

***

Michael Parlane had given me the necessary glowing reference. The safe, security that reporting about life in a small town brought me a degree of happiness. Harry had signed the lease on a little pub at the end other end of town, soon to be a landlord, soon to have a landlady to help him. This hurt Wyn as well, oh he wished his brother well of course and meant it. After all Peggy was a gorgeous looking woman. But everyone had got what they wanted except him. He walked around with the hint of disappointment, a man that had just drawn an ace of diamonds, useless, when lined up with the full set of spades already in his hand.

I had worked hard, I did everything. Typed invoices, wrote reviews for pantomimes. Reports on local football matches. Whist drives, beetle drives, church bazaars, dart leagues, crib leagues, domino leagues. Shoplifters, road accidents, Magistrates Courts, lost and found, cars for sale, houses to let, music lessons, French lessons. I even helped with the type setting. And all the time, something shadowy and overwhelming shifted within me. Self-pity disappeared and I swam slowly away from the plug hole of despair that had gripped me.

Instead of spiralling down and down, I began the steady climb up and away. Until I got a phone call from Michael Parlane. One frosty morning. My new boss let me handle all the calls by now. The noisy clatter of the chaos that was a national newspaper's office rattled out of the speaker and down into my ear drum, causing a membrane stretching sequence of vibrations.

'Jack?' a familiar voice, 'You got the job then?'

'How can you work in amongst that racket?'

Small talk drifted back and forwards across the phone line, I glanced at my watch a couple of times waiting for the gossip, or the question that caused this conversation to develop.

'Listen to this one.'

Here we go.

His behaviour was grandiloquent to the point of triumphant. 'Did you know that Major Watkins was seen in Chelmsford glass-house?'

I said nothing, difficult to speak when someone's punched you in the kidneys.

'Jack, you there?'

I nodded, always a useful gesture down the phone.

'Have you seen him?'

Me?

'Jack? I thought you said they were dead?'

'I've not seen him for months.' Apart from yesterday, pretty much true. Now I had become wary, 'Why?'

A couple of hefty sighs came down the line my way, 'Why do you think? A couple of low-life's are after the three of you. But I guess you knew that. Anyway, I'd quite like a chat with him myself.' I was about to ask why, when he answered the question himself. 'Interesting character, impersonating an army officer during wartime. Up-market brothel keeper and someone brave enough to take on the thugs.'

I nailed one of accusations, Wyn's perfect lie to the military council that helped keep the sentence to a minimum. He hadn't given himself that pseudonym. The newspapers had and made a mistake in the process, putting the wrong name against the wrong face. This fact checked out, his father had fought with distinction at Mons, on the Marne and at Ypres. And come up through the ranks like he did, to reach Major. It only happened a handful of times. No doubt, their father had been a First World War hero. But he had never seen Harry fight though. Furious that his favourite son had chosen boxing before rugby.

Still Wyn's indignant version was believed and his sentence adjusted accordingly. Impersonating an officer became one of simple avoidance of military service. The master liar had managed a rabbit when it was needed most. Three years, became three months inside.

A few minutes silence, frustration hummed out of the phone, Parlane's sharpest knife blunted by Wyn's intrepid lying.

Finally he said, 'Take care.'

I replaced the receiver and smiled to myself, rather like a blind man would do when someone threw a farthing into his begging bowl.

Take care?

Spoken like it was a threat. Two months not looking over my shoulder blown out of the water as the shadows returned. Self-pity bounced back, no slow swim back towards the plug hole of despair.

Instead I began the vertical descent. No spiralling, just down, down and further down the ice face of hopelessness. I sat at my desk and even tried the adult trick that Wyn had mastered years before. Forget the phone call ever happened. Forget anything nasty or untoward ever happens and get on with life. A neat trick and one beyond my limited powers.

Did that make me a realist or a coward? Not the first that's for sure.

***

A couple of days later, I left the office just before five. The afternoon dead as the rabbits lined up on next door's butcher's slab. It had been snowing for a couple of hours. Separate trails of footprints twist across one another. Big flakes flutter down, halo's around the street lights, drifting and blurring the footprints. It just needed a good wind now and we'd be entombed in the house for a day or so. As soon as the thought crossed my mind, all the chaos of the last few months rushed back.

Entombed, incarcerated, buried.

'Stop it!'

I quickly looked around, no one close enough to wonder why I was shouting at myself. That's when I saw him, just a few feet away from me. Drifting as aimlessly as the snow. Snow on his hat, a membrane thin layer covering his glasses. I followed him, twisting the knot of my tie at the same time, as if to remind myself that this wasn't a dream. I was alive, at the moment. I watched as Eyeless stopped, he gave up the unequal struggle and took his glasses off. Staring myopically into the whiteness, a half blind snow leopard looking for its evening meal. Emboldened by my prey's disability, I watched him with all the frostiness of an aloof teacher staring down at a recalcitrant pupil. He twisted and turned, helpless and practically sightless. I looked around for something heavy to put across the back of his head.

Nothing, just snow and the wind beginning to whip the snow into swirling, irregular swarms. Whipping around Eyeless like angry bees swarming after a threatened queen.

Coriolis Effect or inertia?

Why not just call it the beginnings of a blizzard.

Masks of snow covering the occasional car as it went

silently around the market square. Snowflakes chasing after the rear lights causing a kaleidoscope of rapidly changing shades of redness. Eyeless struggled towards the Bear hotel and I watched him stop under the arch, wipe his glasses, place them back on his nose and then scan the wintry scene.

Did he just stare at me?

Probably, but I'd become a man of the shadows and I drifted home, pursued by nothing other than thousands of snowflakes. I wrenched the door and it opened with a deep sigh of appreciation. I looked behind me, how quiet it had become in the garden. Snow, that natural sound insulator. Silence, apart from the irregular moan of wind in the trees. Wailing away, as if the blasphemous night was preparing itself for the end of the world.

1946 – TEDDY

He liked this part of Spain.

This part of its coast had over two hundred beaches and shared two different bodies of water: the Mediterranean and the Menor Sea. Which has an outstretched piece of land called La Manga. Murcia is the capital of the province and got its own University.

The Mediterranean bathed region of Murcia, is not only known for its beautiful beaches, but also for a great number of natural beauties still to be discovered. It is precisely its natural charms and contrasts that makes Murcia outstanding from other regions.

Natural open spaces that look like the most desolate deserts share common ground with lush fertile green lands like the valley of Segura and the valley of Guadaletin modern residential neighbourhoods reaching out to connect with small medieval towns.

'Fuck this.'

He threw the travel guide into the sea. Then the dreams stopped.

Even the one where the baby was thrown out of the third floor window.

Despite the heat, he shivered.

'Where's Eyeless?'

His Uncle Jim said he'd vanished – gone. Last heard of hiding in a gypsy camp near Maidstone. Anyway, Eyeless was too stupid to lie low, dead by now probably.

Did he catch any regret or satisfaction radiating from his uncle?

Everybody likes the return of the prodigal, although he wasn't Jim's boy, he was treated like a long lost, adoring son. He liked the sun, but missed the bars and cafes. The gossip of criminals, the stares of the policemen and the drunks. Old men sat at Formica coated tables, sucking on their roll ups and drinking warm tea.

The women cooing away at him.

'Oh it won't cost you Teddy boy.'

The bitter street smells, urine mixed with overripe vegetables. Here, he had sun and he used its therapeutic properties well.

Good old Uncle Jim gave him a camera. He spent most of his time clicking away down on the beach. Watching couples, intimate couples mainly. Discreet couples that sneaked kisses and touches.

Even better when he fitted a zoom lens.

'I understand you Teddy.' Good old Uncle Jim.

'You're just like all the other tearaways, any little slight and you're off. Someone looks at you the wrong way and it becomes a matter of honour. Revenge is the way you settle any debt.'

'Leave me alone.'

'You fucking listen, why do you think I'm living out here? Same as you, we settled our disputes amongst ourselves. We didn't need a court of law, men of honour? Teddy, its all bollocks.'

'Leave me alone.'

'You can't go home.'

'What?'

'Never probably.'

'Never?'

'Take some photo's – that's a good fucking camera. I took it from some old Jew-boy who owed me.'

'You told me you bought it.'

'Just take some pictures, lie on the beach. Take it easy.'

'I never put the razor across their throats. It was Eyeless.' Teddy stared at the shimmering horizon, 'I want to go home.'

22

1980 – JACK

I always found Inspector Mably a decent sort. A bit dour, but we always got on well enough. As he delighted in telling us the other day, two days into his new career and we were his first interview all those years ago. He interviewed the three of us, constantly staring at Harry's bruises and Wyn's expensive suit. Of course we'd got our story ironed out by then. No evidence apart from blood in the snow and a witness who heard a murderous encounter. But old Bert had actually seen nothing. The whole scene had been played out in a blizzard and vague shadows and a deep layer of snow.

Old Bert was young Bert then and the only police witness to the mayhem. He'd heard the disturbance. Ran up to the police station, swearing that he'd seen a body and heard gunshots. Blood curdling screams and a madman swearing.

It was only Mably's second day in the force and he had interviewed us and Wyn's charm carried the day. The fact that Bert was three sheets to the wind helped as well. The pints of blood in the garden disappeared with the heavy rain that came just before sunrise. Nothing left and no doubt about it, we were lucky – although the worry never left me. Harry's temper worsened about then too and all the time Wyn smiled and breezed through life like nothing had ever happened.

We stood, Stuart restless, shifting his weight from left foot to right and back again. I just stared as Mably studied the old newspaper cutting like an archaeologist would an Egyptian transcript. A dusty old event changing manuscript. But then that's what it was. He rubbed his eyes, another long day. His hands came together, fingers forming a pyramid. He sighed, collapsed the pyramid and started to tap his teeth with his thumb nails and stared down. Finally he pushed the newspaper to one side and pulled an A4 file towards him.

Mably stared up at me and then, rather reluctantly I felt, looked at Stuart. 'I want to speak to Jack alone a minute. Do you mind?'

Stuart raised his eyebrows at me, I shrugged and nodded. He stood and wandered out. Rather like a child turning up for a friend's birthday party, only to be told that he hadn't got an invite.

'What's wrong?' I said,

'Everything that's what's wrong. Bloody lawyers with yet more bad news, evidently there's no forensic evidence, we can't charge him.' I wasn't sure if he meant Patrick. Mably stared fixedly down at the report, 'Why can't they just speak English? Listen to this. The plaintiff is likely to file a writ of habeas corpus ad subjiciendum. This is a legal proceeding in which an individual held in custody can challenge the propriety of that custody under the law. The prisoner can then be released or bailed by order of …'

I sighed, Mably sighed. An outbreak of sighing gripped the pair of us. I said, 'Why don't you want Stuart in here? He's as much a witness as me.'

Mably nodded, 'You know the history, ten years ago and – well it was bad enough her being involved with that little Irish hooligan.'

Her being his daughter, girlfriend of Patrick's at one time and a brief fling for Stuart.

Mably's face took on the appearance of a verger talking about his only daughter's deflowering. 'He used to get her home at all hours, then there was that fight in the Indian restaurant. And just to make things worse, a few weeks later and I catch…'

Her in bed with Stuart.

I said, 'They were young – it's what they do.'

'You sound just like my wife. I find it difficult to remain impartial when those two are close by, both of them are trouble.' Mably straightened his tie and dragged his shoulders back, and tried to focus on the here and now.

'He's grown up these days.'

'Has he now.' Mably's mouth turned down, 'Get him back in then.'

'Before I do, what happened to Patrick?'

Mably groaned, 'He attacked one of my officers, difficult to restrain him, but they managed it eventually.'

We stared at each other, finally I said, 'They never learn, it wouldn't look good in the newspapers. Another beating in a police cell.'

'I try and tell them.' Mably shook his head, 'They're all as thick as planks.'

'I'm sure we can keep it quiet, shall I get Stuart?'

Stuart sat down alongside me and we watched Mably as he lined his pencils up again, rearranged his out tray, leant back and smiled. He'd spent fifteen years policing in Oxford, coming back twelve years ago as the towns' Inspector. Mably spun around in his chair and brushed his thick grey hair back with the palm of his hand as he twisted the squeaking chair from side to side. Mably rubbed his hands together and addressed me as he came back to the matter in hand. 'You both knew her?'

Stuart shook his head and I nodded and said, 'Vaguely, a nice enough woman.'

'I have to ask you this Jack, what were you doing around there?'

I corpsed like a poor actor in a school play, my mouth hanging open.

'We heard that she left the Wheatsheaf with a man.' Stuart took the baton on smoothly enough. 'A few days ago and no one's seen her since, we were worried.'

Mably looked eager, he leant forward, his Springer-Spaniel intensity bubbled away nicely, 'What did he look like?'

My breathing eased a touch, enough for me to shrug naturally enough. I shrugged, 'I didn't see him, a stranger according to the Demon Barber.'

Saved by Stuart's quick thinking and not a lie either. I no longer felt like a Tory cabinet minister, caught in a public toilet with a small boy. Mably shuffled his sparse notes, ran his finger around the notes until he found the name, he brought his eyes up to me. Throughout this brief interview he never looked Stuart's way once. As though he never existed. Mably sat back and began to tap a pencil against his beautifully white and even teeth.

Finally he said, 'I'd have liked to get it all tied up tonight and get off home. But it's pretty pointless until forensic have finished down there. You saw her?'

I shook my head, too scared to cross the threshold. Mably grudgingly asked Stuart the same question.

He shrugged, 'It was just a stinking, smelly, congealed mess. It didn't look like a person.'

We spent ten minutes writing our statements, the desk sergeant came through with three coffees and to collect the statements at the same time. He never acknowledged me and gave Stuart a withering glare.

Stuart said, 'You lot beaten anyone up lately?'

'Ignore that.' Mably stood and pointed his sergeant towards the door. 'All these things going on.' He hissed, 'We've had our legal advice – any forensic tie up and I can't believe that he won't be back in here and we'll charge him.'

Charge Patrick.

He threw me completely with this information.

I felt Stuart tense alongside me, 'There won't be any forensic connection.'

Mably stared at him.

And how would you know?

Stuart smiled at me, then asked the question. 'Can we go now?' A small cloud passed slowly across Mably's face, blocking the well-being of his sun momentarily. He shook his head, 'I've got more questions for you.' We sat in silence, eventually Mably said, 'What's going on Jack?'

He shook his head; Mably looked bemused by it all, dispirited, stirring his coffee like a dejected cricket fan watching live coverage of an ashes series from Australia. He looked up and said, 'Have you ever hit anyone?'

Where did that come from?

'No!' I didn't need to think about that one, 'No.'

He glanced over at Stuart, I thought that he considered asking him too. But that would only be a waste of a good question. Instead Mably shook his head, 'This is all a bit of a fuck up.'

I raised my eyebrows, first time for everything I know, but David Mably swearing? A bit like a middle aged curate suddenly taking up swearing at his aged mother. We sat in silence until he placed his cup carefully back on the desk and said, 'I've had an interesting day. An eventful day, it's time like this that I wished I smoked.'

Here it comes.

'What have you found out?'

'Nothing personally, Don's got his teeth into this one. Anyway, Joseph Lewis, known in the criminal fraternity as Eyeless. Brother of one Teddy Lewis, both thought to have died in a fire. Along with two other men that I now know to be very much alive.'

He looked down and then pushed a photo copy across the desk my way. The same photo that Harry kept in his scrapbook. The picture of Harry with the Southern Area belt held aloft in one gloved hand. His other arm around Wyn, the boxing glove resting on Wyn's expensive shirt. Both of them grinning from ear to ear, one of Harry's eyes shut, but he wasn't winking. Two other pictures, mug shots of Teddy and Eyeless staring at the camera. I stared at the headline and I felt the blood rush up my cheeks.

Boxer perishes in club fire

Written by Michael Parlane, I couldn't take my eyes away from the photograph of Harry and Wyn, arms wrapped around one another. Stood in the middle of a boxing ring. Wyn's sartorial sophistication catching your eye. Bedecked in an astrakhan fur coat, brand new trilby and smiling broadly at the camera. I read on, "Light heavyweight boxer Harry Watkins and his brother, Major Wyn Watkins perished in a raging inferno at The Suede Tangerine Nightclub in Piccadilly. Two others died, one of whom is believed to be business man Teddy Lewis."

I felt Stuart crowding around me, his words in my ear, 'We've got that photo at home... fucking hell. You never told me that ...'

I never told you what – that they were both killed in a fire? I had left that one small fact out of my account the other night.

Mably took a deep breath, rubbed his eyes, then brought them up to mine. The appearance and demeanour of a teacher suddenly having to confront a model student's sudden aberration. He shook his head, 'Where do we go from here?' Mably picked the offending pictures up, inverted and then slapped them back onto the desk, sighed and said. 'She's smart – that young solicitor. For a girl.' He stared hard at me, canted his head and whispered, 'I think the three of you are in need her services.'

'We've done nothing wrong.'

Mably jabbed his finger down at the photograph, 'No doubt about who those two are. And funnily enough, now they've got different names. Major Watkins?' Mably sneered my way, 'He's never been near the army for a start.'

My vow of silence lasted seconds, 'Fighter's names – they all use nom de plumes.'

'No Jack – funnily enough, you're the only one that exists.' Repeating himself now, 'The other two haven't even got National Insurance numbers – they don't exist.'

I stared at the table, you didn't need National Insurance numbers back then to open a bank account. Wyn probably had a dozen different bank accounts, many with different names to them I shouldn't wonder. Neither Harry nor Wyn ever needed a doctor and they were both self-employed. No tax or national insurance to worry about.

I stood up, 'I'm going.'

'I don't think so Jack.' Mably gestured towards my recently vacated chair, 'Sit down. You've all done something wrong... although I haven't figured out what it is yet.' He squinted at me. 'I missed something didn't I?'

I frowned back.

'Down at the old mill.'

'I don't think so, even if you did, it wouldn't look good something coming to light thirty five years later.'

I shouldn't have said that, it sounded like a mild sort of threat.

He stared at me and began to tap his teeth again. Finally he said, 'Please tell me there wasn't some sort of burial ceremony and you lot weren't involved? All three of you will be in tomorrow, lots of questions to answer.'

I stood, rather unsteadily considering I hadn't had a drink, squeezed Stuart's shoulder and said, 'C'mon.' We walked towards the door, Stuart opened it and I turned and said, 'Thanks, we'll talk soon I'm sure.'

'That woman, the dead one, Daphne Miller. She was there when I interviewed you wasn't she? Now she's had her head smashed in.' His mouth turned down and I left him holding the old newspaper headline, as we scurried down the corridor Mably shouted after us, his voice chasing us down the corridor. 'Don't leave the country.'

1980 – TEDDY

'I've got to go home and tidy a few things up. Will you stay here?'

She nodded, 'I'll stay as long as you want me to, honest, I mean that.'

He drove back to Sonning in a stupor, his mind all over the place. What is a life? Not one of those dead-beats sleeping in a shop doorway. But even they had more of a life than my stupid daughter. My stupid daughter… it's so lonely without my stupid daughter.

'Talk to me… Dad, please, you know I can't talk to her.'

Say her name… say her fucking name.

But he couldn't.

What had he just done? He burnt his clothes, but kept the photos.

The photographs, the black girl twenty years ago. Built like a discus thrower. Not the skinny birds that all of the other models looked like. This girl had tits and a spanking arse.

'Do you think I'm too big to be a model?'

The accent, rich Caribbean. She saw him excited, taking pictures of her with a fucking hard-on.

'Shall I take my top off?'

White bra on black – yes. White knickers.

He fucked her in the shoe-box that was his studio. Smaller than the prison cell he never talked…

All that black skin.

'Don't come in me.'

He looked for her photographs. It was there somewhere. Never throw any away, Connie always told him that. Keep everyone, you never know, they might become famous.

So he did.

And all of those of his stupid daughter, it was so lonely without her.

He heard his wife, creep up to the door and knock gently.

'Bernie – Bernie, can we talk?'

'No!'

There was only one woman he wanted to talk to. Only one woman he wanted, only one woman that could save him now. Save him from this latest plunge into the inferno. Shirley would save him.

He leant against the sink, his chest aching. Sweat pumping out of his forehead. He shut his eyes, clamped them tight. Tears can't escape from a locked prison cell.

'Bernie?'

Deep breath, 'Just coming.'

23

1946 – JACK

We sat around the kitchen table. Wyn glanced at his brother who kept his gaze firmly anchored at the door.

Here we are then.

The lights had been flickering all evening, from stark artificiality to Gothic darkness and back again in a split second. Harry's crowbar sat in splendid, solitary isolation on the table. His meaty hand hovered close by.

'Was he on his own?'

I glanced at Wyn, puffed my cheeks out, 'Far as I could make out.'

Why was he on his own? A bit like Harry's crowbar, Eyeless sailed along, a solitary gunboat heading upstream to bump the natives back into line. More than bump, a beating at the very least.

But one man? Harry primed and crowbar at the ready, I prepared myself for a brief and probably bloody encounter. My chest tighter than the skin on a snare drum, my sphincter looser than the pyjamas worn by an inmate of Belson.

Daphne bustled around us, serving our dinner. She leant across me and I stared at the top of her right breast. Through her loose blouse, I could see the top of her bra and just make out the darkness of her nipple against the whiteness of the bra cup. The tension did it, craving to slide my hand inside both blouse and bra. Hold her breast, then fall asleep with my mouth around her nipple.

All the time Wyn gazed my way and smiled at the same time.

Daphne turned away and went back into the kitchen. He

leant close and whispered, 'Do you want some company later – she'll help you sleep if nothing else.'

He grinned and then winked. An understanding father offering his favourite son a generous gift. I took my eyes sharply away from him and across to Harry. He had pushed his dinner across and away, untouched.

You can't fight on a full stomach.

Harry huffed and puffed, stood and paced around the room. I half expected him to start shadow boxing. Instead, just the heaving, great intakes of gulped air. He stared, squinting looks from the door to his cigarettes. Cocked his ear like an inquisitive dog, certain that someone will be along soon. I thought Harry may bark, or more likely, at least growl like an angry, suspicious bulldog.

The lights flickered, once, twice, three and out. Plunged into a world of blackness, a woman's voice from upstairs. 'It's dark.'

'Get into bed and go to sleep, I'll bring you a cup of tea when the power comes back on.' I imagined Wyn smiling away at the implication. His voice came back my way, 'Unless you want to take it up to her?'

'Maybe.' Perhaps I would, then go to sleep with her breasts against my chest. I said it again, 'Maybe.'

'Listen.' The dog growled, cocked an ear to the world outside and then spoke to the door. 'I'm not waiting in here. Let's walk up the lane.' Another growl, feral grumbling deep in his throat. Not human, a primitive warning of danger.

Wyn and me gnawed away at this instruction. Savouring the implications, meet him head on, well that might be Harry's way, but not mine or Wyn's either.

'Why not just lock the door and wait?'

I reinforced Wyn's statement. 'He might not even come down here.' Said more to convince myself, rather than any sense of how things might develop.

'We don't even know if he's alone.'

But Harry opened the door nonetheless and went outside. The wind whistled and snowflakes elbowed and blustered their way past him, quickly settling. A brief life, sharp, clean and cold one second, a tiny puddle the next. Wyn followed Harry and I fumbled my way across to the draw. Felt around and pulled out a carving knife. Slashed the air wildly a couple of times. I shook my head, this was silly. A bit like putting a knuckle duster on a short sighted Boy Scout.

I crept outside.

Total blackout, no lights, but the blizzard and the deep snow meant a strange sort of vision. The ground a featureless desert of white. When Harry's frame passed in front of something snowless, the garage wall in this instance. He stood out like a bluebottle on a white plate of porridge. Blurred movements of the two brothers' drifted along the drive and towards the gate like phantoms. Silent and indistinct, I followed trusting that they knew what they were doing.

I wondered about all the ways possible to kill yourself. This, although probably effective, never struck me as in any way efficient. Jumping from a high window, too messy. A hot bath, half a bottle of whisky and slash the wrists. Half asleep and watch the life drain away, messy again, but relatively painless. Gas oven, not messy but smelly. Hurl yourself in front of a speeding train – the most efficient surely? The messiest as well. Thirty strong sleeping tablets seemed to have the most to recommend it, throw more whisky into the equation and a method that was tidy, silent and trustworthy.

But stood in a garden during a blizzard? A homicidal maniac on the loose, all too random for me. Who would get the baseball bat over the back of the head? Harry probably, and all the while the other two of us would watch and listen to the mayhem. Unable to make out with any distinction what was going on. My mind rambled away; here I was supposedly logical, capable and prepared, stood in a blizzard hoping for the best.

1951 – TEDDY

He woke up in hospital.

'What?'

Uncle Jim said he had been sectioned.

'What?'

Complete mental breakdown.

'You said that you'd been talking to the stuffed fox, he told you to do it.'

'Who?'

'The fucking fox.'

'Made me do what?'

'You boarded the Alicante to Majorca ferry and began slashing at cables until a lifeboat fell onto the crowd stood on the jetty. Lucky you never killed anyone. Put nine in hospital though.'

'The fox?'

'Don't keep saying the fucking fox. I've got you a passport, keep your mouth shut. According to the beak, you're a danger to yourself and others. Tell me something I don't fucking know.'

'The fox!'

'And you can eat the food, no one's trying to fucking poison you, for fuck's sake.'

***

She was nearly sixty, spoke no English, certainly never said no to him anyway. Owned a café, her husband sat and drank most of the day as she worked her arse off.

'A coffee please you slag.'

She wagged her finger under his nose and shook her head, 'No, no en Español por favor.'

'Un café por favor que la escoria.' She nodded and waited.

'Can I fuck you… please?'

She shook her head again, 'No, no en Español por favor.'

'Puedo joder el culo de ustedes?'

She nodded, 'Si.'

He stared at her, what did it matter? Thirty five years

older, what did it matter?

'What did you say?'

'Por supuesto puede.'

'Yes!'

One day a week, every week, every month for three years. She even let him take pictures, he'd never used the time-lapse button before. Teddy stared at the pictures. Her face, her eyes shut, her head back, lips drawn back over her teeth. He never got the movement of her billowing breasts though.

Still, he really liked her. Her husband worked one day a week in the café, while his wife got fucked all day long upstairs. Then she got cancer, gone in three months. He stared at her lazy husband who had stopped working altogether after the funeral. Bullshitting with his mates, how he always kept her in line. He opened the palm of his hand and his cronies all laughed.

Teddy got the best pictures together. Put them in an envelope and gave them to the drunken fucker as he slugged his first brandy of the morning. Teddy watched his face as a terrible realisation gripped.

The old man's face hung open, he pointed at Teddy. 'Usted.'

Teddy nodded. 'Every week mate, she loved it.'

The old man frowned.

'Amaba mamando mi polla.'

'Usted? Hijo de puta.'

'Fuck off you cunt.'

He felt better, the woman had helped, so did letting the old drunk know about what went on.

He felt better, no doubt.

Teddy stood up and walked across to the old drunk and stared down at him.

Finally the old man looked away.

'You need someone to look after this business for you mate.'

'Español por favor.'

'Protection – protección you slag – you need me to look after you.'

Teddy put his arm around the old man and felt him shiver.

24

1980 – JACK

We left early the next morning, well before another invitation to an interview at the police station landed on the front door mat. Stuart drove, leaving me to consider everyone's position. Preoccupation had bound us together, wrapped its cloak of anxiety and a veil of curiosity around his broad shoulders. Wyn sat in the back reading the afternoon's racing card from Kempton Park.

Who had more to worry about? Me I thought, Stuart would disagree with that one sided assessment. His sense of intuition more than niggled and bothered. His anxious eyes searched the road in front as if the answer was to be found on the back end of another car or lorry.

His father and uncle had most to lose that's for sure and Stuart didn't know who to believe anymore.

Always expect lies or half-truths at best.

I guess that's what had drifted his way for most of his life. Stuart glanced my way and said, 'I'm going over and over it all, looking for another road, another route. I've even tried to wind the clock back, unwind the past – trying to unlock events, trying to find that perfect place I need at the moment.' He gestured with his head towards his uncle, 'I know they've got a lot to lose, but I feel threatened too, something, someone is reaching out and trying to touch me.' He quickly touched my arm, 'Touch all of us and I haven't felt like this before – I don't like it.'

The traffic ground to a halt along the Botley Road and we became enveloped in a universe of stillness, Stuart whispered – something about it being like a cathedral. Unable to hear the sound of anything, just driver's faces closed as they sat determinedly patient in the slow moving traffic drifting past in the opposite direction.

He might feel threatened, but my own trap was about to be sprung, I looked at my watch – Mably certain to be prompting Don by now. Someone else aware of the Pandora's Box of deceit. Lies that we'd told to prop up earlier lies, people that were dead, more people that were supposed to be dead, suddenly alive again. At this rate we would all be joining Patrick for a spell inside.

Change the subject please.

Stuart said, 'It's like the Godfather – Wyn looks like Don Corleone anyway.'

I smiled at that one, he did as well, what an image.

Stuart pressed on, 'The old man's in the bunker guarding Mum. On a war footing, which we all know he'll love.'

I said, 'He's too old for all of this.'

Stuart snapped at me. 'He can still punch.'

Father and son, they might have blazed away at each other for the last thirty odd years. But criticise either one and the other will bite your head off.

I stood my ground, this was too serious an issue and I needed to pour cold water on Stuart's idealised image of Harry as still being some sort of omnipotent fighting machine. I snapped back, 'His knuckles are more brittle than overcooked toast crusts. Harry, all of us come to that are too old, except you.'

He stared forwards and never said anything. I didn't want Harry, I wanted Stuart close by, quick, fit and tough. To do what his father did for me for years. My very own Praetorian Guard. Wyn ignored our exchange, apart from a couple of sighs, he left us to it.

Stuart shivered and his eyes went to the chestnut trees alongside the road, the bare branches naked and stark against a blue sky. My mind went back to the earlier conversation we had, then we had exchanged hopeless, bittersweet smiles that said everything, how on earth did we get in this mess?

Stuart jumped the lights by the Royal Oxford hotel, parked on double yellows in Beaumont Street, took a nonchalant glance my way, 'Don't worry, I'll keep my eye on it.'

***

We sat, lined up around a large table, staring at this incredibly smart woman. Slim build, black Wallis suit. The skirt cut just above the knee. Long black hair, cut straight and pulled back behind the ears. Lean face, high cheekbones and you'd have to say it, Jewish looking. She sipped her coffee and sat back. Our newly acquired legal envoy, called Abigail. We had all agreed earlier, to come clean and fall on the sword of justice. Well I'd agreed for them I suppose.

Wyn shrugged agreement at the time and immediately went off on his own merry way. 'Of course we never found out until our accountant died recently.' Wyn's opening gambit, not only a lie, but a barefaced one. 'He'd fleeced us for very nearly thirty five years.' He showed Abigail the palms of his hands. 'What can we do – whose going to believe that, but it's true.'

I covered my eyes with my hands, thought about saying can we start again please. Abigail demonstrated the sincerity that goes with the job, 'My God this is truly awful. I'll draft a letter for the Inland Revenue, we can come to an arrangement I'm sure nearer the time. Don't worry – we can sort this out.'

And I sat there open-mouthed at the brass neck of it all. John Robinson had died recently and he was an accountant in town. A bad one too, defrauded half a dozen over the years. Never handled a penny of Harry's or Wyn's money mind you. No one could ever check that one out though, just before he died, a huge fire had burnt every record of every client he ever had. Wyn's opening ploy was inventive and a decent
beginning for our shaky defence.

But my nerve had gone, after a few minutes of watching Abigail taking notes, I said, 'Whose name are you going to sign the affidavit with? It has to be Wicks; Major Wyn Watkins doesn't exist anymore.' Abigail leaned forward and frowned, Wyn sat back and folded his arms and said nothing. All the time Stuart was watching and listening, constantly watching and wondering.

What is going on?

It had become contagious, I started to lie now. 'Things happened, nothing illegal, I must stress.' In for a penny, I ploughed on. 'At the end of the war, we made a lot of money. Legitimate of course. But we upset some rather nasty people in the process. Bookmakers and criminal types and we left in a hurry, our lives in real danger. We've lived our lives looking over our shoulders since then.'

I took a deep breath.

Here we go.

'Point is, Wyn and his brother have lived under assumed names from that day onwards. If we had stayed in London, they would have been killed… that's for sure.'

I glanced over at Wyn, a hint of a frown, but he nodded at the same time. Wyn shrugged for all of us. He spoke slowly, measured his words like a machinist sizes up a piece of metal in a vice. 'I think that's all we want to say at the moment, the police have suddenly realised who we all are. We were supposed to have died in a night club fire. Even the newspapers reported it that way. We never contradicted it at the time, it meant safety and a chance for a new life.'

He shrugged again, showed Abigail the palms of his hands.

What else were we supposed to do?

That was the first time I could recall him saying anything about those events. Of course he sounded as genuine as the Pope delivering his Christmas day sermon in St Peter's Square.

Abigail swung her eyes along our anxious set of eyes. Made a few notes, brought her head back up and said, 'I think that you had every right to lie low. I'll have a nose around and look for any previous instances that will give us some reference point. Don't worry, everyone knows that you're all pillars of society.'

I heard Stuart snigger at that one, Abigail glanced across at him, their eyes met for a few seconds, before she smiled and took her eyes back to her notes.

'Thanks for getting Patrick out.' Stuart stared her way.

She smiled back, 'They had no right to hold him that long. He should file a complaint, there's no place for that sort of police brutality anymore.' Her eyes flicked his way again. Before darting away again. She fixed on Wyn, did she think he was less predatory?

If only she knew.

We filed out and to be fair to Stuart, he never said anything until we were going south along the Botley road again.

Stuart looked at Wyn in the interior mirror. 'Do I exist?'

Wyn groaned from behind me and I said nothing.

***

We drove back into town with the temperatures already dropping. Shadows lengthening as the sun dipped behind buildings. Into the market place and the shoppers alert, looking for contact – a chance to talk, to gossip on their way home. The sky was a fragile evening blue, the moon already rising in the east, a soft pink blush waiting expectantly for the sun in the west to sink. Dark hills against the sky, mist bubbled up nicely over the canal. We followed the red taillights down Grove Street, the brake lights in front, distorted when he flashed the windscreen washers for the last time.

A long day and now what? He swung the car into the gravel floored car park, switched the ignition off and yanked the handbrake up. Stuart stared out of the window and said, 'That was a waste of time.'

We followed Stuart into the bar. The heat from the fires in the bar did what it always did in wintertime. My glasses steamed and Harry shouted at me. 'Watch where you're going, why don't you get contact lenses?'

I cleaned them with my tie, replaced them and glanced around. We sat, four of us, equally spaced around the table. Stuart staring at Harry, Harry stared down at the table. Wyn stared at the ceiling, I stared at the three of them wondering who would snap first, father or son?

I tried to move things forward, nodded at Stuart and then addressed Harry. 'I've told him everything, cats out of the bag well and truly. We've just had some good legal advice and now we have to stay together.'

Harry never moved, never shouted, slammed his fist into the table or indeed, turned the table over. Just sat there, head bowed and he lit a cigarette, smoke punched out as he spoke. 'Police have been, I've given a statement.'

He'd suddenly turned into the magnetic north and all of our eyes swung his way.

'What did you tell them?'

He stared at me, rolled his eyes. 'What do you think? Nothing, I said I couldn't remember anything. Just the fucking snow.'

Stuart said, 'At least they haven't made the connection yet - the shit will well and truly hit the fan when that happens. He looked at Harry, 'Let's hope Bernard Schwartz and Teddy Lewis never meet.'

Silence.

Harry glanced across to his son, 'Your Mum doesn't even know the half of it.' His head slowly came up and his blue eyes fixed on me. 'You can tell her, you got us into this mess.'

Wyn straightened his shirt cuffs, Harry sighed, Stuart fretted, drummed the table with his fingers and I wondered who would get the call next?'

I sat and dreamt a little, the same feeling I had at the end of the war. It felt safer during the blitz than it did now. At least Shirley wasn't pulling the strings now.

'Where's Shirley?'

The others looked at me and said nothing.

1980 – TEDDY

He liked this game, he'd followed her around for most of the day. Waited outside shops and followed Shirley. Oh yes he liked this game. He even roared with laughter when she came up from Market Street laden with shopping like a refugee's donkey.

They even joked, like they had just bumped into each other.

'Fancy seeing you again.'

'Teddy? You're a sight for sore eyes.'

He got his wallet out, Shirley held her hand up. 'Not a penny more, I'm spent out. I have to pop home, business to attend to.'

'I'll drop you off.'

'Do you mind if I catch the bus, I've got a personal matter to sort out? Don't frown like that, do you mind?'

He shook his head, walked her to the bus stop.

'Can I see you tomorrow?'

He nodded and then rushed back to his car and headed west down the Botley road and out of Oxford. Teddy drove back in a rage, punching the steering wheel, blasting the horn whenever a car or a cyclist or a pedestrian came within shouting distance.

'Fuck off out of the way.'

He drove the fifteen miles back like this. Parked his car and walked into the market place. Looked at his watch, her bus was still fifteen minutes away. He thrust his hands deep into the raincoat pockets. He liked the coat, it felt reassuringly heavy and his wife said that it hung well.

Teddy sighed, she used to say I was well hung.

Caught in a deep reverie, he jumped, when the waitress said,

'What can I get you luv – that's a nice camera. What a big one.'

'An iced bun and a fucking coffee… Please.'

The cake looked jaded, but the coffee was decent. Inside the café it was hot and damp at the same time, a contradiction he felt. It smelt of both straw and wet cement, vinegar and wet dogs and fresh coffee. Teddy stared out of the window at the small shops with their irregular roofs, twisted in the evening sun. The soft darkness giving a pleasant, if odd effect. He liked this time of day, late afternoon and light from the shops radiating across the pavements. The temperature dropping as the shadows lengthened and shoppers went home.

He even got the smell from the newsagents, tobacco smoke and wet coats as he crossed the market place and waited. Hardly Piccadilly, but on market day the streets hummed and throbbed with shoppers. The Chinese restaurant began to kick out smells of garlic and fried onions. Teddy couldn't put his finger on it, the first time for weeks that he'd sensed anything. Smells and buildings and evening light mixing into a familiar mélange that he'd forgotten about for some reason.

Teddy had lost the quality that he'd concentrated so hard on achieving. No longer just a camera that saw things. His senses had started to work again. He dragged air reluctantly into his tight chest, he didn't want feelings and emotions getting in the way of what he had planned. He wanted to be a camera again.

The double decker pulled into the market place and he watched. He knew she would be on her own, but it still provoked a fury within him when he saw her get off the bus. He kicked the door of the tobacconist hard. Too hard and Teddy hopped around for a couple of seconds and then limped after her.

Losing the lights of the market place and into Grove Street's evening world, Teddy's breathing eased and his pulse slowed. Twilight shadows and rats went hand in hand – he followed unseen and happy.

Until he saw the man, in the shadows by her back door. Followed by the embrace, then the kiss, then his hand…

***

He stared at the photo, the policeman and his daughter. The policeman and the blonde.

He's a bit of a lad.

He's going to get some.

Teddy shivered, fucking shithole. Nice little row of terraced houses though, nice little row of outhouses opposite. Used to be toilets, or a place to do the washing?

Fuck knows. He waited.

He'd wait, did she say it?

Yes, she said it.

What did she say? That she'd lost a baby at the start of the war and it was about time she had another one, that's what she said. Mind you that was in 1945.

The eyes.

Not my eyes that's for sure.

The curtains drew back in the bedroom. That fucking policeman.

That policeman wrapped himself around her, Jesus she hardly had anything on. All over each other. He carefully placed the lens cap back on and slid the camera back into the case. He rushed over to the back door, open. She never changed. He thought about rushing in and interrupting their rutting.

Instead he turned and walked away.

Stopped the first person he bumped into.

Where's the library mate?

Thanks.

Into the warmth of the public library, phone book… what was his name, Wilson. Wilson, D. what did that stand for? Dick probably. Finger down the columns of Wilson's – there, that'll do.

'Mrs Wilson?'

'Who's calling?'

'Do you know that blonde?'

'Who are you?'

He put the phone down and made note of the address, then stared at his watch. Time to get home, get them developed and make it back before that dick gets home.

14 Hamfield, what sort of an address is that? Connie was out anyway, she's always out.

Dark room.

He always felt good in here, as if you suddenly sober up and everything in the world comes into a sharp focus. Teddy must have been eleven or twelve when he started. No football or conkers for him, just a harmless little pastime that didn't rely on anyone else, apart from Uncle Jim who helped him set the loft up. Plumbed the tank in, plumbed the waste line did the lot.

Stillness, he never spoke a word while he worked away in a concentrated frenzy. Apart from telling himself to get a move on every five minutes. As regular as the stop-clock Teddy had stolen from Woolworth's.

And there it was a professional dark room. Water tanks, stop- clock, measuring jars, developing solution, running water, everything he needed right down to cotton gloves. Then he stole a camera from the Newspaper offices, a German Voightlander Vito B and it was only a couple of months old. Then he heard the owner moaning in the pub about nothing being sacred anymore, some degenerate stealing his best camera and how was he expected to take decent pictures now.

He took thousands of pictures. Mostly of people, mostly no one realised they were having their picture taken. That's the thing, that's what gave him the buzz, people could be staring directly into the lens and still be unaware they were about to become part of Teddy's photo album.

Bizarrely, developing film fed all of his emotional needs. After the initial doubts that always plagued him at the start of the process he soon soared and flew. Within the space of thirty minutes he got higher and higher. Breathing became irregular and shallow, hands shook when he placed the film into developing tank. Then a calmness, a certainty in a process that he knew intimately. He inverted the tank every thirty seconds, a moment's unease when he removed the tank lid. And then the climax, a sexual pinnacle as perfect images appeared, satisfaction and smugness when he hung the film to dry.

This was the moment – his moment, as the picture appeared he always smiled, some women could be careless with their legs Sometimes.

Her slip worked its way up her thigh as she sprawled over the sofa, the blonde and slips – her indoor uniform. Watching them this morning, irritation as she kissed his neck, he'd taken a few shots of them like that. He struck gold when though, the blonde's eyes on Don, the man's thoughts as transparent as sulphur smoke over a battlefield. Then they wrapped around one another in the window, her falling out of her slip. Him with his hands all over her and then she started rubbing his cock… both of them laughing.

Oh yes, the photographs exceeded his expectations, considering that he froze his bollocks off waiting for them to put in an appearance at the window. He found six of the best, three each in two envelopes and sealed them.

Euphoria.

What was her address?

Mrs Carol Wilson, 14 Hamfield.

Teddy hopped around like a concert pianist with a recently broken thumb, the thought of being a postman delivering bad news always did it for him.

Hand delivered as well.

25

1946 – JACK

'Spread across the garden and stand still.' Harry still in guard dog mode, growled out his instructions.

I tripped, and fell into the six inch deep white blanket.

'Jesus fucking Christ.' From one brother. 'What the fuck are you doing?'

The other more tolerant, 'Careful now.'

Tripped up by one of Harry's garden gnomes. My mind rambled, I couldn't focus. Instead looking for a murdering lunatic at the gate, I picked the gnome up. I sought release by running my finger over it. I laughed out loud.

'What's up with you? Just shut the fu…'

Harry's voice drifted off with the wind and I stared down at the gnome. The smallest of the set. Harry named them all and called this one Gordon. Seven inches long, weighing about the same as a bag of sugar. The baby of the cluster of gnomes that Harry had scattered randomly around his garden. I brushed the snow away, run my fingers across Gordon's pot belly. Wrapped my fingers round it, sitting in the palm of my hand as snug as a hand crafted knife handle.

Knife!

My consciousness ripped back to the here and now. I placed Gordon back on the floor. I fumbled around until I'd recovered my knife. I shuffled my way to the boundary edge. Leant against the garage wall and waited.

Not for long as it happened. A blurred figure appeared, faded in like a ghost manifests on a cinema screen. He stood at the end of the drive. Thirty yards away, snowflakes swirled around him like an angry swarm of bees. Picking his way up the drive, his eyes, like ours by now, well used to the spectral light. But he was moving and we were still. A dusting of snow covering the three of us by now.

Statues, watching a phantom creep towards us. The spectre moved the same way a nervous visitor creeps into an intensive care ward. Expecting the worst, so the cautious approach served him well.

Eyeless stopped mid-way between Harry and me. Wyn was the other side of Harry. The world stopped spinning on its axis. Clock's stopped and hearts too. A man five yards from me and I held my breath. He looked around, wiping his glasses with his free hand. The other hand held something out in front of him, like he was pointing the way forward. I had raised my knife, chest high, remembering Harry's well used method. Holding the weapon out in front, not raising it above your head. Leaning hard against the garage wall. Still holding my breath. A lung bursting lull.

I heard Harry's movement, a wildebeest moving my way. Horns down in the attack position. Hitting Eyeless in the ribs. The crudest of crude rugby crash tackles. The breath oomphed out from the pair of them. One an adrenalin, aggression release. The other one, a rib cracking, breath expelling shock.

I pressed myself hard against the garage wall and braced myself as two bodies came straight towards me. A flash of light, the briefest of camera flashes, accompanied by a gunshot. An instant breaking of glass somewhere close by. And I watched as two bodies came my way with all the uncontrolled momentum of a runaway goods train. Just before impact another flash and crack. I thought about Newtonian mechanics in action. Gravity and mass, bodies in motion. Two bodies in motion. A shoulder hit me in the ribs at the same time as the knife handle was rocked back until it hit the garage wall.

No real noise, just my hand pinned between the wall and something heavy. Warm, wetness spread over my hand and up the length of my arm. My hand began to slide down, dragged in that direction by a collapsing body. A gurgling, grunt. It could have been from either or indeed both of them.

The two slipped down into an untidy huddle in front of me. The knife snatched from my grip somehow. I felt my ribs, why weren't they broken? All that mass, all that momentum and no pain. Harry levered himself up, kicked the body twice. His breathing whooshed my way in red hot blasts. The lights in the house had come back on. Flooding the garden and an unlikely peace enveloped me. Like being stood stock still, under an umbrella as drizzle whispered down on a windless day. The corridor of light from the open door, bathed us in a soft theatre of gold.

I stared down and there it was, my knife buried in Eyeless's throat. Waves of nausea swept over me. I turned and retched at this act of frenzied farce. My head span like a top and I fell face down onto my own vomit. I fell next to the body, my mind telling me to sleep. Lie down, make myself warm and comfortable. Close my eyes and go to sleep, curled up like a dog into a safe little ball.

Harry put his hand under my armpit and dragged me up.

'Don't be fucking stupid Jack.' He brushed the snow from my shoulders and back. Harry held me up and I listened as the brothers whispered. Voices reserved for the company of lunatics, cowards or unwanted wedding guests. My head swam and spun, a burning at the base of my skull. Drifting in and out of consciousness, deeply aware of the smell of fresh snow, blood and vomit. I felt an unbearable weight on my eyelids.

Harry turned to me and whispered. 'C'mon Jack, all over now ... no more, that's it.' Harry sounding like he'd just dug the garden, or ploughed a big field. 'We've still got work to do though – c'mon.'

What?

The three of us stood over a man in peaceful anti-climax. A mountain of a man, his high dome of a forehead hidden by the deep snow. His life seeped away. It wheezed out from his lungs, snot bubbled from out of his nose and blood no longer oozing. A life seconds away from extinction.

1954 – TEDDY

Uncle Jim woke him up.

'Teddy boy.'

He stared up at his uncle.

'You've had a nightmare boy. You ok?'

'Eyeless, I just dreamt about him.'

'You woke Carmen up. Screaming like that.'

'Eyeless?'

'Don't think about that thick as shit, cunt. He was always more trouble than he was worth. Go back to sleep.'

But he did think about him. For the rest of the night. When Eyeless fucked that Maltese schoolgirl. Her gingham skirt up, her white ankle socks stark against her dark skin. He watched as Eyeless pounded against her on the living room sofa.

Minutes later. 'Your turn Teddy boy, have a bang on this.' Was that how the first time was meant to be? Fucking her through someone else's jism?

Eyeless gave her three woodbines and a box of matches. She seemed happy enough.

Later that same night, he lay in bed and lifted the sheets.

The smell of sex, he didn't know whether to be excited or revolted. His erection gave him a clue.

He met the same girl years later. She never recognised him, turning tricks down Coldharbour Lane. Cheap tricks, cheap part of town.

'You want business?'

'Not with you, scrubber.'

'Fuck yourself queer boy.'

He glanced down at the back of his hand, red and stinging. Not as much as her cheek though.

Teddy missed Coldharbour Lane, but not the cold and the rain.

He sat on the beach and did miss Adriana. Dear, fat, old Adriana who gave him peace. Every minute, with her he felt relaxed and happy.

Happy?

He was, she told him that her name meant dark. Dark? Rich like coffee?

He sat on the beach next to Uncle Jim and stared out all the way to where?

Algeria?

Jim said, 'You want to go home, don't you?'

'I miss a good snowstorm, I even miss watching the tarts walking down Coldharbour Lane.'

'Those drippers – stay away from those boy.'

'Football crowds, a good fight.'

'Fight! You've had enough of those here.' They sat in silence, he shivered when his uncle put his arm around his shoulders. 'In a couple of years, we'll find you another passport. But you can never go back to London. You need a good woman to keep you out of trouble... and away from London.'

'I want to see snow blowing across the downs. Howling gale across to Rochester.'

'Couple of year's boy. Think hard though, you know you'll never get caught out here. You're safe. Think hard.'

26

1980 – JACK

Three pints and I slept on the sofa. The restless, sweating sleep of the guilty. Dark visions, murderous images, the same old three pint hallucinations. Harry smirking and saying let me fix this. Then breaking his brittle fist on Teddy's classic profile. Shirley holding hands with Don. Staring into each other's eyes and bidding us good night. They climbed the stairs with his hand clamped on her arse. Wyn watching them like a mournful old hound staring after his fast disappearing, mistress. Then the noise like a bass drum as Harry beat a tattoo on the coffee table with Teddy's head.

Then the voices, 'C'mon – hurry up.'

I sat up, my forehead covered in a mantle of sweat. Eyes flashing round the small living room. The drumming kept on rolling, accompanied by more curses. Someone was trying to kick the front door in.

'Jack – I know you're in there.' Don's voice.

Hoarse and urgent. I walked over and opened the door. The man looked at the end of his tether. Eyes bulging like ball bearings. Spittle flecked his full lips. His cheeks scarlet, the veins on his neck standing out like exposed electrical wiring on against a freshly painted wall.

He barged me out of the way and slammed the door. Hard enough for the glass to groan and mutter and threaten to disintegrate if anyone ever shut the door like that again.

'Sit down – I've had it up to here with you lot.' Don pointed me back into the chair.

'Don, can I get you a drink. Coffee, tea…'

'Shut up.' Don kept pointing, 'Someone's been telling lies.'

Something had opened a valve, one that suddenly opens fully and scattered his emotions all over the floor. I wondered if Don was about to break down and sob or punch me silly. His mind calculating, all the time calculating. An excuse, any excuse would do and he'd pan me.

Don shivered, 'I'd been cold all afternoon, when I got home, I rubbed my hands and walked around in the kitchen. That's the thing with kids.' He stared at me, 'If nothing else it's the noise they generate. If they not asleep or out, then there's always noise. Screaming, laughing, arguing, crying… all the time noise. Not now, the only noise is a loud angry voice hammering away inside my head.'

He's gone.

I got him a bottle of beer. Don sat silently in amongst the silence and drank. He appeared to struggle for breath as his sureness drained away. I bet his temples throbbed – his world had gone quiet. I wondered if he wanted Shirley again and another long night of too much gin and long bruising bouts of lovemaking. I wanted to imagine her legs and arms, how they squeezed him and wrapped around every inch of his body. Instead all I could think of was Carol, standing close by with her hands thrust deep into the pockets on her raincoat.

'What's up – Don, Don. Are you all right?'

He dragged air deep into his big chest. The eyes that had been glazed, slowly cleared. Don shook his head and his breath snorted out. 'I've got the dirt on you lot. Inland Revenue for starters. Bodies all over the place, six in London.'

'Six?'

'Two with their throats cut and four looked like they'd been in a blast furnace. Seven if you count the one that was buried fifty yards from where you used to live. Then last week, your old housekeeper battered to death.' Don stood up and came close, 'Everything's with the legal eagles.'

My turn to struggle to breath, 'Since when has an income tax issue been any concern of yours?'

He never answered for a few minutes. Then he twisted his head a touch and said, 'Income tax?'

Then more silence, apart from his hoarse, rasping breath. A man on the edge of a breakdown and I wanted him out of my house and out of my life.

Leave me alone.

One more question nagged away, then he can leave me alone.

'Anyone in the frame for Daphne yet?'

'Bernard Schwartz.' He shook his head, 'but he's vanished off the face of the earth. Last seen leaving the pub with Daphne. He's that bloke whose daughter…'

'The bloke whose daughter you were sleeping with. That bloke?'

The sudden volte-face on my part shook me, but not as much as Don. His eyes bulged and he began to massage his temples. His breath came out in short bursts.

'Don't twist this around. You're keeping something from me.' He slapped the flat of his hand down on the coffee table. I jumped, the coffee table jumped, my heart stopped for a few seconds. 'I'm going to fix all of you.'

'But what about the girl?'

'Fuck her.' He gasped this as though someone had punched him in the solar-plexus in mid-sentence. Don buried his head in his hands, 'Fuck her. She's ruined everything, that and my stupid cow of a wife.'

'She was just a child.'

'Child! You stupid, queer bastard. You've no idea have you. Child? She made all the running.'

'You used a child, you're finished Don. Some would call it abuse, she was thirty years younger than you for God's sake.' Don sat back down. 'Someone gave Carol some photos.'

I frowned; did I want to pursue this? Yes evidently, 'What was the subject matter?'

'Me with Shirley, me with Celia.'

'Shirley… Compromising?'

Don nodded, 'The ones with Shirley were. If that's not bad enough, my wife's getting fucked silly by a thick as shit, long haired paddy.'

I resisted the temptation to say what's that got to do with anything. But he turned, threw open the door and left me. Evening mist tumbled in the open door. Like fake stage fog, like a dream. I grabbed my overcoat and headed for sanctuary. His rambling thudding away inside my head, what was he on about? Not his threats, or his pumped up macho-man stuff. It was the confused words about his kids. A subject I'd never heard him mention before, conscience maybe? I walked arm in arm with his half declaration of guilt, hand in hand through the front door with me.

Then a sudden thought, perhaps Carol was in danger. Perhaps we all were. I needed a pint. A pint and refuge.

***

Shirley was sat, propped on a stool, staring down at her gin. Harry gestured at her and raised his eyebrows.

Stuart said, 'Are you coming out for a curry later?' He stared at me, 'C'mon it'll do you good.' Stuart's presence nearby reassured and I smiled at his new found role. Happy to take his father's mantle on, defender of the weak and the teller of half-truths. 'Just after eight, Patrick's out celebrating, ok?'

I nodded and watched him go up close to Shirley, who carried on staring down. Stuart put his arm around her, I hadn't noticed, but she had been sobbing gently, just the barest of movement from her shoulders. Stuart pushed her empty glass across the counter towards Harry. Picked her cigarette packet up and said, 'Have one of these for God's sake and tell us what's happened.'

Shirley fumbled around in her handbag, dabbed her eyes with a tissue. Sniffed a couple of times and then sighed. Her make-up had fanned out under both eyes, she glanced over towards me, swiftly averted her gaze and pulled a cigarette out. Took a deep drag and whispered, 'No fool like an old one.'

Shirley hammered her cigarette out and snapped. 'Some people think I was born yesterday.' She shook her head, clamped her lips together and snorted out through her elegant nose. Shirley looked across to Stuart and raised her eyebrows.

Stuart nodded, 'Mum's the word, you know me, soul of discretion.'

Now that was funny, he couldn't keep his mouth shut if you paid him. Stuart stared at his father, Harry looked at me, I sighed, I'd become the master of coming in on the fag-end of conversations. Something else had happened and I knew nothing… again.

***

We walked up together, me and my newly found squire. Bodyguard and the shield between me and Don and Teddy. Stuart talked on the move, 'Did you get what that was all about?'

No I didn't.

We walked into an Indian restaurant midweek in February. More waiters than customers, I lowered the glass of fizzy lager and watched two young men eat with the abandon of two youthful lions. Patrick had propped the menu up, fed poppadum's into his mouth with one hand and slurped beer with the other. Like some sort of continuous, self-feeding manufacturing process. Happy to feed his face and use the menu like a fisherman used a harbour wall against a strong wind.

He spoke through it all, 'Carol's been in the pub and had a slanging match with Shirley. Well, it was one-sided. Shirley just took it – never said a word.'

I lowered the menu and stared his way, dumbfounded and obviously looked the same as well.

'Carol had some photographs.'

'Who from?' I said eventually, my own dire memories of minutes earlier strangling my perception of what was coming.

'I don't know who it was, he didn't leave his name.' Patrick went back to his menu.

Stuart often did the talking for Patrick. That's how it worked it seemed, Patrick told Stuart something, Stuart then relayed it like some ministerial envoy.

'Photographs' of Shirley and Don in an embrace. He hit Carol when she told him.' Stuart placed his menu on the table. 'You can imagine it can't you? She started to lay into him and he slapped her across the face. Hard wasn't it?' Patrick glanced up and nodded.

I'd heard her a couple of weeks ago, arguing with Don on the phone, cat got your tongue? Can't think of an excuse? Trouble is, you only think with your stupid cock.

Don's a big man and I imagined the clear profile of four fingers running diagonally across Carol's cheek, vicious red chevron's throbbing like they had their own pulse.

I took my gaze back to the menu, it was easy to feel sorry for Carol, but strangely, I felt a degree of sympathy for Don too. It explained his rambling visit earlier. I imagined him as he walked away from my house, into a persistent drizzle, slow and sad – shining grey on the slate roofs and black on the tree's bare branches. Occasional umbrellas had drifted past like spectres all morning. It all probably exaggerated his sense of loss. I took a deep breathe.

Then I remembered the young girl, something to balance any sympathy I felt for Don.

Whatever else did he think was going to happen?

Patrick, unshaven, his eyes no longer flashing like black jewels. More like the dull, industrialised, diamond variety. He pushed his thick fair hair back over his head. About time he said something I thought, I waited for something profound.

Finally, he said, 'How many Samosas… six?'

How many?

Patrick stopped chewing, a couple of popodum crumbs around his mouth. Patrick and Stuart stared at each other as they munched away. Sometimes a smile exchanged. It was as if they had suddenly claimed the moral high ground and unused as they were to the rarefied atmosphere of it all. They planned to make the most of it all with a glorious, holier than thou silence.

I decided to puncture this quiet with something profound

of my own. 'Don admitted to me that he'd slept with the girl.'

I stared at Patrick and felt both of them looking my way.

Stuart said, 'What are you going to do about that?'

I shrugged, 'Dunno.' I nodded at Patrick, 'What do you think I should do?'

Patrick slugged some lager back and said, 'I'd tell that inspector friend of yours – get the bastard the sack.'

I needed to know how this worked. Under-age girl with much older men. What were the men thinking about? Apart from the obvious of course.

'Why do you use a girl like that?'

'I never used her.'

We stared at each other. Patrick was a decent poker player and nothing came back. I sighed, 'Why do older men use a girl in that way.'

'Why do you think?' Stuart's agitation apparent as he snapped this at me.

I held my hand up, 'Not you, let Patrick tell me. He's the expert here.'

Patrick slowly shook his head, 'He's right, their age isn't a concern.'

'Well it bloody well should be.'

'Jack… calm down, they want to fuck them. Especially when she looks like Celia. She told me about Don and all of the others. She fell in love with them all and expected the same from them.'

'Which never happened of course?'

He nodded, 'Mostly. Although they told her what she wanted to hear.'

'Even Don?'

Patrick nodded, 'That's what she told me.'

'And you?'

'I never loved her, she never fell in love with me either. Celia thought consummation equalled falling love. No sex – no love. We talked, she talked. Celia was a beautiful young woman, that needed help.'

'You never…'

'No.' Snapped back at me. 'She needed help and got nothing.'

Except men telling her they loved her.

We fell silent as the waiter took the order, Stuart's instructions precise enough. 'Two lamb madras's, one lamb jalfrezi, six samosas and three of the following. Plain naans, pilau rice, Bombay potatoes and saag alloo. And three more pints of pissy lager please.'

I pointed at Patrick's bruised features, 'What are you planning to do about the assault?'

He shrugged, 'What can I do? They'll plead they were just restraining me.' Patrick leaned across the table. 'You know Don stirred them up. Told them I was fucking a suicidal fifteen year old.'

'He knows about you and Carol that's why.'

The hitherto, deadpan features reddened slightly as he said. 'Does Carol know this?'

'I'm unsure. Yes of course she does.'

We sat in silence as the food was shared around the table. Stuart eventually said, 'Getting back to Daphne's murder, that will confuse things even more, fingerprints of a dead man. What can they do? Get the Ghost Squad in?'

'I suppose they'll match the prints soon enough.'

'Then the fun will really begin.' Stuart said this with a degree of enthusiasm that I couldn't share.

I watched them both, little conversation as they raced through the card. Both mopping their plates with some of my naan bread.

They were a handful, Stuart had two cases of assault on his record – nasty one of them, lucky not to go down. The first was just typical Saturday night stuff, you know how it is, ten women in the dance hall and two hundred blokes. The second was in here and it was spiteful. Late night and four noisy drunks were throwing their weight around.

Pissed squaddies, calling the waiters Gunga Din, or worse – one waiter was called a dirty, little fucking wog – nasty bigoted drunks. I thought about that night. Stuart and Patrick were eating – quiet and no trouble. You had to give them their due, they knew how to behave when they were in here and they were in here a lot.

Patrick was with Mably's daughter. She was quite a girl by all accounts, I don't know if she had wound them both up. Anyway, as the three of them left Patrick pushed the noisiest of the louts face straight down onto the hot plate. Fortunately, no smoke, or the smell of burning flesh. Stuart hit two of them out spark out and one of the waiters hit the other with a heavy, cast iron ladle. Pilau rice went everywhere.

Stuart and Patrick, they were always fighting, but rarely started any of it – finished plenty mind. In the restaurant that night, they only did what ninety per cent of the customers wanted to do, I heard that they even got a round of applause as they left.

Patrick stood and made his way to the toilet, I asked Stuart a quick question, 'How long has it been going on?'

'With Carol? A few months, she's quite keen on him. Or perhaps she just hates Don.'

I shook my head, 'Didn't it bother her, being involved with a man who was tangled up with a fifteen year old girl?'

Stuart leant over the table and grabbed my wrist, 'Listen, he wasn't fucking her. Patrick's not like that, anyway, he had enough on his plate with Carol.'

I shook my head, Shirley always said it, Stuart had a fire burning within. A bit like walking past a cottage with the wood burner going, you could smell something burning deep inside. She should have recognised the signs, after all, Stuart did run off with her daughter-in-law.

Stuart said. 'I never had chance to tell you earlier, Bernard's not been home for a few days, his wife's worried.'

Before I could ask him he was in possession of that fact, he told me. 'She rang me just after you left the office. I think she wants to talk. She knows that we're not policemen by the way.'

'What?'

He showed me the palms of his hands, 'It's OK, police

are the last people she wants to talk too, tomorrow.'

***

I felt uneasy about it, most of all meeting at her house. Teddy's house, even if he had disappeared from the face of the earth. My chest tightened as Stuart drove up the sweeping gravel drive. She'd had her hair recently touched up. One button too many of her blouse unbuttoned, tight skirt, too short. Did she look disappointed to see me alongside Stuart?

'Two of you, a case of over-manning don't you think?'

She came up close to me, as if to get a closer look. Squinting, frustration or maybe she had just left her glasses off. Then the glance at Stuart.

I thought you said you'd be on your own.

I offered her my hand, she gave me the briefest of contact, as if I had a piece of rotten fish in it.

She never said anything, sat there watching her cigarette burn down. Sleepless nights has turned her eye sockets cavernous. She stared at Stuart, just the occasional sneaky peep my way. The silence became heavy, the evenings inevitable march into darkness. Mrs Schwartz was just about past the age of reckless ardour. Unlike Shirley, who I always felt could be passionate without being out of control. Curled up on the sofa now, legs underneath, skirt way up her nice looking thighs. Only the clock made any noise, the minute hand masticated the minutes on its familiar circular route, until the irate mechanical chime jolted her back from somewhere nice.

Four o'clock and she broke down. Great big hiccupping sobs convulsed up from her diaphragm and moved like waves across her shoulders. She punched her cigarette into the porcelain ashtray, mascara running and fanning out from each eye, symmetrical like two black opera fans. Her mouth turned down rather like a petulant child who had just been refused a sweet. I passed my handkerchief and another cigarette. She grabbed my hand instead, soft fingers, a touch sticky.

Expensive watch glinting up at me.

'I read it in the evening paper.' Mrs Schwartz held onto my hand, but stared at Stuart. Her sobs receding like tide on a gently sloping beach. 'I never heard him come in, but I saw the blood all over the shirt and jacket. He said he was going to Oxford and he hasn't been home since.'

I raised my hand towards Stuart.

Say nothing.

Let the analyst's angry silence do the talking for us. We listened as the minute hand munched the minutes away, perhaps she only spoke every fifteen minutes, on the chime, four times an hour.

'You know don't you?' Abruptly, she stood up, threw her unlit cigarette at me. 'Oh for fucks sake say something.'

'He's in trouble, that's all I know.'

Mrs Schwartz stared at me, 'He's been in trouble all of his life. There was an assault ten years ago. He got away with it.' She sat down again and wrapped two cushions around her, as if they were a toga. 'He knew that I knew. I was too frightened I suppose. A child I couldn't cope with.' She shrugged and glanced across at Stuart. 'A woman a lot older than him, he beat her up.'

I offered her a cigarette, my eyebrows raised in warning.

Don't throw this one my way.

She nodded and smiled, turned towards Stuart and said, 'Put the light on and get us all a drink while you're up.'

She talked, calmly and freely. 'I met him in Alicante, he had a small photographic business. Snapping the tourists, you know that sort of thing. He was good, a natural talent. I had a modelling agency by now, up until then I used cameramen on a sub-contract basis. A few months later and I had a photo shoot in the sun, contacted Bernard and it… well we hit it off.'

Two glasses of red and the flow had become unstoppable. 'I knew that he must have been in trouble, a cockney boy who had lived out there for fifteen years. Never been home in all of that time. I never asked any questions, he always treated me well enough. He was nearly forty when we met, a good looking man with secrets in his life. A hint of mystery's a powerful attraction for a lonely woman. Plus the fact that he was inexperienced, the way a young man is – around women I mean.' She looked for Stuart's eyes now. 'He'd not been with many women for a while.' She smiled, 'It was like he was making up for lost time, I wasn't complaining mind you. He moved over here a year or so later, we worked well together. Bought this place just before Celia was born. That's when it started to go wrong really.'

Mrs Schwartz poured herself another glass, took a deep breath and carried on. 'He couldn't cope with her, adored her, but couldn't cope. I was anything for the quiet life, agreed with him, did what he wanted all of the time. Celia was the opposite, we thought a good boarding school would help. But it didn't – made things worse in fact.'

She drank half the contents of the large wine glass, 'Celia got into bed with him, just before she went back to school. The day after he caught her in bed with… she needed help, it freaked him. I wanted her to see someone, Bernard wouldn't entertain the idea.' Mrs Schwartz gestured my way for another cigarette, she spoke and punched the smoke my way at the same time. 'She didn't just get into bed with him, she wanted him to…'

Her head dropped, an image so awful had presented itself to her that she crumpled again under its weight.

I watched as her sobs gently filtered into the room. I'd heard enough, 'Has he got a dark room?'

She nodded, 'I'd let you in, but he's got the only key.'

Stuart said, 'Don't worry, my colleague's got a key to any lock.' She frowned, 'I'll show you, I've never been in there. It was his, his to use for the photographs.'

The lock didn't take long and I pushed the loft door open and it was as dark as a crypt, just a hint of wind in the eaves. I stood and waited for my eyes to adjust, finally seeing a light cord hanging in front of my nose then a blinding, naked bulb casting stark shadows around the strangest of scenes.

A camp bed close to the door and snug under the roof trusses. A small cabinet alongside, on top a pile of A4 box files. Running the length of the attic, again snug under the trusses and close to the opposite wall, two trestle tables. Photographic equipment covered them, large trays, cameras, enlargers, lenses, chemicals, funnels, roll after roll of film. Underneath the tables three piles of old newspapers and magazines, there must have been over a hundred.

Someone obviously spent a considerable amount of time up here I thought and I glanced down at the floor. Heavy duty marine ply made walkways, areas around the three light sockets kept clear. A cold water tank an island in the middle.

The smell of chemicals accompanied me as I walked over to the bed, I picked the stack of hard backed, box files up and sat on the bed with them. I soon became involved in an engrossing, macabre voyeurism. I opened the first one, hundreds of photos, some with women carefully posed, all with beautiful backdrops. Then a couple, arms linked together and stood in front of the gates of Trinity College. Plenty of this couple, I stared at one, the location probably Oxford again, maybe Abbey Meadows on a hot summer's afternoon. Lying on the grass, the distances involved made it difficult to make out, but the man's right hand appeared to be inside the young woman's long flowing, summery skirt.

'Who's this man?'

I held the picture and Stuart squinted away. He laughed, 'The geography teacher – that's him. Bloody hell, he's got his hand up her skirt.'

I glanced at a close up of the young woman's face; the exquisite jaw line caught my eye. His daughter, no doubt about it. I gazed on at the pictures of this beautiful, young women. They all looked relaxed and happy and stunning. Smiling naturally at the camera, I picked one, glanced quickly around the room, just to make sure that being engrossed in my own little world and no one could see me kiss the photo and put it carefully into my jacket pocket.

Evidence, but I couldn't be sure how it would help.

I forced myself back to the photos and it was obvious that they had all been beautifully shot. A professional at work. His daughter in soft focus, intense and frowning. I sighed at this intrusion into someone else's compulsion. A chronology began to manifest. Styles from the seventies, sixties, fifties new look. Finally from way back, Shirley, lots of her and I couldn't take my eyes away. It took me back to the most beautiful women I'd ever known. Barely twenty and I stared at the head scarf highlighting her cheekbones, white framed sunglasses and sat in a garden somewhere with a cigarette in one hand and a gin in the other. She looked so gorgeous, the few of her wearing sunglasses could have been comfortably mistaken for Marylyn Monroe.

One of her in just a pair of French knickers, hard, dark nipples pointing towards different corners of the room. Eyes locked at the camera, expression severe though. A mole under her left breast, I sighed. This was as physically close as I had ever been to her and as close as I was ever likely to get.

I shook my head and replaced the photos, closed the file and carefully placed it back in its original position. I lifted the lid on the second box, to begin with they were mostly of birds, birds of all sizes and types. As I worked his way quickly through them, tucked away in the bottom right hand corner – loads of old men sat in Spanish bars. Broken toothed grins, cigarettes welded to their bottom lips.

Lovely pictures though.

Pictures of couples on the beach, all taken with a zoom lens. Unsuspecting couples caught in tender moments. A touch, a kiss, a smile, oblivious to the lone sniper stalking them. I puffed some air out, this was so strange, obsessively so. I picked another pile up, a woman naked and asleep on top of the bed in an apartment room, then one of the same woman stood in front of a mirror, wearing just a pair of knickers and it looked like she was touching her nipples and smiling at the same time.

What did I expect to see? Pictures of couples making love?

Hoped maybe.

'Have a look at this.'

I took the picture from Stuart. A young Teddy on top of a large, dark skinned woman, much older than him. I sighed, a couple making love, it was true. But it didn't excite in any way, instead I shivered and glanced across to the last pile. A black girl on her hands and knees. Bra-less, full breasts hanging down. Her thick lips pouting at the camera. Then her knickers in one hand and a finger of the other hand touching her lips. Eyebrows raised in an expression that said, what do we do next? A close up soon gave me the answer.

Tight pubic hair – semen all over it.

A professional cameraman and young models. Some might say it was just a perk of the job. Still, it was better than putting a razor across their sculptured cheekbones.

I wanted to lay them all out and gaze, it would have been easy to become wrapped up in all of this. Despite the feeling of desecration, I had become morbidly involved. Voyeurism as I well knew, was an addictive hobby.

Stuart's voice crashed into the silence like a jackhammer during midnight mass. 'Is this what we're looking for?'

He held the picture out, I squinted, Shirley wrapped around… Don. I leant in closer, they were all over each other. The strap on her slip had fallen, her left nipple clearly exposed. Don had his hand up the hem of her slip. Bold as brass – framed in the window. I fanned the ones of Don with Shirley across the worktop. One of them stood by an open kitchen door. His hand disappearing up the hem of her slip again. Mouths locked together, a farewell? A coming together? Either way, I would enjoy telling Don of my latest find.

Stuart's more sober assessment brought me crashing down to earth. 'She's in trouble – I think we have to get her out of her house and somewhere safe.'

There you are, I could only see the smaller picture. It's no wonder mind, a woman that I'd known for a lifetime. I knew most of her loves, her weaknesses, her passions. Although that might well be the same thing. I'd imagined every inch of her body pressing against me, imagined her whispering endearments in my ear. Dreamt vigorous couplings and sweet pillow talk. The soft flesh of her thighs pressed against my ears. The feel of her heels in the small of my back.

'Jack... she's in trouble. So is Don.'

I blinked, felt my mouth form a circle.

He placed another photo in front of me. A police car, a young woman and a much older driver.

Both smiling.

I groaned.

'We have to get her somewhere safe.' Stuart gripped my wrist.

I nodded, of course he was right.

But I just wanted to stare at the photographs. I scanned the thousands, until I notice a handwritten letter. Not one, but dozens. Photocopies of an original letter. Someone didn't want to lose it.

My dear, darling Teddy ...

'Jack. C'mon.'

I felt a hand on my shoulder, turned and looked into Stuart's eyes. Waved the letter at him.

'What's that?'

I shrugged, 'Shirley's death warrant I think.'

1980 – TEDDY

Someone with devotion finds nothing but hope, despondency comes to the faithless. Remorse or relief. Maybe neither, just the grim pleasure that comes to those with a taste for disappointment. He used to pull at his father's shirt cuff, then his customary question. His old man looked around and down with the look of wariness and weariness he shouted. 'Why don't you just fuck off?'

Disappointment.

Disappointment, more than that. Disenchantment, disaffection, displeasure, despondency, distress, depression, dishearten. Don't mention that word.

Depression. Depression. Madness.

Hang on a minute. That didn't begin with the letter D.

He went through his list again, what about disaster? That's a good one.

Why?

What was going on?

Concentrate!

Where was his camera?

He looked at his empty left hand. Then over to the right, clasped tightly around a large carving knife.

How did that get there?

He liked lists and went through another in his fevered brain. His cheating first wife, his cheating second wife, Daphne, the policeman, Shirley, his daughter – say her name. But he couldn't.

Say.

Her.

Fucking.

Name.

But he couldn't.

Concentrate, what could he do? Run?

He knew enough people in Spain, he liked the climate, he knew the language. Over sixty, with a flaky erection. What was the point? It worked well enough on Daphne and Shirley. But not his wife, or more fortunately, his daughter.

No – no more running. End it now, tie up all of the loose ends and end things once and for all.

He felt for the letter in his pocket. He hadn't got to see his son either, another loose end. Or had Shirley lied to him again?

Why did he believe everything she tossed his way?

She said nothing about the policeman all the time they were together in that hotel.

Not a word, except for. 'There's no one in my life at the moment.'

That was all she said.

His mind spun away as he thought back. Thirty five years ago, she used to leave the door ajar for him. Now she'd done the self- same thing.

He crept in the kitchen door. Silence.

What did he expect? The two of them writhing around on the kitchen floor. He mind zigzagged back to her little flat in London. Kitchen-diner, bathroom, bedroom. She would be laid across the bed, legs crossed at the ankles. The way the dress clung to her, she might as well have been naked. Buttoned at the front, the top three left strategically undone. The rise of her full breasts always beguiled him. His eyes wouldn't, couldn't fix on anything else. And all the time her eyes drilled into his soul.

He shuddered and crept towards the stairs. Concentrate.

But he couldn't, remembering when he took her to Brighton races one summer's afternoon. Just before he went into prison. Just after the racecourse stopped being an internment camp. He knew all of the bookies. He knew which horse was trying and which one was going to be pulled. He gave her the winnings, hundreds of crumpled notes. Then she fucked him silly in the back seat of the car. In the middle of the car park on the Sussex downs.

Foreplay?

She only needed a bunch of bank notes.

He stopped halfway up the stairs, listened, listened, listened. He crept slowly upwards. One step, listen. One step, listen. Shirley came to his trial. Sat throughout it all dressed like a model and looking like Carol Lombard. His wife stared at her, she stared back. His wife's scar running down one cheek. Standing out like a worm on a white dinner plate. Nobody saw the razor attack, no one fingered him for that. He got six months for punching her in the mouth in Lyon's Tea Rooms in Piccadilly. No that wasn't true, three months for the punch and three months for absconding after being called up.

Two women crying after the judge sentenced him. One crying because of the six months. The other because it was only six months.

Last step, listen. Voices.

From the bath room. The door half open.

'What a mess – Don, I'm so sorry. Have you seen her?'

A man's voice. 'I've seen her parents and the kids. Carol won't see me.'

Silence.

A man's voice. 'Can we go back to bed?'

Silence.

'God, you're such a sexy man. Careful, I'm a bit sore; you'll have to go easy.'

They both laughed.

Then door opened and the policeman came out. He stopped. He was holding a towel around his waist. His eyes bulged open.

The knife slipped into his stomach. Easier than a spoon going into a soft blancmange. The blood ran over the white towel.

'What have you done? No, no.'

The eyes, bulging. The mouth hanging open. The hands trying to pull the stomach together.

'What's up?' A voice from the bathroom. 'Don, what's happened?'

27

1946 – JACK

We all recognised that tranquillity is not a good indicator of a long and prison free life. Eyeless lay face down in the snow, blood scattered around the snow like someone had dipped a six inch paint brush into a full pot of red paint, dragged it slowly out and flicked it hard. The red spots went away in decreasing size. Largest closest and gradually reducing.

What do we do?

Harry darted into the garage, returned seconds later with a spade.

I said, 'You're not burying him are you?'

Harry started shovelling snow, throwing it over the body. Gurgling, bubbling noises still coming from the mouth. Harry shovelled frantically like a lunatic stoker hysterically shovelling coal to regain some boiler pressure. Shovel after shovel after frenzied shovel. Quickly covering the nearly dead man. We watched in open mouthed, wide eyed disbelief.

Harry stared from one to the other, 'What?' Pointed the shovel Wyn's way. 'Breathing space that's all, what should I fucking well do? Lay him out on the fucking dining room table?'

'The lights have come back on.' A voice from the door, Daphne staring at the pantomime scene, 'What are you doing out here in this?'

'Clearing the fucking drive.'

'Make a pot of coffee Daphne – we won't be long.'

'Who broke the window then?'

We said nothing and a few seconds later her shadow moved away and we stood in silence.

'She never saw anything – did she?'

Wyn glanced at his brother, shrugged. 'Don't think so. Is he dead?'

'Yes.' Harry's turn to shrug, 'If he isn't, we won't be able to revive him anyway. The knife went all the way through. Sticking out the back of his fucking neck.'

'Excuse me.' A voice from the end of the drive. 'What's going on?'

I could just make out a snow covered policeman's helmet, thirty yards away, then and a policeman coming steadily towards us.

Wyn whispered to me, 'Get out of those clothes and scrub yourself – quickly.'

I rushed up the stairs two, three at a time. Daphne called from the bottom of the stairs, 'You ok Jack love, I've got a pot of coffee on.' Sounds of people gathering by the door, then Daphne saying, 'Oh hello officer, have you come about the broken window?'

I threw my clothes into the bath and turned the tap on. Filled the sink and scrubbed away at myself. Hands, wrists, face, neck. The red water swirled and gurgled away down the plughole. I couldn't see why Lady Macbeth had so much trouble, I scrubbed up pretty well. I needed the nail brush, apart from that, nothing.

I walked back into the living room, hair slicked down, clean trousers and shirt. A macabre scene presented itself, a squeaky clean policeman. Fresh faced and not a day over twenty. Frowning away and furiously scribbling onto the first page of a shiny, new notebook.

The two older men sat back in arm chairs, talking over the policeman, around him, any which way just to confuse and distract.

'Jack, this is Constable Mably.' Wyn picked a bottle of whiskey up. 'Why don't you try some of this? Jack loves this one. It's good –you can't buy this around here.' A bottle of fifteen year old, single malt Jura hovered under the young man's nose. 'Go on, it's cold out there.'

'I don't drink.' P.C. Mably's eyes followed the bottle like it was a hypnotist's charm. 'Usually.'

'Mably… an unusual name, you're not related to the French writer are you?' I joined in with the game of distraction. 'He was a Stoic and believed in human equality – a noble quality don't you think.'

'Shut up Jack, let him drink his whisky.'

He drank it like a boy drinks beer, too quick. 'Your neighbour says he heard a fight, screams, gunshots – a right set to.'

Wyn shut his eyes for a second.

Give me patience.

'The man's a drunk – this time of night he's always raving. You must have noticed?'

The policeman raised his eyebrows, 'I agree, he had been drinking –but this is a serious charge. We had to follow it up.'

Daphne came through with another pot of tea. 'He's always drunk, got a problem if you ask me.'

Which we didn't, although it helped build our character up as raving lunatic, prone to attacks of the D.T.'s.

'Why were you clearing the drive, you won't be going anywhere tonight. It's a foot deep in places.'

'Supposed to have an early start tomorrow – just trying to clear the decks. I'm going up to London. Buy some new shirts and see a friend.'

Wyn tapped his nose and winked, Mably blinked.

Oh that sort of a friend.

At that moment, the lights went out again. Plunged into darkness again until a candlelit Daphne came through. She placed it on the table for us and said, 'I'm going up to bed now.' She threw Wyn the briefest of glances and left us to it.

Wyn ignored her, 'One for the road?'

The red faced policeman shook his head, four large ones was enough for someone that never drank. He wobbled a touch as he stood. Closed his notebook and slipped it inside his breast pocket.

'I'd better be going – thanks for the drink.'

Harry walked out with the policeman. I imagined him ushering the young man all the way down the drive, bidding him a goodnight at the gates. Staring after him for a few minutes. Guard dog seeing off a wolf. Job done and he rejoined us. The three of us sat in silence.

What do we do now?

1960 – TEDDY

Widest lens aperture, shortest focal length and stare. Did he catch any regret or satisfaction radiating from his uncle? Everybody likes the return of the prodigal, although he wasn't his son.

'You still putting the squeeze on that café down the road?' Teddy nodded, waiting for the reprimand.

'Be careful boy, Jesus, sometimes I think you just don't get it.' But Uncle Jim turned a blind eye. He even tried to contact Eyeless again, all in vain as it turned out. Not a trace, disappeared from the face of the earth. Most of the time they sat on the beach a lot, they both liked the sun. Jim watched Teddy snapping away. A more expensive camera every year.

'Poor old Teddy boy. What are you thinking?'

His mind drifted back to the pubs, the gossip of criminals, the stares of the policemen and the drunks. Old men sat at Formica coated tables, sucking on their roll ups and drinking warm tea.

The women cooing away at him. 'Oh it won't cost you Teddy boy.'

The bitter street smells, urine mixed with overripe vegetables. He missed all of that, but here he had the sun and he used its therapeutic properties well. Best thing good old Uncle Jim did for him, buying the camera all those years ago. Now he'd got a Russian camera. The Zenit-5 was the first of the motorized SLR cameras. Despite the camera's bulk, he loved the sound of the motor winding the film on.

He spent most of his time clicking away down on the

beach. Watching couples, intimate couples mainly. Discreet couples that sneaked kisses and touches. Even better when he fitted a zoom lens.

Then he saw her. Connie wasn't Spanish, despite her dark hair and tanned skin. Her cameraman was a poof as well. Well he wouldn't be giving her one. That was always reassuring.

The girls, all five of them were skinny. Beautiful, but skinny. He zoomed in on their chests for confirmation – all five flat as a nun's chuff.

The stinking dog that had become his constant companion, sat the other side to Uncle Jim and watched as well. Waiting for a scrap. Dogs didn't argue, he liked this thing.

He pointed, 'Hey perro… vamos… por favor.'

He liked the dog, but didn't want to look like some deadbeat with that woman close by. She looked classy as she herded the girls around like a terrier snapping at the heels of a small herd of cattle.

He liked bossy women. Attractive though.

He stared at her – zooming in and out and his mind was everywhere. How old was he? How long had he been here, fourteen, fifteen years?

He followed the gaggle of fashion models back to their hotel, the Hospes Amerigo. He sat in the bar drinking a fruit juice – nothing mixed with the tablets he was on. Not Spanish brandy anyway, or cerveza. Certainly not that sangria piss.

He watched them, she bossed the cameraman around too. Made sure the girls ate nothing but lettuce leaves. He felt inside his pocket – five reels to develop.

She was suddenly in front of him, pointing. 'Me estás siguiendo?'

'No.'

'Estaba tomando fotos de mis chicas.'

'De ninguna manera! Just fuck off will you, I'm not following you. Anyway it's my fucking beach.'

'Oh my god.' She smiled. 'You're English?'

'Yep and my Spanish is ok, yours is shit. And I was taking pictures of you, not those skinny birds you were bullying.'

She smiled again, 'I'm Connie. Can you show me the pictures? I need a local man, the ability of these agency guys is so variable.'

'How do you know I'm local?'

'Your tan, your not flabby and pink like most Englishmen out here.'

She held her hand out, 'Like I said, I'm Connie.'

Who was he?

'I'm Teddy, no, I'm Bernard, call me Bernie.'

'Bernie, show me the pictures, get them to me tomorrow and I might have some work for you.'

'Tomorrow? What's your room number?'

***

She was sexy and knew all about him. Didn't know who he was, but knew that he was a runner. Something odious in his past. Something disgracefully, monstrously illegal. Something violent.

All of those and more, if only she knew what exactly. But she never asked questions, just hinted now and again.

'If you ever went back to England, where would it be?' He played the game. Laughed when she said, 'I bet you can't go back to London?'

He rented an apartamento. A small flat near the beach. It had a shared garden, a pool and play area. Connie stopped there whenever she came over.

Teddy had found peace.

Even when she said, 'I live in the countryside, it's not London. Do you think you could live with out in the sticks with the country bumpkins?'

Goodbye Uncle Jim.

Back home, not London, but home nonetheless.

28

1980 – JACK

My mind buzzed with dozens of beautifully photographed images and a single photocopied letter written by Shirley. We left Connie's house to be greeted by snow, not a whiteout yet, but a heavy, soundless blanket of tumbling snow twisted its erratic way into my face. Then the tortuous drive home in rush hour traffic. Happy to leave the busiest traffic behind, somewhere between Streatly and Blewbury. The eastern edge of the Berkshire downs, with snow settling on the meadows and hedgerows, tyre tracks visible on the roads. And all the time feeling of déjà vu overwhelmed me.

'Like this was it?' Snow and the implication not lost on Stuart either. He glanced over, 'Bring back memories?'

'Bad memories.' I nodded. 'It was worse than this, a blizzard.'

By the time we had crossed the roundabout at Rowstock, driving had become difficult. I felt safe enough with my chauffeur, it was the others snaking and twisting and braking that unnerved me. We stopped at Hendred and I used the phone box to ring Harry. No use, some moron had ripped the phone out and it sat on the floor in a miserable isolation. I swore my way back into the warmth of the car.

'Vandalised.'

'Relax - we'll get back soon enough.' I couldn't smile at the optimism of a young man.

I craved something sweet, some of Wyn's strong black coffee laced with sugar, or a jam doughnut. Now that would hit the spot. Instead my throat remained dry and my hands sticky and damp. I fumbled for my cigarettes, just the thing when your throat's drier than a Saharan pebble. He drove into the pub car park, spun through one hundred and eighty degrees in a decent impression of a rally driver.

Stuart jumped out and ran around the car. He opened my front door, watched me as I pulled my cap low on my head, crossed my scarf and buttoned my coat.

'My Mum dressed me like that when I was six.'

I told my chauffeur to fuck off, and braced myself for whatever the evening had in store for us. Stuart stared down at me, his hands came my way and he lined my scarf precisely up at my throat, patted me on the head and took my hand.

I shook him off me, 'It's not funny.'

'C'mon, it's likely that Shirley's on her sofa, watching the television.'

I stared at him, he might be right. I hoped that I looked at the face of a survivor. Not much guile, but strong with a brutal edge. Fear never travelled along their bloodline, bred out over the centuries. Selective breeding in action, Stuart smiled, raised his eyes and tipped his head a touch.

Here we go then.

I said, 'You shouldn't be here.' My turn to feel uneasy. He had three young children and a wife close by. You think that might make him a touch more cautious. More careful with his life, many more things to hold him to this world than me. But repercussions and nervousness weren't apparent in his make-up. Stuart just saw it as an opportunity to fight and a chance for glory. Never just an exercise in self-sacrifice either.

'Why don't you go and have a pint?'

I said nothing, just hurried after him, my last day on earth and once again I followed someone like a well-trained poodle. A poodle whose temples throbbed like that of an Olympic sprinter. I walked on, my vision blurred by the snowflakes tumbling into my eyes. Or perhaps they were tears. Civilisation had ended, the silence broken by an owl somewhere in the distant, hooting away, telling me to go home.

I trudged after Stuart, the unspoken words between us perfectly audible. The muffled, soundproofed world of snow.

The soft, feathery stuff drifted down from a windless sky. It clung desperately to branches and crunched underneath our feet. The terrace of twenty odd houses had the angles and edges of rooftops blurred by the snow. The one streetlight midway down the length of the houses, turned the scene to crystal where the shadows disappeared. What struck me was the normalcy of the scene, gas heating outlets vented their steam, windows condensed, water trickling down in irregular channels. Wood smoke mixed with that of coal. Fighting for dominance. The smell a mixture of the sulphur and burnt wood. A cat looking for a snow free haven, scuttled across in front of me.

Was it black?

Shirley lived opposite the solitary streetlight, Wyn used to say that the light cast by the lamp, set the most erotic of moods in the bedroom. Soft light merged with vague shadows, a light for love making. Oh and Shirley's presence helped the ambience as well.

Stuart's signal slid into my world, a finger up to lips. He nodded towards an open back door. I groaned silently, Shirley rarely locked the bloody doors. I watched Stuart as he slipped through. Turned and waited for me. His murky figure stood stock still. Listening and sniffing the air like a lion out on the prowl. Stuart's shadowy features deepened by the gloomy light. Deep shadows ran across his face, ageing him, hardening him into a wanted picture of some tough criminal.

We stood in the small kitchen, the radio filtering in from the living room. A nauseating country record's lyric taunted me.

"Everyone considered him
The coward of the county"

Stuart smiled at me and tiptoed to the door and stared into room. The radio teased away.

"Walk away from trouble if you can"

Seconds later he turned back towards me. Gestured with his eyes, skywards - upstairs. I screamed, the silent scream that those in fear of their lives are familiar enough with.

The layout of the house was simple enough, two down, three up. Stuart placed one foot on the stairs, I grabbed his sleeve and pointed at the open knife draw. Gaping like some lantern jawed freak - mocking me with its implied threat. He shrugged and crept up the stairs. I followed and heard two people talking.

Not the hushed, low voices of lovers.

The middle of an argument more like.

What were we doing here?

We stood at the bottom of the stairs with a lover's sense of the highly strung. Temples pounding, we stood on the brink, a couple of pearl divers about to take their leap into the emptiness. The soft light cast a corridor of blurred radiance that tumbled across the small upstairs landing.

Instead of the hushed tones of lovers, a small noise, a grunt. Not of pleasure either.

Shirley's voice broke into the groan. 'No, please. Not this way.'

Was Shirley's whispered instruction a command or a plea? Had we crept in from a twilight, snowy world and intruded into a lover's province?

No, another groan, a low moan. A deep sigh and then air whooshing from – who?

At the top of the stairs, a pair of bare feet.

I peered around Stuart. Don was lying on his back staring at Stuart with glazed eyes. His mouth hung open, the usual olive skin a deathly white. Both of his hands holding a three inch gash together in his stomach. A towel soaked in blood. Pints of it laying on the carpet. Sticky like a puddle of bitumen.

A voice from the bedroom, my heart stopped for a second when Teddy said, 'You lying, fucking scrubber.'

'Please no…'

Stuart stepped over Don and pressed himself against the

wall of the short landing. I did the same, only at a slightly wider angle and I could see into Shirley's bedroom. The end of her double bed and what I saw punched me between the eyes. A pair of highly polished, handmade, black brogues of someone sat on the edge of the bed.

Shirley stood in the middle of the room, a silk robe wrapped tightly around her. The stomach still flat, narrow waist, breasts heavy, but no longer the gravity defying miracles they once were. The rise and fall of her chest an indication of the tension inside of her. Pale skinned and natural. Stars glitter and die, but Shirley had remained ageless. Apart from her neck and the tell-tale lines. Just beginning to criss-cross and encroach, looking a bit like the lines on a map of the railways. Making their inevitable, creeping routes and their predictable indicators of the march of time.

I stared, transfixed, rooted to the spot. She saw me, just a slight raising of the eyebrows, never tried to cover herself up. Never acknowledged me, never screamed, never called me a fucking pervert. Never shut the door, just stared at the man lying on the bed.

Then a voice deep and loaded with distress. A voice that found all humankind to be the biggest collection of two faced liars and back stabbing women.

That voice.

'He was fucking my daughter.'

Those few words became a starter's pistol for Stuart. He went around the door and into the room.

1980 – TEDDY

What to do?

She looked good, freshly bathed and he guessed, not unreasonably, recently fucked. Why did he like to fuck after someone else had been there?

She looked good.

'Is he dead?' Who? Silence.

Make her wonder. Then.

'You lied to me.'

'When?'

He put the knife down and pulled the letter out. Watching her all the time. He smoothed the letter out and began to read it.

'My dear, darling Teddy'

He stared at her, knowing every word, comma and full stop he recited in a monotone. Shirley's eyes closed and she began to shake her head.

'Please don't.' He carried on.

'My dear, darling Teddy, I love you so much and I always will. I have to go away, I almost miscarried when I heard the result of the fight. They betrayed us, they made a fortune and cut me out completely. I'm in an infirmary and likely to be here for all of my confinement. On my back for months and not to have you close during that time breaks my heart. I'm in the Radcliffe hospital in Oxford and after that I don't know. I'm alone, everyone's left me except you. Please come and visit me. I'm sure your baby will be fit and well. Please come and see me soon.

Always your adoring Shirley.'

He wiped a tear from his cheek.

'Anything to say?'

'I meant everything, I loved you so much.'

'Not even my baby was it?' Silence, the silence of the guilty?

'Catastrophic Schizophrenia, that's what the Spanish doctor said. What else would he have to say about me? Complete breakdown, listen will you. Catastrophic schizophrenia has an acute onset and rapid decline into a chronic state often without remission.'

He couldn't stop laughing.

She never thought it was funny.

'You can still get away. Why don't you just slip off?'

'Has he just fucked you?'

'Don't, please – let me call an ambulance? Please.'

His mind wandered again, just malicious gossip, that was her stock in trade. Everything speedily memorised. Whereas he couldn't think straight, a tectonic shift is taking place, namely the transition from a man in which information is transmitted down the pyramidal structure that used to be his mind. Now he couldn't form an opinion or make a decision about anything.

The room began to spin, as he saw all of these slags swimming about in a protoplasmic mess of titillating supposition. No doubt about it, he thought, he lived in an interregnum between madness and complete lunacy and in such times, as Marx observed of political interregnums, the strangest of bed-fellows will arise.

'Teddy? Don't cry, you know it upsets me when I see you crying.'

He shook his head. She came back into sharp focus.

He spoke slowly.

'I used to take her out in the car. When she was six or seven. We laughed and talked and loved each other. That flabby cunt out there was fucking her. Barely fifteen and he used to take her out in his police car. Did you know that?'

'No, please let me ring…' She gasped.

Movement in the door caught his eye. A man hurtling his way.

What the?

Where's that knife?

29

1946 – JACK

We had waited until four in the morning, our arguments for the course of action we were about to take seemed impeccable. After all who would ever believe us? In all likelihood, we'd be hung and if not, a prison sentence meant certain assassination by Teddy's friends. We had no choice, apart from how we disposed of the body. It might be days before we could get the car up Lock's Lane. It had to be tonight and quick.

We wrapped Eyeless in an old rug, Harry threw the big man over his shoulder and carried him over the footbridge and along to the paddock. The big house was two hundred yards away. A bizarre convoy made our way in the fag-end of the blizzard. Snow easing all the time, not the wind though.

Buffeting us down through the darkness.

Wyn had scrapped the snow away, then carefully removed the turf. Laying the neatly squared turf out exactly as he had just cut it from the ground.

'C'mon for fuck's sake, hurry up.'

'Patience – let's do it properly.'

The ground still firmish after days of frosts. A day later and it would be saturated. Harry made the most of it and dug the four feet or so down in a blind fury. I stood guard like a panicky sheepdog.

The snow had stopped by now, soon after broken clouds scudded across a full moon. When it peeped through, an eerie, silvery world exposed itself and a maniac digging, another man leaning on a spade and a length of rolled up carpet laying close by.

Twenty minutes later Harry leant on his spade, sharp

breaths snorting out from his mouth. He stayed like that for a few minutes. Took a couple of deep breaths, walked over and picked the rug up. Grunted and expelled the air like a champion weightlifter. Lined it up, lowered it feet first, then let it go. Immediately started to shovel the earth back into the hole. Jumping up and down to compress it as he went along.

Despite all of his efforts, a fair amount of soil remained. He scattered it around a thirty yard radius. Then Wyn began his systematic turfing, lining every piece up like a jig-saw champion.

'C'mon for fucks sake. It'll be light soon.'

'Shhhh... let's get it right.' Wyn patted his turfing down with the spade. Then the methodical spreading of the snow back. 'We'll have to see how it looks in the daylight.'

The rain started as soon as we got home. Cleansing the blood stained snow from the garden. Washing any evidence away down the hill and into Letcombe Brook.

I walked by the paddock the next morning, alone and in the rain. The horses had walked over the grave by now. Hoof prints had churned the whole area, milled it into something resembling a First World War trench in November. No one could ever guess what lay beneath.

Except me.

1974 – TEDDY

He never went anywhere near London until they both took Celia to the Shaftsbury Theatre. Afterwards, they ate in a small Greek restaurant in the Charing Cross Road.

Celia? He'd just said her name.

As they walked north, Celia pointed at the garishly lit strip clubs and the queer boys clubs along Old Compton Street.

'Can we walk down there, please daddy?'

The street names came back and smacked him between the eyes.

Right down Wardour Street. Quick left along Peter Street.

Right turn into Lexing Street.

There.

He couldn't look, but his eyes went upwards... there. Beak Street.

He hurried her along, his chest tight. Pulse throbbing.

'What's the rush?'

Into the broad avenue that was Regent Street and his breathing slowed.

'Are you alright?'

He nodded, Regent Street, the last time he walked along here...

Him and Eyeless- both bathed in blood. He stopped and held onto a lamp post.

'Daddy...'

'I'm a bit dizzy babe. Give me a minute.'

30

1980 – JACK

I stared, for the briefest of seconds I thought I was having a stroke, my eyes blurred and it felt as if someone had punched me on the temple. I steadied myself against the door jamb. Not a stroke, just fear and I couldn't suppress its rise through my body. I had gone mad and craved an arm around my shoulder.

Seconds before, Stuart had just raised his eyebrows. Gestured with a flick of his head for me to get out of the way. He tiptoed around the door and launched himself across the small bedroom. An Olympic sprinter out of his blocks. I leant around the door and watched the human missile throw himself at the man sat on the bed.

He drove his forehead into Teddy's face, connecting in a bone crunching collision.

Teddy's eyes went from wide eyed shock as he watched Stuart close the gap between them at an alarming velocity. Wide eyed shock to eye rolling unconsciousness within the time it takes to crunch an egg shell under your foot. Egg shells breaking, that's exactly what it sounded like. Teddy rolled back across the bed. On his back, one arm draped across a pillow.

I heard a groan, but not from the bedroom. I glanced down.

Don!

I quickly glanced into the bedroom, then doubled back down the stairs. I rang for an ambulance, never mentioned a knifing. An accident I said, a man bleeding to death. The police would be here soon enough without me tipping them the wink. I rushed back up the stairs and knelt alongside Don.

'Hang on Don. Don – Don. Won't be long.'

He blinked, in slow motion a couple of times and then they closed.

Forever?

I'd seen three men bleed to death in front of me. This looked like becoming a four-timer. I leant over and looked into the bedroom.

Two men on the bed, one dressed like an undertaker in his black suit and Stuart. Sat up groaning and holding his head like one of those bad actors in an Aspirin advert. He had swelling above the right eye, which had begun to close. Like a cartoon swelling that manifests in a split second. He just needed some cartoon birds twittering their way around his head to complete the scene. The memories of Harry's boxing opponent's eye closing in the same fashion came sweeping back. Perhaps an ending was close by – maybe.

Shirley's voice jolted me back. 'Are you ok? Stuart? Stuart?' I stared at her stood wrapped in a deep red, silky dressing gown around and tied it off at her waist, she stared at me. 'Have you rung the police?'

I shook my head.

'Don't either.' Stuart, with just his left hand on the point of impact now. He brought his head up and looked at me. Rather like a man shielding his eyes from the strong sun. 'Ring Dad and Wyn.' Stuart took his glance across from Shirley and lined me up. 'Get them both down here. Don't stare at me like that, just get them down here, quickly.'

The knock on the head had scrambled his brains. But my mind was knotted too. My heart wouldn't stop thumping. I wondered if my fear could be catching. Contagious like an infection. I was a carrier of panic and I didn't have a cure.

'We have to get the police and finish this charade once and for all.' A thought swept over me, making me shiver. 'Please don't tell me that you're going to bury the body?'

'Get me some ice Shirley.' Stuart glanced over at her and attempted a smile. 'You didn't have to get dressed up just for me.'

She stonewalled that remark, walked across to the bedside

table. An ice bucket and a half empty bottle of white wine nestled close by a box of chocolates. A long night had been rudely interrupted. She fumbled around in a draw, found a sock, grabbed a handful of ice and poured it down the neck of the sock.

'Go and sit with Don.'

Shirley stared at me, never moved for a second or two. She sighed and moved towards the door.

I grabbed her wrist, 'I know about the letter and I know that you rang the military police.'

'Know it all don't you.'

I pointed at her, 'And you told Eyeless where we were living.'

'Leave me alone – you know nothing about me.'

She shook her hand free and walked towards a dying man.

Stuart whispered, 'What was that all about?'

He clamped the ice onto the point of impact and groaned again, softly. Slowly merging between a groan and heavy sighing breaths. A sound so evocative of Harry in the car, holding onto his bandaged hand. All it needed was a curse or two. 'Fucking hell, Jesus fucking Christ, why did I do that?' He blinked his good eye my way and shouted. 'Go and ring them... quick.'

My voice cracked as I said, 'Have we got two dead men in the room?'

Stuart turned and for a pulse in the neck and nodded.

'Does that nod mean that he's dead or alive?'

He nodded again, 'Alive.' He groaned again, pursed his lips.

'Ring my old man now, please.

Down the stairs again just to have Harry shouting down the phone at me. I quickly explained and went back up to the grisly scene. Shirley was stroking Don's cheek with one hand and a towel was compressed over his gaping stomach. I didn't dare ask how he was. Stuart, stood up by now, he glanced at me and said, 'Two men in Shirley's house, both unconscious, she certainly knows how to finish a man off.'

She stared back, pointed at Stuart and shouted, 'I'm not in the mood.'

Shirley began to sob. Racking, shoulder heaving sobs as the spectre of safety dragged her away, from what exactly? Teddy still had her biggest carving knife by his side. The other man had probably bled to death. Through her tears she asked the same question as me. 'Is he alive?'

At that moment Harry burst through the door. Wyn close behind. They looked at the scene. Pretty mild compared to what they'd been used to. Two sets of raised eyebrows, two mouths open. Harry noticed Stuart's eye, came up and stared into his face. 'Did he hit you?'

Stuart shook his head, 'I stuck my head into his face.'

Harry smiled, 'Good man – hurt's doesn't it?'

Wyn came up to Shirley, 'Can I get you anything – cigarette, coffee?'

She nodded, 'Both please.'

'What happened Shirley? We need to get the story straight.'

'I don't know, never locked the door I suppose. Never saw anything. One minute Don was …'

Pumping away?

'We never heard a thing, just this noise. Don came out of the bathroom and…'

Wyn came back in with coffee and cigarettes, 'I've rung the police. Don't look like that, how long does it take to get our stories straight for God's sake?'

He walked over to Shirley, lit her cigarette and passed it over to her. There had always been this iron bond between them. Despite their many separations and her betrayals, they were tighter than a welder's joint. She told him everything and he understood it all. They whispered away to one another now. A meeting within a meeting, heads together like twins.

Harry took his eyes away from them and back to his son. He kept winking at Stuart. Harry always told him that foreheads do more damage than a fist.

That's my boy.

'What's the story then?'

I said, 'Well we've rescued a policeman and a damsel in real distress. Caught a murderer. It makes things easier — perhaps they'll gloss over the past.'

Please gloss over the past

'Not me, Teddy hit me, remember?' Stuart took his one eyed gaze around the room, 'Let the old boys save everyone. Teddy stabbed Don and then knocked me out. Dad and Wyn rescued us. It looks better for them, a thirty five year vendetta knocked on the head by two old men.'

'Less of the fucking old.'

Is it possible to stare death in the face and become a better man or woman? Stuart suggested that it could happen that way. He looked pretty smug mind, but that's a reasonable emotion in a moment like this. It did paint the others in a truly positive light as well.

'We followed Teddy down here. He stabbed Don in front of our eyes. Pity we can't get him dressed. How do we explain that away?'

I stared at Shirley, 'That's Shirley's to explain away.'

Her nose flared and Wyn squeezed her shoulder. 'It's all right. It will sort itself out.'

The ambulance men arrived five minutes before the police. The debate began, any shifting of Don and the probability was that what little blood he had left in his body would soon siphon away. But they had no choice, he would die either way. One ambulance man tried to staunch the flow as Stuart took one end of the stretcher.

Mably and his troops arrived at the same time as the stretcher left the back door. He stared down at his sergeant, 'What the ...'

Stuart gestured towards the inspector with his head. 'The murdering bastard's been laid out upstairs on the bed for you. Worked out nicely Inspector.'

They came slowly up the stairs, tiptoed around the pool of blood and stared into the bedroom. The inspector gave me one of those suspicious police looks. A frown, another glance at the carnage. Another frown back at me. 'Who's that? Bernard Swa…'

'Or Ted Lewis, I think you'll find his fingerprints all over the caravan. He laid Don out and Stuart. Harry laid Teddy out.'

'But that's Bernard Schwartz, I saw him at the coroners.' He puffed his cheeks out. 'Did Don know who he was? How many of you knew?' Mably nodded, 'Only the whole bloody world and his wife. Everyone, apart from those that should have known. Jack, Jack we've got some serious talking to do.'

I stared at Harry. Unlike a cat at the hint of trouble, their first instinct is to get as far away from humans as they could. I took on the mantle of a dog, seeking safety by getting as close to their owners as possible. I walked and stood next to Harry. He slipped his arm around me and whispered. 'Don't worry Jackie boy.' Harry held me up just like he did after Eyeless's demise. He frowned at Mably and said, 'Don't worry about that pompous prick, it's all over now. All over.'

It felt like the mangled knot that had strangled my heart for years had been severed by a slashing blade. I could breathe again. I stared at Harry's gnarled old fist resting on my shoulder. Hard hands, knotted from years of punching hard heads in boxing rings. Good job he hadn't hit anyone, I imagined broken, splayed fingers defying cartilages, bending away at odd angles and then the nerve screaming pain.

I glanced down at pool of blood. My relief had become tempered with a simmering rage. I wanted to tell Shirley it was all her fault. But she'd be swearing and blaming the spider. Forgetting that she had spun the web all by herself. The web of secrecy demanded time and money and inventiveness. Defeat costs marriages and more stares from the neighbours. She knew life, affairs, jealousies and the oddness of the sexual nature.

But little about common sense most would say.

Except Wyn of course, he said it often enough, "who would say anything if it were a man behaving like that? None of you, she enjoys life too much for you hypocrites". Eyes fluttered to ground as a man's one sided love affair meant defending her had become a life time exercise. He had become her own listening service. Someone that can be told anything without fear of criticism. He had heard and done worse himself.

Whatever came his way, never incited anything but a calm understanding. We all felt an affectionate emotion for this gorgeous woman. But it was all a trap in a way, Shirley was an authority in the provocation of just such feelings.

Or perhaps I was just jealous.

Perhaps we had all forgotten what started this nightmare off. A young suicide called Celia. No one asked about her any more. I stared at her unconscious father – well who could ever imagine what he thought about anything.

***

Carol didn't come into work the next day, sat by a hospital bed watching her half dead husband's laboured breathing. A man soon to be cited for bravery, trying to rescue a woman held hostage by a lunatic. What he was doing naked in Shirley's house was never made public. She had a champion for a husband. No wonder Carol sounded so happy on the phone, husband just about alive and back in the fold. Unable and probably unwilling to stray again.

For a while anyway.

Stuart said one word. 'Carol?'

I nodded and glanced at my younger colleague. His eye had taken on the appearance of a multi-coloured closure. Shut and likely to remain so few a good few days yet. Still he'd be dining out on that for weeks to come and who could blame him. Another hero whose spouse accepted his sudden
absences. Hours and days at a time – working, chasing a criminal mastermind. Well mastermind was how he described Teddy to his wife.

Just a blundering, psychotic more like.

And Stuart, his father and uncle never tried to keep the truth a secret either. Apart from their police statements, they told anyone and everyone pretty much as it was. Principle one thing, reality another. I suppose the truth was seeping into Inspector Mably's consciousness. But he'd just shrug it away. Thirty five years earlier and a novice policeman missed out on murder and mayhem. Mably didn't need reminding of how we talked him out of that.

Retirement loomed, he didn't want questions about buried criminals coming back to spoil his last year as the bastion of propriety. Carol would hear these same rumours, like Mably she'd shrug them off as petty jealousies spouted by small minded, rumour mongers.

Even problems with the Inland Revenue receded as corrupt accountants fleecing innocent, law abiding men became their legal eagle's mantra. The real threat of assassination the motive for a change of identity. It had all slipped into place so neatly.

I could readily visualise that gorgeous solicitor of ours, "Of course my clients want to repay every penny to the Inland Revenue. It may take a long time however and considering that they've already paid the monies once …"

Stuart jolted me back, 'Wyn's taken Shirley down to Cornwall for a few days.'

I shrugged, that was his predictable response to any of Shirley's crisis.

Stuart sat back in his chair and swung his legs onto his empty desk. Clasped his hands behind his head. Wearing his wound like a street fighter's medal of honour. He turned his head my way. One eye shut, but just like his father in the photograph, he wasn't winking.

I had to say it, 'You look just like Harry.'

'What five foot five and fat.'

I smiled, 'Something like that.'

'Wyn was right, you're lucky Jack.'

I sat up; it wasn't anywhere close to being an accurate assessment. But I smiled and thought, there's worse things to have on your headstone.

Lucky Jack.

1980 – TEDDY

He woke up in a bed, surrounded by curtains. The smell of hospitals and dying old men.

It stank of a prison hospital.

Even the nurse looked like some kind of rodent. His eyes followed the ugly nurse, which type of rodent? Small eyes too close together, big ears.

Some sort of intelligent rat.

The androgynous haircut reminded him of his sister. But despite the appearance, his sister was sexy and in an aggressive way too. Throwing any man in her immediate vicinity the challenging stare of the sexually voracious.

Not this little rat.

He wondered if his sister was still alive, she had the clap once and never went to work. She used to show him her chuff when he was little.

Teddy sighed, people don't understand hatred, never realise its true value or how to use it. Teddy could hate and Eyeless could fight. Eyeless didn't hate and Teddy couldn't fight.

Funny old world.

Why did Eyeless try and finish them off? He did it for me.

Good old Eyeless.

His mind flew randomly around like a moth battering into a light bulb. He didn't understand, didn't know anything, or what it meant anymore.

No, no... he never understood anything. He fingered his jaw. Soup for weeks rat face had told him. He went to cuff her, but a sharp pain shot up his arm. He blinked at the handcuff, shook his hand, a dry, metal rattling alarm went off.

Handcuffed to his fucking bed.

He drifted back, what was the name of that old trailer? The Bone Yard. That's what the old lags called it.

A trailer in the prison yard used for overnight visits of

wives. Or in his case, Shirley.

They both knew the guards would be watching. It turned both of them on. Give them a proper show.

Prison.

Prison.

Prison sex.

It didn't take long to remember the prison sex. Not with Shirley. The trailer was a privilege granted to the chosen few.

What about real prison sex?

It took longer to remember just exactly what happened. The little poof blowing his cock.

Not that. Watching.

Binding the poof's hands. The pretty little poof.

He was so young and vestal.

It must have hurt him, but was still breathing afterwards. His head down, eyes closed, and his throat wide open.

A lamb and a martyr, so precious.

The others all found some release in sodomy. Except the poof.

His hands bound, his head down, his eyes shut.

They all found some brief moment of sanity in amongst the shit and blood and semen.

He looked so precious. Poof.

He woke later, lying amongst sweat soaked sheets. He must have a fever or something. Irritable and uncomfortable in an indefinable way.

Like a cat that runs for cover on the night before a disaster. He remembered. They might have handcuffed him. But the stupid fuckers hadn't searched him.

Properly searched him.

He felt himself smiling at what he had concealed.

An aluminium tube that usually encased a small cigar. A petite corona – about four inches long and a half inch in diameter. An aluminium tube with a screw top. Uncle Jim told him that the smoking time of the cigar was twenty five minutes.

He had to put plenty of Vaseline around it and he winced

when it went up his arse. It never had a cigar in it. A stainless steel switch blade, slim, highly polished. A three inch blade.

Toledo steel and he bought it in Spain.

'Nurse, nurse – I need a shit.'

The rat hustled through the curtains. 'You're not supposed to shout with that jaw.'

'Hurry up I need a shit.'

The guard walked him to the toilet and insisted on coming into the cubicle with him.

'Leave me alone. Are you fucking queer or something?'

'No fucking about then Teddy. Quick shit and out.'

He flushed and rinsed the shit off his fingers and the blade. It winked away at him.

The guard walked him back to his bed.

The guard was thick.

'Don't chain both arms.'

'Regulations Teddy.'

'I want a wank.'

'Teddy.'

'I have to hold it – I can't sleep, please?' The guard left his right hand free.

Whenever he closed his eyes he saw Eyeless as a young boy, splashing around in the moonlit mud at low tide. He heard the screams of men burning to death, pleading, begging to be let out. Eyeless always called him a dog, one that wagged its tail, but snarled at the same time – he liked that one.

Life had become like one of his photographs, one that he'd cut in two and stuck back together. Careless with the gluing, the two halves not aligned. The image forever distorted, causing him to blink like a short sighted man squinting into a sandstorm.

Try to sleep again, except he kept waking as if he was still in a dream. Despite being adrift in a dream, he felt safe again. Some animals develop an intuition for these things. He became reluctant to drink at the waterhole. A dangerous place to go. But he went anyway. He caressed the feeling of security, the umbilical of the handcuff. Whenever he woke, it felt like some kind of heaven.

Surely the smells were real? The scent she wore, the perfumed soap she used, the sweet smell of young woman. Her tight schoolgirl skin tinted a carroty orange by the firelight.

Stay here, safe at last.

He sat up and it was as if he had woken from the dead.

All the others with their roasting rectitude – fuck them all. His mind whirled away, searching for answers, desperate for a solution.

My guilt, my blame, my blood, my fault.

I am not innocent. I'm not innocent.

No one is innocent. No one is innocent. No one is innocent.

No more rotting in some lethargic being.

There's a shadow, cloaking every breath. Making every promise empty, pointing every finger.

Murder or suicide now the chosen path.

Trust me. I want what I want now.

Not on my knees and on fire. My piss and shit are the fuel that set my head on fire. So smell my soul burning. I'm broken, looking up to see the enemy.

Murder or suicide?

He felt inside his underpants. It felt hard. Not his cock.

The knife.

Shiny and so smooth. He pulled it out.

Getting the blade open. Hold it in his manacled hand.

Lean across.

There.

He'd armed himself to fight. It's all he had left.

There's only one choice.

He's shameless, nameless, nothing and a nobody now. But his soul became steel and his fear no longer naked. No longer naked and fearful.

No longer dead inside.

Loathing, weakness, and guilt keep him alive. For how much longer?

Celia crawled away from him. Slipped away. He tried to

keep a hold, but there was nothing he could say. She slid and crept away and there was nothing he could say or do.

The policeman didn't mean fuck to him.

He stuck the kitchen knife in.

This is love.

This is true love for Celia.

'Nurse, nurse!'

'Don't shout.'

'Now.'

Say you won't go. Dancing in quicksand.

Why don't you watch where you're wandering?

Why don't you watch where you're stumbling?

You're wading knee deep and going in. And you may never come back again. Gone under two times.

Struck dumb by Celia's voice that speaks from deep beneath the cold black water. It's twice as clear as heaven, and twice as loud as reason. It's deep and rich like silt on a riverbed.

So comfortable... Too comfortable. Shut up.

Shut the fuck up.

Baptized by Celia's voice.

I'm back down. I'm in the undertow. I'm helpless and awake in the undertow. I'll die beneath your undertow. It seems there's no other way out of this undertow. Euphoria.

Here comes the nurse.

Time to cleanse and purge.

'Nurse, I've got something in my eye – it's hurting like fuck.'

'Which eye?'

Murder or suicide?

Suicide or murder?

She leant over him.

Her mottled neck inches from his face.

He couldn't stop his hand.

Push the knife against the soft flesh.

Push and slide. Blood.

Pints of blood.

31

1980 – JACK

I sat in my office, tapping my teeth with a pencil. I glanced down at my watch, just before midday on a frosty Wednesday. Copy for the week finished and a long lunchtime beckoned. Stuart sat back in his chair, with his feet on the desk, hands clasped behind his head. I smiled, back to normal kept resounding inside my head.

'You going for a pint?'

Back to normal!

I raised my eyebrows at Stuart, 'What do you think?'

'Where you going?'

I shrugged; Stuart's insistent questioning meant that he was angling for an invite. I sighed, 'Wednesday, it must be King Alfred's Head.'

Stuart began to count his change, I sighed again. Nepotism comes at a high price.

We lapsed into a comfortable silence.

Carol glanced over to Stuart and then back to me. 'I can lock up if you two want to get off.'

The recent upheavals in her life hadn't changed her sweet nature. Before I could thank her, my phone clanged into the collective consciousness of the small office. Stuart's feet lifted clear and he swivelled his chair my way, sitting to attention at the same time. Carol's eyebrows went up, she took all the calls, only two people had my extension and we all realised the potential significance of this call. My pulse quickened, only the second time this month it had rung and we all knew how that developed.

A soft, even voice, instantly recognisable. Inspector Mably said, 'I know you've probably wrapped up for the week, but you should know. Teddy Lewis has escaped.'

'How?' I stood and immediately had a violent dizzy spell. I rested my free hand on my desk and tried to remain standing.

'Held a knife or a razor to the nurse's throat and made the guard undo the handcuff. Ordered the guard to handcuff himself to a radiator, then handcuffed the nurse to the guard.'

As my head span, I tried to reason things through. No money, no clothes – he won't get far. Was this statement an accurate assessment of how things would develop? Or more likely just a blind hope based on my own sense of impending terror.

Mably's voice came out of the speaker. 'Jack, Jack…'

'Jack – what's up?' Stuart insistent urgency came from the other side of the office. 'Jack, what's happened.'

1980 – Teddy

Christ it was cold.

Too cold to be clambering up a building in some one horse town anyway.

Up the fire escape until he reached the top floor. He blew hard, the full moon highlighted the steam as it rushed out from his mouth. He looked at the window. It was the one; he had no doubt about that. He pressed the uninjured side of his face against the glass and kept dragging huge amounts of icy air into his lungs. The tears felt so cold as they trickled over his broken cheekbone.

Move!

At least the drainpipe was cast-iron. He gave that idea up quickly enough, men over sixty had enough trouble climbing stairs, let alone drainpipes. He clambered up onto the curved rail of the fire escape. Nearly pitching over at the same time.

Not yet!

He balanced on the top rail and looked down.

The moonlight picked out the corniced wall that had smashed her head open.

Not yet!

His face hurt.

Not as much as his heart though.

Why did Celia get into bed with all of those men? Why did she get into bed with me?

The stupid … god how I miss her.

He stared at the wall.

How high was he?

Sixty feet?

How many seconds? One?

Two at the most.

Teddy took a final deep breath and then pitched forwards, shouting as he fell.

Just enough time to shout her name.

'Celia...'

The End